TEMPTING JUPITER

An Arena Dogs Novel

Charlee Allden

Sign up for new release announcements.
www.charleeallden.com

Books by Charlee Allden

CHAPTER ONE

The Renegade
Earth Alliance Beta Sector
2210.146

Jupiter had heard of the fiery afterlife the humans called Hell, but he'd never expected to end up there. It wasn't that his soul wasn't black enough; he just didn't think the humans would allow an Arena Dog entry.

Flat on his back, muscles turned to molten metal, he battled the fogginess in his brain.

Flames crackled around him, eating their way closer. A chemical tinge burned his nose and turned his stomach. The heat of the flames intensified until one side of his body crawled with sizzling prickles. He tried to roll away from the danger, but his efforts gained him nothing.

He forced his eyes open. His heartbeat hammered against his chest and his gaze raked over the room. The smoke gathering overhead hung close to his face. Apparently, Hell had low ceilings.

A loud pop outside his visual range focused his mind like the air-shot at the beginning of an arena match. With the added clarity, he realized a restraint stretched across his chest, holding him in place. An attempt to dislodge it with his right hand brought a sinking realization. His right arm wasn't moving and he couldn't feel his fingers. That would have raised his heart rate if it hadn't already been beating too fast to count.

The flames licked closer. Was he being set on fire as a special punishment, or was this just the usual hellish welcome to new residents of the afterlife? He laughed at the thought, then coughed violently when he sucked in a lungful of smoke. Suffocating spasms seized control of his body. The memory of Seneca, the last time he'd seen his pack brother, formed in his mind. When he closed his eyes he could still see the pale blush of Seneca's lips, blood splattered across his face, etched lines of pain bracketing his mouth, and regret glazing his eyes. Jupiter's lungs burned. His body ached. And the sure knowledge that he was to blame for Seneca's injury made Jupiter contemplate surrendering to the flames.

But he'd never been one to quit.

He was alive, despite injuries that had been more extensive than Seneca's. He wouldn't give up hope that Seneca might also live.

Jupiter glared down at the restraint. His eyes stung from the smoke and he blinked in an attempt to focus. He pushed against the material with his left hand and found it stretchy and thin. It clearly wasn't meant to prevent him from getting free, but it might be meant to keep him from rolling out of the strange bed in his drugged stupor. Yeah, his system had definitely been pumped full of drugs. The pounding at the base of his skull and the jittery twinge of his muscles left no doubt. He flicked out the claws on his good hand and the material fell away in a shredded heap. Rolling to his side, he tried to get a look around, but didn't recognize a single thing. He swung his legs over the edge only to double over in pain. His left hand shot to the throbbing ache in his middle. A soft square of flex-bandage clung to his skin. One quick look told him someone had patched him up with a stark white bandage.

A door to his right… and down… whooshed open and the flames jumped higher, licking the ceiling like a viper tasting the air for prey. *Whoa*, Jupiter's brain complained as it registered that his feet were dangling a meter above the floor. He looked down, judging the distance. A sharp bark drew his spinning head back up, and he was jumping down to the floor before his brain had a chance to engage.

An unfamiliar Arena Dog stood in the doorway. "Fire suppression is offline." The Dog had the tall, broad, more than human build, wide face and pointed ears of their kind, but he was dressed more like a human. The Dog threw a white canister toward Jupiter. He tried to reach out to catch it, but his damn right arm failed him again. The cylinder hit him in the chest and he cradled it against his torso.

The Dog who'd thrown it grabbed another and held it in front of his body. "Point the nozzle at the flames and press the red button!" He had to shout to be heard over the noise of the fire and something mechanical grinding metal against metal in the distance.

Jupiter struggled to work the fire canister without the use of his better hand, but somehow he managed. A blue powder sprayed out, dousing the flames as it bubbled and expanded wherever it landed. It changed the stench of the fumes—no less vile—but it dulled the burning in his lungs.

"What's happening?" Jupiter choked out the words. He still had no idea where he was and he wanted answers. He stood in an aisle with two beds like the one he'd crawled out of, stacked one above the other on each side. Across the aisle, both beds had been empty and were now blackened with soot beneath the blue skin of the suppressant. He jogged farther along the row and doused more of the flames.

The other Dog followed, shouting to Jupiter as they worked. "You're onboard a resistance transport. We snuck you off-planet and were trying to get you to our haven."

"We're not on Roma?" He'd known Roma was only one of many planets and that the arena spectators came from other worlds, but the idea of being anywhere else seemed implausible.

"No." The other Dog answered over the last of the dying flames. "We're in a transport vessel."

The Dog tossed his canister to the floor and barked for Jupiter to follow back the way he'd come. "We have to keep the attacking ship's crew from boarding us long enough for the pilot and the mechanic to make the repairs and get us moving again."

Jupiter had never heard of the resistance or been aboard a ship of any kind, but he was used to adapting to unexpected situations. He followed the man, but as he approached the bunk he'd vacated moments before, he spotted the still form on the one below. The Dog's ice white hair had been twisted into a single rope and pulled over one shoulder. His long lashes rested against his cheeks. Bandages wrapped his torso. "Seneca!"

He dropped to his knees and pressed his ear to his pack brother's chest.

The stranger shoved at his shoulder. "We have to go."

Relief flooded through Jupiter at the faint rise and fall of the chest beneath his ear. Seneca's heart beat strong and steady. Jupiter looked up to meet the gaze of the Dog who was still trying to get him to move. "He's alive."

The Dog nodded. "He's deeply sedated. He's smaller, lower

body mass. It'll take him longer to come around."

Jupiter wanted to stay with Seneca, to wait for his lavender eyes to open, but he understood they were in danger and had an enemy to fight. He lurched to his feet and sprinted after the Dog, knowing the best thing he could do for Sen was to keep whatever danger approached from reaching his slumbering body. They thundered along a narrow corridor of dull metal walls and grated floors that shook beneath their weight.

The Dog ahead of him slapped a palm against a panel next to a door and it slid open. Jupiter followed him into a narrow space that led to a larger room. He caught a flash of a console full of lights and screens before two men trudged through what appeared to be an external hatch and right into their path. Jupiter had a split second to identify the uniformed men as humans carrying burst weapons. He dived low as the miniature explosion of the guns blasted over his head.

The other Dog collapsed to the floor beside him. Most of his chest was so much bloody meat and the only thing keeping his head attached was a fragile column of charred bones. Jupiter had been the instrument of too much death to be shocked by the gore. He bunched his leg muscles and lunged toward the two men still standing in the hatchway. He kept low, aiming for their legs. One of the men had angled his body away from Jupiter and shot his burst-gun in the direction of the lit panels. The other man had fired at Jupiter, singeing the decking where he'd been standing only seconds before.

He struck their legs and they tumbled to the floor around him, their limbs tangled with Jupiter's body. The ache in his abdomen spiked into his awareness before he once again pushed it from his mind. He crawled over the closest downed man and struck a fast, sharp blow to his throat. The satisfying crunch of the human's trachea fueled his determination. Jupiter made a grab for the other human, trying to wrestle the burst gun from his grip as the man thrashed against him. When he couldn't break the man's hold, Jupiter snapped the man's arm near the elbow. The man squealed.

"Wait!" The shout of a human drew Jupiter's head up.

Damn! On the other side of the hatchway at least a dozen men aimed weapons at him. They wore an unmatched array of body armor, most of which seemed never to have seen battle. Jupiter rolled, pulling the downed human over him as a shield, but no blasts fired. "Don't shoot him," the man warned. "He's worth more alive." The small army of men kept quiet as their leader yelled orders.

Jupiter couldn't believe his luck. The weapons were the only chance they had against him. Hand to hand, no number of humans would stand a chance. He shoved the man on top of him aside and bounded to his feet.

"Wait. Heel. Whatever the fuck you call it." The leader stood well behind his team with his hands up in the universal sign for stop. He wore no armor, but he did wear a uniform of some kind. Something Jupiter hadn't seen before.

Jupiter growled, drawing back his lips to show more teeth, at the men who still pointed weapons at him. He wanted to give them an eyeful of the deadly incisors he'd been cursed with, but experience kept him frozen in place instead of lunging for his prey.

The men closest to him edged back, feet shuffling, weapons aimed.

"Listen." The human leader paled, but he stepped out from behind the armored bodies that had provided him cover. "There's no reason to fight. Even if you kill us all, what then?

Where are you going to go? Your pilot's dead." He pointed to the far end of the room and the proof of his words.

Jupiter's nostrils flared and he snarled, backing the man away. He knew a man was dead where the leader pointed. He'd smelled the blood, singed flesh, and the rotten odor that comes from a man when his insides are exposed. Now he let himself take in the remains. The pilot faced them as if he'd turned to fight. He sat slumped forward, strapped into a chair and surrounded by view screens and controls. Half his torso was gone, but he was clearly human.

Why would a human have been helping Arena Dogs escape the powerful reach of The Roma Company?

When Jupiter looked back to the enemy leader, the man grinned. It was the grin of a whip-master before he announced the number of lashes he intended to rip into a Dog's back. The grin of the game-master before he stepped onto the platform where he handed down arena verdicts. It didn't bode well.

"Unless you can pilot a spaceship, there's nowhere to go." His eyebrows wiggled like orange worms arched over his eyes. "Can you? Are you a pilot?"

The mockery in his voice should have outraged Jupiter, but he didn't have the energy for rage. He swayed on his feet, thinking of his vulnerable pack brother in the compartment down the corridor. He should fight. The thought flickered in his mind, but his body didn't respond.

"Or," said the human, "we could just wait here until you bleed out."

Jupiter's chin dropped. Crimson splashed at his feet and a blood-soaked bandage stretched across his torso. Another stream of blood trickled across his collarbone and down his pectoral muscle. He touched his fingers to his shoulder and found it wet and slick. He pressed hard against the wound, hoping the jab of pain would provide a much needed surge of adrenalin, but it was too late. He'd already lost too much blood.

His legs buckled and the jarring impact of his knees slamming into the decking sent agonizing shockwaves through his body. His eyelids fell. The rush of weakness could no longer be put off. It left him powerless.

He thought again of Seneca. Regret and longing for his pack brother settled in his chest. As the humans circled closer, he huffed out his bitter shame.

For the second time in as many days, he was going to die.

CHAPTER TWO

The Salley Ho
Earth Alliance Beta Sector
2210.146

When Feeona heard the commotion in the hall outside the *Salley Ho*'s one-cell brig, she checked the time. A brief jab beneath her ribs made her sit straighter. It could've been a symptom of her worry over the damage Captain Walter Fitzhew's side-trip had inflicted on her schedule. More likely, it was a cramp from the way she'd been sitting for hours—her back to one wall, ankles crossed, legs stretched along the cell's built-in metal bunk. In her defense, it was the only piece of furniture in the monotone gray cell and sitting made it easier to maintain her remote link with Bug. The miniature terminal access drone and the neural implant she used to direct it were the best investments she'd ever made, but it did take a lot of her concentration to control it. At least sitting kept her from walking into walls or, more importantly, the shimmering energy field that blocked the cell's entrance.

She uncrossed her feet and swung her legs over the side of the bunk, slipping into the boots she'd left on the floor. Fitzhew and a small mob of his crewmen, all toting weapons, had two prisoners in tow. She wasn't surprised to see they were both bloodied. Fitz was a small man with a narrow face and a bushy cap of carrot-tinted hair that he was currently raking his fingers through. He didn't have any particular reputation for violence, but she knew he could be utterly ruthless when the need arose.

Bug's DATA UPLOAD IN PROGRESS message flashed in Feeona's left eye. Opting to remain seated as long as possible, she smoothed her palms down her soft black trousers then tugged at the hem of her matching pullover. She propped her forearms on her thighs and leaned forward, studying the controlled chaos in the previously unmanned security station.

Two members of the crew dragged one of the wounded men directly to a spot in front of her cell. The prisoner was unconscious and obviously taller than his captors. His feet dragged behind and his head hung forward, obscuring his features, but the pointed ears were hard to miss.

"Crap, he's a heavy fucker," one of the crewmen complained, chest heaving with exertion.

They'd each slung one of the prisoner's arms across their shoulders. Those arms were thick with muscle and lined with veins that bulged against his skin, as if to deny any lack of vitality that his unconscious state implied. Narrow silver scars marred his shoulders and bruises mottled his coppery skin. Blood, thick and crimson, coated his bare chest. The sticky stuff clung to the curve of muscle as it oozed from shoulder to abdomen to the shallow dip of his navel.

The second prisoner tugged against the restraining grip of his minders, but they'd restrained his hands behind his back and shackled his legs. The stretch of his arms showed off a leaner physique, and his unusual coloring hinted that he might have a bit of alien blood. White silk hair hung past his shoulders. His skin was a dusky white that made her think of the pearls of Old Earth. His face seemed more human, but too stunning to be real—jaw and cheekbones too sharp, an elegant nose and lushly full lips. His concern for the unconscious prisoner filled eyes that were lavender, large, and expressive.

"He needs medical attention." His voice was as lush as his eyes. She'd bet, even with the odd features, he'd look and sound amazing singing in a shower. The kind with real water. Hot and steamy.

One of the crew standing guard over him gave a nod and another crewman elbowed lavender-eyes in the ribs. He huffed out a pained breath, but he stayed upright. Bandages had been wound around his middle. Blood stained the white in several places. The patches of red expanded as more blood seeped through the cloth.

The readout in Feeona's left eye flashed UPLOAD COMPLETE.

Finally.

She sent Bug a RETURN WITH STEALTH command and shut down the link. Bug's programming for autonomous flight was very basic, but Fee trusted it to return undetected. Most of the ship was dealing with the aftermath of their recent battle and wouldn't notice Bug zipping past over their heads.

She stood, put her palms against her lower back, and stretched. "Hey Fitz, did you forget about me or does this mean I'm getting upgraded accommodations?" When he stomped over to stand eye to eye with her, she fluttered her lashes and gave him her best you're-an-idiot-and-I-hate-you smile. "Anything with a mattress will do."

"Oh, you're not going anywhere, Mattie." The muscles around his mouth jumped with annoyance as he called her by the alias she was currently using. "You're staying right where you are, only now you'll have company."

Feeona flicked a look over Fitzhew's shoulder. The prisoner might be unconscious but he was also big.

She let her voice climb to be heard above the commotion of the crew trying to manage the prisoners. "Uh, Fitz. This cell is a little small for two."

"It's the only cell I've got, and I'm not trusting either one of you on this side of the pulse field until we reach Karona Station." His lips pulled tight, then gave way to a grin that crept from one side of his face to the other. "If you can't do the time, don't do the crime." He snorted at his rhyme.

Feeona snickered. "You're real proud of that gem, aren't you? You do know it's an Old Earth saying? About as ancient as stardust and ten times as common."

The mirth slid from his face. "Back off."

Her barb had hit the mark with more force than she'd intended. He must have heard the rhyme recently and thought he could claim it. He was always trying to appear more clever than his perfectly average IQ could support. A tiny smidge of pity knocked at the door of her hardened heart. Luckily, that door had been reinforced and welded shut. She held her hands out in surrender. "Whatever you say, Fitz."

His face and ears turned scarlet. "I meant back off, literally. Back away from the pulse field."

Two more of his crew took up positions just on the other side of the barrier and aimed stinger-shooters at her. She edged back into the empty corner at the foot of the bunk.

Fitzhew punched in a code on the control panel and the pulse field flickered and disappeared. The two men carrying the unconscious prisoner dragged him into the cell and dropped him. He landed half in, half out and as motionless as the dead.

The prisoner still in the hall, snarled and slammed into one of his guards as he tried to break free.

Fitz's hand hovered over the control panel. "Hey!" He shouted to be heard over the tussle. "Cut it out or I'll cut this one in half."

The prisoner stilled, swaying on his feet.

"I mean it," said Fitz. "If I turn this on maximum now, he dies."

Lavender-eyes propped a shoulder on the corridor wall, breathing hard. Pain etched deep furrows into his unusual but appealing face. "Don't. Hurt. Him." There was agony in the demand and it had nothing to do with his injuries.

Fitz lifted a shoulder in a half shrug. "I'd rather have him alive, but that's up to you."

Feeona wanted to sock Fitz and tell the soulful prisoner he didn't need to worry. Fitz had no intention of killing either of them. It was written in his body language. She was good at reading people and she saw frustration in the tense set of his body, not rage and not cold calculation. The urge to speak up spiked, but she couldn't get involved any more than necessary. She had other priorities and a timeline that was being blown all to hell.

She dropped her arms to her sides and rolled the worry from her shoulders, then stepped forward. She squatted down by the unconscious man's feet and dragged his legs across the danger zone. "If I have to share my microscopic cell, fine. But can you all go the hell away now and let me get back to napping on this oh-so-comfortable metal bed?"

Fitz frowned. "Don't be such a bitch. That bastard is an Arena Dog. If he smells that bitchiness on you when he comes around, he might get confused about whether to eat you or fuck you."

"You're all charm, aren't you, Walley?" She ignored Fitzhew's bluster and focused on the prisoner swaying in the corridor, just outside the room's entryway.

The man's lavender eyes had darkened and gotten impossibly larger. She could barely see any white in his eyes at all. "Help him." The demand was soft, slipping along the floor and into her ear like the stroke of velvet. "Don't let him die."

Throwing his voice was a neat trick, but it couldn't change the fact that there wasn't much she could do. She got to her feet and met Fitz's glare, letting no sign of her frustration show on her face or in her body language. Sometimes the icy control she'd had transfused into her veins came in handy. "Can I at least have a blanket? He's bleeding all over the floor and I have to sleep in here."

"Brice, toss her a blanket and the med kit." When the crewman grabbed the kit from a compartment in the wall, Fitz stayed his movements with a hand on his arm. "Take out anything she could turn into a weapon first."

Brice nodded and complied, then tossed it to her. Then the blanket.

"Gee thanks," she said. "I'm not a medic, you know."

The pulse field flickered back on. Fitz tipped his head. "No, I think we all know you're nothing more than a common thief."

Feeona watched the men file out of the room. As he was being led away, the prisoner shot her a glance from beneath long lashes. His big eyes blinked then caressed the prone form on her floor.

As they disappeared, Feeona kneeled next to the bleeding man and popped open the kit. She pulled out some gauze pads and tugged him onto his back.

There was a lot of blood.

The wounds weren't new. Traces of bandage and sealant residue clung around the injuries. The reopened puncture wounds had been deep and could have killed him. They still could, but she wasn't going to let that happen. Someone had taken the time to patch him up, and it would be a shame to let that effort go to waste.

She leaned over him, her lips near his unusual ears. "Lucky for you I'm not really a common thief," she said. "I'm a *brilliant* thief." She laid the gauze over the big wound in his abdomen and pressed down hard. She engaged her link with Bug and redirected the small mechanical assistant to locate the med-bay. Bug wasn't really designed for carrying things. It would take a few trips to get everything she needed. First priority was a shot of blood-doubler. She sent the command, leaving the link open in case Bug needed additional input.

"Hang in there, big guy." As Feeona kept pressure on the biggest wound, she studied his face. He and the other prisoner might both be Arena Dogs, but they didn't look all that much alike. In addition to his dark copper coloring, this one had a wide jaw and nose and his wolf-like ears were much larger. She couldn't tell about his eyes. "I can wait," she told him. "You sleep and get some rest. I'll see those eyes when you're feeling better."

He had plump lips and the tips of overdeveloped canines pressed against them. It all added up to something not quite human. Maybe they were both alien. But what she'd heard of the Arena Dogs had always led her to believe they were of Earth descent, just like the original gladiators they were meant to recreate. She'd never seen one, of course. And the sum total of her knowledge came from transmissions advertising luxury excursions to Roma—home to the sector's legendary and brutal Roma Rex Arena. Proof of that brutality had been carved into this man's body. She could only guess what it had done to his soul.

She shifted, still hunched over him, letting her weight do most of the work. It was all she could do for him while she directed Bug to the medical area, but she found her attention divided. The stranger's chestnut hair had been cropped close, leaving his softly curved ears exposed. They looked soft as velvet and thin as parchment. She wanted to stroke them and see if they were as soft as they looked. The thought of indulging that whim made her belly clench. With his eyes closed and his face slack, he looked vulnerable, something she'd bet a big man like him would deny.

She couldn't help the smile that forced its way onto her face. "I hope you don't turn out to be a total ass. It would ruin these little fantasies forming in my head." And she couldn't remember the last time she'd fantasized about any man. She normally avoided the bruiser type as much as she could. If this guy was what it took to wake up her feminine hormones, she was in trouble. "No. You're not any ordinary bruiser, are you?" But she figured she was right about the trouble.

CHAPTER THREE

The Salley Ho
Earth Alliance Beta Sector
2210.146

Jupiter woke to a sharp spasm in his belly and a confusing mix of scents. An unfamiliar figure leaned over him. Acting on instinct, he tried to shove the shadowy attacker away, but his muscles were weak. The silhouette hunched over him blurred at the edges as light bled around to reveal hints of the creature's identity. Clothed, small, bloody—with Jupiter's blood. When he lurched forward, the flex of his abdominals shot shards of icy, strength-stealing pain through his muscles. His right arm didn't respond at all, and the left moved only inches before it bumped benignly against his torturer.

"Hey, hold still, big guy. I'm working here."

The voice was gruff, annoyed, and female. As she looked up from her task, light painted her features and Jupiter's vision adjusted to his current reality. She was human. He lay on the floor and she knelt beside him. There was something chemical overpowering her feminine scent markers. What he *could* read from her, told him she was anxious but not why. Despite her demanding tone, she was not a guard. Not a threat.

"What are you doing?" Forcing out the words helped focus his mind. Roma had few females on staff. Most were medics.

"I'm trying to close this wound. I've got sealer here, but it's a mess."

He lifted his head to look down his body. The woman's hands were steady, but she was trying to push the edges of the wound closed with only her fingers and they kept slipping in the blood.

"I said hold still, damn it. You'll only make it bleed more." She reached for a crimson-soaked wad of gauze and wiped futilely at the blood. "Crap! The sealer won't bond if I can't get the edges together. I think the major repair job inside is okay, but you've ripped the wound open and torn it even farther. What did this, anyway? Looks like someone tried to punch a hole in your chest."

The memory of the spike stabbing into his chest flashed in and out of his thoughts. It had been an accident. A misplaced elbow and a spiked gauntlet worn by his opponent. Jupiter's thoughts went to Seneca. They both were meant to die in that match. The ache of worry for his pack brother rivaled the pain of the hole in his gut.

"Damn." The woman's curse refocused his attention on the present.

Her focus was entirely on her task.

It was going badly.

Where were the tools of her trade? He'd spent enough time in the med center to know them all on sight. Clamps? A suture threader? No arena healer lowered themselves to the floor to treat a Dog. No, she was no medic. He looked around but recognized nothing. The unadorned walls were close. A bunk hung from one wall, and an energy field of some kind filled the only exit.

Jupiter tried again to lift his left hand. His arm stretched out along the floor until it bumped against the woman. He managed to bend it, but lifting it clear of her was beyond his strength. "Help me pull my arm over you."

"Uh, I'm a little busy—"

He growled with all his strength to stop her flow of words and gain her compliance.

Her head lifted and she met his stare with wide, surprised eyes. The vivid green of them startled him when everything else about her was muted and unadorned. She wore her hair in a skull-hugging style that ended in a knot at her neck. Her clothes were a dull black and they covered her skin, neck to toe.

"Do. It." He ground the words out between clenched teeth.

"Oh-kay. But if you die, it won't be my fault." She stopped and twisted to wrap her hands around his left forearm.

She ducked under it and then brought it close to his torso. His nostrils flared as he got a better whiff of her. Beneath that chemical tinge that masked her scent, there was none of the stench he associated with humans. Her subtle female essence coiled in his lungs, soft and tempting.

"You're human," he accused. Her scent shouldn't stroke his senses.

She leaned over him again. "Yeah, you got a problem with that?"

"Yes." He flexed his hand and his claws flicked out.

Her startled gaze darted to his and she studied him through her lashes. She swallowed as if her words had lodged in her throat then sat back on her heels. "Well." A false note of teasing lilted through her voice. "I suggest you wait until after I'm done patching you up before you kill me."

He dipped his chin in agreement. "That was my plan." He

strained to better see the jagged tear in his chest, then hooked one claw into the edge of the wound. He ignored her indrawn breath and pulled the flesh toward the opposite side.

"Alright then." Her tongue slipped out, depositing a line of moisture across her pink lips. "Will you be able to get your... claw out if I apply the sealer across it?"

"You'll have to help, but yes."

She nodded, but it wasn't directed at him. Her eyes were on his injury. "Okay. That'll work." Her hands shook as she pressed the tube of sealer to his injury, but he didn't think it was his threat or the gore of her task that disconcerted her. She didn't seem to know much about Dogs and he suspected it was the disadvantage of being in unfamiliar territory that had her rattled.

"I can't feel my right arm." It worried him. He'd thought before, it might have been an after-effect of the sedative.

"Trust me, it's still there."

"I know that."

"Thought you couldn't feel it."

"I can't, but my eyes are working well enough."

"Glad to hear it and thrilled to hear you're a glass-half-full kind of guy. A little optimism never hurts in a challenging situation." Head still bowed over his abdomen, she continued to work. "I haven't had a chance yet to patch up the injury on your shoulder, but it doesn't look too bad."

"Not being able to use my hand is serious." He kept still, not wanting to slow down her work.

She huffed. "Yeah, well, you won't be able to use anything if you're dead."

"True," he muttered.

A laugh bubbled out of her. "Careful. If you start acting all reasonable, I might get soft and fuzzy over you. The ability to be reasonable is rare in your gender. It puts you ahead of ninety percent of the men I've met."

He knew she was making a joke, but even imagining a bonding between them shook him. It wasn't that human women had never chosen him for pleasure, but they had always treated him as a thing, a curiosity. "You were surprised by my claws?"

"Yeah, I've been a little preoccupied with keeping you from bleeding to death. I hadn't really looked at your hands."

If she didn't know Dogs, she couldn't be working for Roma. "Who are you?"

"I'm the human trying to get your bleeding stopped. If you've forgotten that already, maybe I should check for a head injury."

"I haven't forgotten," he said through a tight jaw. "But it tells me little."

She blew out a breath and rested her hands on his abdomen as she straightened. "Done. Since you're awake and making such delightful conversation, I guess the blood-doubler I gave you is working." Her mouth curved in a grin that plumped her cheeks and stretched her soft lips tight.

The weight of her hands, a casual touch rather than a task-oriented one, made his stomach twist.

"You can call me Fee," she said.

"What kind of name is that?" Fee meant payment in his mind.

"Short for Feeona, but let's keep that between us, okay? I'd offer to shake hands, but mine are all bloody and yours are, well…" She shrugged and it turned into a shoulder roll. "I'd better look at that other wound but let me clean my hands first."

She started to stand and he wasn't ready for her to go. "Wait."

She stopped and looked at him, eyebrows arched high over those intelligent green eyes.

"Help me free my claw first. It will require putting your hands in the blood again."

She nodded. "Tell me what to do."

He bent his hand back to try to work the curved tip out. "Press against the skin around the claw." He cut his instructions short when he saw that she understood exactly what he intended. Her palms rested flat on his belly. The heat of them burned her touch into his memory. Her fingers pressed, gently working his claw out of the injury. When she had it mostly free, he flexed his hand to retract his claws. The trapped one slipped free.

She seemed to shake herself, then stood and strode over to a cleansing station in the corner. "You got a name?"

He could think of no reason to hold back the name chosen for him by the masters of the arena. "Jupiter."

She looked over her shoulder as she held her hands out toward the cleanser. "Suits you."

"Does it?" He'd never bothered to ask if the name had meaning.

"Sure." A chemical mist soaked air whooshed across her hands, removing all traces of his blood. "Old Earth mythology, right? God of sky and thunder."

They'd named him for a god. The thought galled him.

She threw away the gauze in a waste disposal unit. When she returned, she went back to work, treating his injuries with calm efficiency. Her graceful movements reminded him of Seneca. Smaller and leaner than other Arena Dogs, Seneca had mastered every frightening technique that relied on dexterity, agility, and precision. It had honed him into something deadly but fluid and sensual.

Jupiter needed more information if he was to find his pack brother. "Who brought me to you?"

"Captain Fitzhew and his crew, but not to me specifically. I'm not a medic. I only know the basics." She pressed her fingers gently around the edge of the shoulder wound. "Injuries are always a possibility in my line of work."

Gentle as her fingers were, pain spiked through his shoulder. He clenched his teeth and kept his misery to himself. "Your line of work?"

Eyes on his injury, she pressed again. "It doesn't look infected, and the original sealer is mostly intact." At the sound of the groan he could no longer contain, her head lifted. She studied his face with a grim expression. "I get things for people who want them."

He didn't understand, but he was grateful that she'd returned to the conversation. And what did he know of the human world beyond the arena? "If not for your healing skills..." He stopped to catch a breath. "Why did they bring me to you?"

"Like I said, they didn't. They brought you here, and I just happened to already be here." Her lips pressed together in a grim line. "As far as I can tell, whatever's wrong with your arm isn't related to this shoulder wound." She waited until he nodded then got to her feet. "This is the brig, by the way. The lock-up onboard Fitzhew's ship."

He barked his frustration at his own lack of knowledge.

"Relax. It's not so bad." She tapped the bed above him. "It even has a shiny metal bunk. Only one. Could be crowded." She shrugged, then closed the box of depleted medical supplies. "Oh, right. Almost forgot, you're going to kill me." She turned away and began to clean up. "Maybe that's what Fitz had in mind. I guess if you do, you'll have the bunk to yourself."

He watched her work to clear away the used gauze and stow the supplies under the bunk. Like one of the exotic beasts the masters occasionally brought into the arena, she behaved like no other creature he'd encountered. The unpredictability of those animals made them the most challenging foes. "Why are you helping me?"

"I was tempted to let you bleed out. So I could keep the bunk to myself. But I didn't want to sleep in here with your dead body." The cold sarcasm drained away. "And your friend is a hard man to say no to. He asked me to help you."

"Seneca." The knowledge that he had survived the attack lifted a weight from his chest. He breathed a little easier, but he needed to be sure his pack brother was still okay.

She crouched over him again. "Is that his name?"

Jupiter nodded. "How long ago did you talk to him?" He tried to sit up, but her hand on his chest stopped him.

"You're not strong enough for whatever you're thinking. Seneca's fine for now. He was walking on his own, and Fitz wants him alive."

Jupiter used his good arm to get some leverage. "You don't understand."

She quirked a narrow eyebrow as she met his gaze. "I did mention this is the brig, right? Even if you get on your feet, you aren't getting through the pulse field."

"I have to get to Seneca." She couldn't understand their bond. Even among Arena Dogs, his bond with Seneca was special.

"I told you he's fine."

"If he thinks I might die," he said, "he'll risk his life to get back to me."

"So you're both going to get yourselves killed." She scowled and grabbed at the bottom of her shirt. "At least I'll have the bunk to myself." She tugged the long-sleeved shirt she'd worn over her head, revealing a tight-fighting undertunic that did little to obscure the size and shape of her breasts. Beaded nipples pressed against the material.

He hated the flare of need in his groin.

"Is this why they put us together?" he growled. "So the beautiful human female would distract me from any attempt to escape?"

She wrapped the thin material of the shirt around her hand and used it like a sponge to wipe away the blood staining his chest, stroking along his muscles with a touch that was as gentle as it was thorough. "I told you, they're probably hoping you'll kill me. They aren't my biggest fans." Her features softened and her lips tipped in a secretive smile. "You think I'm beautiful, huh?"

He scowled. "Spoiled human female. Don't think I'll pleasure you in payment for your aid."

Amusement flashed through her features. "A bit full of yourself, aren't you?" One last stroke across his abdomen and then she tossed the sodden shirt into the corner. "I think you're getting ahead of things here, big guy. Even if I did want that, you're in no shape to do anything about it. And before you feel the need to defend your prowess, let's get you up on the bunk, out of this puddle."

She reached for him as if he were no danger to her. He wanted to snarl and show his teeth, to startle her into a more respectful demeanor, but the blood loss had added invisible mass to his body, weighing him down as if his muscles had turned to damp clay and his bones to solid lead.

She guided his good arm over her shoulder and he worked his feet under him. He panted as he dragged one foot after the other.

"Wait." Frustration roughened his demand as he used his one good arm to steady himself against the wall of their cage. "The blood soaked into my waistband. It itches and I want to be clean."

She raised her eyebrows at him. "You're sure?" When he said nothing and instead stared steadily back at her, she took a deep breath and squared her shoulders as if she would be the one making the treacherous journey to the cleansing unit.

"Okay." She did an adequate job of aiding him, but the moment he arrived in front of the cleanser he realized the flaw in his plan. Did he instruct her to steady him while he tried to remove his training pants one-handed or ask her to peel the clingy material from his legs?

She huffed. "Just steady yourself. I'll do it."

He suppressed the urge to growl. He hated that he needed her help at all. It pricked his pride to allow her to handle such a personal task. At least his cock cooperated. Between the pains in his chest and shoulder and the strain of standing, there was little that could have raised his interest in that moment. She managed to strip off his pants with swift, efficient movements and started the cleanser without a word. She stood behind him and put a hand on his good shoulder to steady him. He almost growled but quickly realized she was pushing his trousers into his hand.

"Hold this under the spray. We don't have any spare pants on hand." Her voice broke like she couldn't get enough air.

In the end, after he and his pants were dry, she got him back to the bunk and helped him get his pants back on. With the task complete, she reached for a blanket, laying on a corner of the bunk. She pushed it into his chest. "You need to stay covered, both for your health and my sanity." Her cheeks were pink.

She strode back to the cleansing unit and triggered an army of soft-bodied cleaning bots that ghosted across the cell's floor like living sponges, cleaning away the blood. As they disappeared back into the cleansing unit she returned and stood propped against the wall, eyes not quite meeting his.

Her scent had shifted. The idea that she might be fighting the same attraction that had made him so aggravated made it harder to think of her as the enemy. He shifted on the bunk to make a spot for her near his legs. She accepted the unspoken invitation and sat, tucking one leg beneath her as she turned to face him.

They sat in an awkward silence for a handful of seconds before she spoke again. "You know that numbness in your arm could just be a joint injury or a pinched nerve. Do you want me to take another look?"

He nodded his acceptance of her offer and watched as she scooted forward. Her eyebrows drew together as she tentatively pressed cool fingertips to his flesh. The barely-there touch slipped across the ball of his shoulder and became a firm flat stroke of her palm. Her fingers kneaded as she explored the heft of muscle, the stretch of sinew, and the unyielding structure of bone.

"Tell me if anything hurts." She didn't look up as she spoke, but her breath whispered across his skin.

Jupiter said nothing as she dug her fingers firmly into the muscle, searching for the joint. He could feel her touch even if he couldn't move the limply-hanging arm. There was no discomfort... until there was. A sudden, sharp stab flashed bright white in his vision. He clenched his teeth and focused on his breathing. This was something he could understand, something more familiar—humans causing pain.

CHAPTER FOUR

The Salley Ho
Earth Alliance Beta Sector
2210.146

Seneca pulled deep breaths in through his nose as his guards shoved him along the corridor. The unremarkable walls did nothing to help him make sense of his surroundings, but the smell told him there were no other Arena Dogs in this place. He'd awakened with restraints on his wrists and armed men urging him to his feet. Before that, the last thing he remembered was being dragged across the arena grounds. It wasn't the first time he'd been treated like so much trash to be cleared out of the way, but he'd fully expected it to be the last. He'd heard the death verdict from the game-master after he and Jupiter had lost on the field of battle. The loss had not been unexpected. The verdict, though, that had come as a terrible shock. But that was past.

Here, there was cold metal beneath his flex boots instead of dusty, hard-packed soil. They moved forward between smooth, alloy walls not unlike the hallways that led to the arena medical facilities. The men surrounding him, weapons trained at his head, were not whip-masters. They didn't even appear to be employees of Roma, the company that owned him. These men were not as well trained.

If he knew where he was, he wouldn't hesitate to take advantage of the many openings they gave him to break free. The restraints on his hands were sturdy as were the ones at his feet, but neither would stop him if he chose to fight. The weapons were the only real threat and he would be willing to take the chance to get back to Jupiter.

Seeing the bigger Dog unable to stand, dragged along as his blood spilled, had terrified Seneca. The woman's eyes had promised aid, but she'd been human. When had a human ever aided a Dog?

What if she tortured Jupiter instead of tending him? Seneca's pack brother was strong, he'd survive. Jup could surely take whatever one small woman might do. And if she did tend his wounds, Jupiter might not thank him for urging the human to save his life, but he'd have a life and that was all that mattered. Jupiter had taught him that and proven it true many times over.

"Go on," said the man poking a weapon between his shoulder blades.

Seneca looked up to see a short hallway leading into a large, round room with low, uncomfortably familiar lighting. His heart raced like a mouse running from a clee-cat. They couldn't have taken him back to the pleasure house. The lighting, so much like a patron's luxury suite, brought back memories he rarely allowed. His muscles quivered with remembered shame. Inside those rooms, he'd learned to loathe himself as much as he loathed the humans that took him there. Light had glinted from hidden nooks near the ceiling. It had oozed from beneath furniture and from behind the decorations on the walls. The dim, glowing lights had done nothing to hide the avarice and cruelty in the faces of the many patrons he'd served.

"Move." His guard poked him again.

Seneca shook off the memories. He wasn't in the past. He would never go back and this place was nothing like that one. He stepped across the threshold. His eyes adjusted to the lower lighting, bringing the details into focus. Here the soft lights came from readouts and displays and other things he couldn't identify. People were bent over the colorfully lit panels. Many stopped to watch as he was led to the center of the room.

He'd learned to ignore the arena crowds that watched them fight, but those damn memories of quiet rooms and thoughtless humiliation never seemed to fade. *They look at you and see a warrior.* Those were the words Jupiter had whispered countless times as the roar of the arena crowds had threatened to send Seneca cowering in the dirt. *They look at you and see a warrior.* Seneca repeated the words in his head over and over as the hushed men around him slapped at him with their eyes. His spine remained straight. He held his chin up. They couldn't undo the man Jup had made him. Seneca wouldn't let them.

The leader of the armed men, the one the woman had called Fitz, stood in front of him. Foolishly close. He jabbed a finger into Seneca's ribs, digging into a bloody wound. It was easier to ignore the jab than it had been to ignore the watchful eyes.

Fitz whistled. "That looks painful." He held up his fingers as if Seneca needed to see the blood to be convinced.

There hadn't been a question, so Seneca said nothing. No need to explain that the claw marks on his chest were too shallow to trouble him. They'd been inflicted for show, for the crowds. The cracked ribs beneath were more serious. When he decided it was time to fight he'd risk a break that could puncture a lung. The life-threatening gash across his wrist had been sealed somewhere between his losing consciousness in the arena and being hauled from a bed by Fitz's men. Nothing was making sense.

Fitz wiped his bloody fingers across Seneca's abdominal muscles. Seneca's insides crawled with loathing at the touch, but his stony defenses held. This man wasn't a threat to the most dangerous cracks in his barricades. His digging fingers wouldn't find the place where Seneca was most vulnerable. He'd learned to read men's eyes. This one saw him through the cold filter of greed. Greed didn't frighten him. It could make a man do unthinkable things, and there were some types of greed that could dip into the vile and perverse, but that wasn't the case here. This man's greed was for the most ordinary of things: simple profit. It made a commodity of Seneca, but he had been that since birth. It wasn't even close to the worst thing he'd been.

Fitz narrowed his eyes and frowned. "What's going on in that head? Nothing stupid I hope."

A sarcastic reply tripped over the tip of his tongue and he swallowed it back and bowed his head. He needed more information before he could act. He needed this man to ramble out something useful. "I only wish to understand. Where are the whip-masters? Why have I not been taken to the kennel?"

Fitz laughed. "Could it be you don't know?" The grin stretched across his face was as cold as his eyes. He slapped Seneca's shoulder. "You missed your brief bout of freedom. Some do-gooders busted you out of Roma's tender care and now you're in mine. Captain Walter Fitzhew, that's me." He thumped his chest. "And you'll find that, if you mind your manners, you'll be treated well. At least so long as you're here."

Seneca understood what Fitzhew wasn't saying. That he wouldn't be there long. Since he still didn't know where he was, that didn't mean much.

Fitzhew turned away, as if taking Seneca's silence as compliance, and for the moment, he'd be right. "Tommy, get Owens on the com channel."

The mention of Owens helped fill in some of the missing pieces. The man who'd been in on the creation of the arena and the Arena Dogs had owned Seneca from birth. If Seneca truly had been free, Fitzhew must intend to sell him back. And Owens would pay, if only to ensure his death.

"Com coming up, Captain." The voice came from one of the men leaning over the colorful consoles.

A subtle hush swept across the room as a large screen flickered to life. Grand Owens filled the screen. The silver-haired man sat behind his desk with the arena filling up the skyline over his shoulder. His glance settled on Seneca, and a slow smile plumped Owens' too-smooth face. "Seneca, good to see you alive, pup." He didn't wait for a response. He'd know better than to expect one. His gaze shifted to Fitzhew. "Captain. It looks as if we have a bargain to strike."

"Indeed we do." The captain sat in a throne-like chair and propped one booted foot across the opposite knee then settled his hands along the armrests. Seneca had seen the stance before and knew the captain was trying to make himself look larger, more imposing, to the older man on screen. He could have told the captain not to bother. It wasn't possible to intimidate a man who owned nearly a hundred fighters and a quarter-interest in hundreds more.

Owens' smile didn't waver. "How many did you recover, Captain?"

"There's another one, but he isn't likely to live more than a few hours. I'm afraid getting them was a nasty job. I lost two of my men."

Owens shook his head. "Was that you, our sinful Seneca, putting up such a fight? Or was it Jupiter?"

Seneca counted his breaths to keep them even and held his body still. If the captain didn't want to provide specifics to Owens, maybe he had other plans for Jupiter. Something that might give him better odds at escape than returning to the arena.

Owens' smile snapped into a straight line, but he dropped the question. "Fitzhew, have you been able to download the data from the ship's navigation system?"

The captain shook his head. "Afraid it's scrambled. Might be recoverable, but it will take an expert. I don't keep someone like that onboard."

Owens tapped his fingers rhythmically on the desk. "I need to know where that ship was headed, Captain. Someone is stealing my property and I can't let that stand. I need the location of their base of operations. I need to know where they're hiding my Dogs." His tapping had stopped and he slammed his fist on his desk. "I'll want the remains of any dead, the ship, and the crew."

"About the crew." The captain leaned forward. "Some of them were human. They all fought hard—none survived."

"Disappointing."

Fitzhew nodded. His scent changed and small beads of sweat broke out across his forehead, but his smile stayed in place. "We can bring back the ship, but it's too big for our cargo hold. We'll have to tow her and that will take time, fuel, and extra personnel for security. I'm sure whoever is behind that ship won't want her getting to you." He leaned back in his chair. "Now that you've seen the proof, take some time to consider what you might be willing to pay for, and give me a call in an hour. I don't want to be sitting here, dead in the black, so to speak, any longer than that." With a wave of his hand, the screen winked off. "Good job, Tommy. Let the pompous old ass stew for a bit."

"Thank you, Captain." The man's voice rattled like a pooch-snake wagging its tail for attention.

Fitzhew hopped out of his chair and came to a stop in front of Seneca. "Sinful Seneca, eh?"

Seneca kept his growl from escaping.

"Since you were so good," said Fitzhew, "I'm sending you to the medic for a stitch-up."

"What about Jupiter?"

"Your big friend in the brig? He's already proven he can't behave, so he stays where he is."

"You told Owens he would die."

"He might, but if he doesn't, it would be nice to have a card up the sleeve."

Seneca didn't understand the reference, but the tone told him what he needed to know. Jupiter was still alive and relatively safe… for now.

CHAPTER FIVE

The Salley Ho
Earth Alliance Beta Sector
2210.146

By the time Feeona finished with the big guy's shoulder, he'd disappeared behind eyelids edged with long, delicate lashes. Those lashes had to be the only delicate thing on the man. They'd settled against the puffy purple shadows that stained the skin below his eyes. In sleep, all the guarded gruffness had drained away from his features. Feeona smoothed her hand over his short, dark hair. She'd learned as a child that pain could make a man lash out, but he'd taken the hurt she'd had to inflict until it had shut him down.

She sat on the bunk, fascinated by the wounded beast taking up most of the space. Even in sleep, he was a big, powerful man, but his presence was more reassuring than threatening. She couldn't say why. It couldn't be the fact that he clearly meant something to the other Arena Dog. Even the worst of men had friends. It couldn't be that he hadn't killed her when he awoke to find her crouched over him, when he clearly hated humans. That had been in his own best interest. It couldn't be that she saw a familiar combination of vulnerability and inner strength in him. Why should she care one whit?

And Feeona was getting off this lousy ship in… she started
to check the time, then realized, she needed to reconfirm course
and speed to update her schedule. And that meant getting Bug
back to an unsecured terminal. Feeona got to her feet and paced
to the wall. She slapped her palms against the metallic reminder
of her confinement and pressed her forehead to the cool, flat
surface. The chill did little to sharpen her focus.

She'd been too damn preoccupied with the injured lug when
she should be concentrating on the plan. Her plan. She had a job
to do. Getting to the meet with her buyer had to be her top
priority. She needed the money he'd pay for the navigation charts
she'd stolen off Fitzhew's computers, charts Fitz still didn't
know she had, and she needed to get back to *Petro-5* before
Toolman decided to sell the cargo waiting for her there out from
under her.

Her thoughts drifted back to the lavender-eyed Arena Dog
who'd asked her to help his friend. Her gaze settled on the man
sleeping in the cell's only bunk and the small wedge of space
where she'd sat while working on his shoulder. His chest rose
and fell in the relaxed rhythm of deep sleep.

She needed to work with Bug to get updated data from the
navigation system and then she needed rest, but that wedge
wasn't really enough space to ensure she wouldn't end up on her
butt on the floor if she did actually unwind enough to sleep.

The rhythmic hum and shimmer of the pulse field added
hazard to the unappealing deckplates beneath her feet. Eyes
tracing the cold, unadorned walls of her cell, Feeona turned in
place. Definitely not the corner with the cleansing unit. Her
patient and the bunk he occupied were the only inviting things
in the room.

One step and she was beside the bunk. She sat, slipped out of her boots, and swung her legs up onto the bed. Pushing away the memory of how he looked in the buff, she carefully turned onto her side and wiggled into a semi-comfortable position. She stretched one leg over his, wedging her toes beneath his muscled calf to ward off any urge to roll away and off the bunk.

His tight black pants ended just below his knees and his boots stopped at his ankle. For a half second she wished she'd taken off her socks so she could feel his heat, skin to skin. The broad, bare expanse of his chest offered a much more effective temptation. Avoiding his injuries, Feeona wrapped an arm across him and pressed her cheek against his good shoulder. His warmth soaked into her, relaxing her muscles. Beneath the scent of cleanser, a masculine hint of leather teased her nose.

She closed her eyes and activated Bug where it sat hidden in the air vent. She sent the remote looking for a terminal. The controls were sluggish. Bug needed to charge after all the heavy lifting it had done to get supplies for her patient.

Even with her focus on Bug, she could feel the man pressed against her, his chest rising and falling in a steady rhythm. With a thought she activated the sensory overlay that would allow her to *see* what Bug *saw* as it moved through the ship's environmental conduits. Using the ship's schematics, Feeona guided Bug toward the nearest terminals. There were two that looked promising. One in the ship's tiny science lab and another in the medical center. Fitz probably didn't even have a qualified science officer, so there was unlikely to be anyone in the lab, but Bug had gotten in and out of the medical center several times without being noticed. No reason to think it couldn't be done again.

As Feeona directed Bug to the riskier choice, she told herself she wasn't checking to see if lavender-eyes... Seneca... had gotten medical attention for her own benefit. If she could reassure her cellmate with that information, it would just be a bonus.

As the darkness of the conduit gave way to the light of a nearby vent, Feeona's mind briefly rebelled at the new sensory input. With light came a clearer image of surfaces and shapes, but also a Bug-sized sense of scale. The air vent filled her field of vision like the opening of a gigantic cave. The distance and the drop-off to the surfaces below seemed terrifyingly enormous until her intelligence won over animal instinct and her perspective snapped into place. Bug hovered in the conduit and the drop to the floor was no more than a couple of meters, and Feeona lay safely tucked against the big guy's side.

"My injuries are minor." In the room below, Seneca's muscles tensed and bulged as he spoke to the medic in deceptively soft tones. "Jupiter is the one who needs medical attention."

Bug's predictive programming suggested the Arena Dog could easily break his restraints, but he was trying the honey tactic before turning to brute force.

Wise man.

🐾 🐾 🐾

Seneca strained to keep his voice calm as the medic sealed his wounds. "Your leader might be angry now, but when his temper cools, he'll remember Jupiter is far more valuable alive than dead. If Fitzhew is like the arena masters, he'll blame you for his poor judgment."

The medic snorted and bunched his lips in a pouty grimace. "Captain knows what he's doing. Sometimes crew morale is more important than profit."

"The dead men?" Seneca had smelled them when they'd

brought him into the room.

"If you know about them, you can understand why your pal's in the brig."

The bodies weren't in plain sight, but they weren't far. Maybe in an adjacent room. "I don't know what happened, but I know Jupiter does not attack without cause, not even humans."

The medic snorted again as he finished his work and stepped back. "Just doing their job. Had families, plans, the same as the rest of the crew."

Seneca watched him cross the room and reach into a cabinet. He had to get to Jupiter. Jup meant more to him than his own life.

He tensed, preparing to break out of the ridiculously weak bonds, when a strange noise stilled him. The noise had been there for some time, blending in with other mechanical and electrical noise, but it had changed. The rhythmic pulse had transformed into something more like speech. His ears pricked as he focused on the sound far outside the audible range of the human in the room.

"Jupiter's okay." The tiny almost-voice repeated the message as the medic loaded a small vial into an injection gun.

The voice agitated Seneca's nervous system like the buzzing of an insect in his ear. He shook his head to rid himself of the sensation. He needed to act, if he meant to take the man by surprise.

"I took care of him, like you asked." The voice refused to go away. "He's safe for now, I promise."

Could it be the woman from the cell? A transmission, perhaps? Did he believe her? He had no reason to believe her.

But he did.

A prick against his arm startled him. He'd gotten so

distracted, he'd lost track of the medic. Lethargy crept through his muscles and his mind dulled.

"Don't be afraid. It was only a sedative." The tiny voice probably meant to reassure him. He rarely feared for his own life, but being drugged and unaware—that still terrified him.

"It's okay," the voice assured. "If you're anything like Jupiter, that won't keep you down long. We'll talk later."

The voice had moved closer. Seneca struggled against lead-lined eyelids as his vision softened. Sound dulled. Sensation drained away. He tried to ask about Jupiter, but the muscles of his throat refused to obey. After that, he thought the voice promised to watch over him, but it seemed to emanate from a silvery-winged being that hovered over him as he slipped into unconsciousness.

Feeona watched Seneca through Bug's mechanical eyes. The sensors told her that his heart beat slow but strong. She backed Bug away. More and more of this second Arena Dog came into focus until she had a clear view of the entire tempting package. In his own way, as tempting as the man pressed against her body.

There was no bulkiness to Seneca, but even as he slept, she could see definition on every muscle-covered inch of him. Jupiter would want to know his friend's condition, but she didn't have to ogle him to find out. Her scan told her that his injuries had been treated, ribs recently mended. That was good.

Bug's low-power warning flashed across her virtual vision, reminding her of the other pressing matters that needed her attention. She guided Bug to a terminal in a corner of the room, maneuvering the remote into a nearby hiding spot. Bug needed to be close for a near field hack and power siphon to work. With

Bug out of sight, she got to work on updating her schedule.

CHAPTER SIX

The Salley Ho
Earth Alliance Beta Sector
2210.147

Jupiter deepened his breathing and kept his eyes closed. His lungs filled with the warm, mysterious scent of the woman pressed against him.

At least he knew where he was—sort of. In a metal bunk, in a spaceship that was likely taking him back to Roma Rex. That was as specific as he could be. He didn't know how far they were from Roma or what other worlds might be close. He'd rarely concerned himself with the universe beyond the domed city where he'd been engineered to fight and die in the arena—to be born and die a slave.

His past experience with human women hadn't prepared him for how good the tickle of this female's breath would feel against his bare skin. Her arm pressed lightly against his chest, positioned precisely between the two wounds she'd treated. No human woman he'd met previously would have inconvenienced themselves for a Dog. Feeona's legs were tangled with his, her bent knee resting just inches below his cock. If he wrapped his hand around her thigh, he could pull that leg up and thrust against her. Would she turn into him? Rub against him? Would she turn submissive like many of the females of his kind? Or would she use him for her own release and leave him aching as the human women at the Lady's Wall so often did?

There were no chains here. No drugs to prevent his orgasm. No guards standing over them with stun sticks. He could take what he wanted from her. She wouldn't be able to stop him. He could take away her choice as the patrons had done to him with their drugs and grasping hands and cold hearts. The memory stirred the coals of his anger.

Adrenaline surged through him. His heart pumped blood through his arteries. His senses expanded until the scent of the woman filled his nose and the sound of her breathing filled his ears. The beat of her heart pulsed against him, everywhere their bodies pressed together.

He knew the moment she realized he was awake. Her breathing changed. A thread of tension wove through her muscles, then they wound tight. She was going to move away.

He surged over her, rolling her to her back as he dragged her to the center of the small bunk. Well, that proved both his arms were working again. He lowered his body until the swell of her breasts cushioned his ribs, then pushed his hips against her, nestling his cock into the dip of her belly and giving her no room to move. He wrapped his good hand around her neck and tightened his fingers, enough to ensure she understood the threat, but not enough to restrict her breathing or mark her delicate skin.

His eyes raked over her surprised face. Pink lips opened on a gasp, tempting him to taste them… or slip his tongue inside and fill the moist cavern of her mouth.

Her eyes widened and then blinked, slow and measured.

"Does this mean you're finally feeling fit enough to kill me?"

Even as he ground his teeth in frustration at her lack of fear, he fought the urge to chase after the tongue that flitted across her lips.

Her hips lifted in a motion that caressed his aching cock. "Or did you have something else in mind?"

He tightened his grip around her neck to silence the taunt she surely intended to follow.

Her choked gulp for air made him grin with satisfaction. She'd probably thought she could trick him. Use his body against him. She'd use him to fulfill her needs with no intention of meeting his. It was the way of human females. But this woman didn't have the drugs the patrons used to torment a Dog until he begged for their body, then take their release and leave the Dog with aching balls, cowering in humiliation.

Jupiter growled in the back of his throat. He dipped his head until her narrow little nose brushed his. "I haven't decided yet."

She strained to swallow beneath the grip of his fingers on her throat. If he decided to kill her, it wouldn't be this way, he realized. She'd saved his life. He couldn't allow her to suffer the slow agony of strangulation. It wouldn't be a fit repayment.

His grip eased, but her breathing didn't deepen. It came in short, shallow pants. Her pupils had dilated. Her heart beat a rapid tattoo beneath her ribs. Fear?

Or arousal?

Her body didn't struggle against him. She didn't beg for her life. Her natural scent had strengthened. His senses told him in that moment she was all warm, willing female—an almost irresistible temptation.

He eased up, a small push-up meant to test his own strength and give her the illusion of freedom. To test her compliance.

She slipped her freed hands to his sides, pressing into his muscles. "Umm, this is nice and all, but are you sure you're up for it? I mean, I know you're up," she tilted her hips to make her meaning clear. "But are you really up to it?" She gave him a smile that hinted at mischief and stroked her hand against him, following the contour of his muscles. She ruined the seduction by raising and lowering her eyebrows in a ridiculous manner.

Jupiter had to fight not to laugh. In the end, he gave in to the humor. His lips trembled, his cock twitched, and his belly tightened on a chuckle—and that shot a jolt of pain through his chest. He held back the groan that tried to force its way up his throat, but she must have seen something in his face.

"Yeah." Her hands flexed against him. "*That's* what I meant." She shoved gently. "You shouldn't be straining those seals."

He let her ease him to the side, then sat with his back against the wall and his long legs stretched out along the bed. "Are you sure you're not a medic?" Those careful hands were already checking the dressings over the wound in the center of his chest.

Her eyes did a little roll. "Smart ass." She let her fingers trace one of his older scars. "With as many injuries as you've had, I'll bet you could have done a better job with that sealer than I did."

The ghost-like touch of her fingertips should have tickled. Instead, it sent a call straight to his cock. "Maybe."

Her eyes flashed up to meet his. "If you'd been conscious."

Likely, he'd have bled out if she hadn't aided him. He frowned at the thought. She was human and might well have another motive for her actions, but he hadn't seen any hint of it. He closed his hand over hers to stop her distracting touch. "No matter your motives, you might well have saved my life. Until I discover what profit there was in it for you… I thank you."

Her eyes sparkled with merriment. "That must have been

painful for you." She pulled her hand free and placed it over her chest. "Be still my heart. Dare I believe you've decided not to kill me after all?"

Jupiter rubbed at his shoulder and tested the movement of the joint. Whatever she'd done had left him with only the mildest of pain. He stretched then turned on the hard metal bunk until he could put his feet on the floor. "I have decided to wait on that decision—for now."

She slapped at his arm and laughed out loud. The fastener that had been holding her hair back had disappeared. With laughter lighting her face and her hair in curls down her shoulders, she was transformed from plain to beautiful. Her laugh wasn't the sharp, cruel jeering of the patrons. It was soft and sensual and tempting.

As she quieted, her head tipped and she studied him. Her lips were still curved in a half-smile, but her eyes had gone from sparkling to intense. "Has anyone ever been kind to you just because they didn't have a reason to be cruel?"

"Arena Dogs treat each other with respect."

"That isn't what I asked."

Jupiter didn't understand her question. What was kindness after all? His pack brothers watched his back. They shared whatever they received equally. Food. Blankets. Whatever. Was that what she meant?

She stretched, then slipped off the bunk and pulled on her boots. There wasn't much room in the small space, so he remained seated. An unfamiliar tension crept through his muscles under her scrutiny. Her arms hung loose at her sides, her hands open. There was no threat of violence, but that fact didn't put him at ease.

"Do you ever relax?" She frowned and that unsettled him.

Had he done something to cause her shift in mood?

He nodded. "When I'm with my pack brothers and there is no arena match to fight, no training left in the day."

"Well..." She reached out and touched her fingertips to the thin, silvery scar that ran from his shoulder to his wrist. "I can't conjure up your friends, but there's no match and no training to worry about. We're locked together in a cell with nothing to do for at least—" She blinked and paused before going on. "At least the next hour."

As her fingers traced the scar down his biceps, she wedged between his legs and kneeled on the floor at his feet. She settled one arm over his thigh, her hand lightly gripping his quadriceps, and used her free hand to lift his palm to her face. He watched, curious, as she pressed her lips to his wrist where the scar ended. "What are you doing?"

She smiled against his skin. "I'm being nice to you."

Lowering her gaze to his wrist, she twisted his arm to reveal the vulnerable network of veins. He tensed instinctively, prepared for an attack, but the flick of her tongue, hot and moist, against his pulse sent a spike of surprise through him that tensed his muscles for a whole different reason.

He thought he'd grown immune to the teasing touches of human females, but this woman with her smiling lips and intelligent eyes had his heart racing and his cock hard. Perhaps it was her scent. It drew him, despite the heavy chemical tinge of the color she wore on her skin. He steeled himself for the frustration that would come when she showed her true intentions, but he couldn't find the strength to push her away. So he watched and indulged in the visual and sensual treat as her soft lips closed over his skin again and again, each slow press of lips taking her farther along his forearm.

Her hands stroked his thighs, edging higher and higher. The first brush of her thumb grazing his cock rippled up his abdomen and sucked the air from his lungs. His head snapped back against the bulkhead and his eyes shuttered as she repeated the caress.

His belly jumped at the unexpected press of her mouth to his abdomen. "So many injuries." Her lips dampened a spot where the end of a lash mark wrapped around from his back to stop just below his ribs. "Old... and..." Her lips moved higher to press near the puncture wound she'd sealed for him. "And new."

She'd moved forward and her body pressed all along his. The pressure on his cock was almost painful. He forced his eyes open and looked down into her gaze.

Her face tipped up. She studied him as if memorizing his features. "You let me patch up your injuries. Will you trust me a little longer?"

"I don't need to trust you for what you imply."

"No?"

"No. I only need to prepare for disappointment."

Her eyebrows lifted and her eyes widened. She looked as if she might speak, then she shook her head and pressed her hand directly over his cock. He couldn't control the moan that started low in his chest and escaped from his throat. He should stop her. Push her away. But he couldn't. His body whispered that the pleasure of even a few minutes of her touch was worth the price he would inevitably pay.

She held his gaze as she stroked down his length and then up, only to repeat the motion until perspiration slicked his skin and his heart thumped wildly in his chest. Still, he was ready for her to stop and laugh, or demand he service her, as the arena patrons had done when he'd been younger, weaker, and chained to the wall.

Bending her head, she pressed her lips where her hand had been and nuzzled him. Her fingers tugged at his pants, giving his cock room to straighten. He pushed his palms hard against the bunk beneath him to keep from reaching for her.

Her tongue laved his tip. He pressed harder against the flat cool surface beneath him, torn between feeling every moment to the fullest and trying not to feel at all.

Her tongue stroked around him, as if she were exploring his shape, noticing each curve and angle. She pulled harder at his pants, freeing more of him from the tight, stretchy material.

"Help me," she coaxed.

Still waiting for the moment she'd turn the situation to her own ends, he lifted his hips long enough for her to slip the pants down to his thighs. Without hesitation, she returned her attention to his erection, licking a trail of moisture from the tip to the base. When she completed the return journey upward, she opened her mouth and took his throbbing shaft inside that hot haven. Sensation blazed through him. She took him to the back of her throat, wrapped her lips tight around him, and stroked up, then down and up again, each time taking him a little farther.

His hands were off the bunk and reaching for her before he knew what he was doing. He stopped and pulled them back as he fought for air, panting with want for her. He surrendered to the delirious pleasure as she stroked him with her mouth again and again.

When she couldn't take his cock any deeper and it pressed against the soft stretch of her throat, she halted on the very next stroke. "Don't stop," he pleaded. The words were out before he could call them back. He'd gotten weak. Somehow, he'd gotten weak and fucking pathetic.

"I won't," she assured. "I'm not." She clasped his hands and pulled them to her lips. She kissed his knuckles. "It's okay."

When she released his hands, he was torn. Touching a patron would never have been allowed. But she was no patron. He laid his hands over hers where they again clung to his thighs. She sank back onto him, taking him deep into her mouth. His hands clenched, closing around hers. He wanted to hold her there. To wallow in the hot, carnal bliss. But there was no need. She kept him there until he pulled against her, fearing for her discomfort. He urged her up until he could see her face. There was no look of superiority or cunning. She blinked at him as if his actions confused her.

Jupiter leaned forward, heedless of his wounds pulling against the seals. He wrapped his hands around her head and cradled her jaw with his thumbs, tipping her face up to meet his lips. Had he lost his mind? He kissed her, nipping at her lips and enjoying the touch of her tongue as it met his.

He pulled back, no longer caring if he'd gone crazy or would regret this a moment later. They studied each other and he was glad to see her breathing as hard as him. Her nipples pebbled against her tunic, and her breasts lifted with each inhale.

She smiled, a slim smile, sexy and mysterious, then returned to her task, taking all of him in a pace more purposeful than before. Jupiter indulged in the heady pleasure of using his hands to guide her, setting a pace that stopped his breathing and tightened his balls... and then, and then, and then the blinding white ecstasy of release ripped through him.

She swallowed him down, drawing out his pleasure so completely he thought he must be delirious from lack of oxygen. But he was breathing, and finally she released him with a touching reluctance. A pang unrelated to his injuries sparked in his chest and confusion clouded his mind. Something in his world had shifted. Something fundamental. Something in his very core. He might not understand it yet, but he knew the touch of this human female had left its mark.

CHAPTER SEVEN

The Salley Ho
Earth Alliance Beta Sector
2210.147

Feeona eased back, sitting on her heels, and licked her lips. Jupiter was a tantalizing mix of salty and sweet on her tongue.

"Why?" He still had a hand around her skull, fingers tunneling in her hair, and he was waiting for an answer.

Her position between his knees was suddenly awkward and uncomfortable and she had no idea what to say to him. She wasn't looking for an angle; she just wasn't comfortable with the truth. She'd done it because he'd managed to push her buttons. She'd done it because he'd needed it. She'd done it because she'd wanted to.

She liked the big grumpy jerk, but no matter how much she wished things were different, she'd be leaving him behind to whatever fate Fitz had planned for him.

She flexed her hands against his obliques and forced her lips into a smile. "Why else? To give you motivation to put off killing me a little longer."

His frown was almost cute, the way his dark brows bent toward one another. The way his lips plumped against the tips of his canines. Saints, she wanted to kiss him. To have him kiss her again. Instead, she slipped her grip down to the waistband of his trousers and tucked him away.

His thumb stroked her scalp as his fingers clutched tighter. "I—" His thumb found the bump of her implant hidden beneath her scalp. It curled behind her ear, at her hairline.

She tensed, ready to jerk away. "Careful," she warned.

"What is this? A scar?" His frown deepened and his touch was light, but he didn't release her.

"Not exactly." The implant was as durable as they came, but she had no doubt those big hands could damage it and her without much effort.

He pulled her forward and pressed her face against the bare, hot skin of his abdomen. Gentle but determined hands searched through her hair until he found the raised evidence of the tech. She knew what it looked like. She'd seen it on others. Talked to people who had one before she'd made the decision to get the implant.

A five millimeter circle marked the top of the implant. From there, a narrow ridge curved downward. He traced it from top to bottom with his finger. A shiver chased down her neck, raising goose bumps in its wake.

"It tingles against my skin." His deep, masculine voice jerked her out of her thoughts and brought her back to the sharp reality of the hot skin beneath her cheek and the implications of the male flesh hardening against her collarbone. Something fluttered in her chest.

She couldn't have sex with him in the brig. Well, at least not any more than she already had.

Jupiter had only just had his release and he still wanted her.

She'd given him pleasure and had taken nothing for herself. He didn't understand. All he knew was he could still smell her arousal, but she was pushing away. Even as she clutched at his thighs, she shoved gently against him.

He wanted to hold her there. To press her velvet cheek against his cock. He wanted to drag her onto the bunk and under him. What he did was let her go. The moment his hand left her, she was on her feet.

For a moment she seemed lost, eyes dilated, jaw slack. She blinked, then huffed out a single puff of air. As she took her next breath, her features returned to her normal amused expression.

"Wow. That was something, huh? If we ever end up in the same place and in the vicinity of a nice soft... large bed, we'll have to explore that a little further." Her cheeks plumped as she ramped up the smile. She turned and plopped herself onto the edge of the bunk beside him. In a move more playful than tempting, she slapped one hand against his thigh. "If you're up for it, of course."

Jupiter growled low. He would not be dismissed so easily.

"Oh all right, maybe it wasn't as good for you as it was for me." She scooted back on the bunk and lay on her side. "You should at least be relaxed enough to go back to sleep now."

Another growl escaped him. "You're insane." Did she think he would forget what she'd done, or more to the point, what she hadn't done?

"Don't need much sleep, huh?" She curled an arm under her head. "Well, I've learned the best way to pass the time in a cell is to sleep."

Then she closed her eyes as if that's exactly what she had in mind. Again, she tried to dismiss him.

"Perhaps if you spent your whole life in one, you might choose another tactic."

Her eyes opened. "What are you saying?"

"I've lived in some type of cell all of my life. Even when we're training, we're still caged."

Feeona sat up and reached out to touch him. "You're not talking metaphors, are you?"

He didn't understand her words, but her dismay was clear. "I'm an Arena Dog."

"Right. Fitz mentioned that. You're some kind of gladiator at the Roma Rex Arena, but what's that got to do with living in a cell?"

"That's where they keep us," he explained. "They call them kennels, but it's all the same. Even the arena is just a bigger cell."

She pulled her legs into a crossed position and leaned forward. "Is the arena some sort of prison program?"

It hit him. She didn't know. Would it make her look at him differently? "We're slaves," he said, waiting for her reaction.

She paled.

Jupiter turned away. Would she have taken him in her mouth if she'd known? Would she have touched him at all, even to save his life?

The warmth of her palm against his shoulder startled him. Her color had returned in a flush of pink across her cheeks. She crawled closer and slipped under his arm, wrapping herself around him. Everywhere she pressed against him was a balm to his spirit.

"Slavery is illegal." She thundered. "How can they get away with that?"

She didn't wait for an answer. Her arms slipped away and she bounded off the bed. "And now Fitz is taking you back to them.

Damn it." She paced along the pulse field like a crazed hyrax-
badger.

Her reaction reached deep inside Jupiter. A crazy sort of
satisfaction rumbled through him. She was angry.

For him.

She didn't regret touching him. Not at all.

He snagged her hand as she paced past, forcing her to stop
and face him. She didn't resist as he pulled her closer and settled
her on the bunk. When he stretched out over her, she let out a
soft, breathy moan. Her body fit against his as if she'd been
designed for him. The soft yielding heat of her sent his blood
racing to his cock. He wanted to pleasure her and learn what
other small sounds he would discover. "Perhaps I will pleasure
you after all," he whispered against her ear.

She groaned, planting both her hands on his chest. "No." The
word sounded dragged past her lips. "We are not having sex."

Her denial didn't worry him. She didn't think him less for
being an Arena Dog. That fact pleased him. Whatever her
reasons, he would deal with them. He lifted his head to read her
face. "You're still angry. Why?"

She didn't answer him for a long moment. Then she slipped
her hands up to cradle his face. "What they did to you was
wrong. So wrong." She bit her lip. "Your friend. He's an Arena
Dog, too."

Jupiter stiffened. Guilt ate at him. He'd been thinking only of
himself while he had no idea what Seneca was going through.

He moved off her and swung his legs over the side of the
bunk. Bracing his elbows on his thighs, he bowed his head into
his hands. "I have to find him."

She shifted to sit by his side. "He's in the med-bay. They're
taking care of him." Her hand settled on his spine. He recognized

her attempt to use touch to reassure him, because he'd used the tactic often enough to reassure Seneca. After all the Dog had been through, Sen should've hated being touched, but he'd never shied away from Jupiter.

He couldn't keep himself from turning to look at her. "How do you know where they're keeping him?"

Her teeth bit into her lip as she got to her feet and stretched. She put her back to the cell entrance as she faced him. "There's a camera in the guard station."

He hadn't thought to look for cameras, but that didn't bother him. There was no privacy in the life of an Arena Dog. His frustration surged, but not because their captors watched or because she hadn't answered his question. He realized now how often she'd kept her back to that chamber, blocking her actions from the camera. He didn't like how naturally she censored her words, how deception seemed second nature.

Jupiter had lived his whole life being watched in one way or another, but he'd had little experience avoiding security. On Roma there'd been no point in trying.

"The audio receivers for the camera are suffering from a malfunction." She spoke softly. "I can create interference or short loops on the cameras, but I can't get away with that for long."

Interference? Loops? He didn't understand, but still he waited.

With a small movement of her hand, she urged him to stand and come to her. When he did, she slipped her arms around his waist and pulled him close. "They can't see much if we stand close."

He allowed himself a moment to take pleasure in her embrace, breathing in her scent. "Tell me."

She studied him, again weighing her choices. This time he realized he wanted her to trust him with her secret… for reasons that had nothing to do with needing truth.

CHAPTER EIGHT

The Salley Ho
Earth Alliance Beta Sector
2210.147

It was a risk, but Feeona's instincts had her calling for Bug. The small mechanical device flew a careful path from the vent where it had been hidden. She eased back from Jupiter and held her hand open between them. Bug landed on her upturned palm.

Jupiter scrunched his wide, flat nose and his nostrils flared. She didn't tell him how adorable it made him look.

His head tilted. "It's a machine." His voice was a soft rumble, pitched low.

"That's right. It's a remote terminal access unit. It has a metal alloy body and synthetic wings." She brushed a finger over one of the four semi-transparent structures. "They're incredibly strong."

Bug trembled in her hand, then launched into the air. Its flight was silent, but Feeona saw Jupiter's ears twitch, listening to some sound that only he could hear as the small device circled overhead, then landed again on her hand.

"I call it Bug." She let a smile curve her lips. "It's very good at search and surveillance. Not so good at retrieval, but it

managed to carry back the blood-doubler and the sealer from the
med-bay." She tilted her hand slowly sideways and Bug crawled
upward with the movement, seeking the topmost position on her
hand, imitating the behavior of its namesake. "It took two trips,
but Bug did it."

"You used this to get medical supplies?"

She nodded and then sent Bug back to the duct. "I control it
using the neural implant." She tapped the spot on her head.
"When I'm linked, I can see what it sees."

"And that's how you know of Seneca. You saw him in the
medical center through this bug machine."

"That's right," Feeona agreed. "And he's fine." She slipped
her hands to his waist and urged him to step back. He felt too
good, too solid, in her arms. It had been a mistake to let him get
so close again. She wanted more of him, but it was more than
lust. Giving into desire would only make the situation worse.

Slipping free, she returned to the hard metal bunk.

"You distracted me earlier." He followed and sat beside her,
crowding into her space. He pulled her legs across one of his as
if he wanted her as close as possible. She didn't resist, but she
lifted her eyebrows to question his actions. Would he admit that
he liked having her near?

He met her gaze directly. "It will be expected."

His answer disappointed her. It might be true—after the little
gift she'd given him, anyone watching would expect them to
behave like lovers—but she doubted it was the real reason he
was still touching her.

"When I felt the implant, you changed the subject." His grip
tightened on her thigh. "You didn't intend to tell me about the
machine."

"No." She hadn't planned to tell him anything. Or had she?

Damn. She'd given him her name right from the beginning, when she hadn't known anything about him. What had she been thinking?

"Why tell me now?" He reached up and stroked a finger along her forehead as if he wanted to soothe away the frown lines where her eyebrows drew together.

"You needed to know I was telling the truth about your friend—"

"Brother. Pack brother." His hand settled along her neck, his thumb tracing along her jaw.

Feeona willed her body not to react, but her pulse sped at his touch. There was something in the way he looked at her that made this touch different from the other times he'd touched her. She was practically in his lap, but it was the gentle brush of his thumb that did it to her. Lowered her defenses. Something she rarely allowed. And with him, something she'd done long before she'd realized.

She nodded. "Your pack brother." She reached up and banded his wrist, her fingertip settling over old scars. "And slavery is so wrong. Even the word gets me steamed. Injustice infuriates me."

"And yet you're a thief." He made the statement with no insult in his tone.

She grinned, eager for the turn in conversation he offered. "Remembered that, huh?"

"It just came back to me." A playfulness she hadn't seen before glinted in his dark eyes.

She snorted her opinion of his memory. "Convenient."

Jupiter made a sound, half-humph and half-growl, then tried to pull her closer, his gaze dropping to her mouth.

He was going to kiss her. Or he was going to try. Feeona

resisted. She needed to remember that she was going to leave him behind when the time came for getting off Fitzhew's ship. And that time was getting very close. Damn, she wished she could help him.

She tugged his hand from her neck and pulled her legs free from where they'd been stretched across his lap. She tried to scoot away, to get some distance, but Jupiter followed her across the bunk. Her back was against the wall and he was rapidly closing the distance between them.

"So. Ah, back to Bug." She cleared her throat and tried again. "Listen. If Fitz finds out about Bug, it would screw things up for me."

His eyebrows lifted. "You're imprisoned on his ship. Aren't things already going wrong for you?"

"Looks that way, doesn't it? But no, not really. And Fitz knows me as Mattie. I'd like to keep it that way."

With his hands braced on the bulkhead on either side of her, his big body crowding her, she could barely move. Jupiter had her caged far more effectively than Fitz. Her body didn't seem to mind. Her stupid nipples were painfully tight in response to the proximity of his hard musculature. She was breathing too fast and her whole body was starting to ache with need. How did he have her rethinking her no-more-sex-in-the-cell decision?

Feeona had lost her mind. Forgotten all the rules. She couldn't even claim fear as a reason for telling Jupiter about Bug. He hadn't threatened her. Not really. She'd given him something he could use against her for no better reason than she wanted to put his mind at ease.

But it was time to get control of her runaway mouth and get some control over her oh-so inconvenient attraction to this man. As far as Fitz knew she was Mattie Hairo, a small-time claim jumper. All it would take was a simple DNA test for Fitz to ID her as Feeona Traveler. If that happened, getting away from Fitz would be the least of her problems. He'd go to the Alliance Enforcers and they would hitch all of Mattie's alleged crimes to her one clean identity. She couldn't allow that.

Jupiter waited for her explanation.

She sighed. "We should really focus on what's important. Finding you a way to get off this ship."

He looked at her with suspicion. "Why would you want to help me do that?"

"It's like I said. Injustice offends me." She pressed her palm to his warm cheek. "You can trust me on this. No hidden agenda about this. No promises, but if I can help you find a way off this ship, I will."

A lightning-brief narrowing of Jupiter's eyes, there and then gone, let her know he didn't miss the carefully worded assurances. On this one thing, he could trust her. She'd left herself plenty of room to maneuver. She didn't understand why she bothered to avoid lying to him, but somehow it was important.

Jupiter eased back, giving her room to breathe as he considered her words. "I don't know much about spaceships, but I've been told they're the only way to travel through space."

She nodded confirmation.

"Unless you have a ship alongside this one, wouldn't it be wiser to force the crew to take us somewhere before attempting to get off?"

She swallowed a chuckle. His logic was sound, but his question made it clear he didn't know anything about the *Salley Ho* or space travel in general. Why would he? A slave wouldn't have any need for that kind of knowledge. The thought brought all her anger surging back, but he was waiting for her to answer. "This is a big ship. It would be almost impossible to try to take it over or force its crew to do anything for very long. They know the ship and the technology. They'd have the advantage. You might be half right, though. It might be better for you to try to get away from Fitz once they get you to Karona Station. The problem there is getting off the station. It's a bigger place to hide, but without connections and help, it would still be unlikely you could get safe passage out or hide indefinitely."

Jupiter's jaw tightened as she spoke. "Tell me about this ship and its crew."

It was a good question to start. "*Salley Ho* is a salvage ship. It's big and designed for hauling things or dismantling them in place. It's equipped with cranes and cutters. Large storage bays. There are five decks and a sixty-man crew." When he didn't ask any questions, she continued. "Fitz goes to places where things are being decommissioned—big things like ships, buildings, a port—and he helps haul away the junk. He gets paid for the hauling, but he also gets to sell anything he can salvage. Raw materials and that sort of thing. But the real money is in finding abandoned things and staking a claim. Like your damaged ship out there. If the owners of something like that abandon it, he could legally take ownership of the ship and the contents."

Jupiter's fist clenched. "The ship I was on wasn't damaged until they attacked it."

"Funny thing, that. The *Salley Ho* isn't an ideal ship for attacking a passenger vessel. There must be an enormous amount of credits at stake for Fitz to walk away from a claim." The salvage job where he'd found her and assumed she was trying to claim-jump. Letting him grab her had been the only way to get onboard the ship. "Since the *Salley Ho* hasn't moved a single kilometer since they brought you onboard, I'd say he's after more than just you and Seneca. That ship out there is important, too, for some reason."

Jupiter had been listening intently. "I don't know anything about the ship we were on."

"Well," said Feeona. "It's a mystery then, and this whole business has put a real crimp in my schedule."

"Schedule?" He tipped his head and narrowed his eyes, revealing tiny lines at the outer corners.

She smiled. "The key to any successful endeavor is a plan, and the key to any good plan is a schedule."

"Now you sound like Mercury." Annoyance colored his tone, but his face softened and those muscular shoulders of his relaxed.

"Mercury?"

A small, gruff noise came from deep in his throat. "The leader of our pack. He always talked strategies when we had to fight as a group."

"Oh, damn. Tell me he isn't somewhere onboard." That was the last thing she needed.

"No," he said. "But I will tell you what I often tell him. Even an excellent strategy cannot guarantee success."

"If something can go wrong, it will go wrong?" She wrinkled her nose. "Damn, you're a pessimist. I hate pessimists."

Secretly, Feeona agreed with him, but she had no intention of telling him. Plans and schedules were her way of minimizing the number of things that could go wrong. They gave her a sense of control that helped her keep a calm head. It was the best way she knew to deal with those things that inevitably did go wrong. "I—"

Jupiter tensed. His ears flicked, then he sprung to his feet in a blur of motion. He faced the doorway like a man ready to go into battle.

Feeona froze. "What is it?"

His ears flicked again, but he didn't face her. "Someone's coming."

She got to her feet and put a hand on his shoulder. "I thought you were going to wait until the ship got to the station to try to escape."

A muscle in his jaw ticked, but his stance eased.

She smoothed her palm along the bare muscle in a caress of regret, then let her hand fall to her side. He radiated heat and his body was all muscle. He was solid and vital and real and that made it all the harder to focus on the reason she was on the *Salley Ho*. "They're coming for me, not you. I wish there was something more I could do to help you, but I can't stay and I can't take you with me."

He looked at her then. His eyebrows bunched together and she knew he thought she was losing touch with reality.

"If you don't start trouble," she said. "Fitz won't hurt you. He wants you and your friend alive. Believe that, if nothing else I've said. That will give you power and some room to work in."

"Seneca is with them." Jupiter spoke softly, as if the words were for his own benefit rather than hers.

Feeona tried to inject some much-needed optimism into her voice. "That means he's okay, right?"

Jupiter nodded.

"That's great. So, good luck." In all the universe, why had he landed in her path and why now? Her stomach bunched. If things were different...

The sound of boots in the corridor drew her attention back to the doorway. Jupiter must have amazing sensory abilities.

He'd alerted her long before Bug would have been able to detect the men approaching.

"Damn." She'd forgotten Bug, and that was a measure of how distracted she'd been by the man in the bunk. Feeona closed her eyes, disrupted the camera and sent the call for Bug.

By the time Fitz strode through the doorway, her eyes were open and Bug had crawled into her recently re-coiffed hair. Jupiter had been right about Seneca. He was there with a half-dozen men pointing stingers and pulse pistols at him.

She could almost feel the tug between the two Arena Dogs, but Jupiter backed away, giving Fitz no reason to delay opening the security field. She wanted to hug him for being so cooperative.

Feeona focused her attention on the captain. "If you're thinking of putting three of us in here, Fitz, I'm going to have to file a complaint."

Fitz approached the hand control pad and waited as one of his men poked Seneca in the ribs. The jab didn't seem to bother the Arena Dog, but Seneca stepped forward, hands secured behind his back.

Fitz eyed Jupiter. "Stay right there, or your friend here will have a zero distance pulse blast through the back. Mattie, you're stepping out. You," he said to Seneca. "You're going in."

Fitz didn't even bother to sneer or take any verbal jabs at Feeona and that worried her some.

"Problem, Fitz?" Feeona kept her voice light.

Fitzhew scowled at her. "We have an Alliance patroller grabbing on. Apparently, they tracked you to me. They were looking for you because you've got warrants." Fitz humphed. "Knew you were a damned criminal."

He triggered the controls and the pulse field fizzed off.

Feeona stepped out as Seneca stepped in. She thought she heard a low-pitched "thank you" as they passed, shoulder to shoulder. Behind her, the pulse field buzzed back into place.

"Well, at least the Alliance has better accommodations." She kept the chipper note in her voice, but the tightness in her throat made it difficult. Leaving Jupiter and Seneca behind made her stomach churn.

One of Fitz's crew grabbed her arm and yanked her around, putting her back to him. It left her facing the small cell. She watched the two Arena Dogs as the guy behind her jerked her lower arms together. The cool press of plasmold restraints against her wrists didn't worry her, but she wished the incompetent bastard would hurry. The connection clear between Jupiter and Seneca squeezed her heart and Jupiter's glance her way only added to the constriction in her throat.

He wasn't expecting anything from her and she owed him nothing. So why was walking away making her head hurt and her belly ache? She had other priorities. Life and death priorities.

Sometimes the universe was a bitch.

CHAPTER NINE

The Salley Ho
Earth Alliance Beta Sector
2210.147

The *Salley Ho* crewman pulled Feeona into the hallway. Fitz led the way down the corridor. The crude banter between the crew made it clear that word of her being-nice-to-Jupiter gesture had made it around the ship. She let the comments roll off her shoulders. She should banter with them. That's what she would normally do, but the taste of Jupiter, the tug of his fingers in her hair, the press of him against the back of her throat wasn't something she wanted to turn into a joke.

Fitz led them to one of the secondary cargo bays and through the maze of stacked crates that filled the space. As they rounded the last crate, Feeona finally had a clear view of the ship-to-ship spanner rigged to the exterior hatch. She let herself study Stone and Barney, since she wasn't supposed to know them. They'd done a creditable job of cleaning up enough to pass as Alliance patrollers. Barney had left off her usual arrangement of metal studs, gauges, and spikes, making her piercings less noticeable. Stone had shaved off the few scraps of graying hair that normally dotted his mostly bald scalp and his height gave him the illusion of authority. The weapons they carried were the only real giveaways—they were considerably overpowered for escorting one small-time thief onto their ship.

Stone and Barney both focused intensely on Fitz's men. A shiver crept down Feeona's spine. If she was assessing the situation without any expectations, she'd say they were waiting for all of Fitz's men to clear the crates. Ensuring they were in the open. Easy targets.

Damn. Something was very wrong.

Fitz's men were armed, but with her hands restrained and Stone and Barney's weapons trained on her, the crewmen had relaxed. Their weapons pointed at the decking beneath their feet. Some had even shoved their weapons into a holster or pocket.

Fitz approached Stone, too tense about having patrollers onboard to see the danger. "Here she is and, ah…" Fitz cleared his throat and shifted his stance, clearly nervous, but she'd bet he was nervous about the wrong thing. "Since she already has a long list of charges against her, I don't see a need to file a report and add my complaint to the lot."

No, Fitz was worrying about the wrong thing altogether. He'd just attacked a ship, probably killed the crew, and now he had the Arena Dogs in his brig. He was probably eager to get the men he thought were patrollers off his ship.

Feeona scanned the bay for the closest cover. Stone and Barney wouldn't have been carrying weapons that size unless they expected trouble. What had gone wrong? Until she knew what was going on, there was nothing she could do.

Stone frowned at Fitz. "Right. No need for trouble. No need for anyone to get hurt."

"Hurt?" Fitz's body jerked taut as if the volatility of the situation had finally struck like an electrical jolt. "We—"

Whatever Fitz would have said was cut short when Stone aimed his gun more pointedly in Fitz's direction. Fitz's hands lifted up in the universal assurance of cooperation and lack of weapons. He took a half step back. "Ah, I don't know what the problem is, but—"

"If you like your chest without a hole in it, you'll stay right where you are." Stone looked as serious as Feeona had ever seen him.

Barney had her big cannon aimed at Fitz's men. Anyone who knew weapons would know the cannon's blast could easily put them all on the deck. With their weapons already pointed at their feet, Fitz's crew had become teetering statues on the edge between playing it safe and doing something stupid enough to send them all crashing over the edge.

It was time to find out what was going on. Feeona kept her stance relaxed and open, not exactly an easy look to pull off with her hands restrained behind her back. She aimed her smile at Stone. "Maybe we could resolve this situation without anyone getting hurt, if you tell them what you need from them."

Stone's frown deepened even further, but he spoke to Fitz. "We intercepted your communication with Grande Owens. You've got an Arena Dog onboard. We'll be taking it off your hands."

Feeona's stomach turned at Stone's use of 'it' for the men she'd left behind in the brig. It didn't help her digestion to know that she'd given Stone the means to listen in on that transmission. She'd wanted him to be able to monitor the *Salley Ho* in case Fitz got a crazy notion in his head, like dropping her off on some lifeless rock before the planned rendezvous.

Fitz's placating demeanor flipped in a flash of anger. "Holy Hell, man. You seriously don't want to screw with Owens."

Stone belched. "I don't imagine Owens cares who he does business with. No reason we shouldn't be the ones to collect on the reward. We'll even let you keep the ship you've been prepping to tow. We got no way to haul that thing. Plenty of money to go around."

Fitz stomped his foot like an angry child. "You think I'm going to let you just walk onto my ship and take what you want?"

"That's exactly what I think," answered Stone. "First, you're going to unlock Mattie and she's going to walk over to the com panel with you. Then you're going to order your crew to bring the Arena Dog to us."

Fitz grabbed Feeona and shook her. "You! You're in league with them." His pale face flamed to a red as bright as his hair.

"Hey," shouted Stone. "I said release her restraints. Do as you're told unless you want to lose every man and woman in this room."

Fitz let go of her arms, but she knew she'd probably have bruises from the way he'd gripped her. He turned her and released the plasmold ties.

Stone shifted his focus to Feeona. "Sorry, Mattie. Can't pass up this kind of money."

Everything went from unfortunate to plasma-storm in a flash. Fitz shoved her toward Stone. She tried to get her feet under her, but she crashed into him. She didn't actually register the sound of the blast as Stone fired his cannon no more than ten centimeters from her face. Everything went eerily silent. She could see Stone shouting. Muzzle-flashes flared and winked out. Sparks danced in her peripheral vision as projectiles from a stinger weapon hit the bulkhead near her. It all happened in complete silence. That had to mean the blast had taken out her hearing.

Her journey down to the decking as she tumbled down Stone's body seemed stretched, as if time were an elastic string pulled just short of breaking. A fiery sensation blistered across her shoulder as a burst round burned into her arm. When she finally hit the deck, the entire bay was an explosion of motion. Some of the crew were down. Some had made it up and over the crates and were returning fire, but that wouldn't last long. Stone and Barney were blasting their way through the freight at an impressive rate.

Fighting for breath, she rolled to her side and scooted to the nearest crate.

Out of the direct line of fire, Feeona fell back on the decking and took stock. She couldn't feel her left arm and she was starting to shake. Not good.

A quick check assured her she wasn't bleeding all that much. She'd taken a few pieces of shrapnel, but that seemed minor. It had to be the plasma burn on her shoulder that was flooding her body with adrenaline and endorphins.

She could probably get to her feet, but it would be safer to let her unfortunate choice of rescuers drive the crew out of the bay and out of her way. She needed time to think anyway. Closing her eyes, she sent Bug airborne.

She looked through Bug's eyes as she sent the device speeding down the corridor. The sudden shift in perspective, combined with her fogged brain and damaged inner ears, gave her an uncomfortable dose of vertigo.

She sent Bug toward the brig on instinct, not certain yet what her next move should be. If she wanted to play the optimist, she might hope Stone and Barney would still get her out of there. She had what she'd come for. Why should Stone's decision to claim the bounty on the Arena Dogs mean anything to her? She'd

just walked away and left them. She could do it again. Getting to
the cargo that waited for her on Petro-5 had to be her top
priority. But before that, she had to get back to her ship and
collect her earnings for this job. Stone was unlikely to cooperate
if he had his eye on the bigger bounty of the Arena Dogs. No
way she could pay him more than he could collect from Roma.
She could play along with Stone, then help Jupiter and Seneca
down the line. But if Stone didn't come out victorious in this
skirmish, she'd be even more screwed than she already was. No.
Working directly with Jupiter and Seneca was the better choice.
It was a risk, but all the risk was on her terms, the way she liked
it. Her instincts told her to go with Jupiter. It was her best bet.

Leaning heavily on the crate for support, Feeona climbed to
her feet and started moving slowly toward the hatchway leading
to Stone's ship. She wobbled her way through the spanner and
found Stone's hatch sealed tight. There was no exterior entry
panel, which meant it would take a remote to open. Damn it.

She headed back through the spanner to the *Salley Ho*. The
big bay was still too motionless. Stone and Barney had chased
after what remained of the armed crew. The stench of singed
flesh and fresh blood made her last meal consider abandoning
her. She swayed on her feet and moved forward, hand skimming
along the crates and then the wall, for balance and to avoid
smacking into anything she might miss seeing while she focused
on controlling Bug. Her ears had started ringing and the false
signals competed with the auditory signals Bug sent directly to
her implant. At least it meant her hearing would recover.

She stepped carefully over the bodies of the fallen crew
members and made her way to the corridors that would take her
further into the innards of the ship. She needed to keep in range
of Bug and get to her final destination—the only option she had

left. Trying to navigate the corridors, control Bug, and avoid the fighting would be a challenge. Her chest heaved in a silent laugh, shooting pain along her ribs. Despite the pain, her heart and her mood had lightened. Jupiter might be right about her being crazy.

CHAPTER TEN

The Salley Ho
Earth Alliance Beta Sector
2210.147

The moment the crew disappeared with the woman, Jupiter gave into his thumping pulse and reached for his pack brother. When Seneca stepped back, Jupiter hesitated. His belly clenched and his muscles stilled to stone. He hadn't seen that hesitation from his friend in years. Was that small step a natural show of respect for Jupiter's greater size in the small space of the cell? Or a memory from his past, dragging fear or shame into the present? If anyone had harmed Seneca… brought back those feelings with their actions, Jupiter would find them. He'd rip off every body part that had touched his pack brother. No, he'd hold them down and let Seneca do it for himself.

Jupiter waited, letting Seneca speak to him with those soulful eyes of his. Eyes that told him Sen didn't want the distance he'd made between them. That he needed Jupiter close. In truth, Jupiter needed that too. Slowly, he put a hand on Sen's shoulder. On the training field or on the battlefield Jupiter allowed no distance between them. There, hesitation could be death. There, everything was clear. There, only survival mattered. But in this, nothing was as simple as it seemed.

Seneca closed the distance, moving in until only a few centimeters separated them. He bowed his head and Jupiter mirrored the movement. The press of their foreheads was a gesture they'd shared for years. It was familiar and comforting, but with their recent brush with death blazed freshly in their memories, it wasn't enough. Not for either of them. Tension vibrated through Sen's body. His scent let Jupiter know Sen would welcome a move for more closeness. Jupiter pulled his pack brother into his arms and the smaller Dog melted against him, clutching him tightly.

Memories of their last moments in the arena shuddered through Jupiter, leaving him shaken. He cradled Sen's head in his hands and tipped it up, cupping him from smooth jaw to that silky fine hair at the curve of his skull. "I thought you died."

Sen's hands stroked his back, wiping away the memories. "We're alive."

Jupiter nodded as his chest filled with pride at the fierce set of Sen's jaw. His pack brother was strong. In some ways, even stronger than Jupiter. He slipped his hands back down to the smaller Dog's shoulders and squeezed before easing away. "Now, we just have to *stay* alive."

"I saw Owens." The words rushed out, as if Seneca couldn't stand their taste any longer.

Hatred fired through Jupiter at the mention of the man who'd owned them all their lives. "Owens is here?"

Seneca shook his head. "Owens was talking to the Captain over a long range communication system. He thinks he can use the ship we were on to find the people who helped us."

Jupiter wanted to howl. Regret that he hadn't been able to defend their rescuers turned his anger inward. "The men from the ship are dead. No one else survived when they boarded the ship."

"I don't mean the crew," said Seneca. "Owens believes they were part of something bigger. He wants to use the ship's computers to track back to their home base. There might be others there. Other Dogs." Seneca pressed his palm against the center of Jupiter's chest. "We can't let Owens find them."

That thought churned in Jupiter's gut. "You're right." He put his hand over Sen's and pressed it more firmly against his skin. "There's no reason to think we were the first to be freed from the arena."

"Someone saved us from death." Uneasiness laced through Sen's voice.

"Hmm," Jupiter grunted and let his hand fall away from Sen's. "Our brothers must think we're dead."

"Yes." Sen settled onto the metal bunk, freeing up more space for Jupiter to move. "Dogs die in the arena all the time. How many of them are still alive?"

He didn't care, Jupiter realized as he stared at the top of Sen's silver-white head. He didn't care as long as Sen was one of them. Alive and strong. "There had to be someone working with them, someone working for Roma."

Sen straightened and looked up. "A trainer or a guard? Maybe a medic?"

Jupiter pictured the faces of all the possibilities and couldn't accept that any of the humans would help the Dogs. "No way to know."

Sen rolled his shoulders and Jupiter wished they had room to spar. He needed to stretch his muscles, but simple stretches were never enough for him. He needed something more energetic. Always had... and why did that lead him to thoughts of the woman? Just because she'd had a…satisfying way of relieving his restlessness, that didn't mean he should be wondering if she was still on the ship.

"Okay." Jupiter announced. "We make destroying that ship our priority. If there are more Dogs out there, we have to keep Roma from finding them."

A sense of purpose settled into him and the weight of helplessness fell away. They had a goal. A priority. With those came direction and focus.

"Agreed," Seneca said, eyes serious and somber. "If Dogs are living free…we'll ensure they *stay* free."

Jupiter nodded and they shared a moment of silent accord.

Seneca tilted his head to the side. His ears twitched and his eyes narrowed as he climbed back to his feet.

A buzzing sensation tickled Jupiter's ears with a familiar melodic zing. The noise came from down the hall, and they both peered through the shimmering barrier that formed the front of the cell, waiting for the source to appear. Fee's small flying machine zipped into the main room of the brig and flew straight to the panel that controlled the cell door.

Seneca turned his face to Jupiter and raised an eyebrow. Words that had started to form on his lips froze in place as a discordant rhythm came from the small device.

Jupiter shook his head, uncertain why Fee's small flying machine, Bug, had returned, but he didn't think it had been part of her plan. "Something must be wrong."

The pulse field flickered, then winked off. Bug jerked away from the panel and headed toward the hallway. He and Seneca leaped across the invisible line where the barrier had stood.

"She wants us to follow." Seneca was already trailing the device.

They stayed close as Bug zipped along the corridor near the ceiling. Fee's voice echoed in Jupiter's memory...*if I can help you find a way off this ship, I will.* Was that what this was? Had she found a way to help them?

As he and Seneca ran easily, side-by-side, he considered the situation and his own surprising reactions. When he'd seen the device, he hadn't even considered that it might be a trick. He trusted Fee, possibly the first human to earn that from him. But why did Sen seem so willing to follow her blindly? He studied his pack brother. "How do you know about the device?"

Sen's brows drew together. "She used it to speak to me in the med center and just now in the cell." Sen's eyes shifted away. "She saved you."

She'd checked on Seneca just as she'd told him.

Seneca shot a glance at the flying device that had returned to hover closer. "He can't hear you," he said, clearly not talking to Jupiter. "Our hearing is different." They locked gazes and Sen spoke again. "She says to tell you she has a plan."

Of course, she did. Jupiter remembered her lecturing him on the value of a good plan. "She probably has a schedule too," he mumbled.

Seneca kept pace with Jupiter as they ran behind the winged machine. With their natural healing abilities and good medical care, they were both recovering quickly. Seneca's muscles heated and stretched. Strength pounded through him. Despite the uncertainties surrounding them, the moment felt right as they settled into the rhythm of the run.

Against his will, his thoughts drifted to Jupiter and the woman and speculation on what had happened between them. He'd bitten back the temptation to ask Jupiter when he'd first entered the small cell. Their scent, not distinct but intertwined, had been everywhere, but especially on the bunk. And her scent had been on Jup's skin.

Arousal had been there. Jupiter's arousal, dominant and distinct. Seneca might not have scented it often, but that scent had been seared into his memory—it featured in all his impossible fantasies. He'd known Jupiter was attracted to women. Females of their kind were scarce. But recently a female had been given to their pack. She and Carn, one of their brothers, had bonded as mates. It was their way to share all things. And when the female was willing, a mate most of all. It created a bond that ensured they would all protect and provide for her. They'd all fucked her. All but Diablo, the least stable of their brothers. So, Seneca had known Jupiter desired females. It had been the strength of the scent that had shocked him. But the moment for questions had passed and they ran in silence.

They followed the little machine through the ship as bland hallways gave way to an even blander gray metal bulkhead. The space opened up around them and they ran at full speed for more than the length of the arena field. It gave him a sense of the ship's size. Big.

The tiny flying machine stopped in front of a hatch, latching onto a control panel. Seneca found it hard to stop moving and wait. His muscles were warm and his genetically engineered body hummed.

"Seneca." The high-pitched mechanical voice snagged his attention. "Stand clear. When the hatch opens, don't go through. You guys hang in there."

He relayed the message to Jupiter with a shrug. He could hear the woman's words, but that didn't mean he understood what she was up to.

Jupiter nodded, but Seneca knew he wanted to demand details. Patience had never been his strength.

When the door slid open, they looked inside to see a small room outfitted with padded benches and heavy straps. The door slid shut again and Bug took-off down the passageway. They sprinted after the thing and followed it down the long, straight corridor.

"I think this is the exterior bulkhead." Sen pointed to the bright red CAUTION: DECOMPRESSION AREA boldly printed across a rectangular section that might be a hatch.

Like most Dogs, Jupiter couldn't read the human language, but he would understand the color and bold print always meant danger. Seneca had learned to read at the knee of one of the arena patrons who thought he was doing him a great favor.

The little robot stopped again and went to work on a second hatch, identical to the first. Only, this one was at the point of an intersection with another passage, so they were exposed on three fronts.

Jupiter paced as they watched Bug do its task. "Did she say anything about what we're doing?"

"No, but—"

"I don't...have...time." The small mechanical voice didn't provide the explanation Jupiter wanted, so Sen kept the broken speech, which could mean anything, to himself.

The sound of men with no care for hiding their footsteps echoed down the hall. "Humans," said Sen. He tilted his head to get more of the sound. "Three. They must have discovered our escape."

"And they sent only three?" Jupiter scoffed under his breath.

The familiarity of preparing for a fight pushed everything else out of Seneca's mind. "No match unless they have weapons."

Jupiter muttered softly. "Clever woman."

"What?" Seneca hadn't heard the woman speak through the device again.

Jupiter shook his head, then grinned. "The woman said they'll want us alive. We can use that."

Seneca nodded his understanding.

The crewmen never slowed, as if they were unaware of the danger. They would be carrying weapons, but Jupiter's words were all the strategy he needed to deal with that likelihood. They'd fought together so often, the rest would come naturally.

Jupiter surged forward, leading them toward their opponents. As long as the enemy would not fire lethal shots on their direct approach, the closer space of the corridor would be to the Dogs' advantage. The crew skidded to a stop—two males and a female. As Jup predicted, they held simple stun guns.

Seneca felt the first jolt roll through him. He flew forward, taking one of the males to the decking. He fisted the man's hair and smacked his head solidly against the metal plates beneath them. He was hooking an arm around the legs of his next opponent the moment the male's eyes rolled back in his head.

The female came crashing down, all flailing arms and elbows. Pain exploded in his right eye as one of the bony joints connected. He seized one of the legs already in his grasp and twisted until he'd won a satisfying cracking sound from her fragile human bones.

He took a quick second to assess their situation. Jupiter had dealt with the third opponent, who now lay unmoving on the ground. Another unpleasant pulse of energy fired through him, jerking his attention to the female.

She'd found the weapon she'd dropped and was about to hit

him with a third stun blast, one too many, when the weapon went flying and her arm dropped limply from the power of Jupiter's kick.

She fell back right into Seneca and, carrying them both to the ground, she writhed in pain. Seneca shoved her lower limbs off him and reached out to take the hand Jupiter offered.

"Put them in the pod." The mechanical voice was back. "Don't get trapped inside."

The device had finished its task. The door to the small room stood open. "She wants us to put them in there."

Jupiter raised an eyebrow, but complied, dragging the two men into the crowded space. Seneca carried the woman. He gave some thought to strapping her to one of the benches. The straps must be there for a reason, but the warning against getting trapped stopped him. In the end, he dumped her inside and stepped back.

The doors slid shut and the mechanical device launched into the air. It headed down the corridor, so they followed. It finished with a third hatch without interruption, then sped along again. This time it led them on a path complicated by turns.

The bare metal walls were long behind them and Seneca realized the corridors had started to look familiar. "This is the way back to where we entered the ship."

Jupiter barked low—a vague sound.

"Why is she taking us there?" Seneca couldn't hold back his concern. "The captain said the ship was damaged beyond repair."

Jupiter barked again with more certainty. "If they think we have no reason to go there, it might be a good place to take cover."

"They'll search there eventually," Seneca pointed out,

surprised the more dominant Dog had answered at all.

Jupiter nodded. He lifted his nose in the air and his breathing turned slow and deep. "She's up ahead. Her scent grows stronger."

When the flying machine turned into a corridor that was different from the others, Jupiter slowed. Seneca looked at the expanse as Jupiter must see it. Half-meter square sheets of metal lined the floor, looking as if they'd been hastily thrown down to make a path. The rest of the floor, walls, and ceiling were made of a heavy textile stretched over metal ribbing.

"This is how they joined the two ships together," Sen explained as he stepped into the tube-like structure.

Jupiter followed close behind. "It is stupidly made."

The concern in Jupiter's gruff complaint warmed Seneca. "It's not far, Jup."

"Humph," was his prickly pack mate's only reply.

The deep breath Jupiter took and the alert position of his ears stole the moment of ease. In an instant, everything about him had gone on alert. There was something bad ahead.

CHAPTER ELEVEN

The Renegade
Earth Alliance Beta Sector
2210.148

Jupiter stepped onto the decking of the smaller ship. Smoke-tinged air filled his lungs and overpowered Fee's scent. "This place still smells of fire and death."

"And plasma discharges," added Sen.

The bodies of the dead crew had been removed, but there had been no other attempt to clean up. The melted pilot seat sat empty in a ring of singed metal. Blue lumps of fire suppressant splattered the hallway leading to the back of the ship.

Jupiter lost sight of Bug and he didn't see any sign of Fee. "Do you hear the device?"

Ears alert, Seneca tilted his head. "No."

Jupiter sniffed at the air and found the scent of the woman who'd slept with him and pressed her lips against his skin. It was there, hidden beneath the other more noxious odors and the chemical tinge that always accompanied her. He followed it deeper into the ship and found her lying on a bench in a two-meter square room that had no obvious purpose. Her chest rose and fell in an uncertain rhythm. Her hair was a tangled cloud around her face. With those green eyes closed, she looked ordinary. He saw little to hint at the vital, spirited woman who'd given him ecstasy with her mouth. A muscle in his jaw twitched with tension. The scent of blood and burnt flesh mixed with her softer essence. An open med-kit sat on the floor beside her and a white cloth lay across her shoulder.

Jupiter crouched down beside the bench and wrapped his hand around hers. "Fee?"

Her eyes fluttered open and her hand tightened on the fingers he'd curled under her palm. "You're clear." Coughing interrupted her words. "That's good. Seneca?"

"I'm here." Sen stood in the doorway.

She'd wrapped a dark blue cloth around her arm, but he could taste the taint of the dried blood beneath. It was the shoulder that worried him. She tried to sit, but Jupiter quickly pressed his palm over her chest.

"Be still," Jupiter complained. "You're injured."

Her muscles relaxed and she fell back. Her lips curved in a hint of a smile. "I think... I like you bossy."

Her eyes fell closed and she said nothing more.

He leaned closer and breathed her in. There was definitely a burn under the white cloth. Burns could be serious, fatal. "Fee?"

Her eyes snapped opened. "Hmm?"

The wave of relief he felt was short lived, but he refused to show his fear. "We need to treat your injury?"

She humphed and her eyes narrowed. "Yeah, but right now we need to get deeper into the ship and keep out of sight."

Jupiter wanted to return her humph with a bark of his own. She was near losing consciousness. "Are you sure your wish to relocate isn't just part of a quest to find ever more uncomfortable resting places?" He reached for the cloth pressed to her shoulder.

"Don't!" Her fear-filled demand startled him.

"How bad?" He couldn't move her until he knew.

This time her bright green eyes stayed open and wide. They were glassy and serious. "It's a plasma burn. But it's superficial. Didn't shred the muscle. I'll heal."

He wasn't sure he believed her assessment. He wanted to see for himself. "Let me tape it for you, then we'll move you to wherever you want to go."

"After. You can tape it after." Fee shoved against him, in another attempt to sit-up. "It's stuck to the wound. It won't slip."

A shock wave rippled through the hull. Jupiter stretched an arm across her to keep her from falling to the floor.

"What was that?" Sen crouched in the hallway, ready to defend them.

Feeona patted Jupiter's hand where it had slid up to grasp her uninjured shoulder. "That was the nearest of the escape-pods disconnecting and engaging its thrust engine."

Jupiter frowned. Her words made little sense to him. "Escape-pods?"

"Yes." She nodded slowly. "Small vessels the crew can use to leave the ship in emergencies."

"The small rooms your device opened," Sen said. "Those were escape-pods?"

"Three of them," she answered. "This ship has dozens. Standard safety feature. We need Fitz to believe we got off the ship. It's the only way they'll stop looking long enough for us to find a better place to hide."

She pulled against Jupiter's restraining hand and this time he decided they'd played out this battle for dominance long enough. He slipped an arm under her knees and one under her shoulders. She hugged her injured arm close to her chest as he lifted her.

She was trembling, but her free arm curled over his shoulder. Jupiter chuffed his approval.

When Sen looked to him for direction, Jupiter considered what needed to be done. "Clean-up anything that could give away that we're here then follow."

Jupiter carried her deeper into the ship past the many rooms that lined the hallway. At the end of the corridor a spiraling ramp led to the lower decks. They went one level down and stopped when the woman moaned in pain.

Jupiter growled in the back of his throat. "You need medical care."

Lips pressed together, tight and bloodless, she nodded. "There might be a med-bay. Most likely place is this level."

He hadn't been in a med-bay, but it had to be something like the medical center in the arena. He'd recognize it.

Sen had followed them down the stairs. He slipped past and started down the corridor, opening doors as he went.

Jupiter followed, cradling Fee close.

"Here," Sen said, as he stepped aside.

Jupiter entered the small room that looked much as he expected. Familiar instruments were neatly stored in purpose-made bins that attached to the walls and ceiling. He strode to the med-bed in the center of the room and started to put Fee down.

"No, wait," she protested. "Over on the bench."

He hesitated. A molded shelf, barely suitable for seating, extended across one short wall. It had to be a joke. "I assure you the examining table will be uncomfortable enough to suit you."

"Gee, thanks." Her attempt at a grin did little to hide the strain tightening her features. "Sweet of you to think about that for me, but the supplies I need are over there and I'll be able to find what I need more quickly than I can tell you."

Not sure of the wisdom of his choice he put her down where she wanted, near the compartment-covered wall. She ran her fingers from label to label as she read. "Here." She opened a shallow drawer. She pulled out a hypo-injector then shoved the drawer shut, moving on to the next set of compartments. Another drawer yielded rows of tiny injection cubes.

With shaking hands, she dropped the tiny cube into his palm. "Load this one."

His fingers fumbled and Sen came in and took it from him.

The woman retrieved a pre-filled spray from another drawer. "This is it."

"You need more than pain meds and quick patching," Jupiter argued. "The burned flesh could become infected, if it's not removed and it will scar if it isn't stitched."

The Arena Dogs were allowed to scar because Roma wanted them to look tough, not because the Dogs wanted it that way.

Her lips lifted weakly and she patted his cheek with her good hand. "You sure *you're* not a medic?"

"It is as you say. I have had need of much medical care." His voice came out softer than he intended. She was growing shakier, and he could no longer find the spirit to banter with her as if nothing were wrong.

"The injector isn't a pain med, it'll speed up the healing. The spray will debride the burn. After the spray, you'll need to use the silver nozzle built into the overhead to neutralize the enzymes and clean away anything still in the wound." She gripped at his shoulder, ready to be lifted back into his arms. "I'm not worried about sutures or scarring. I just need you to do the nozzle part and then slap a bandage over it. You can do that, right? I expect to be unconscious pretty quick after the spray."

As he carried her to the med-bed, he couldn't look away from her eyes. The sparkle of mischief that normally resided there had faded, but they still captivated him. Her inner strength impressed him. Her obvious faith that he would take care of her when she lost consciousness amazed and humbled him. He'd done nothing to earn her trust.

Seneca moved to stand at his side. "We'll take care of it."

"I will," Jupiter added his promise. He reached for the overhead unit mounted above the bed then pulled it down to an easier reaching distance.

"The hypo-injector," she demanded with her hand outstretched.

Sen kept the hypo. "Just tell me where."

Her face showed strain. "Oh, yeah, okay. You can put it near my left shoulder blade. As close to the wound as you can make it." She angled her body giving him better access to her back.

"Just press it to the spot and pull the trigger?" Sen gently pulled down the torn neckline of her shirt.

She sucked in a breath as the material clung to the wound. "That's right. Don't worry. It's hard to mess up." She gritted her teeth and waited.

Sen pulled the trigger and she nodded. "Well done." She reached for Jupiter's hand and squeezed. "See the blue and green stripped nozzle up there?" She pointed to the overhead equipment rack.

He reached for it.

"Spray a little of that on the bandage. Then I need you to hold my arm still when your friend pulls off the steri-cloth."

He did as she asked. The strain in her features urged him to move quickly. He reached for her injured arm. "Where is it safe to hold on?"

"Doesn't matter. I'm only feeling the burn right now."

She didn't let go of her death grip on his right hand so he braced her arm with his left.

Sen set aside the hypo and gently lifted the cloth.

Fee panted in pain.

He pulled a little more and they could both see that the tissue below was a blistered and raw gash of muscle. What was left of her shirt had melted into the wound.

"Fuck," Jupiter muttered. "Fuck those bastards all to hell."

"Amen," she panted.

Sen pulled a little more. She gasped and would have jerked away hard had Jupiter not been holding her steady.

She spoke through gritted teeth, tears welling in her eyes. "Just get it over with." She braced. "Make sure all of the cloth is out of there, okay?"

Jupiter pressed a kiss to her forehead. "I'll take care of you."

Seneca didn't give her a chance to respond. He pulled the cloth the rest of the way off in one continuous pull. Not so fast as to add to the rips already gouged into her flesh, but fast enough to cause considerable pain until it was done. Feeona went limp momentarily then clenched her good hand against him.

"Let go, Fee. I'm here." Jupiter cradled her closer to his body as Sen pushed her hair out of the way and sprayed on the debriding enzyme.

She groaned and her body sagged as she blessedly passed out. Jupiter sighed in relief. At least she wouldn't be feeling pain. He repositioned her on the med-bed and reached for the silver nozzle. He looked up to Seneca. "See if you can find some grabbers, a suture threader, or maybe that spray-on artificial skin the medics use."

Sen nodded. A moment later, he handed Jupiter a pair of

grabbers and laid out the other items along the edge of the bed.

In silence, they worked to fix her. She would heal well and there would be no scars. Of that, he would make sure. When he was satisfied with his task, he sprayed a graft-bandage over the injuries. It formed a white crust, like an armored skin.

Sen carried away the used instruments, dropping them into a compartment with a bio-hazard symbol. "She's an unusual human."

Jupiter understood the unspoken thoughts behind the words. He'd never aided a human in his life. He hated them, but this small woman *was* different. He knew Sen was warning him to be cautious. Just because the woman had aided him didn't prove she could be trusted. Humans were manipulative creatures. Sen had more reason than most to hate them, but he'd never been vocal about it. Maybe because his own people had not always treated him well either.

Jupiter frowned. "Call me a fool if you wish, but I trust her."

Sen returned with a fresh set of instruments. He met Jupiter's gaze steadily. "I don't judge you or question your actions."

The simple statement of support should have steadied him, but Jupiter felt wholly unbalanced.

Sen spoke softly. "We should tend to her other injuries while she's unconscious."

They'd heard no sign of anyone investigating the ship, so Jupiter went to work on the rest of her. Blood had soaked through her clothes in several places. He cut away the material to get at the tiny bits of shrapnel embedded in her flesh. Small shallow wounds on her arm were easily closed, but his hand shook as he dug into a particularly deep puncture.

"Let me take over for you," Sen offered. "You're still weak from your injuries."

Jupiter growled instinctively and followed it with a sharp bark. "I can do it." Jupiter started again, this time with steadier hands and a calmer voice. "See if you can find a warming blanket and anything else useful."

Sen slunk away into the shadows. Jupiter regretted the sharpness of his response. Something that Sen might have interpreted as censure when he hadn't meant it that way. The Dog was so loyal, so capable, so necessary for Jupiter's peace of mind.

But he needed to deal with this himself. He slowly set about removing the metal shards, cleaning and spraying over each small wound.

Sen reappeared at his side with the asked-for blanket and some packaged water. He stretched the blanket out across the woman.

Jupiter laid his hand on Sen's shoulder. "Thank you, my brother. I couldn't have gotten through this without you."

A thud that rattled through the small ship and the deck beneath his feet disappeared as the artificial gravity failed. Jupiter scrambled to pull the now floating Feeona tightly to his chest. Another shock wave rippled through the hull. The lights flashed then went dark. He lost all sense of direction. He was in the air, anticipating a hard landing. He curled his body around Feeona as best he could, unsure where or when the impact would come. Dim red lights appeared above him. The gravity reengaged and his body became a stone dragging him toward the deck. He slammed against it, taking the impact with his back. His head hit the decking hard enough that he expected a pounding headache. He managed to ensure Fee didn't land beneath him, but the fall had to have jarred her. Fortunately, she'd stayed unconscious through it all.

He looked for Sen and found the Dog lying on his side a meter away, propped on an elbow and his smiling face painted red by the odd lights.

Jupiter growled his annoyance. "What are you fucking smiling at?"

Sen's lips softened. "Sorry. This day just keeps getting stranger." Sen looked thoughtful. "Actually, it's turning out to be the best day I've had in a while."

Speechless, Jupiter stared.

Sen shook his head, still smiling. "The woman will heal. And we're alive."

"So far."

Sen's face turned serious. "We're free. And we're together."

"You and the woman will get along." Jupiter adjusted her in his arms then got to his feet. "Damn optimists." He shot Sen a look to see he'd also gotten to his feet. He settled Fee back on the table. "Come on," Jupiter barked. "Let's finish this and find out what's happening."

CHAPTER TWELVE

The Renegade
Earth Alliance Beta Sector
2210.148

"You must wake." A soft touch on Feeona's good arm accompanied the words. Seneca crouched near the edge of her bunk. They were no longer in the med-bay and she didn't see Jupiter. All of her pains were still with her, but they seemed to be dulling. They must have given her pain meds after all. She tried to sit and got one shoulder off the mattress before the pain knocked her back down. She couldn't help the groan. Okay, maybe dulling wasn't the right word to describe her level of pain.

"Easy," Seneca urged. "You'll re-open your wounds." His voice was smoother than Jupiter's, like good brandy to the punch of aged scotch.

The thin bedding beneath her was only slightly better than the bunk in Fitz's brig. That thought brought Jupiter's dry teasing to mind and she realized she missed him, if that was even possible. She didn't know Seneca and his serious expression didn't put her in the mood for small talk. She tried again to sit, focusing on using her core to compensate for the injury, but the rest of her body failed to cooperate.

"Let me help you." He wedged a large hand under her good shoulder and eased her into a sitting position.

She tucked her left arm against her chest and bent her legs to the side, turning toward him. "Thanks."

He dipped his head slowly in acknowledgement, big lavender eyes fixed on her face.

"How long was I out?"

"Not long," he said. "Your injury is serious. I wish I could let you rest and heal, but I fear we need your help."

She heard the thud, thud, thud of shoes against decking as someone came toward them, moving fast. Her whole body tensed and her heart accelerated.

Seneca didn't move. Still and calm, his hand slipped away. "It's Jupiter."

The bigger man appeared through a hatchway. He loomed over them, larger than she remembered. That wasn't exactly true. She remembered him being large—it was just that her brain had been telling her he couldn't be *as* large as she remembered. But he was. Large and alive and looking healthy. The mends she'd made seemed to be holding. The injuries were already starting to heal—miraculous. Soon they would just be two more scars on a body covered with them.

He frowned. "You must be in pain. Why are you awake?"

"I'm okay," she fibbed. "I might even give standing up a try, if you're willing to catch me if I start to fall on my ass."

Jupiter stepped closer, scowling and Seneca moved out of the way.

Instead of pulling her up, Jupiter squatted down in front of her and kissed her forehead. The soft heat where he pressed his lips sent warmth through her core and then out to her extremities. When he leaned back his scowl had softened. "No sign of fever."

"I'm okay." She held his gaze and let the warmth he'd shared with her, beam back at him. "And I owe you my thanks. I mean, really, thank you." She ignored the pain and smiled at him again. "Now, why don't you tell me what's happening?"

She thought he might not answer, but after a moment and a glance to Seneca and back to her, he relented. "The door to this craft has closed. We're trapped in here."

She didn't manage to keep the shock off her face. She could feel it lifting her eyebrows and tightening her face. "They know we're here? No," she asked and answered her own question, thinking aloud. "If they knew, they wouldn't just close us in."

"We don't know what's happening." Jupiter wrapped a warming-blanket around her shoulders. "The ship rocked and the lights changed, and when I went back, the hatch had been closed."

She closed her eyes to engage Bug. Dizziness engulfed her. She opened her eyes, desperate for some reference. Strong hands clamped around her biceps. She leaned into him. His body stiffened against her, but she needed his strength whether he liked it or not. "You missed an easy opportunity to kill me." She muttered against his chest.

His hands tightened gently. "For Arena Dogs, easy is usually a trap."

She laughed a single release of breath. "I need to lean on you for just a minute, okay? It's kind of embarrassing, but I'm not exactly steady here, big guy."

"I'm here," he reassured with a soft, low rumble.

Feeona pressed her forehead against his chest and relaxed into his hold. She closed her eyes and checked Bug's power reserves and sensors. Power was low, but Bug was still functional and right where she'd left it, clinging to a tangle of wires hanging out of a control panel on the flight deck. Through Bug's vision, she could see the closed hatchway just as they'd said.

"What is she doing?" Sen spoke softly. "Did she lose consciousness again?"

"She is operating the remote device," Jupiter explained. "She must concentrate to control the machine."

There wasn't enough power for Bug to take flight, so Feeona tried for a wireless hack into the ship's systems. The baseline interface came up, but all she could get out of it was a systems lockout. She tried a back door into the power stats, a system that didn't usually get a lot of protection.

"Bingo." She spoke unintentionally, the word heartfelt but barely a whisper.

"What is bingo," Jupiter rumbled.

Feeona welcomed the small surge of adrenaline that came with success. "Old Earth saying. Means I win or, in this case, I get into the computer system."

"That's good?" His question vibrated beneath her cheek.

She pressed more firmly against him, deciding she liked feeling his voice rumble up from his chest when he spoke.

The ship's response came back with power consumption levels. She could have sworn the *Salley Ho* had been feeding the ship power, but there was no sign of any external power coming into the system now.

"Good? Yes," she answered. "Just checking the logs for the past twenty-four hours."

"What will that tell us?" He released his hold on her biceps and settled his arms around her. His warmth chased away her chill more effectively than the warming-blanket around her shoulders.

She reexamined the figures and her heart surged into her throat at the only possible explanation. She opened her eyes and looked up at him.

"I need to get up to the flight deck." The one-million things she hadn't checked before she'd passed out flooded her tired brain. Like what ship systems were still functional. She pushed at Jupiter's torso, panic and hope driving her to move, but he didn't release her. He didn't budge a centimeter.

Jupiter's dark eyes fixed on hers. "Tell me."

She took a breath, in and out, struggling for a calm that wasn't going to come. Her brain hadn't decided if the situation was disaster or miracle, but her body just reacted to the certainty that she needed to be ready. "The power consumption shows a substantial loss. The link to the *Salley Ho* is… gone. I… I think we're floating free."

Seneca spoke from outside her peripheral vision. "The captain told Owens this craft is damaged beyond repair."

"People lie," she warned. "It may be damaged, but there can't be a hull breach or we'd already be dead. The power is low, but it obviously isn't out completely. And since we're all still breathing and not floating around weightless, the grav-generators and environmental controls are working well enough." She took a deep breath and released it. "But Bug's power reserve is nearly drained so I can't know anything for sure until I can get up to the flight deck."

"Wrap your arm around my neck," Jupiter encouraged.

As she did, he slid his arm under her butt and stood, lifting her with him.

Seneca appeared at their side. He tucked the dislodged warming-blanket back around her. "Why would they disconnect?"

Feeona gritted her teeth against a fresh wave of pain. "I hate to speculate, but my plan to trick them into thinking you were in the escape pods might actually have worked."

Jupiter carried her through the hatch and down an unfamiliar corridor. "You didn't think it would?"

She let her head rest against his shoulder as she answered. "The *Salley Ho* is a salvage ship. It has all sorts of exterior equipment. Things they'll be able to use to recapture the escape pods. I thought they'd catch at least one, probably two, of them before they got completely away from the ship. I figured they'd shoot down the other."

Jupiter made an odd, but not unpleasant, noise in the back of his throat. "Owens wants us alive."

She smiled, remembering their earlier conversation. "He does. Even if Fitz didn't blast the pods out of existence, he still had to deal with Stone and Barney."

"Stone and Barney?"

"The, uh, Alliance patrol. They were actually a team I paid to act like a patrol and get me off the *Salley Ho*."

"You knew you would be caught and need assistance," Jupiter summed it up correctly.

"All part of the plan. The key to survival in my business isn't never getting caught, it's making sure the mark never knows you stole from him."

"But you were caught before you could steal from the captain." Jupiter reached the ramp back to the upper levels and started up.

"That's what he thought, until my damn team decided stealing you from Fitz would earn them a better payday than I could provide. They double-crossed me. And damn it, if they didn't let Fitz know they were working for me. Now he'll question everything and probably figure out I was there to copy his navigation charts."

"So, you weren't trying to steal from him, just copy these charts?" He sounded like he wanted to mitigate her actions.

She hated to disappoint him, but she had an inexplicable need to set him straight. "Fitz might see things differently. Those charts give him an advantage over his competitors. An advantage they're eager to negate."

They'd made it to the top level and headed toward the pilot's station.

Seneca followed close behind, ears alert. His gaze met hers over Jupiter's shoulder. "So, what does all this mean for us?"

"That," she admitted, "remains to be seen."

"Where?" Jupiter stood in the middle of the scorch-marked space, waiting for her guidance.

"The pilot's console." Fee saw that the top half of the chair was missing. Some of the charred material melted into the seat had probably once been a part of the pilot. The thought did nothing to relieve the nausea brewing in her stomach. Too many damn meds.

Jupiter set her on her feet and steadied her until she found her balance.

Back straight, teeth gritted, she brushed the debris off the surface of the wide stretch of the pilot's interface. The rubble fell to the floor in a discordant percussion that sent a new round of stench into the air. She found the sensor station intact, but the display was dark. Resting one hand on the edge of the console for stability, she leaned over and put her palm against the inactive display. It came to glowing life. "I think I forgot how slow it can be to interface this way." She would have gone for Bug if she thought she could actually make it across the deck and back, but that wasn't happening. The arm she was using to prop herself up was her injured one and the muscles were already starting to shake.

She scrolled through the readings with the tips of her fingers. "Some of the external sensors are down, but there are enough of them active to confirm the *Salley Ho* isn't out there anymore."

Her arm collapsed on her suddenly. The inevitable impact with the console never came. A strong arm wrapped around her hips. "I've got you."

Jupiter. Strength and warmth radiated from his body to hers. She put her injured arm over his. "Can you get to that?" She pointed to the square pressure pad she could no longer reach.

He bent over, stretching and that shift pressed him more firmly against her back like a blanket of solid muscle wrapped around her.

"Press down," she instructed.

He did and the metal alloy wall in front of them hummed to life. Tiny droplets of charged silica appeared across it, like dew clinging to leaves. It spread to a thin layer then the colors changed to form the external view display.

Jupiter straightened suddenly. Seneca strode quickly to his side.

"Neat, huh? I remember the first time I saw one of these," she teased. "I thought it looked like the hull was melting away and that we'd go flying out into space."

"If that were the case, we would have felt a change in air pressure," Jupiter said, voice flat.

She met his eyes over her good shoulder. His face showed no hint of emotion, but that fact spoke volumes. He was being brave. "Not impressed, huh?" She hoped to lighten the mood, but his features remained stoic.

"There are many things we'll have to learn to survive outside the hell of Roma," he said. "But we are not completely ignorant."

The flatness of his voice almost crushed the satisfaction she was feeling at seeing the empty space around them. "I never thought you were, Jupiter." She turned to break free of his hold.

He let her step weakly free of the safe circle of his arms. She lurched her way through the wreckage, clinging to whatever she could reach, to retrieve Bug. By the time she reached its hiding spot, Jupiter was there too, lifting her back into his arms. She pulled Bug free from the snarl of exposed wires, then spoke without meeting his gaze. "Thanks. Back to the pilot's panel, please." When they reached it, Jupiter put her back on her feet. She placed Bug on the console. She adjusted its position and began a power siphon.

"Now what?" Jupiter asked, some of his stiffness gone.

Good question. There was still too much to do and too much that could go wrong, but sharing her concerns would benefit no one. "Now, we find out if we can fix this hulk, at least well enough to maneuver, before Fitz or Stone realizes you weren't in those escape pods and comes back."

Seneca leaned a hip against the opposite end of the control station as he watched her work. "How long will that be?"

"With any luck, they'll still be at odds and slow each other down. And I programmed a little surprise into the pod systems that should cause a minor explosion if they try to bring one of the pods onboard. Not enough to do serious damage, but enough to cause some confusion and make a mess. That's if they try to bring it on board and if they don't take precautions against a power overload."

"What are the odds they won't take precautions?" Seneca folded his arms across his chest, but the move looked all wrong on him.

"They won't expect you to know how to rig something like that, but they should at least be considering that I might and that I might have been with you. And since they're a professional salvage crew, I'd say the odds are pretty damn long against us."

Jupiter gently squeezed her good shoulder. "Now who's the pessimist?"

CHAPTER THIRTEEN

The Renegade
Earth Alliance Beta Sector
2210.148

Seneca watched the way Jupiter interacted with the woman. He'd never seen him show anything but hate to humans, but it wasn't Jupiter's concern for her health that surprised him the most. It was the easy verbal sparring, as if they'd known each other for years.

"You think you can fix the ship?" Jupiter kept a hand on her shoulder.

"I'm no mechanic," she said. "So if there's anything big wrong, I doubt I'll be able to do much. On the other hand, I'm a wiz at computer systems. There's obviously some systems damage, but I may be able to reroute things enough to get the ship back in functional condition."

The woman was swaying on her feet. She'd avoided the seat, but eventually had no choice but to use it. She needed rest and time to heal, but time was something they didn't have.

Jupiter paced as the woman worked. Yes, they'd followed Mercury as pack leader, but they were used to doing their own share of the fighting. Waiting made Seneca feel useless. It had to be even worse for Jupiter. It didn't take long before more lights and computer displays began to flicker on. A shudder rumbled through the decking and then faded away.

Feeona turned her chair to face them and rested her forearms against her thighs. She'd started to shake again. "I have good news and bad news."

"What's the bad news?" Jupiter's scowl had deepened.

"The maneuvering thrusters aren't responding at all and the standard space drive is only functioning at half capacity. It won't get us anywhere."

Seneca hoped the rest of her news outweighed the bad. "You said there's good news."

"Sure. Lots of it. Like, no sign of Fitz or Stone yet." She tapped the console with one hand. "The *Renegade* here has enough power to continue to run the grav drive and enviro for the next year or so."

"So we aren't in immediate danger," Jupiter concluded. "But we have no way to get away from this place and the other ships will return eventually."

The woman lifted her head. The circles beneath her eyes had darkened. She needed rest. "Yes and no. All interstellar ships have two drives: the standard drive for short distances within a system and a skipdrive for long distances. The skipdrive may still be functional."

Jupiter strode over to her and squatted down in front of her. "Why are you unsure?"

"The skipdrive is tied directly into the navigation systems and right now I'm completely locked out."

Seneca remembered the conversation he'd witnessed on the human ship. "Owens asked Fitz if he was able to retrieve the navigation data and Fitz told him he was unable to do so."

"Easy to see why." The woman shook her head as she spoke. "I've never seen this kind of encryption on something so innocuous as nav controls."

Seneca carefully chose his words. He wasn't sure what information to reveal to her. "Fitz and Owens seemed to think the ship's crew attempted to protect information about where the ship came from."

"That fits." She turned her attention to him briefly, then returned it to Jupiter, still directly in front of her.

Jupiter took one of her hands and cupped it in his. "This is why Fitz was planning to tow the vessel, so better technicians could attempt to break the encryption. We must not let that happen. We have vowed to destroy this ship before letting them retrieve that information."

It made Seneca uneasy to see Jupiter place such trust in her. She'd helped them. Saved Jupiter's life—something that had earned Seneca's gratitude. Despite that, they knew very little about her and her motives.

"Okay," the woman answered easily. "I can understand that." She sat straighter, pulling free of Jupiter's hands. "But I may be able to clear the existing nav charts and load Fitz's data. That way I could use the computer to do the *skip* calculations without actually using the ship's nav history."

Jupiter stood, towering over her with his powerful body. "Good solution."

She looked up to meet his gaze. "Thanks, but it will take me time to implement and once we get where we're going we'll be just as dead in the black as we are now."

"Anywhere would be safer than here," Jupiter answered.

She rested her good hand on the console as if preparing to get back to work. "I agree. So, I'm going to give it a try."

Jupiter held her gaze with that look of his, the one that brooked no refusal. "What can we do to help?"

She didn't hesitate. "You can look around to see what we've got. First priority, any weapons you can use in case we don't get out of here in time. Second priority, locate the engineering section in case we need to do anything down there to get this ship moving. While you're looking, take an inventory of food and water. I'll need to plan our *skip* so that we don't run out before we can get off this ship. Take note of anything else you think will be useful, fresh clothes, meds. Whatever. I'll open ship-wide coms, so we'll be able to hear each other."

Jupiter barked for Sen to go and search, but it was clear Jupiter had no intention of going far from the woman's side as she worked on the computer. She was perilously weak. Jupiter might be restless, but someone needed to make sure she didn't lose consciousness.

It was the right course of action, even if it did feel all wrong to Seneca. They were a team. They worked together. Or they had. Now Jupiter had the woman and Seneca would search the ship alone.

Jupiter wanted to go with Seneca. Something was troubling his pack brother, but it would have to wait. He would have to be content with the reassuring sound of Seneca's voice across the ship's com system as he searched and reported back what he found. Fee had closed her eyes, connecting to the ship through her device. She sat eerily still except for the barely perceptible sway or twitch of muscles struggling to keep her upright. He wanted to hold her so she could relax, but that might prove counterproductive. If she relaxed, she might lose her battle to stay alert and do… whatever it was she was doing.

He left her for brief moments to investigate nearby. In the strange square room that he had previously believed served no purpose, he found that pressing on the wall panels revealed hidden cupboards. Some held equipment or unopened supplies while others held what looked to be personal belongings. Several scented of Dog when he opened them and held coats, boots, even pouches of coins or small gems or pieces of plascard with writing on them. All things no Dog on Roma would possess. None contained weapons, so he returned to check on Fee.

She sat motionless as before, but Bug had taken flight. It circled her like a pooch-snake, a common pet of the patrons. The view screen still showed the space outside the ship. One of the distant dots grew larger as he watched.

Jupiter barked a warning. "They're coming."

"I know. I know." Fee's voice was little more than a mumble. "We're going to have to try to *skip*."

"Fee." Jupiter shook her shoulder until her eyes blinked open. "How can we help?"

Bug abruptly zipped off down the corridor that led deeper into the ship.

"Follow Bug and take Seneca with you. I have the nav system and skipdrive controls, but it needs a hard reset." When he frowned, she reached out and pushed at him. "Just go! I'll tell you as we go."

The dot on the display was large enough to make out the shape of a bulky vessel. He turned and bolted after her flying machine. He found it hovering over the ramp downward. As soon as he had it in sight, it headed straight down, floor after floor. Jupiter ran, pushing his muscles for maximum speed. Around and around until he could see what had to be the bottom of the ship still a few decks below. Planting a hand on the safety rail as he continued to move, he vaulted over the side and fell down through the center. He hit hard at the bottom, but he let his knees bend, ducked his body into a tight ball and led with his shoulder as he let momentum tumble him to the decking. He managed to roll and come up on his feet. He spared a heaving breath to bark for Seneca, then dashed after Bug.

Jupiter wove his way through an unfamiliar landscape made of metal, hulking blocks bolted to the floor and walls and cylindrical columns that stretch from floor to ceiling. A low mechanical hum rumbled around him and the stench of death hung heavy in the air. Some of the crew must have died down here, then been removed. The smell would be stronger if the bodies were still there.

Bug hovered in front of a control panel on the face of the biggest object in view. It filled one end of the compartment completely, with snakelike conduits stretching out in all directions and disappearing into the decking, walls, and ceiling.

"Look for a row of glowing red buttons." Fee's voice echoed from the ship's com system.

"There are things glowing red all over this panel," Jupiter growled.

"Look for five in a row. They are square, not part of the display screen. Actual raised buttons that you have to press in order from left to right. Look where Bug is hovering."

Seneca appeared at his side. "Look." He pointed. "They are numbered below."

"That's them! Push them, now!" Panic edged Fee's shout.

As Seneca pressed each button it changed from red to green. When the last button had been pushed, Bug darted over to another area of the control panel.

"Flip these red switches, top to bottom."

Jupiter flipped each switch as Fee continued with her instructions.

"When you finish that, the big lever to your right will be engaged. You have to pull it down to bypass the safety system and engage the skip-field generator."

The lever she referred to was easily as big as Sen. Jupiter reached for it and pulled. His biceps bulged with effort, but it barely moved. He stepped sideways to get a better grip and give Sen room to help. They tried together and the lever moved, but only a small portion of the way. It was nowhere near the bottom where it needed to be.

"Now, guys! We're running out—"

"Mattie!" Another voice carried through the ship and for a moment Jupiter thought Fitzhew had already boarded the ship.

Seneca grabbed his arm before he would have released the lever. "It comes from the other ship."

"Come on Mattie. I know you can hear me. You're not going anywhere in that ship. Let's talk. We can make a deal."

Jupiter and Seneca pulled together, making progress centimeters at a time.

Fee didn't bother to respond to the captain. "There has to be a metal bar that locks into the side of that thing for leverage." Her words were clipped, fast. They had no time for searching for the bar.

Sen barked. Jupiter saw his intention and braced for the full force of the lever. Sen released his grip and moved back. He took a few steps then launched himself at the machine, bounding up its face until he could wedge himself between the ceiling and the lever, now beneath his feet. Aided by his own weight, Sen pushed with his whole body. It gave, moving to half the full distance.

Jupiter barked. "Again." This time he added his weight. Sen pushed against the ceiling and Jupiter pulled himself up until his upper body was above the lever, his arms extended downward and his feet no longer touched the floor.

The lever gave way. Seneca and Jupiter landed sprawled on the floor. The ship shuddered beneath them.

"We're in skipspace." Fee's voice broadcast relief more than celebration.

Jupiter reached out and grabbed Sen's hand. "Victory," he whispered.

Sen squeezed his hand in return. "Victory."

CHAPTER FOURTEEN

The Renegade
Earth Alliance Beta Sector
2210.149

Seneca flipped the rehydrated meat that stretched over the heating elements. "Food's almost ready."

"Smells good." Jupiter appeared at his side and leaned forward to get a closer look.

The barest brush of shoulder to shoulder and the familiar scent of him made Seneca's gut tighten. Jupiter put a hand on his growling belly and chuffed his approval of the food.

They'd chosen the largest living area on the ship, not for its size, but because it had everything they needed in one room. Tucked in the corner, the small food preparation area had been a welcome surprise. They'd found nothing like it in any of the other quarters. The cooking contraption had taken Seneca some time to figure out, but it had been worth the effort. Their unique physiology would keep them alive for long periods without food, but that didn't mean they enjoyed it. This would be their first meal since the arena.

Seneca watched Jupiter pad across the room to where the woman lay on the bed. The table where they would eat their meal and the oversized bed the woman slept in, were like no other furniture on the ship. Big and sturdy, the pieces were perfect for their larger than human bodies—as if they'd been designed for Arena Dogs. There had been plenty of room for all of them when they'd grown fatigued and curled up in that bed beside the woman Jupiter called Fee.

Jupiter adjusted the blanket around her. His movements were tentative, gentle. His big, muscled body curved over her in a protective stance. What had she done to win Jupiter's regard? The pale patches of sealer the woman had used to close his wounds stood out starkly against the coppery expanse of Jupiter's chest. She'd done a good job of it. For that, Seneca could only be grateful. He still didn't know if they could trust her. Whatever her motives might be, so far, the net effect of her actions seemed to benefit them. For the second day, they were together and they were free.

Seneca kept his voice soft to keep from waking the woman. "How's she doing?"

Jupiter pressed his fingers to her forehead. "She's cool. No sign of fever."

"That's good." He might not trust her, but Seneca didn't wish her any further harm.

Jupiter sat on the edge of the bed. "Fee, we have food prepared." He too, spoke softly.

If she still needed sleep, they would let her sleep. But her body also needed fuel to aid the accelerated healing injection they'd given her.

Eyes still shut, she stretched her good arm over her head and pointed her toes, stretching out everything in between.

Jupiter watched intently as her movements shifted the blanket. "How's your shoulder?"

"The pain seems manageable at the moment," she said. Her voice was sleepy and warm and Jupiter responded with a soft growl that did funny things to Seneca's gut. Did it affect her the same? He didn't miss the way Jupiter leaned toward the woman, breathing in her scent. That didn't affect anything so low as his abdomen, it tightened a fist around his heart.

"You haven't tried moving the arm yet," Jupiter teased.

She opened her eyes and frowned. "There's no rush, is there?"

Jupiter barked under his breath. "You can stay in bed as long as you like, but I have no intention of letting my food get cold."

Feeona lifted her head from the bed, eyes taking in her surroundings. "Well, why didn't you say the food was warm?"

Seneca stilled, making himself just another item in the room. He wasn't ready to know if she would include him into their banter or use her wit to put him firmly on the outside.

Jupiter moved off the bed and squatted down within her reaching distance. "Do you want something for the pain before you try getting up?"

"No." Her head dropped back to the bed with a thump. "I don't want to pass out again. How long was I out this time?"

"A day," Jupiter rumbled.

"Not too bad." She reached for Jupiter, using her good arm. She wrapped her fingers around his biceps and used him to slowly pull herself up into a seated position. She touched him like a woman sure of her mate.

Seneca had to look away. The ache in his chest insisted. But her scent, her voice painted a picture in his mind.

"Good," she said. "Plenty of time for a meal before I have to check on the ship's systems." There was a buoyancy to her voice that Seneca found appealing. He could see how that might draw

Jupiter.

Seneca's own weakness defeated him and he let his gaze slip back to his pack-brother and the woman.

Jupiter lifted her out of the bed and into his arms. The night before, he'd urged her out of all but her under-things and into a Dog-sized tunic. It left her legs bare from just above the knee. When they'd found the tunic for her, they'd also found the clothes they were now wearing.

Jupiter carried Feeona to the table. She wrapped her good arm around his neck, pressing against him more than necessary, but not enough to be overtly seductive. She liked being in his arms—Seneca couldn't fault her for that.

Jupiter put her down in one of the Dog-sized seats. Her bare feet didn't reach the floor and she looked almost child-like. The lines of strain etched into her face, the way she held herself stiffly upright, made it impossible for Seneca to dislike her. She didn't complain. She didn't demand consideration. There was no need. Her quiet resilience did more to focus Jupiter's attention than any play for his interest. His pack mate grabbed a pillow from the bed and stuffed it behind her back. She relaxed instantly, a result that stamped satisfaction across Jupiter's face.

"Well, hello-there, Seneca." Her words snapped his gaze to hers.

"Hello." He'd been too busy studying Jupiter's focus on her to realize hers had shifted to him. He went back to portioning the food onto platters. "I hope you're hungry."

"Starved." She sniffed the air then pressed her lips together and made an mmm of approval. She shot him a smile, then her eyes went wide as she took a look at the cooking equipment. "Wow. That's not your average food prepper."

Seneca dipped his chin in agreement. "This room seems to

have been converted for the use of Arena Dogs."

She chuckled. "I'll say. Looks like the standard nutrition processor units have been ripped out and replaced." She narrowed her eyes. "Is that real meat?"

Jupiter chuckled. "We found packs of them in the ship's supplies."

"Yes." Seneca turned to offer the server of food and the motion shifted the shirt he'd pulled on when he'd crawled out of bed. He hadn't bothered to fasten it and the movement gave Fee a fair view of his chest. It surprised him to realize she noticed. He'd been ogled by humans plenty, but her momentary fascination didn't bother him. Especially after she realized she'd been caught looking and her embarrassment showed on her face. He smiled pleasantly to let her off the hook then handed the server to Jupiter.

His pack mate took the food, but his gaze was fixed on Feeona. He was still shirtless and he quickly captured her attention. She seemed to find it hard to keep her concentration on Jupiter's face. Seneca understood the temptation of Jupiter's body, but *he* found Jupiter's face even more fascinating. Those broad, masculine features and brown eyes warmed as he soaked in her appreciation.

"Sorry," she blurted out. "You're both just damn distracting freaks of nature. In my experience, men don't look like you."

Jupiter's eyes flashed and she threw up a hand to stop his anger. "No," she said firmly. "*That* was a compliment."

Seneca swallowed a chuckle at her bluntness.

"Less compliments," grumbled Jupiter. "More eating." He dropped into one of the seats and forked a piece of meat into his mouth.

Seneca set Feeona's portion on the table in front of her. She peered down at the meat he'd cut into small strips for her. She poked at the pieces of a purplish root vegetable he'd heated and mixed in. He thought she might push them aside, but then she popped one in her mouth and chewed.

"Good," she said to no one in particular.

Seneca sat down with his own portion and they ate in a peaceful silence. They were too busy filling their bellies to talk.

By the time the woman leaned back and pushed away her plate with a happy sigh, he and Jupiter had already started on a second round.

Jupiter grabbed her plate. "More?"

"Nope," she answered, sounding well contented. "I'm good. Besides, we should talk."

Jupiter made a noise of agreement then pushed another strip of meat in his mouth.

Feeona watched Jupiter intently. Seneca couldn't decide if she'd caught a glimpse of Jup's fangs or if she'd been caught up with the way his tongue smoothed across his lips to catch every bit of flavor or maybe it was the way his throat worked as he swallowed.

When Jupiter stopped chewing to raise a questioning eyebrow, her cheeks pinked. "Uh, assuming we make it to Karona Station, we need to figure out how to keep you safe."

Seneca kept his voice low and fluid. "Will Captain Fitzhew follow us there?" He wanted her attention. He wanted her to look away from Jupiter.

She glanced his way, and he saw that the pink had left her cheeks. "He won't be able to actually follow us. But he could easily guess where we're going. It's the closest station and that's where he was headed next. We don't need to worry until we come out of skipspace."

"How long will that be?" Jupiter added a subvocal growl of reassurance that only Seneca could hear.

Damn it. How did his pack mate always know? Jup had picked up on the fear he tried to hide. Hopefully, he'd take it as a fear of recapture. He hated the idea of recapture, but it was the woman sitting at their table that fueled his deepest fear.

"About twenty-four hours." Feeona answered, showing no sign that she'd picked up on Jupiter's subvocal communication. "Before we arrive, I'll see if I can bounce a com signal out to the station. I'd like to have a tug-tow waiting to pilot us to a landing bay. The faster we move the better."

She pulled her knees up under the tunic so it covered all but her bare feet then wrapped her arms around her legs. "I have some business to do on the station, but I want to leave again as soon as possible. I'm already behind schedule." She looked from Jupiter to him and back. "Do you have any idea what's next for you?"

Master Owens' words came back to Seneca. They would try to use the ship to find the freed Arena Dogs. The room they sat in was proof that they existed. "We need to ensure this ship doesn't get back to Roma."

Feeona smiled at him. "I remember. Consider that taken care of."

She made it sound easy—of no concern. He knew so little about how that could be done. He had many questions.

Before Seneca could form a query, Jupiter spoke. "Is there a way we can find out what has happened to the other members of our pack?"

Feeona rested her chin on her knees. "I can try. How many are in your... pack?"

"There are three others." Jupiter's voice shifted low with

worry.

Seneca noticed he hadn't counted Hera as pack. She was mate to a pack brother, but she did not fight at their side and she'd only been with them a short time. Still, they had both made the pack bond with her.

"Oh, okay," Feeona replied. "I'll need names and whatever identifying information you can give me." She sat a little straighter and nibbled her lip before continuing. "I imagine we could find out something just by looking at the arena match schedules and recent results. That's publicly available."

Jupiter reached over and cupped her cheek. "Just knowing they're alive will be a great relief to my mind. Thank you."

She leaned into the caress in an almost submissive response. Not a side of her Seneca had seen before. He could see that her action aroused Jupiter. His eyes darkened and his nostrils flared. His instincts would drive him to protect a submissive female. But the gesture was at odds with her unmistakable determination and strength. Was this softness real or a ploy of some kind? They already knew she was comfortable with deception.

"I get why you would want to know," she said, pulling away and sitting straighter again. "But then what? Have you thought about where you'll go? What you'll do?"

Jupiter shook his head. "We can't help the Dogs on Roma without assistance. We need to find the free Arena Dogs, but I don't know if that's even possible."

Jupiter was right. Seneca hadn't thought beyond staying free. Wherever Jupiter went, he would follow. No matter what came, Seneca vowed, he would be grateful for every day of freedom they had together.

Jupiter stood and began to pace. "But even if we don't find them, eventually we will have to return to Roma Rex. If our brothers are… dead… we will have to return soon."

"What?" Feeona released her hold on her legs and her feet slipped free of the seat, as if she might bound to her feet. "You're kidding, right?"

Jupiter halted and met her appalled gaze. "We have a duty to our brothers."

Feeona suddenly relaxed back into the pillow behind her. Her body went soft—spine curved, the bend at each joint of her limbs angled to suggest complete relaxation. It was utterly false. Her cheeks were pink again. She was embarrassed by her outburst, but it was more than that.

"You do realize that statement started with *if our brothers are dead?*" Her voice feigned idle curiosity. "What duty would there be after death?"

Seneca recognized her deception because he'd used that affectation himself, when he needed to hide how important something was to him. When he knew his masters would use it against him. It was a knowledge he didn't share with any of his brothers. They were honest to the point of bluntness. In the arena, a Dog could lose everything at any time. The only thing expected of them was to train and to fight. Survival was the reward. Poor performance brought punishment. There was no subtlety in their existence.

For most of his life, Seneca had dwelled in a din of subtlety where nothing was as it seemed. Caring about anything had been handing his masters the means to destroy him. Not his body, but his soul. He knew, rationally that this wasn't the same, but his heart beat harder with the memories.

Unable to stop himself, he reached for her expertly limp hand and enfolded it in his own.

"One of our brother's has a mate. If they die, the female will have no protection." Seneca smiled his most flattering smile and slid a hand up to circle her arm just above her wrist, fingertips resting over her pulse point. "The female is not like you. She has no clever skills. She's not a fighter. Without the pack to protect her, she'll suffer."

Touching her confirmed his assessment. Beneath her relaxed façade and her silken skin, her muscles were stone and her pulse raced.

Jupiter appeared at her other side, pulling a chair up to face her. "It's our duty to protect her, if they cannot. But we have no reason to think they're dead. Not now."

Feeona raised her eyebrows. "But eventually. All Arena Dogs die in the arena eventually, right?"

Jupiter frowned. "Yes."

Feeona's face fell as her pretense crumbled. Unshed tears made her eyes glossy. How could she have such sadness for people she didn't know?

"It wasn't true for us." Seneca squeezed her fingers gently. "Thanks to you."

"Thanks to your resistance." She deflected his attempt to credit her, but her lips tipped up in a near-smile and some of the sadness left her eyes.

Seneca was glad. He didn't know where his words had come from. Her conclusion had been correct for the most part. As far as they knew, no Dog had ever grown old. The certainty of early death had been the reason for the bonding custom—at least in part. He'd been told things had been different when there had been female fighters. There had been fewer of them than the males, but many of the females had avoided the mating bond. They preferred to share themselves generously without committing to any particular Dog. But there were almost no females of that type left. The masters had begun to give the Dogs females from the pleasure houses—females engineered to be submissive and weaker than the Arena Dogs. In the world of the arena, those females depended on a mate for survival. Or so it was thought. Having more personal knowledge of what it took to survive life in the pleasure houses, Seneca suspected Hera would quickly adapt to whatever new pack she was given to. None among the Dogs of House Owens would harm a female. They were too precious.

Feeona blinked away the moisture in her eyes. "You've found me out. I'm kind of a softy about oppression and I didn't get you off the *Salley Ho* to let Roma recapture you. They have a long reach."

Jupiter growled. "Owens won't rest until we're recaptured or dead."

As Feeona's attention shifted back to Jupiter, Seneca released her hand and settled back in his chair.

"I might be able to help you find your people." Her eyes drifted away from Jupiter. Was she simply pondering how? Or did she have something to hide? "I have a lot of connections. I'll do everything I can. But I won't be able to help you until after my next pick-up and deliveries."

She'd refocused on Jupiter who was frowning. "Pick-up and deliveries?"

Her cheeks tightened into one of her ready grins. "I don't spend all my time being a thief."

Jupiter's frown faded and something passed between them that brought back all Seneca's insecurities.

CHAPTER FIFTEEN

The Cavern
Karona Station
Earth Alliance Beta Sector
2210.150

Jupiter stepped out of the ship and into the space station's cavernous docking bay. The main arena could have fit inside, were it not for the enormous machinery everywhere. Feeona had made the arrangements to get them and the ship safely into what she called an off-the-logs entrance. He wanted to stop and study the place, but Feeona was striding with purpose.

Sen waited at his side. "I believe she expects us to follow."

They did follow but at a slower pace. Cautious. Wary. A shared glance with Sen set them both into motion. Splitting up, they each took a wider path. They would not be ambushed. They would not walk blindly into a trap. Feeona glanced over her shoulder but seemed unconcerned when they moved away.

There was no need to keep her in sight, her enticing scent left a clear trail through the sleeping giants that must be spaceships. They covered the floor in every direction. A week back he'd never seen such a thing, now he'd ridden aboard two of them. He crouched low to slip beneath the belly of one of the monsters. Scorch marks marred the surface, but no heat came from the slumbering machine. He'd learned much and freedom had more to teach him, more to be experienced. But he mourned the separation from the other Dogs of the pack. He needed to find a way to get them all back together and free.

He heard her voice before he could see her.

"I need a tuck away, Peety."

"You know the upcharge." The second voice was male, but weak. "I can't keep a prime spot occupied indefinitely without something to show for it." There was complaint in his tone, but no sign of strength to stand his ground.

Jupiter rounded the machinery blocking his view and melted into the shadow of a structure overhead. Feeona stood close to Peety. The thin human, with a burn scar that melted one side of his face, leaned away from her as if he feared being too close.

Feeona smiled. The angle of her stance allowed Jupiter to enjoy it. Those soft, plump lips had been around his cock. Not to tease him. To give him relief. She'd healed him and saved Sen. Saved them all. And so far, asked for nothing in return.

She put her hand on the man's shoulder. "How about this? You can have the damned thing on the condition that you keep it out of sight for the next week and that you scrap the ship's computer and salvage the rest as parts."

The man's eyes glimmered with a hint of interest. "She's a running ship."

Feeona scoffed.

"Oh, don't be hard on the old girl," the man said. "She got you here."

Feeona brought her hand back to her side as she lifted one shoulder. "That's the deal. Take it or leave it. The value of parting it out for one week's storage."

She stood confident, feet apart, ready for anything. The man shifted from one foot to the other. "Lemme check one thing." He shuffled his way behind a counter Jupiter hadn't even noticed. There was a frame or structure of some sort around it. All of that had blended with the surrounding metal crafts. A jumble of color and metallic surfaces created an effective camouflage.

A blue glow lit the man's face as he stared down into a screen.

Feeona never flinched or looked uncertain. She waited calmly, though he knew she was worried. Jupiter could see it in the way she clenched one hand behind her back, the stiffness in her spine. He'd learned a lot about her in the few days since they'd met.

The man looked up, studying Fee as if weighing her. His lips bunched then shifted side to side. "All right. I might regret it, but I'll go for it."

Fee stepped forward and reached a hand across the counter between them. "You know you're getting a great deal here."

The man took the offered hand and shook it up and down. "And it won't even take up the storage time. I have a team available to chop her later this sleep cycle. Won't be able to find two pieces left together by morning." He grinned as if he'd won a prize.

"Perfect," said Feeona. "Then you won't mind waiving my current storage balance."

"Ah, Mattie, a man needs to make a living."

Jupiter couldn't see her face now and she didn't answer. The moment stretched out until the man's shoulders slumped and he offered a disgruntled "agreed."

Fee leaned against the counter and angled her body across it. "I need your discretion on this. You haven't seen me or a ship like this one."

"Ah, hell, you know I'd never rat on you." A nervous laugh escaped the man's narrow lips.

"Thanks, Peety. Next time I'm back this way I'll bring some of those red berries you like."

His frown flipped, turning into a grin in a flash. "Now you're after my heart."

Jupiter wasn't certain of all of the expressions common beyond the gates of the arena, but he did know he didn't like the way the man watched her. Eyes focused on her breasts with occasional glances down to her hips.

"I have to go up to my ship for a few minutes then I'm going into the station. I want to leave in four hours. Can you have things ready by then?"

"Sure. No trouble."

🐾 🐾 🐾

Feeona knew the Arena Dogs were around somewhere, but she wasn't prepared for how fast they appeared when she stepped out of Peety's sight. Jupiter materialized out of a shadow and Sen came from somewhere off to her left.

"The little man is going to chop the ship?" Jupiter's nose scrunched in confusion.

"Fitz will guess we're here, but I don't want anyone to be sure of anything. Peety's crew will take the ship apart and sell those parts so no one will be able to find a piece big enough to identify it. And they'll destroy the ship's computer, so Roma won't get their hands on any data."

"You said you had cleared the data." Seneca's voice was free of accusation.

It rarely showed any sign of emotion unless he wanted it to.

Even having spent more time with him, he remained as mysterious as the day they'd met. The only thing she knew for sure was that he was completely devoted to Jupiter.

"Trust me. Roma can afford to hire an army of experts to find a way to get something out of the computer's corpse. With data, nothing is ever one hundred percent except melting down the hardware."

A twinge of guilt tugged at her conscious. After two days aboard, she'd learned everything there was to know about that ship. Everything she was doing her best to keep safe was backed up on her neural processor's storage. She hated that melting down that computer also ensured the value of what she had. She didn't want to think she would ever use the info except to help Jupiter and Seneca, but if that was true, why hadn't she told them she had the location of the resistance's base? Old habits. Always hang on to your aces.

She traced her fingers over Bug's rigid surface, where it hugged her neck like a gaudy piece of jewelry.

"I have to go into the station, but you two need to stay out of sight."

Feeona led them to the edge of the maze of machinery and ships, then slid her palm over the almost invisible control panel. She traced her fingers over the images that appeared on its surface to open the small lift. It hadn't been designed to accommodate the bulk of two Arena Dogs, but she stepped in and urged them to crowd in around her.

Jupiter maneuvered her to stand with her back pressed against his chest. She looked over her shoulder at him. When he lifted an eyebrow, she smiled a closed lip smile.

Then they bolted upward. To his credit he didn't panic, but his muscles tightened and his breath hitched. She hadn't considered that he might not have been in a lift before. She'd only wanted to keep where they were going a surprise. She reached for his hand and squeezed.

"It's a lift," explained Seneca. "To take us to another level."

The answer seemed to satisfy Jupiter. Odd that one of the men would know and the other wouldn't.

Seneca stared down at her. "There are lifts in the arena, but Dogs don't ride them."

She wanted to prompt him for more, but the door slid open before she could formulate a question. They stared out onto a similar but much smaller maze of ships. They hung from above. Beneath them there was only space. No floor—just a network of narrow metal grated walkways.

Jupiter and Sen followed her onto the walkway, alert and soaking in their surroundings.

"It's an impressive sight, isn't it?" She directed them to look down. "That's a clear drop to the level we were on earlier, so be careful up here."

"I can see it, but something obscures the view," said Jupiter, hesitation in his voice.

"Some sort of energy field?" added Seneca.

"Yes, but nothing solid enough to break your fall if you go over the edge."

Jupiter tipped his head to the side as he studied the obfuscation field. "It's like looking through a basin of water."

"From down there, you can't see the ships stored here." Fee stopped in front of her sleek black craft. "The extra layer of security is expensive but worth it."

"Didn't you say this is a secret landing port?" Seneca sounded only mildly curious.

"Mm-hm." She ran a hand over the ship's satin hull.

"A secret within a secret?" Jupiter followed his question with a low growl.

Feeona turned to face him. Despite the growl he didn't seem angry at her, but the mood definitely needed lightening. "Not everyone who ends up in a brig doesn't deserve to be there, big guy."

"I'll remember that the next time I end up in one." His sober tone broke the humor.

Feeona's smile faded. She reached out and pressed her cool palm against the healing injury on his chest. "Let's see if we can all stay clear of lock-up. Okay?"

As Feeona worked to open her ship's hatch, Jupiter took a moment to study them both. Beneath the dull shine of the ship's hull lay a network of old injuries. The ship had been damaged and repaired many times. Fee put a hand on a silver rectangle near the hatch, making a security panel appear. She entered a code, then the seal popped open. The whoosh of air exchanging flared and then disappeared. She pulled the door open. Her slim, graceful body hid a surprising strength. The door was thick and her injured shoulder needed more time to heal. He could see the strain in her movements. He wanted to aid her but feared she'd take it as an insult.

With the door fully opened, she reached in to grasp handles just inside the door. She pulled herself up and into the hatch with a hop. He followed her lead, landing softly inside on textured flooring. The space smelled subtly of that illusive scent of hers. Each breath he took pulled her essence into his lungs. She'd moved further into a second entryway then bent to loosen the straps of her boots. The position displayed her ass nicely.

The whisper of movement behind him alerted him to Sen's entry in time for him to brace. Sen landed just behind Jupiter, pushing into him from behind. The light weight of his hands settled at his waist as the smaller Dog steadied himself. Jupiter waited for him to get his footing then stepped forward and out of his way.

Fee slipped a pair of fuzzy shoes onto her feet. She straightened, eyes closed in a look of pleasure, flexing her feet beneath the fur. "Mmm. That feels good."

Seneca chuckled. He'd moved forward to stand at Jupiter's shoulder.

Feeona's eyes popped open. A narrow eyebrow lifted. "What? A girl shouldn't enjoy getting out of her boots and into something more comfy?"

Not waiting for an answer, she turned and led them deeper into the vessel.

"Your shoes are fuzzy." Jupiter stated the obvious.

"Mm-hm. I'm sorry I don't have any for you two."

The entryway opened into a bigger room. Large, bench-like furnishings ringed the room. Soft colorful cushions covered them and dotted the floor along the walls. The center of the room was bare, covered only by more of the soft texturing.

She stopped in the center and turned to them. "Alfred, close the hatch please."

A mechanical noise started behind them, but Jupiter's senses didn't detect any sign of a stranger. No out of place scent.

"Welcome home, Captain." The smooth male voice seemed to come from everywhere at once.

"Guys, it's okay. It's just the ship's computer. You're safe here, I promise."

The heat of Sen's back against his own made him realize

they'd instinctively shifted to a fighting stance. He shook off the surge of adrenaline as Seneca returned to his side. "Your ship's computer speaks and has a name?"

"I should have warned you. I'm sorry. It's not unusual to have a voice interface, though Alfred is a bit more sophisticated than most computers."

Jupiter looked to Seneca and was reassured by his nod.

"I've seen computers respond to voice commands before." Seneca shifted his gaze to Feeona. "But they didn't have names. They were just called computer."

Feeona shrugged her good shoulder. "Well, that just seems unimaginative to me. But I can't take credit for the name. He's had it since I first came aboard." Her lips turned up in a hesitant smile. "Alfred, Jupiter and Seneca are my guests. Please take good care of them while they're here. You'll respond to their voice commands."

"Acknowledged, Captain. Voice prints on file."

"Good." She gestured toward an opening on one side of the room. "Pilot's station is that way. At the moment it's locked down, so there's nothing to see." She pointed to the other side of the room. "Quarters, galley, and more ship's systems aft. I need to go get a few things from my quarters before I go out. Please make yourselves at home."

"Feeona." She'd already started to leave the common area, but she stopped when he called her name. "We need to talk."

In his peripheral vision, Seneca sank down onto one of the seating benches and stretched his body out with a sigh of pleasure. The *Renegade* had been comfortable enough, but without luxuries.

Feeona turned back to the doorway and started moving. "Walk and talk then. I want to have this business over and done as quickly as possible. Every minute we wait the more of Fitz's crew or Roma's goons there'll be searching for us."

"Seneca and I are grateful for your help, but it would be safer for us to find our own way from here."

"Safer?" She turned and headed up a steep, curving staircase.

Jupiter followed her, realizing as they went that it became almost a vertical spiral, taking them up to the next level.

"Safer for you," he clarified.

"I see." Her tone clearly conveyed her disapproval. "So, where are you going to go?"

The stairs opened into a corridor. The wall they faced was actually a pair of doors, etched with images of beasts he'd never seen before. One had a long horn on its snout and the other was a similar creature with wings sprouting from its back.

"Don't laugh. I was sixteen when Roland had this done for me."

It wasn't laughter that sparked in his chest. "It's beautiful. This Roland must value you highly."

Feeona flashed him a wide smile. "He adored me." There was no doubt in her statement.

Jupiter choked on the warmth in her voice for this man. "Will he return soon?" And if he did how would he react to the presence of two males?

Fee's smile dimmed. "He died a few years ago. He was—" She shook her head then slid a finger in a strange pattern on a touch screen panel at the edge of one of the doors. "We were talking about where you're headed next."

The panels of the door slid apart to disappear into the corridor walls. He followed Fee into a room as large as the seating area where he'd left Sen. In this room, the walls were covered in a velvety fabric. An enormous pallet that had to be meant for sleeping dominated the space to the left. It was covered in soft fabrics in shades of gold. Feeona strode to the right where clothes hung from a long pole almost to the corner of the room. Shelves covered a three-meter stretch of the side wall. Everything from more clothes to shoes to things he didn't have names for crowded the box-like spaces. Feeona stepped into a nook that started where the shelves ended, and her Bug flew up to the top shelf.

"I know you wish to leave here quickly, but—" Jupiter lost his words when Feeona slipped off her trousers and tossed them to the side. He was used to nudity. His life had allowed for no modesty, but the humans seemed to cling to their clothes like a good suit of armor.

"I know. I promised to find out about your pack brothers, and I will." She pulled her shirt off over her head. "Actually, Alfred can help you get started while I'm out. Just explain it to him and he can search the public data logs for you."

Much as he'd pictured it, her body was athletic with toned, lean muscles. She'd done nothing sexual but his body hardened at the sight. She faced the wall. He wanted her to turn so he could see her breasts, the folds of her sex. Holding back a growl of frustration, he forced words to form. "We still need to talk, as soon as you return."

She pressed a hand against the wall and water flowed down over her body. "Absolutely."

"Agreed." It was all he could get out of his suddenly parched mouth. The water flowed down her body, stroking the muscles of her shoulders and trailing down her spine to her enticing ass. He wanted to grab her hips and bend her forward in search of the hot, wet channel that would squeeze his cock as he thrust into her.

"Great. We can brainstorm a bit when I get back." She lifted her hair off her back and worked a sudsy substance into it.

The water pooling at her feet turned muddy as it circled a drain he hadn't noticed. There was a lip in the flooring as well, keeping the water in the nook. As his gaze traveled back up her body he saw the caramel-colored streak the water had left along her skin. The unexpected sight held him transfixed as she worked the suds along her skin until she was a uniform tone all over. The water stopped and she pulled a cloth from some hidden compartment and wrapped it around her body.

She turned and stepped out of the space a different woman than she'd been before. The chemical tinge that had muddled her scent was gone—washed down the drain. Her hair was a darker shade. Her caramel skin was so perfect it made him think of the patron women who used creams and powders to get a similar look. Jupiter stepped closer. Unable to resist the call of her body, he traced the curve of one generous breast.

He lifted his head enough to meet her eyes. The green was gone. They were a warm brown that suited her natural appearance.

She seemed at ease. "I wish I had time, big guy." She stretched up on tiptoes and offered her lips. He bent down to meet her and waited. She pressed her lips gently against his then spoke with her lips a breath away. "Maybe when I get back. After we talk."

She eased back until she stood flat footed again.

Jupiter straightened. His heart thudded heavily. "When you get back."

CHAPTER SIXTEEN

Karona Station
Earth Alliance Beta Sector
2210.150

In a corner of the station's busy market sector, Fee stared at the impossible message. ACCOUNT TRANSACTION FAILED. The exchange with her buyer for Fitz's nav maps had gone smoothly. She'd watched the trader transfer the payment to her account. She'd checked her account balance and it had all been there. So, why couldn't she transfer the funds to her contact on Petro-5?

"Hey beautiful. Can I buy you a brew? Tavern's open."

The too close voice startled her.

"We're on a 24-hour station. The tavern is always open." She let the full measure of her annoyance chill her voice as she walked away.

She'd pulled her hair back in a loose ponytail. Her slacks, tunic, and coat were all worker-gray. She'd hoped the serviceable style would discourage men like that one from approaching.

It had been her only choice. She had no way to know which aliases Roma would have connected to her. Her own identity had been the only one she felt safe in.

Fee left the noise of the market's main thoroughfare behind and strode quickly toward the next most popular lane on the station—the treasure handlers. She needed answers and her money, now.

She turned the corner and slowed. All of her senses screamed at her. Something was off. She walked forward eyes straight ahead until she'd passed Billy's offices and reached a corner. She turned again and then stepped into the first doorway. A hungry-eyed money-lender sat behind a desk. Just beyond the middle of life, the woman had left her hair naturally gray despite obvious signs of other cosmetic treatments. A slender man, not more than 20, sat at her side and two burly enforcers lounged in ancient chairs, backs to a wall. The enforcers were the kind of big that came from popping cheap growth pills. She doubted either of them could get out of their chairs before she could get to their boss and put a blaster to her head. Not that she wanted to. She smiled. "How much to sit in one of your chairs for fifteen minutes?"

The lender steepled her fingers and smiled a smile that never went beyond her lips. "Name's Celia Morris. No need to bring credits into it." She waved a hand toward an empty seat near the door.

The man at Morris's side froze, a pleasant expression gracing pretty features—a slender nose and a firm chin.

Feeona returned Morris's smile. "I need fifteen minutes with no interruptions."

Morris sat back more deeply into her chair. "Of course."

Fee activated Bug with a thought. The small mechanical creature tickled as it uncurled from around her throat and launched into the air. She opened the door for Bug to fly out, then closed it and settled into the seat.

She closed her eyes and tapped into Bug's vision. At least three men in the area near Billy's place stood exactly where they'd been when she'd passed them. They were waiting for her. Damn. How had they gotten to her account so fast? She had dozens, all carefully protected and tied to different identities. How could they have found the one account she would use?

She waited until someone opened Billy's door then Bug slipped inside. It flew over the heads of the tellers and down the narrow hall to Billy's office. He was sitting with his feet propped on his desk, talking to a hologram standing in the space next to him.

Bug landed on the toe of one of his nice dress shoes. Billy froze for a moment then abruptly ended his call. Bug's auto-safety features kicked in to keep it safely in the air when his feet dropped to the ground with a noisy clatter.

"Shit. You can't be here."

She landed Bug on his workstation and tapped into his speakers. "Strictly speaking, I'm not there."

Billy scooted closer and lowered his voice. "As good as." He poked a finger at Bug and the AI flicked Bug's wings as a warning. "This thing can't have that much range. Truth be told, if you're on this station, you're too damn close." His voice had lowered word-by-word until it was a fierce whisper.

"I need my funds and the account is frozen. You're supposed to be a strictly independent treasure. No government interference. Not Alliance, not planetary, not even the station government. That's why you have my business."

"This isn't government interference. It's Roma. And they have more money than any government. Money means power. You know that."

A sudden heaviness hit her belly. "Are all the accounts

frozen?"

Billy's face scrunched and he tapped his fingers on his desk. "All the accounts I know about."

That was it then. Billy had helped her put her protections in place. There was only one account he didn't know about and that one never had more than a few credits.

His fingers tapped the desk again. "They have your electronic fingerprint. They own every piece of information about you. You need to get off this station and out of this sector."

Stone and Barney must have talked. Damn them for not being good enough to get away. There was a limit to how much they knew. She didn't trust anyone with everything, but Stone had known her a long time—he was an old acquaintance of Roland's. But under one of Roland's many false identities. She stopped a moment to consider Stone's fate. Had he sold her out right away or had they hurt him to get the info. With the harm already done, she hoped he'd found a way to profit rather than get himself tortured or dead.

"To leave, I need funds." The men in the hall hadn't identified her. Had she ever been caught on vid as herself? Would they eventually make that final connection?

"Sorry. I can't help you." Billy sat back and sagged in his chair. "They say you have something of theirs and they want it back. They're very determined."

Her breathing accelerated and it got harder to focus on her connection with Bug. "That isn't an option."

"For God's sake, Fee. Give them what they want. Or get the hell across the border with Gollera."

She considered a dash for the border for a split second. They were at the ass end of human controlled space. There were two sector-borders in the vicinity: Gollera and Delvinci. But neither were an option for her. She had plans she couldn't change.

"I can't." She had to find another way.

Billy scrubbed his hand over his face. "Nothing is worth dying for."

That's where Billy was wrong. There were a lot of things worth dying for.

She launched Bug into the air and got it carefully out of Billy's office before handing control back to Bug's artificial intelligence. Bug would return to her without further instructions, because Bug was the best remote AI of its size money could buy.

And there was her answer.

Her eyes fluttered open to Morris's face, less than a meter from hers. Feeona jumped in her seat, heart pounding.

The money-lender's round hazel eyes, set in a narrow face, were cold an assessing.

"You okay, dear?" She straightened and inched back. "I was getting worried."

Feeona was still breathing hard from the anxiety her conversation had caused. She met Morris's eyes. "I'm fine."

The woman shook her head. "Can't fool a money-lender, dear. Accessing people is part of the job. Who will take the money and run? Who is good to their debts? You, I'd say, are in a bit of trouble. Something I can do to help?"

Feeona's instinct was to get away from Celia Morris as quickly as possible. But, then what? "What makes you think I'm in trouble?" The money-lender wouldn't need any skill at reading people, if she'd connected her to a station-wide manhunt.

Celia lifted an arched eyebrow. "Aside from the panicky breathing?"

Feeona grimaced. "Yes, aside from that."

"You're in money-lender row and hiding out in my shop. You

are hiding, aren't you?" Morris waited for a response and for once nothing snappy came to mind. Fee was totally screwed.

She deflected the question. "What do your instincts tell you about what kind of risk I am?"

Morris returned to her seat behind her desk and leaned back. "Ah, so it is a financial problem. I'd say you're the type to be true to your debts. But not currently in the position to do so. No, you wouldn't be a good bet for a loan."

"My accounts are frozen." Fee explained. "I have the funds. I just can't get to them."

The young man watched their interaction, face still blank as a doll. Why did he look familiar?

"Well, I'm a simple money-lender," said Morris. "I don't employ these two," she gestured to the hulks. "For their code hacking skills. I might not be the most ethical lender in the row, but I don't break the law."

"I didn't mean to…"

"In your situation," Morris pointed a finger at her. "We lenders rely on collateral. Have anything worth value you can leave with me?"

And that quick they were back in the vicinity of her only option. "My remote." She said it flat out. Like it was no big deal. Like the thought didn't knot up her belly.

The money-lender snapped her fingers at the goon standing near the door. He pressed the control and the door swung inward.

Bug zipped in and landed on Feeona's shoulder.

Morris leaned forward to take a closer look. "I had some business with a fella who had one of those. Not exactly like that one. But I have an idea how much it's worth."

Bug's wings flapped and then it circled Feeona's throat to

form a decorative piece attached to the slender chain hanging there. She'd given the command before it was in her consciousness.

Bug was a part of her and she could only tolerate the thought of giving it up, because the alternatives were even worse. But she'd only be leaving it as collateral with a chance she could get Bug back.

Morris reached for a com pad. "I can see by that look, you've decided. I know a surgeon."

"A surgeon, wait, I—"

"You were thinking I'd hold just the remote for you." Morris laid the pad back on her desktop. "This model requires a matched neural control implant for smooth operation and data transfer. The match is hard coded. It can't be controlled from an external interface or from any other implants. If you don't make it back, for reason's not your own, where would that leave me?"

"I don't have time for surgery." And if she had the implant removed, it was unlikely she could ever get another. Even with the best surgeon, there would be scar tissue.

"Life is about tough choices. I understand, if you're not interested." Morris returned her hand to her desk and her fingers moved in a rhythmic pattern against the com pad. A smile slinked into place. "Good news, the surgeon can do the surgery immediately. If you decide that's what you want to do."

Fee died a little inside, but she wouldn't betray Jupiter and that was the only other option. "I'm sending you the details now. You'll set up a holding account for me and transfer the money directly into the account after I let you know. You'll have to keep my identity off the record and—"

"You let me worry about the accounting." Morris's fingers never stopped moving. And she'd already messaged back a counteroffer on price.

Fee frowned.

"I'll be covering the surgeon's payment," said Morris. "Rush work isn't cheap and you're in a hurry, right?"

Roland had told her never to trust a money-lender. Make sure they're making a good profit and that's the best bet you have to keep them from turning on you. Fee would take the offer. "You'll need to arrange to get me back to my ship after the surgery. Some secrecy will be required."

Morris smiled. "Don't worry, I'll handle everything."

Fee didn't like extending trust to a stranger, but what choice did she have? The cargo waiting for her on Petro-5 was too precious to lose.

Yeah. She was screwed.

CHAPTER SEVENTEEN

The Hawley
Karona Station
Earth Alliance Beta Sector
2210.150

Seneca sprawled across one of the comfortable benches in the common area of Feeona's ship while Jupiter paced its length. The relaxed pose was an attempt to put Jupiter at ease. It hadn't worked. Jup was well on his way to wearing a path across the floor with his pacing.

"Alfred, please explain that in more detail." Seneca had taken on the task of talking to the computer when it became clear Jupiter didn't feel comfortable doing it. So often, Jupiter took the lead, but this was one situation in which Seneca could easily bear that burden.

"The Arena Dogs called Mercury, Diablo, and Carnage are not currently listed on the Roma Rex active roster." Alfred's calm, artificial voice did nothing to soften the statement.

"But you also said they haven't been listed on the death roll." Seneca's gaze followed his pack-mate's progress across the room. He didn't miss the hesitation in Jupiter's gait at the mention of death.

"Correct. I can confirm their existence based on previous match announcements and results available from multiple gambling services."

Seneca huffed a breath of frustration, then a thought occurred to him. "When was their last match on record?"

"2210.140. Featured match. Main Arena. Mercury, Diablo and Carnage against Jupiter and Seneca. Mercury, Diablo and Carnage listed as winners. Would you like me to read you the match description?"

"No." He definitely didn't want to hear how their masters had sold the match to the patrons. "Jupiter, no report of death has to mean they're still alive."

Jupiter stopped his pacing and met Seneca's gaze. "Then why haven't they been scheduled for another match? It's been ten days."

"That's not so long. Not if their injuries were severe. I know you ripped into Mercury pretty deep." It had been after he'd seen Mercury aiming a cudgel at Seneca's head. He'd overreacted. They both knew Mercury would never intentionally cause either of them serious injury.

Jupiter's hands clenched at his side, knuckles white. "We're free and they're still there. What if they're punished for our escape? Damn it! I don't even know what questions to ask the damn talking machine."

"My programming is quite advanced." Alfred interjected. "As an example, I can anticipate that you might be interested to know that you were both listed as deceased after your last match and your records have not been updated, even though Roma now knows Seneca is alive."

If Seneca didn't know better he'd think Alfred had taken offense at Jupiter's damning him. But Alfred couldn't have feelings. No offense, no worry, no fear. Jupiter's emotions were real. The sense of helplessness eating at him was as clear to Seneca as the training walls that had kept them imprisoned. "Alfred, can you run a broader search and tell us if there's any mention of them…anywhere you can search, after the last match?"

"Of course, Seneca. The search is running now. I should have the information for you momentarily."

Jupiter returned to pacing. Seneca wanted to go to him. To hold him and sooth him. Instead, he kept his seat and waited.

"Search complete. One record found. The Arena Dogs named Mercury, Diablo, and Carnage were named on a list of assets included on a secured manifest declaration."

Jupiter growled. "I don't know what any of that is."

Seneca shifted on the soft bench. "I'm not sure of most of it, but I think that if they're listed as assets, then they'd have to be alive."

"That is correct." Alfred's confirmation seemed to ease some of Jupiter's tension.

A chime sounded, startling them both.

"We have a visitor outside the ship," said Alfred. "He is requesting entry."

"Alfred." Seneca sat straighter. "Identify the visitor and assess the threat."

"The visitor is a human male. Caucasian. Age approximately nineteen Earth standard years. Weight approximately sixty kilograms. No weapons in view. Facial recognition reports 60% match to a human male that traveled on this ship 2200.045 to 2200.50."

That managed to surprise Seneca. He couldn't imagine Feeona taking passengers. "That would mean the man was a

child at the time." Feeona would have been young then, too.
Seneca got to his feet. "Alfred, what is the man doing?"

"He is striking his fist against the hull and asking for entrance.
His current activities and level of force will not harm the ship."

Seneca glanced to Jupiter and rolled his eyes at Alfred's threat
assessment. "Alfred, how is he dressed? Is he wearing a
uniform?"

"Would the ship be able to tell that," Jupiter rumbled low.

"He is wearing pants, a shirt, and shoes. There is no insignia
to indicate a uniform and he is not carrying a security ident-card
or tracking device." Jupiter and Seneca shared a moment of
hesitation as Alfred paused. "Would you like to see him?"

Neither of them had seen that coming. "Yes. Can we speak
to him without leaving the ship or opening a door?"

"Yes. Shall I engage the com?"

"Yes." Jupiter barked.

A projection of the space along the walkway outside the ship
appeared on the main wall.

"I know you're in there." In the image the visitor, barely a
man, still pounded a fist against the hull, making a dull noise.
"The Angel is in trouble. Or don't you care about that?"

"Angel," Seneca questioned quietly.

"Feeona," said Jupiter. "Has to be." He vibrated with tension.

"It could be a trick," Seneca warned. His heart twisted at the
evidence of how important Feeona had become to Jupiter.

"What?" The man in the image straightened and rubbed his
hands down his pants. "Hello? It isn't a trick. I mean…me
coming here isn't a trick. It's the Angel that's being tricked."

"Who are you?" Jupiter growled the demand, apparently
more comfortable talking to a computer generated image of a
real person than he'd been talking to the computer.

"They call me Ears." The young man's voice carried a note of impatience.

It was an odd name, but Seneca didn't know the naming customs of other worlds. On Roma, their owner had named them when they began training.

"I work for Celia Morris—she's a money-lender. Your friend came into her office earlier and made a deal with my boss. But somebody named Owens had a bulletin out for the Angel and they offered my boss more money. She's going to turn the Angel over to somebody who can extract the information they want from her implant then kill her." The young man wrung his hands. "Please. We don't have much time."

Jupiter's body tightened.

Feeona had said it wouldn't be safe to leave the ship. They'd be recognized. But Seneca knew Jupiter wouldn't be willing to wait. "Close com."

"What—" the man began.

Sen really had no choice. "Alfred, let the man in."

Jupiter raised an eyebrow in question.

"I will listen for a lie," Seneca offered as explanation.

Jupiter scowled but nodded. Seneca would have to be close to the man, to touch him and gain his trust. Seneca hesitated. He wouldn't be using the skills Jupiter taught him. This skill had come from his life before Jupiter. All the reasons *that* might anger Jupiter weighed on his heart, but he couldn't worry about that now.

The pop of the hatch opening and the sound of feet striking the steps swung them both around to face the man called Ears as he appeared in the entryway. His eyes widened and his forward progress stalled. "It's true, then. You're Arena Dogs. But they said it was only one."

"Come in Ears, we mean you no harm." Seneca took a small step toward the man, reaching out a hand as if welcoming a friend. He softened his voice, relaxed his shoulders and tilted his head forward, letting his hair fall around his face. It completed his transformation from fierce Dog to something less threatening, almost feminine. It was a role he'd played in the pleasure house often, but he'd never let Jup see him this way. His stomach twisted.

When Ears took his hand and let Seneca pull him closer, Jupiter growled low in the back of his throat.

Ears flinched, but Seneca held fast. He edged closer and put an arm around Ears' shoulder. "It's okay, Ears. He's house broken. I promise." He chuckled and the boy accepted the unspoken invitation to join in. "Tell us what's happened to our friend, Ears. We're so glad you came to warn us."

Ears nodded, his body relaxing in response to the thick warmth in Seneca's voice. "It's like I said. She made a deal with Celia. She's going to have a surgery to remove her implant so she can sell it. She needs money. Roma's looking for her and they put a hold on her accounts."

Seneca flicked a glance to Jupiter over the boy's shoulder. They both knew why Roma had done it. By helping them, Feeona had been pulled into their trouble. Seneca furrowed his eyebrows as he returned his attention to Ears. "They can do that?"

"They can do anything. Money talks, you know."

"No, I didn't know." Seneca smiled gently, teasing for more information.

"This whole place, the station, it's all about money. People who have it get what they want. It's the same everywhere. And Roma has enough money to make them gods here on the station."

Money gained from the pain and deaths of Arena Dogs.

Seneca's smile wavered. "They were god-like on Roma, too."

Ears settled a hand on his shoulder. "I'm sorry. It isn't right what they did to you, and it isn't right what they're trying to do to *her.*"

There was no change in the young man's skin temperature or respiration or heart rate. Being able to sense those things by touch was one of Seneca's talents. Useful for a whore. Not so much for a fighter.

He released Ears and shed the role like an old skin. His shoulders stretching back into place and away from the young man's touch. "He's telling the truth." He met Jupiter's eyes, refusing to hide from any judgment he might find there. He saw only confusion, a reaction he could live with. He was almost glad there was no time to explain. Helping Jupiter get to Feeona was more important.

He turned back to Ears. "Can you tell us how to get to her without being seen?"

Ears shuffled back and his gaze darted between him and Jupiter.

"Answer," Jupiter demanded.

Ears jerked out of his thoughts. "Tunnels. We'll use the tunnels." He headed for the hatch. "Come on. I'll explain on the way."

Fee fisted the cloth of her surgical gown in one hand and put out the other to stop the med-tech trying to put the anesthetic wrap around her arm. "No, thanks. I'm good with a local."

Dressed in a blue med-suit, the technician frowned.

"Standard protocol—"

"I said no. And I've been through this before." Fee turned her head to the surgeon, working at the terminal on the end of the med-bed. "Doc?"

The man looked up and nodded. "It's fine. Better actually, if you aren't squeamish."

"Not a bit." Fee breathed easier at the answer.

"Just use the restraints." The surgeon dropped his gaze back to the terminal.

Fee's gut lurched. Her first instinct was to refuse the restraints with as much determination as the general anesthetics, but her original surgeon had done the same. So, why was anxiety gnawing at her nerves, giving her second and third thoughts about the wisdom of letting the surgeon cut into her head. His office seemed professional enough. A brightly painted medical symbol hung on the wall outside his offices. A sympathetic reception worker had been seated behind a counter explaining to an unhappy patient that their procedure had to be rescheduled. The patient hadn't looked as if he were escaping a face-off with a hatchet man. The surgeon looked perfectly average. Average height. Average weight. Average brown eyes. Maybe it was his averageness that was setting her off.

"Okay," said the medic. "I've turned off the sedative, but we still need the monitors."

Feeona scowled as the man wrapped the padded sleeve around her arm. He didn't seem to mind her attitude. He smiled blandly as he moved to the end of the table, and she struggled to remember why she'd been scowling.

"Now, just relax." The tech patted her shin with a gloved hand.

Think of the cargo, she reminded herself as the first restraint locked into place around her ankle. Think of the cargo waiting on Petro-5.

His hand wrapped around her free ankle and the absence of a visual to go with the contact made her realize her eyelids had closed. Damn him. Turned the sedative off, my ass. She reached for the arm wrap, but nothing happened. Her muscles barely twitched in response to the mental command.

The sound of a door opening and voices whispering raised her heart rate and pumped much needed adrenalin into her bloodstream.

She pulled her right leg free of the aide's reach just as a wall panel crashed to the floor.

Jupiter. His brawny form appeared in the newly made opening and it took her a moment to decide he wasn't just a drug fueled dream. He stepped through. The lines of fury carved into his face helped to convince her. In her dreams she was pretty sure he'd have been looking at her with a very different heat in his eyes.

Startled shouts and booted feet had her scrambling up to a seated position. Fear fueling her muscles, she twisted, reaching for something to defend herself with, but her hands came up empty.

She didn't recognize the people coming in through the door, but the lead man had a thuggish look with a nose that had been broken and healed badly. There were too many, but Jupiter and Seneca didn't hesitate. Both Arena Dogs surged across the room. Jupiter slammed into the crush of thugs like a wrecking pylon, before they got off a single shot, and then they were all too close for pulse weapons.

The med-tech and surgeon disappeared, leaving Feeona to focus on freeing her ankle. She pulled against the restraining band, using her leg strength to drag herself down the table until she was practically wrapped around her foot. Her free leg hung over the edge of the table as she wrapped her arms around her restrained leg. Knee pressed against her chest, she tugged at the restraint. The thing wouldn't budge. A dot of light flashed defiantly, proof of locking circuitry at work.

The clash playing out just a few meters away crushed her concentration. Jupiter fought in the center of the armed men and Seneca danced around the edges, sending more of them to the floor. The sight mesmerized her. Like watching a blaze from the heart of a fire as a ritual dancer dragged away and discarded half burned branches until all the fuel was gone.

The slender man from the money-lender's office brushed her hands away from the restraint. "Let me help you."

Where had he come from?

He made quick work of the locking mechanism and held out a hand.

She took it long enough to hop off the table and get her balance. "What the hell is going on?"

"It's okay, Angel." He grabbed her arm and urged her toward the opening in the wall. "It's my turn to rescue you."

She studied his face, looking for that hint of familiarity she'd dismissed. "I don't know you," she said, but it was almost a question.

A small smile curved his lips. "It's okay. It was a long time ago and there've been a lot of kids since me."

He lifted his wrist to show her. Oh, God. The tattoo marring his skin looked so much like the one she'd had removed on her sixteenth birthday.

She shook her head. "You shouldn't be here." But concern for Jupiter and Seneca stole her attention. She looked over her shoulder. "We have to help them."

"They're doing fine." He put an arm around her waist and urged her toward the damaged wall.

He was right. As she watched, Jupiter lifted one of the remaining men by the neck and slammed him against a wall. The man's feet kicked and shook as he clawed Jupiter's hand at his throat. Seneca had the last attacker backed into a corner.

A loud thump drew her eyes back to Jupiter. He released his opponent and the man's lifeless body spilled to the ground. The back of the man's head was coated with blood.

Feeona swayed, feeling dizzy. It had to be the drugs in her system. She'd never fainted at the sight of blood before. Not knowing what was going on always made her edgy and she was seriously in the dark. She took a steadying breath and turned back to her young rescuer. Her fists clasped his tunic as she tried to make sense of things. "Tell me what's going on."

"Roma knows you're here." Jupiter's rumbling bass at her side was an impossibly welcome comfort.

Jupiter pulled her against his chest and framed her face with his hands. "Are you hurt?"

The heat of him soaked through the surgical gown and chased away the chill that had stolen into her bones.

"I'm fine." She wrapped her arms around him, no longer able to remember what had distressed her. Her fingers dug into the solid mass of his muscles and his familiar masculine scent enveloped her. Her panic settled and Seneca came into focus at Jupiter's side.

"We really need to go now." The kid's insistence had turned desperate.

His presence brought her back to the harsh reality of her situation with a jolt.

"Damn it all." She needed the funds to pick up her cargo. "The surgeon. I need –"

"We're getting you out of here," Jupiter insisted.

Seneca stalked through the room, ending at the back wall. "The medics are gone. There's an exit back here."

She would've turned, gone after them, but Jupiter held her still. She reached up and pressed her hands to his cheeks, meeting his gaze, trying to make him understand. "You shouldn't have stopped them. I need the funds I was going to get for this."

"The money-lender betrayed your trust. The doctor would have turned you over to them." Jupiter spoke softly, like a rough-hewn blanket to ease the bad news.

Fee glanced over to where the thugs lay on the floor. The big lug had gone from lethal to comforting in a moment. For her.

Jupiter's thumb brushed against her cheek, urging her to look at him. "I'm sorry we brought you this trouble."

Fee loosened her hold on him, slipping her hands down to lie against the tempting expanse of firm muscles across his chest. "This is so not your fault."

"When these guys don't report back, there'll be more." The kid picked up Bug from the med-cart and shoved it into Feeona's hand.

"There won't be any place on the station that's safe." With that thought, she linked with Bug, powering up the small device. The familiar sensations buzzed through her brain and suddenly she could think clearly again, despite the weakness lingering in her body.

"Come. We must go back to your ship now." Jupiter wrapped one of his hands around hers as he pulled her toward the opening in the wall.

His hand was cool and slick with blood, but she clutched it

like a lifeline. Getting back to the ship was smart, but what then? If she didn't have the funds, there would be no point in going to Petro-5. Toolman was a hard ass. There was no way she would get to the cargo without paying upfront.

When they stepped through the hole in the wall and into a maintenance tunnel, the kid stopped. "Just go back the way you came," he said to Jupiter. He shifted his attention to Feeona, lifted a hand and smiled. "Let them protect you, Angel. We can't lose you."

She acknowledged his words with a nod and watched as he disappeared down the opposite end of the tunnel. There was no doubt left in her mind, that he was one of her kids. And it no longer mattered that she didn't have the funds. Not yet. Not going to Petro-5 wasn't any kind of option. She had to get to her cargo. There was no way she was leaving her next load of children to die.

CHAPTER EIGHTEEN

The Hawley
Karona Station
Earth Alliance Beta Sector
2210.151

Jupiter climbed into the ship behind Feeona. The thigh length garment she wore made it hard not to notice her sleekly muscled legs and the curve of her bottom as she moved. A quick glance to Seneca confirmed that the sight hadn't gone unnoticed by his pack brother.

"Alfred, start launch prep." Feeona stopped in the middle of the entry room and fixed her gaze on his. There were questions and explanations swirling in her eyes and they had time for neither.

She stepped forward like a youngling walking barefoot over rocks—like every step hurt and had the potential for serious injury. Taking his hand and then Seneca's, she stood close. The subtle scent that was uniquely her permeated every breath Jupiter took. Her smaller hand tempted him to fold his carefully around the fragile flesh and bones.

"You know you can't stay on the station. It isn't safe." There was none of her usual sarcasm or spark in her voice.

He and Seneca both grunted their agreement.

"We haven't had that talk." Fee said.

She was worried about taking away their choice. He remembered her outrage when he'd told her he'd been a slave. He saw only acceptance on Seneca's face.

"We choose to leave this place with you." He held her gaze, letting his certainty show in his eyes.

Her lips curved into a small smile. "Good." She squeezed his hand then spun on her heel and led them toward the pilot's station. "This way."

They followed her up several steps, then through a hatch to a generously sized room with a control panel and view screen dominating one wall. With a wave of her hand, she indicated two seats and showed them how to strap into the harnesses.

She dropped into the large, curved seat centered in the room.

Alfred's voice filled the space around them. "Welcome back, Captain, launch sequence underway."

Data flowed down the screen like flickering glow bugs.

"Release docking clamps and negotiate launch guidance with the Cavern."

Lights blinked to life around them.

"Launch guidance confirmed."

"Engage launch guidance assist." Feeona locked her harness with a click. "Here we go."

"Launch guidance assist engaged."

The ship lurched and Jupiter tightened his grip on the arm rests of his seat. Feeona rotated her seat to an angle where he could see her face.

"There'll be some tight turns," she said. "And we'll feel it until we cross out of the station's gravity field. The launch will knock us up and back hard, but things will smooth out after that."

Jupiter nodded, grateful for the information. He and Seneca had been unconscious when their journey on the resistance ship had begun and during their escape from Fitzhew they had already been drifting free in space.

The Owens kennel, the place where he had been imprisoned and trained on Roma Rex, had been near the spaceport. He'd heard and felt the percussion of ships launching, but being inside the ship when it launched was new to him.

Seneca's body showed no sign of stress, but his ears were alert as he listened.

Feeona shifted her attention back to the data readouts. "Alfred, follow the nav-guides out of the bay and chart the closest safe skip-point."

"Acknowledged, Captain. Shall I begin skip calculations?"

Feeona's gaze flicked toward Jupiter, her face pale and lips pressed tightly together. "Yes, Alfred. Calculate the first skip using gamma approach for Petro-5 as our destination."

"Yes, Captain."

The grim press of her lips eased, softening her expression. When she spoke again her voice was lighter and her words were for him. "God, I'm tired."

Jupiter reached for the straps holding him in place before his brain caught up with instinct.

Feeona shook her head. "No, stay strapped in until we're free of the nav-guides and the standard engines kick-in."

She'd warned him about the launch, but his urge to care for her had momentarily overpowered his sense. He wanted to blame it on lust and the memory of her wet and naked, but all he wanted in that moment was to scoop her up and carry her to her cabin where he could tuck her into her bed and watch over her while she slept.

He should be thinking of the Dogs that remained on Roma Rex. Of the pack brothers whose fate was as yet unknown. Not the physical needs of one small human female.

He wrapped his hands around the straps, white knuckled with his internal battle. Then a brush against the bare skin of his arm snagged his attention. It was Seneca, reaching out with the barest of touches to refocus him.

Seneca's lavender eyes were shades darker than normal. "We'll find a way forward together."

"As brothers," he answered by rote. It didn't help his mood that it had always been him aiding Seneca. Not this. Not him being the one struggling and off balance.

By the time Feeona got them safely into skipspace the remains of the drugs the med-tech had snuck into her system were gone, but Jupiter insisted on carrying her to her bed. Seneca trailed behind at a discreet distance.

This was the moment when she had to decide. She didn't fully understand their relationship, but it was clear there was a special bond between them. If she wasn't having them both in her bed, she needed to make it clear now.

Jupiter's big body radiated heat, easing her muscles. She pressed her nose against his neck and breathed him in. The essence of the man. Something rare and comforting. Safety. If safety had a smell that's what Jupiter smelled like to her. When had someone last gone to battle for her, or more importantly, simply been there when she needed saving?

Roland. He'd have piloted through a star to reach her. Not her flesh and blood mother or father—just a man. A good man.

Jupiter wasn't Roland and the feelings growing for him were

of a very different nature, but he was a good man, too. If she hadn't figured it out for herself, she would have known it by the way Seneca looked at him. She looked over Jupiter's shoulder as he carried her into her room. Seneca's gaze had been searing into Jupiter's back, but he met her gaze over the muscular curve of Jupiter's shoulder with those clear lavender eyes. She curved her lips into a smile for him as she loosened her grip on the man carrying her. Sen was impossible to read, but she suspected deep emotions hid behind the careful expression. She didn't know him yet, but she knew she didn't want them to be adversaries. He was too important to Jupiter.

He hesitated just inside the door as Jupiter laid her on the bed. She closed her eyes and listened as Jupiter rumbled an awkward request to Alfred for a warm water shower. It was Seneca's voice quietly asking for cleanser and then drying air. A few minutes later the blowers stopped, and Jupiter slipped into bed behind her. His body fit around her, but he made no move to demand anything more. She'd known he wouldn't.

"Sleep," Jupiter commanded softly as his hand stroked the curve of her shoulder and down the length of her arm.

A quick glance and she found Seneca back hovering at the door, He'd put back on the same clingy black pants as before and his snowy hair was now braided and pulled over one shoulder. Feeona studied the still empty half of her big bed. Roland's room was across the hall from hers, but there was no reason to send him away. They were only going to sleep. She was pretty sure they'd all slept together on the resistance's heap of a ship. But sleep would be followed by waking and this time there would be no recent injury to detour Jupiter. Did she want Seneca there when sex was finally on the table?

She didn't know Seneca as well as Jupiter, but she realized she wanted to know him better. He was beautiful and strong and seemed to come as part of the deal. He'd been right beside Jupiter when they'd come storming through the wall and if she didn't yet know him well enough to trust him completely, that was okay. She'd had sex with men she didn't trust before.

Damn it. She trusted Jupiter. Really trusted him.

Feeona let that sink into her psyche then gave Seneca another smile. She reached out and patted the empty space. "Come on," she said, gaze on the quiet stranger across the room. "Let's all get some sleep."

His face stayed blank, but he moved toward them and slipped into the empty space. The man lay on his back. No part of him touched her. Had she been wrong to think he and Jupiter came as a pair?

"Sleep." Jupiter commanded more firmly.

Seneca's eyelids closed and his body sank a bit deeper into the bed.

And they slept.

CHAPTER NINETEEN

The Hawley
Earth Alliance Beta Sector
2210.152

Feeona woke in her own roomy bed for the first time in a month. Jupiter's heat blanketed her back. His hand lay relaxed against her belly, and his morning oh-so-happy-to-wake-up-with-you nudged against her ass. The promise of that helped her contain the urge to indulge in her usual morning sprawl and stretch. As she lifted her eyelids, the expanse of empty sheets in front of her left her both eager for the man at her back and confused. She remembered Seneca's inscrutable face when he'd laid down next to them, but he had joined them to sleep.

Jupiter nudged more firmly against her bottom and thoughts of anything but the size and heat of him fled. Size didn't make a man a good lover, but something about the combination of all that muscle and the tender ways he touched her made her melt. He nuzzled against her shoulder, teeth scraping against her skin. She stretched her neck to give him access and his lips followed the slope of her shoulder to the sensitive skin under her jawline.

She moaned happily. "Good morning."

His answer was a sexy growl and a hand stroking her skin. His big palm spread heat everywhere he touched her. Her thigh. Her hip. Her belly.

Then he reached down, unerringly fitting his hand between her legs. She had a breath to think it might have been nice for him to touch her breasts, but then the heel of his palm pressed a small circle over the still hidden nub of flesh that was suddenly begging for more direct contact.

Her hips shifted of their own accord. She hadn't made a conscious choice to move but her hunger for this man was irrepressible. His fingers hadn't yet burrowed into her, and she hadn't touched him at all. It didn't seem to matter. She arched her back and whimpered when his hand shifted to her leg to pull it across his thigh, opening her more fully to his touch.

He growled again then his hand was back where she wanted it. One of his long fingers settled into the newly exposed valley. The touch made her aware that she was already wet and moist and open for him. She squirmed beneath his fingertips, now tracing along her soft wet flesh. His hips rocked against her in small thrusts against her bare bottom, but he made no move to fuck her. She rocked against him until they both needed more.

His hand slipped away, and she whimpered at the loss. He captured one of her wrists and guided it down and between her legs.

"Claws." His voice was so raw and growly she almost didn't understand the word.

She hadn't even considered his claws. Hadn't had the presence of mind to think. The pace of things should have worried her, but her body was somehow keeping up with what he was doing to her.

He put his hand over hers and pressed her finger where his had been a moment earlier.

"Put your fingers inside." His words, hot and colored with need, stroked inside her ear and she shivered.

She knew why he wanted her to do it. He was a big guy. If she was going to take him, she needed to be prepared. The moment of choice, comply or don't comply, allowed other thoughts to creep in. She shouldn't be doing this. They were in a bad situation and there was a lot she wasn't telling him.

The soft rumble that came from the back of his throat had her looking over her shoulder. For a moment their gazes locked. Raw need filled his, but there was something more—vulnerability and reassurance. Despite his animal need for release, it was still her choice. There was no choice at all.

She'd wanted him for days. She'd just been too tired and hurting to do anything about it until now. Something about him reached inside her and she couldn't let what might come later steal him from her now.

He must have seen her decision in her face. His eyes darkened and his breathing deepened. The heat in that look was all sex. Like he was fucking her with his eyes.

Her body responded with a flood of cream that had her following his instructions. She pushed her fingers inside, one at first, then another.

His hand over hers encouraged her to use more pressure than she would have, and it was incredible. She felt connected to him as she'd never felt before.

He watched her squirm as his hands roamed over her. She was rushing, but she couldn't stop. Her skin felt tight everywhere he touched her. She fought for more contact where it would push her into heaven. Her body was revved and ready and she couldn't breathe and—

Jupiter pulled her hand away. Air flooded back into her lungs, but she wanted more.

Feeona reached behind her, wanting him in her hands, but there was no space between them. Her hand ended up clutching the taut flesh of his ass. Her fingers dug into the unyielding flesh as if to urge him even closer. He grunted in approval as muscle flexed beneath her ungentle touch.

She whimpered again as he shifted away from her, leaving her back exposed to the cooler air. Then her back pressed against the sheet and he settled between her legs. He slipped one arm under her to lift her toward him. He looked his fill as he gripped her thighs and positioned her where he wanted her. He was like a god kneeling there. The broad expanse of his chest captivated her. Powerful muscles wrapped around him, made strong by physical labor and brutality. She could see every muscle beneath his skin, beneath the scars—silvery lines, thin traces and thick reminders of old injuries. Without the fire burning in her belly, she might have been distracted by them, but the need he'd stoked burned too hot. She reached up and traced his muscles from the curve of his pectorals and down. She brushed lightly across his belly and his muscles jumped against her fingertips. He growled and she shivered.

Jupiter pulled her closer and thrust deep. She gasped. He grunted and stilled his hips. He tipped his head back and howled.

She couldn't breathe and she didn't care. She clutched at his hips and fought his grip on her thighs to tilt her hips for him, to encourage him to move. She was full of him and couldn't get enough. "More," she said on a moan.

He didn't make her wait. He reversed his grip and pushed her thighs wider as he leaned over her and thrust harder. One, long, deep, shove after another filled her with the length of his cock and put pressure on her clit. It dissolved her ability to think.

Every thrust forced a sexy noise from him and sent her soaring.

"Yes," she whispered. "Yes." The word escaped on a breath.

On the edge of paradise, she forced her eyes open to watch him move over her. He was looking down along the length of their bodies. Intense concentration sharpened his features. His muscles bunched and stretched as he moved. The sheen of exertion sparkled on his skin. When had sweat become sexy?

Her barbarian conqueror lifted his head, face tight with concentration. His gaze locked on hers as he changed the angle of his movements. Feeona's vision filled with white hot sparkles and her body tightened almost unbearably. Sweet, hot, pleasure swept her away and left her shaking beneath him. He lowered his body, wrapped his arms around her, and followed her over the wave.

It took several minutes for Feeona's heart rate to return to normal. As she became more aware of her surroundings, she realized he'd shifted to lie on his side, pressed against her. His lips pulled up at the ends as he traced a path across her collar bone and down to the curve of her breast. Her cooling flesh tingled beneath his touch.

She licked her lips and grinned. "Something tells me that was only round one."

His eyes flicked to hers then went right back to eating her up with appreciation. "Hmm." The sound, gruff and low, made his agreement clearer than any words could.

That was all good. The sexy vee from his hips to his cock, begged to be worshipped with hot kisses and they had time.

Her stomach chose that moment to growl. "Unless you can arrange breakfast in bed, maybe we should go find food first."

She let out a silly, over the top sigh. "While I still have enough energy to walk to the galley. There's no reason we can't come right back up here after food."

"You won't need energy, I'll carry you." Jupiter's tone was playful, but somehow, the mood had shifted. He pulled away from her and crawled out of bed.

"Hey, what's wrong?" Feeona sat up and waited for a reply while he pulled his pants on.

"Seneca has been gone too long."

"If there was anything wrong, Alfred would let me know." She wrapped the sheet around her and sat cross-legged on the bed.

Jupiter's face went full scowl. "It is not his safety that worries me. It's that he left at all."

She reached over and gave his hand a squeeze. "He probably wanted to give us some privacy."

"Yes." Jupiter sat on the edge of the bed with a sigh. He reversed his hand to hold hers against his chest. The small gesture turned what had been really good sex into something sweeter. "That is the problem. It isn't our way."

She couldn't stop the smile. "What isn't your way, privacy?"

He didn't smile back and she instantly regretted her words. Of course, slaves didn't necessarily get privacy. How could she have forgotten? "I'm sorry. I—"

"It isn't privacy, in general, that worries me. It's privacy for sex."

She didn't understand why he looked so sad, but she knew exactly what to do. Listen. She leaned in and pressed her check against his shoulder so he wouldn't have to meet her eyes and he wouldn't read into what he saw or didn't see in her face. "Tell me."

"Arena Dogs have little. What little we have—blankets for warmth, food to sustain us—we share equally within our pack. There were few female fighters from the beginning. Their numbers only grew scarcer over time. But a year ago, we heard the news that the surrogates used to give us life, had died. They would carry no more young."

"Surrogates?" Feeona didn't understand.

"They created us in their labs, but the attempts to grow us in artificial wombs always failed. The Dogs created that way never thrived."

Jupiter lifted his arm and pulled her into his lap. "There were more females of our kind that had been created for the pleasure houses. The masters thought that by giving us some of those females as mates they could encourage us to breed."

Feeona's throat tightened with a mix of anger and sorrow for the inhuman way his people were treated.

"Still, their numbers were small. Never was any pack given more than a single female. It's in our nature to bond with a mate. But our other needs complicated things."

"Needs?"

His fingers stroked idly over her arm as he talked. "Yes. The need to share with our brothers and our instinct to protect the female."

"So, you found a solution."

"The females solved the problem. They would bond with one male, but they would share sex with all males in the pack. They knew any male that was a sex partner would feel protective and sharing themselves freely would prevent tension among the males."

She resisted the urge to lift her head and meet his eyes. She wanted to know what he thought about that solution. "Did it work?"

"For the most part."

"Your pack had a female." Unexpected tension zipped along her nerves. She'd never thought to ask if he had a mate or children, but Seneca had said their brother had a mate, not Jupiter.

"Her name is Hera. We all swore an oath to protect her." There was no emotion in his voice to give her any hint of his feelings, but what he'd said made it clear all the males in his pack had sex with her.

She couldn't stand it any longer. She looked up desperately needing to read his face, after all. "You think Seneca considers you being with me as a betrayal of her?"

He wrapped a hand around her jaw and met her eyes. "No. The bond we share with our brother's mate is not that sort of bond. If she were my mate, I wouldn't have wanted your touch. Something changes inside us when a mate bond has formed. Nothing about you is betrayal. You are only good."

Guilt roared to life. Good was so not the word to describe her. She wanted to help Jupiter and Seneca, but she feared she'd end up hurting them. If sex with Jupiter turned that fear to fact, she would just have to find a way to keep her distance.

"I can see you are blaming yourself, Fee. And you're wrong." He bent down to capture her mouth.

He pressed forward with a deep, no-holding-back kiss she couldn't find the will to resist. When he broke the kiss, his features were lighter. The damn Dog was pleased with his effect on her.

He stroked her cheek with his thumb. "I'm concerned because Seneca didn't feel welcome in my bed."

"Technically, it's my bed. Don't you think that might be part of the problem?"

"No." He shifted his hand to wrap loosely around the back of her neck. "I was here, so it was my bed as much as yours and he should have known it was also his. Whether you accept him as a lover is your choice to make, but that fact and his presence would not stop me from fucking you."

That pronouncement should have raised her anger, but instead it fueled a need to have him inside her again. "Jupiter…"

He chuckled. "There will be plenty of time for us to learn each other."

Damn, she needed to rebuild some of her defenses. The man was dangerous. And she wasn't the only one to think so. She thought of all the times she'd seen Seneca watching Jupiter with longing in his lavender eyes. "Jupiter, you and Seneca have such a strong bond. Is it possible that he might be… hurt, by our being together this way? Maybe sharing isn't what he wants."

He shook his head and frowned. "Our bond is strong, but there is no reason he would be hurt by this."

"Are you certain? I mean, has there ever been anything physical between you?" Jupiter's scowl deepened and she instantly regretted her words. Maybe it wasn't her place. "I shouldn't have—"

Jupiter shook his head. "No. It's alright. It's just that I could never ask Sen for anything like that. I could never risk hurting him that way."

"Hurting him?"

"I fear he bears deep scars from his time in the pleasure house. He spent years there before he came to us. He isn't the same Dog now, but he carries the weight of the past."

"Of course, he does." She cleared the anger and sympathy from her throat. "Tell me about Seneca. I can't believe gladiators are sent to the pleasure houses all that often. Wouldn't that be dangerous?"

Jupiter scooted further onto the bed to put his back against the wall, taking her with him. He gave her room between his thighs and she settled her back against his chest.

"You're right. In the arena and the kennel, they chain us to walls and drug us when they let the female patrons use us. But the Dogs that work in the brothels are not chained. The females were engineered to be docile. But the males that go there aren't. They go there as pups, too small to be dangerous. He was just a child when they took him."

A fist of outrage slammed into her abdomen. Using slaves for sex was reprehensible, but using children that way... The tight feeling in her throat magnified, allowing her no air to speak. She didn't think she could get a word passed the constriction. Jupiter's arms slipped under hers and wrapped around her middle as if he could sense her disquiet.

"Seneca was created two birthings after mine, but his group shared the same juvenile facility. He was always smaller than the other Dogs in his group. And... beautiful. Even humans thought so."

Fee could hear Jupiter's appreciation and love in the way he talked about Seneca.

Jupiter softly stroked her hair as he spoke. "The Master gave the use of him to one of the patrons as a gift. A man who liked young boys. Seneca told me he tried to fight, but he hadn't been trained. The man overpowered him easily." Jupiter's voice became rougher as he spoke. "There were others. He has never said—" Jupiter's voice broke.

Feeona tugged his arms around her and wrapped hers over his in a semblance of a hug. "He survived. He didn't let them destroy his soul."

Jupiter nodded, brushing his chin against the top of her head. "Years later, when they brought him to the kennel, he was weak and far, far behind in training. He tried to learn, but he didn't have the muscle mass or stamina to keep up. Other young Dogs like Sen had been brought to the training grounds before. Most didn't survive long."

Feeona hated the sadness in his voice. Her heart was breaking for both men.

"Seneca was different. There was a spark of determination in his eyes. But that spark wasn't enough to overcome his lack of training, his small size, and lack of a pack. With no pack to sleep or eat with, he had to stay in the training yard all the time. Many of us tried to take him food, but the trainers wouldn't allow it. They said we needed our food to stay strong for training. He survived eating scraps, but he only became weaker and weaker. The only water he got was when they irrigated the grass in the training field." Jupiter's muscles tightened as he spoke.

Feeona rested her arms over his, stroking his skin. "They deserve to be tied up in a low oxygen atmosphere and left to see if they'd suffocate or starve first."

Jupiter chuckled. "You have a devious mind, my Fee."

She lifted her shoulders in a shrug.

He leaned down and rubbed his chin against her temple. "I think the trainers enjoyed seeing one of us brought low. When there was a break in training, I would sit with him. He was so thirsty he would lick the perspiration from my skin. I think his body needed the salt as much as the water. He was so close to death in the end."

Jupiter's arms tightened around her as if he'd gone back to that moment. "One evening after training, I went to look for him. I hadn't seen him at all that day. He'd curled up in a corner away from everything. He couldn't even lift his head. He had such a strong will to live. I couldn't let him die. I carried him inside. The whip-master tried to stop me, but my pack brothers backed me up. He didn't want an open rebellion so he told us we would all have to take lashes for our disobedience."

Feeona closed her eyes and fought the toxic emotions roiling inside her. He spoke of unspeakable cruelty without any sense that it shouldn't, couldn't, be allowed.

"The whip-master laughed and said we were only drawing out his death. That we shared our water and food only if our performance didn't suffer. If we performed badly, they would kill him outright. Mercury, our pack leader made sure we gave him only what we could without weakening ourselves, but he stood with me and he saved Sen every bit as much as I did. Now Sen is a full member of our pack, as valuable a fighter as any other. His body has recovered, but a Dog is more than flesh and blood."

Feeona sat up and turned to him. "Go to him. Give him the reassurance he needs."

Jupiter looked at her like she was made of pure starlight, then pressed a final kiss to her forehead and got to his feet.

Seneca's fists ached, but he couldn't stop hitting the training target. The tension inside him had to go somewhere. He'd found a surprisingly well-equipped training room on the main level. The gear looked very different from the blunted swords, metal shields, and staffs he'd trained with on Roma. He did recognize the square of striking surface, surrounded by sensor readouts. On Roma they trained for the primitive and deadly weapons of

Old Earth, but Master Owens spared no expense on technical gadgets to improve their strength and battle skills.

Jupiter entered the room on softly thudding bare feet. "You'll overload that target's circuits, if you don't give it a rest. Maybe you need something else to hit for a while."

Seneca threw one more punch, then met Jupiter's gaze. "You want to take the target's place?"

"Whatever you need, Sen." Jupiter held his arms out to the side, as if he might be waiting for an embrace. No. He wasn't waiting for that. He was offering himself up as a more satisfying striking target.

A flash of violence ripped through Seneca, and he had to hold himself still until the urge to punch Jupiter's treasured face faded. "There's safety gear," he offered instead.

Jupiter's eyebrows lifted. Seneca shrugged. The bigger Dog's eyes lit as he charged right at him in a sloppy move more play than training. Jupiter tackled him around the middle and carried them both to the ground. Seneca didn't want playful. He wanted to pound and be pounded on. He needed to numb the pain. Not the pain in his hands, the ache lodged firmly under his ribs. The large organ that pumped blood through his heated body had become an open wound.

The sound of Jupiter's howl when he'd joined with Feeona had stabbed him with more force that he'd expected. He slammed a fist into Jupiter's ribs and was rewarded with a small grunt of pain. Seneca pressed the advantage, twisting beneath Jupiter and landing another firm blow a few centimeters from the first.

Jupiter let him twist, pushing with the motion. The world flipped and Seneca's back hit the training floor with a loud thump. Jupiter pressed Seneca's body against the floor. The heavy masculine weight of Jupiter over him, the hip pressed against his groin, dug into Seneca like a rusty spoon.

"Fuck," Seneca grunted and bucked then reached for Jupiter's head, trying to get some purchase."

Jupiter didn't budge. "What's eating you, my friend?"

"I'm fine," he growled back, still trying to dislodge his pack-mate.

"Then why did you leave the bed to come hammer away at training targets?"

Seneca snarled. "We're free now brother. A Dog should have his female to himself the first time he claims her as mate."

Jupiter's concentration broke. Seneca was ready. He threw Jupiter off and leapt into a defensive stance. He waited for the next attack, muscles vibrating with tension. When nothing came, he realized the Dog had gotten to his feet, but stood still, jaw slack.

"A mate claim?" Jupiter shook his head.

Seneca wanted to roll his eyes. The Dog operated on instinct and had rarely studied his own feelings. "Don't be too worried. The two of you fit." And that was what was shredding his guts most of all.

Seneca didn't wait for a reply. He took Jupiter down in a clean efficient move. Now that he'd said it out loud, it seemed he could manage the emotions better. He grinned as he pinned the bigger Dog beneath him. "We're even now."

"Not even." Jupiter reversed the pin with a show of brute strength.

Seneca couldn't move. Jupiter had him pinned tight. He knew his best move was to relax. Stop struggling. But fuck. He could feel Jupiter all over him, his broad chest crushing him. His scent and the smell of sex filling his nose. Jupiter wasn't aroused. No

doubt Feeona had sated him. Seneca wanted to slide his knee up
to press gently against Jupiter's balls. Just to see if he could
change that. Jupiter's powerful thighs, locked tight against him,
wouldn't allow him to move a centimeter closer to that
temptation.

Seneca hated how easy it would be to get off. The grip of
Jupiter's strong hands holding his wrists above his head
screamed sex to his corrupt mind. It would only take one or two
thrusts up against the Dog who had no idea how often he played
center stage in Seneca's thoughts. The one thing Jupiter couldn't
miss was the iron length of his dick, pressed tight between them.

Jupiter chuckled low in the back of his throat. "You wouldn't
be so uncomfortable now if you'd stuck around in bed a little
longer."

Seneca growled. His dick had only gotten harder with
Jupiter's laugh. "Let me up, damn it."

"Serves you right for that mate crap you used on me."

That reminder should have done more to dampen his over
sensitized nerves. His vision dimmed and he realized he was
breathing too fast, too hard, without getting any air.
Hyperventilating.

Jupiter released his wrists then pulled him up and forward.
"Fuck, Sen. Calm down."

Seneca couldn't think, he was drenched in sweat and
shivering. Jupiter moved around him, never losing contact, never
giving him the break he so desperately needed.

"You're okay." Jupiter pressed up against his back. Not
restraining now. Chafing his arms and murmuring softly.
"Breathe slow. In and out. That's it."

Seneca responded, in spite of himself. Obeying an alpha.
Following the guidance of the Dog he trusted most in the

universe. The concern, the love in Jupiter's voice, soothed him. This was the love Jupiter could offer. It had been enough for him before. It would be enough again.

He cleared his throat of panic's leftover tension. "I wasn't … joking."

"Don't try to talk."

Seneca looked over his shoulder. "I'm okay. But you, my friend, are in love."

Jupiter's face twisted in a half frown, half grin. "Maybe."

"Definitely." Seneca ran his tongue over his parched lips.

Jupiter's mouth stretched into a full, beautiful grin. "If it's true, you have even more reason to stay in our bed."

The pack bond. It was the way of the packs. He stifled a sigh. At least he'd managed to distract Jupiter from his own inconvenient distress and the undeniable fact that his own heart was breaking.

CHAPTER TWENTY

The Hawley
Earth Alliance Beta Sector
2210.152

After the evening meal, they were all sitting around companionably in the common area. Feeona didn't remember how it had gotten started, but somehow she'd ended up reciting children's nursery rhymes to them.

"Wee Willie Winkie runs through the town, upstairs and downstairs in his night gown."

Jupiter frowned. "That seems unlikely. Why would a child do such a thing?"

Seneca adjusted the pillow he'd been leaning on. "At least it isn't about chopping up small sightless animals, like that one about the butcher's wife." Seneca shivered as if the story actually had the power to unsettle him.

He'd seemed relaxed since he and Jupiter spent the morning sparring. She'd found them working out when she'd finished her shower. It had been fun to watch and she'd been relieved she hadn't broken their relationship.

Feeona smacked Jupiter's shoulder with the back of her hand. "You didn't let me finish. It goes... Tapping at the window, crying at the lock. Are the children in their beds, for it's now eight o'clock?" Fee stroked Jupiter's shoulder, rubbing away the sting of her earlier smack. "There's more, but I think those Old Earth people had a good idea about getting to bed." She wiggled her eyebrows.

Jupiter stared back at her with a single eyebrow raised high. A moment later he sprang into motion. He'd been holding her feet in his lap, but they were moved unceremoniously to the floor.

He stood and offered a hand to help her up. "The best thing you've said in hours."

Feeona shot him a look. "I am known to have good ideas on occasion."

He pulled her into his arms and pressed her body up against his, meeting her eyes with fierce concentration. Slowly, he lowered his head and pressed his lips against hers, kissing her with small nips. His tongue slipped out to tease her lips open and he pushed into her mouth.

She kissed him back. Her senses were full of him. His scent. The heat of his body pressed all along hers. As slowly as he'd started he withdrew, leaving her bereft and glorious at the same time. Her heart beat strong and impatient. Her lips tingled. Heat from somewhere inside her pressed against her too tight skin.

Jupiter's lips slowly stretched into a wide smile. "I have plenty of my own ideas right now. You can take the rest of the night off."

Ideas? Oh yeah. They'd been talking about good ideas. She let her happiness escape on a laugh. She peeked around his shoulder to Seneca who was still sprawled on the cushions. "How about you? Do you have any good ideas we should consider?" It was her way to let him know she wanted him to join in the game they were playing.

Seneca raised his silver eyebrows. "I have ideas, but I'm content to follow Jupiter's lead."

She winked. "Me too. He *is* the biggest."

"Pleasingly so, I'm sure." Seneca's gaze shifted to Jupiter's ass in his form fitting training pants.

She shifted her attention to Jupiter's well-deserved smirk. He was big all over and she remembered just how good that had felt. "Can we go to bed now?"

"Demanding female," Jupiter complained. Warmth coated the mock gruffness in his voice.

Seneca shifted across the cushions then stood. "I think she deserves a little indulgence."

Jupiter lifted her up and guided her thighs to his hips. "I agree." He pressed one more soft kiss to her lips then carried her up the steps.

Looking over his shoulder, she had a great view of Seneca flowing up the stairs behind them. Despite being all Dog, his body was part dancer, part cat. Grace and lazy confidence. Whatever had been in the way before, had been resolved.

Tonight, she would have them both.

Seneca watched as Jupiter pulled Feeona's clothes off with more patience than he expected. Jupiter took every chance to press kisses to her lips, to stroke her caramel skin. He pushed her top up, licking the curve of her breast. His teeth grazed her skin but he didn't bite. If it were Seneca, would he allow himself to be more aggressive? Sen would beg for Jupiter's big canines against his skin, but he wanted that tongue and those soft lips, too.

When Feeona took over getting her tunic off, Jupiter stroked back down to her hips and pushed her clingy trousers down just far enough to uncover her ass. He molded his big hands along the tempting curves and pulled her up against him. She made a sexy little moan of pleasure.

The memory of Jupiter's body pressed up against his that morning, swamped Seneca. He didn't blame Feeona for moaning and wrapping a leg around his thigh. He'd nearly done the same. He couldn't blame her for Jupiter's attraction to her either. The problem here wasn't Feeona or Jupiter. They were doing what came naturally. Seneca was the one wishing for something he could never have when he should be relishing the excuse to be close, to touch, and glory in the scent and heat of the Dog he loved.

Feeona clutched at Jupiter's shoulders as if she wanted to climb him. She was a little too short to align her anatomy up with Jupiter's. Seneca stepped up behind her. "You're being cruel, Jup." He gave her the boost she needed to press directly up against Jupiter's dick. Her breath hitched, then accelerated.

Jupiter growled in response. "I want more time to touch her." No longer needing to support her weight, Jupiter shifted his hands.

Feeona moaned again. "Don't talk like I'm not here."

"Oh, I know exactly where you are." Jupiter rocked his hips. Feeona moaned again. "I didn't get to touch you enough this morning, Fee."

"That was…" He was touching her now. Her rough breathing made that clear. "Your choice…. I…" She dropped her head down against Jupiter's shoulder. "I wasn't rushing you."

"Yes, you were." Jupiter pressed a kiss to her temple. "And you're doing it again now."

Seneca almost regretted stepping up to join them. He was too close to see what Jupiter was doing to her. He'd watched and been watched, with no choice, and he'd learned to take his pleasure where he could. His hands were just above her hips, digging into soft, warm flesh. She didn't seem to mind. She squirmed under his touch, but she wasn't trying to get free. She was rocking up against Jupiter. Seneca nudged aside her hair and pushed his nose up against the back of her neck, breathing her in.

She smelled female, but not like other humans or any of the female Dogs he'd known. Her scent was unique and he liked it. Jupiter's scent had been the first thing to attract him. Back then he'd been too intimidated by the size of the gladiators to get turned on by their rough beauty.

Seneca lifted his head enough to whisper in her ear. "Put your arms around his neck and hold on."

She obeyed without hesitation. Her prompt obedience left him free to squat down and pull her pants the rest of the way off. He stayed put for a moment and Feeona lifted her legs to circle Jupiter's hips.

Seneca's position at their feet gave him a clear view of Jupiter's hand between her legs. He was teasing her, circling his fingers around her clit without touching. Her pussy was pink and swollen. The scent of her arousal filled his nose. He wanted to press his nose into the fragrant valley between her legs. Moisture coated her flesh and Jupiter's fingers. As Seneca watched, Jupiter finally stroked directly against her clit. She made an "ung" sound in the back of her throat. It was a pleading noise.

Seneca's dick hardened. He couldn't get enough of the view of Jupiter's big hands and the slippery sound of his fingers sliding against her. He could see that Jupiter was doing well at keeping his claws under control, but he was also avoiding taking the next step when she was clearly ready. Well, Seneca didn't have claws to worry about. He lay his hand on Fee's back to let her get used to the idea of him touching her then slid it down between her legs. Seneca put his other hand on Jupiter's calf on the pretense of steadying himself. The strength and heat of the bigger Dog seeped into him. He slipped two fingers deep into Fee's cunt. She gasped and Jupiter's chest rumbled. Seneca stretched her pink flesh, moving his fingers in and out, stretching her for Jupiter's big dick.

Jupiter made a gruff noise and his hand disappeared from Feeona's swollen pink flesh. Seneca stood and backed away, relieved that he didn't have to hide his arousal. Any Dog would be turned on by Feeona's pussy. Jupiter's fingers at play and that precious moment of skin-to-skin contact had been Seneca's private bonus.

Jupiter shucked off his pants and carried Feeona with him as he crawled onto the center of her big bed. Seneca's heart pounded in his chest. He was too turned on to get on the bed with them. He'd never resist the urge to touch Jupiter. He backed against the nearest wall and willed himself to disappear into the shadows of the room. The lights were dimmed but not out. It didn't matter. Jupiter and Feeona were absorbed in each other.

They were beautiful together. Jupiter's copper-skinned body moving over Feeona's caramel curves. They pressed together everywhere, stroking each other with lingering touches. Jupiter worked his way down her body, kissing and tasting her skin. He circled a brown nipple with his tongue then took it into his mouth. Feeona's spine bowed and her fingers caressed Jupiter's short, cropped hair. Jupiter worshiped her body from head to toe. Seneca couldn't stop himself from imagining Jupiter touching him that way.

He watched Fee's chest rise and fall and her hips squirm as she stroked Jupiter's skin. The bunch and stretch of Jupiter's muscles drew Seneca's eyes and it drew moans from Fee's lips. When Jupiter finally raised up to position himself to fuck her, Seneca watched Jupiter's fully erect dick stand proud before it disappeared between her thighs. Her spine bowed again, and she tipped her head back as she groaned her pleasure. Jupiter lifted her thighs and pushed her legs back. It gave Seneca a better view of Jupiter's dick glistening as he pulled out.

"Jupiter, please," Feeona breathed.

"Greedy." Jupiter's voice was all growl, despite his obvious approval. He thrust back in and joined her in a pleasured groan.

It hadn't been this way with Hera. Their pack brother's mate hadn't encouraged them to linger or take their time. She'd accepted them, one after the other, with little enthusiasm. Seneca knew Feeona wouldn't be that way with him, but he wasn't sure how she *would* be.

She and Jupiter found a rhythm that pleased them both and made Seneca's heart ache. Feeona moaned her pleasure and encouraged Jupiter with sensual touches. She strained with an orgasm, twisting in her mate's grip.

Jupiter barely slowed. "Again. Come for me again."

The deep raspy command stroked Seneca's need as if Jupiter had been speaking to him. He pushed down his pants and took his own dick in hand. He squeezed hard and stroked, down then up. He smoothed his thumb through the pre-cum that beaded thickly at his tip. He matched his strokes to Jupiter's, pounding his own flesh with punishing pressure until he was on the verge of coming. He kicked out of his pants and reached between his legs to jerk tight on his balls. He wouldn't come. Not yet.

Jupiter released Feeona's legs and dropped down, pressing his long body over her. His spine curved, shifting the angle of his strokes as he seemed to try to thrust even deeper. Feeona screamed. Jupiter lost his rhythm. He thrust hard again, body straining.

Seneca's dick was leaking a nearly steady stream of pre-cum as he imagined being pinned beneath Jupiter, that demanding dick pounding into him.

Jupiter howled his release. Seneca pulled on his balls again to keep his orgasm at bay, but he couldn't stop his howl from joining Jupiter's.

When the last echoes of their howl faded away, Feeona and Jupiter were still clinging to each other. Jupiter rolled over, taking her with him, so she sprawled boneless across his chest. He'd satisfied her. Satisfied them both, for the moment. But Jupiter was probably almost as hard as he'd been before coming. Stamina was an Arena Dog trait.

Seneca had waited as long as his arousal would allow. He crawled onto the bed. Straddling Jupiter's legs, he nudged his dick against Feeona's ass. She sighed a languid response.

Seneca stroked his hands up her back and then around her to cup her breasts. Slowly she came back to life and sat up to give him better access. The position allowed him to look over her shoulder, down her beautifully female body and to Jupiter's half hard dick, stretching toward his navel. Seneca rocked against Feeona, moving her against Jupiter. The big Dog hummed his appreciation. Seneca's belly tightened at the sound. In a hurry now, he pulled her hips up and eased her shoulders forward. He was as long as Jupiter but not as thick. She was well prepared to take him. One smooth stroke buried him in her hot, wet heat.

She was tighter than he expected and they both panted heavily at the sensation. He could feel Jupiter's gaze on him, but he let the physical pleasure of fucking take him where not much could reach him. He flexed his hips in a rhythm born of instinct. A small, very physical part of him wanted to pursue a quick release, but his heart and his pride wanted to take Jupiter with them.

Seneca pulled free, wrapped his hand around Jupiter's dick and indulged in a single stroke up and down his length. The satisfying sound of Jupiter's groan tightened Seneca's balls. He steadied that big dick with one hand and adjusted Feeona's hips into position. Her juices flowed over Jupiter's tip then his length disappeared inside her. Seneca closed his eyes and counted to five to resist the urge to shove his dick in alongside Jupiter's. She was still too tight and he wasn't sure any of them were ready for that. Jupiter might never be ready and he'd have to accept that. Seneca positioned his now slicked dick in the valley of Feeona's ass. He avoided the temptation to push into her tight pink rosebud and let his dick slide between her cheeks. Arm wrapped around Feeona's belly, he pulled her back up into a sitting position, her back pressed to his chest. He angled them both forward until her breathing hitched. "There we go," he rumbled. "That's the spot, isn't it Fee?"

"Yes," she hissed.

"Let's send Jupiter to heaven."

"Oh, yes."

"Already there," Jupiter growled.

"We'll see," Seneca teased.

With both arms wrapped tight around Fee—one beneath the soft curve of her breasts and one at her hips—Seneca guided her movements into a grinding serpentine movement that had Jupiter panting in a flash.

The position and the movement were a delicious challenge for Seneca's out of practice thighs and groin. He barely registered

Fee tugging at the arm he had wrapped under her breasts until she pressed her fingernails into his skin. It threw off his rhythm for an instant as he let her pull his hand away. She guided him to Jupiter's torso and pressed his palm below Jup's collar bone. Before he could think better of it, he stretched a thumb out to brush Jup's nipple. The answering groan sent tingling fire to the base of his spine. He slid his gaze to Jupiter's flushed face and for a brief second, he could believe there was something more than blind lust in his eyes. But the pleasure quickly took them all back to the edge.

With Jupiter and Fee lost in sensation, Seneca had license to enjoy the beauty of their bodies straining together, the ecstasy of his balls brushing against Jupiter's thighs. Every move tugged at the rim of his dick where it was pressed tight against Fee. Fuck, he was going to come.

Jupiter bucked beneath them then threw his head back and roared. The straining tendons in his neck made Seneca want to lick them and that beloved masculine sound pushed him over the edge. He spilled slippery splashes of hot cum along Fee's back. Her rhythm broke and he was certain the breathy sounds she made meant she'd followed them into release. She collapsed along Jupiter's chest and Seneca flopped onto the sheets beside them, breathing just as hard.

It had been the first glorious time he'd felt like he was giving Jupiter his orgasm. He owed Feeona for allowing him that. He needed to get up and clean them up, but after that he would sleep well tonight. They all would.

CHAPTER TWENTY-ONE

The Hawley
Earth Alliance Beta Sector
2210.156

After five nights with Jupiter and Seneca, Feeona should have been sleeping, but that feeling of waiting for the other boot to drop plagued her the moment the ship got quiet. She was awake when the alert-tone whistled softly through her quarters. Jupiter's ears twitched and his eyes opened. She smiled to put him at ease.

"Alfred's letting me know it's time to go attend to navigation." She propped up on one elbow and leaned over to plant a kiss on his broad nose. "Go back to sleep. I'll be back in a little while."

His nose scrunched and he chuffed in the back of his throat. A second chuff softly echoed from the other side of him. Seneca lifted his head and acknowledged her with a lazy blink of his eyes. The light was on dim, but that just added sexy shadows to the sleek masculine skin on display. They generated too much body heat to need covers, so nothing blocked her view of the curve of Jupiter's shoulder and hip as he lay on his side. Or the rippled muscles of Seneca's abdomen and the tempting vee that drew her eyes down to his soft masculine flesh.

Feeona looked away before she risked shrugging off what needed to be done in favor of another round. She wasn't sure she was ready for more just yet. With nothing to do until they reached Petro-5 sex had become one of their favorite ways to pass the time. It left her body achy and sore, but in a good way.

The more time she spent with them the more strongly she believed that Jupiter and Seneca loved each other, but neither would act on those feelings. Was she making the situation better or worse?

She stepped over the clothes they'd thrown on the floor and snagged her robe on the way to the door. She didn't allow herself to look back as she pulled on the soft material that covered her down to her thighs.

When she made it to the pilot's station, she checked the navigation controls and made the necessary adjustments. They'd come out of skipspace and transitioned to standard propulsion without so much as a bump.

"Alfred, please verify that our guests are still in my quarters and alert me if that changes."

"Verified. Instructions understood." Alfred's reply came without delay. "It's not polite to spy on others, Feeona."

She couldn't complain at the admonition. She'd been the one to teach it to him. "That's right, Alfred. But every rule has its exception."

"Yes, Captain."

"Close the door to the pilot's station, please."

The door slid shut. It was unnecessary. The doors to her quarters were already shut. There was no way Jupiter or Seneca could hear her, but caution was a habit that had served her well.

"Alfred, display any incoming coms." A list of respondents

filled the main screen. She'd gotten a message from each of the contacts she'd broadcast to before their last jump. "This is good. Let's hope someone can come through for us. Display full messages in sequence please, Alfred."

The first came up on screen. "Would you like me to read the replies to you, Captain?"

"If they're all this brief it'll be quicker to do it myself." The first message read simply, *Not Interested. —DQ.*

The next six were equally succinct. Then the no's got longer. Damn it! It didn't surprise her, she was offering a high-risk deal, but that didn't make her any less frustrated. The best response she'd gotten was a request for direct contact from one of Roland's oldest friends. She wanted to be optimistic, but after so many blunt refusals it wasn't easy.

"Alfred, attempt a direct contact with Gulliver. He says he's in the area." She stretched to open her personal storage compartment and pulled out Jacky the Unicorn. She adjusted her robe and hugged the soft stuffed toy to her middle, ready to settle in for the wait.

"Connection ready, Captain."

"That was fast." He must have been waiting. She shoved Jacky behind her, twisted her hair back in a knot and straightened her shoulders. "On screen one."

Gulliver's rugged face flicked onto the screen in front of her. His hair and beard were still salt and pepper, but the lines in his face had deepened further than last she'd seen him.

"Are you alright, bonnie-girl?"

She folded her arms across her chest. "Do you have to assume I'm in trouble?"

"Hell, yes." His eyebrows lifted so high they disappeared into his still full hair line. "When you reach out to half the sector, offering up the *Hawley* for funds, yes."

"You're exaggerating. It wasn't that many." She should have known Roland's friends would spread the news to Gulliver. "And I'm not selling the ship, just putting her up as collateral for a loan."

"Same difference. Never bet what you're not willing to lose." He scowled and it bunched up one side of his puffy, reddened face. He had the look of a man who'd enjoyed his liquor all his life. Even when less damaging intoxicants were available, he and Roland would pass an evening together over a carton of scotch. "I know Roland taught you that lesson."

Feeona forced her arms to her sides and lowered her shoulders. Body language for beginners had been another lesson Roland had taught her. She wasn't above leaning on their long history and his lifelong friendship with her mentor, but she needed Gulliver thinking of her as an open-book teenager again. "So, how about it? Are you going to be my knight in shining armor?"

"I'm sorry my bonnie-girl. It's not my way to do bad business and fronting you money for the *Hawley* is a deal so stupid I wouldn't do it even for my old mother."

Feeona's jaw tightened and she smiled to hide the frustration bubbling up inside her. Showing emotion would only reinforce his opinion of the deal she'd offered. "You know I'm good for it, Gulliver. I've never had a shortage of work and I don't run out on my debts. I'm just pressed for time right now."

His scowl softened. "You're a thief and a grifter, my girl, and that line of work is never certain." He shook his head. "And before you go defending yourself, think on it. The *Hawley* is essential to your business. Give her up and you'll have a hard time making a living. More than that, she's your home. Could you really giver her up, if it came to it?"

She blew out a breath that lifted the strands of hair that had come loose around her face. "It won't come to that. One job and I'll have your funds back to you."

"Will you, then? And how do you plan to get work when bounty hunters from Madeley-4 to Ellington Colony are looking for you?"

Damn. That was news she didn't need to hear from him. "I'm resourceful, Roland always said so." And she wasn't giving up. Gulliver was the only one on her list who'd even bothered to talk to her.

The older man nodded. "Yes, but I'm no fool."

"What if I make it a sale, plain and simple? I'll send you an electronic deed as soon as the funds are transferred." The words were out of her mouth before she'd thought them through.

Gulliver frowned. "Do you mean that, bonnie-girl?"

Did she? Would she really give up the *Hawley* to get just one more shipment of kids off Petro-5? It could take her years to earn enough to purchase a suitable ship before she could haul another shipment. Would she risk that to keep Jupiter and Seneca safe?

"Yes. I do mean it. I know an electronic title wouldn't normally be enough, but I swear to you, Gulliver. I swear to be good to the deal." It would take her a few weeks to distribute the cargo and get the *Hawley* to him, but there was no need to go into that. "Please."

She didn't bother to hide the pain in her heart. The pretense of keeping emotions out of it had long since failed. Maybe her pain would translate into sincerity.

She waited, watching untold thoughts flash across his face as they came and went in his head.

He licked his lips then smoothed his beard. His head shook, providing her answer even before he spoke. "Just can't do it. Come visit me awhile. I'll keep you hidden and safe and you'll still have the *Hawley* when your troubles blow over."

Would they blow over? She had a feeling Roma had a long memory. What had she gotten herself into?

"Thanks for the offer." Her emotions were running strong, but gratitude wasn't among them. "I'll find another way."

She reached out and cut the connection manually. "Damn it." She pulled Jacky back into her lap and hugged him tight. He'd been a gift from Roland that first year. His colors were faded, but he still had his shiny black eyes. "My options have gone from bad to worse, Jacky. Worse than worse. Damn, damn, damn."

"Perhaps a cup of tea would make things seem better, Captain." Alfred's calm suggestion made her snort despite the constriction in her throat.

"I don't think that's going to do it, Alfred." She shoved Jacky back into his bin, then got to her feet and rubbed at the tears that were definitely not falling down her cheeks. "I'm going to go break out a carton of Roland's scotch. I want a connection to Morgan St. Germaine open when I get back." She needed some liquid courage before dealing with the vilest man she'd ever had the misfortune to meet.

"You said we weren't dealing with Morgan ever again, Captain."

"Desperate times, Alfred. Desperate times."

Two shots of scotch, a trip to one of the downstairs lavs, and a rushed round of solo brainstorming later, she'd come up with the best *bad* plan she could. And she'd made her deal with the devil.

"No matter how much Roma Rex offers or threatens, you *will* give me a chance to outbid them." Feeona kept her expression light, her voice firm and all thoughts of consequences and worry out of her mind. Okay, maybe the last part of that was a total lie.

She sat in her pilot's chair, feet on the floor, back straight but angled toward the recorder. She'd wound her hair in a braid around her head and added a quick spray of makeup. She did her best to emote congeniality while squashing out any sign of softness. It was a hard look to pull off, but acting was always part of the gig.

"Of course, Poppet. Everything will be just as you wish." The man on her view screen was slender and polished. "You have finally come to me after these many years of staying away from the trade. I wouldn't dream of doing anything to jeopardize the business we could do together."

Morgan didn't look like evil. He looked like a wealthy merchant—something that was true as far as it went. The clothes he wore had no doubt been hand tailored and they flattered his otherwise unremarkable image. He was younger than most of Roland's cohorts. Naively, she'd once thought it was his age that had prompted Roland to keep him away from her. He never looked at her with fatherly affection like Gulliver or the others. When she'd learned the truth, she'd realized he'd been protecting Morgan from her as much as the other way around. She'd been more of a hot-head then. If she'd known Morgan's merchandise was people, she would have shoved a pointy object through his cold heart.

Morgan had been after her to smuggle for him since the day Roland died. He didn't know her reasons for dismissing him out of hand and so he'd been relentless. Telling him she didn't deal with slavers hadn't been enough of an explanation for him. To him it was all just business. His lack of comprehension served her purpose now. With no better alternatives at the moment, she couldn't discount him as an option when her kids' lives were at stake. If there was another option, she'd find it and walk away from the deal that had her insides so tangled she feared the contortion might be lethal.

"Good, and don't you even think of caving into any of Roma's threats."

She hadn't wanted to tell him about Roma, but logic told her that Roma would insert themselves into the situation no matter how cautious she was.

"I don't scare that easy." Morgan grinned, reminding her of a clee-cat—opportunistic and fearless, the cats were known to take down prey triple their weight. "Those Roma pussies put their trousers on one leg at a time, like the rest of us."

"Excellent, then we have an agreement." Feeona's self-loathing compounded with the words. As much as she might tell herself this was only a back-up plan, there was no Plan A in sight. Dread squeezed her heart with the merciless grip of the damned.

CHAPTER TWENTY-TWO

New Telford, Petro-5
Earth Alliance Beta Sector
2210.160

Feeona and Jupiter stood at the edge of the jumble of people surrounding the gate that led to the factory entrance. It had been that way as long as Feeona had been coming back to the factory. They clustered there hoping for day work. Most of New Telford's colonists worked in the finishing or packing plants. Only the desperate would willingly seek employment at the giant factory, where so many never left.

But the crowd benefited her. It made it easy to approach and get the attention of a guard willing to carry in a note to Toolman. She had Bug busy circling the sky, keeping a watch on the ship where they'd left Seneca to wait for their return.

As they approached, Jupiter closed the distance between them. He walked so close they brushed against each other with every step. Feeona halted in the middle of the crowd and looked up into his hooded face. The shadows of the garment he wore hid him from a distance, but up close it was easy to spot the less than human features that marked him as an Arena Dog. Those features came together in a face that already meant the world to her. A face she'd pressed kisses against, a face she'd memorized, a face she would likely see in her nightmares after today.

"Maybe you should stay here. We don't want one of the guards to notice you."

He scowled. "I didn't let you leave the ship alone. I'm not going to cower in hiding now, when you also risk being recognized."

She grimaced. "I suppose you're right." She gripped his forearm and met his eyes. "When we get to the fence, turn your back, okay?"

"I won't give us away." He wrapped his big hand around her jaw, tracing his thumb along her cheek.

With any other man, she wouldn't have tolerated the proprietary gesture, but it felt right when it was Jupiter. She suspected he'd be delighted if she reciprocated with a possessive move of her own. He wasn't like other men who wanted to control her. He wanted to keep her safe, sure. But just as he respected Seneca's abilities, he also respected hers. He trusted her. How bittersweet to see the warmth and confidence in his eyes, when she could only dim that light. The only thing she could do for him now was to keep Seneca safe. If she'd had any doubts before, days of watching the two men together had left her certain that the connection between them was strong and mutual, even if they hadn't quite figured it out for themselves.

Her throat had tightened beyond speaking without giving away her grief, so she nodded and led him to the primitive looking fence. Three meters high, made of interlocking metal wires, it wouldn't resist any serious intruder, but it effectively kept the hopeful and doomed at a comfortable distance from the actual entrance to the building.

Jupiter did as she'd asked, turning his back to the armed

guards. He kept her close, blocking her in against the fence as he surveyed the crowd. Feet solidly planted and head above anyone else there, he looked like a paid bodyguard to her respectable merchant. It was impossible for a man his size to go unnoticed, but the illusion was a believable one that neutralized curiosity and fit the persona she'd painstakingly built for Petro-5.

Feeona let her gaze settle on a nearby guard, motioning him over when he noticed her looking.

The guard took in Jupiter's size with a frown, but quickly dismissed him. "You have business here trader?"

She extended her hand, offering a coin in the local currency. Offering too much would only arouse suspicion. "I have a message."

"I'm listening."

She waited until the man accepted the coin. "Tell Toolman, his promise-daughter is in town. I'll be at the Crooked Path."

Skepticism flashed in his face and then it was gone, and he nodded then moved away.

Toolman lived at the factory and had the rare privilege of being allowed to come and go as he wished, so it made sense that she would come looking for him here. It was less likely that Toolman had ever had a close enough friend to be named a promise-father or that anyone would actually trust him with a child. Other than factory management.

Feeona brushed Jupiter's sleeve and led him back through the crowd. When they were once again out of eavesdropping range, she slipped her hand in his and led him down the first side street.

"It will take some time for him to get the message and there's something I need to show you."

Jupiter took Feeona's hand and let her lead. Her hand felt small and cool. Today she looked as cool as she felt. She'd worn one of her disguises. She'd painted her skin almost white and done something to make her hair even whiter. She'd pulled it back loosely with a clasp at the base of her neck. Her ivory clothes were plain but finely made.

As they moved down the side-road together the shops turned shabbier. They didn't have to go far before they reached the end of the block. There were no stores beyond that. Fee led him through a maze of squalid houses. The people that came and went there looked as neglected as their shelters.

Jupiter's nose burned. The smell of death and waste lingered in the air. The people who made their homes along the path were unwashed, but not filthy enough to account for the foul odor. Filthy was not dead.

Fiona pulled the scarf around her neck up till it covered her mouth and nose, protecting her from the rancid air. She fished a similar scarf from her pocket and helped him arrange it around his face, then lifted the hood back onto his head. He didn't tell her there was really no use. His senses were too sensitive and already flooded with the stench.

"Sorry, I should've warned you. I'm afraid it's going to get worse."

"It's all right." Jupiter squeezed her hand.

"No. Really. It's about to get very bad." Fiona frowned.

Jupiter just nodded. He wanted to lift her up and carry her away from whatever noxious thing lay ahead. He hated her being anywhere unsafe. Always, she was leading the way into danger.

For a moment, her footsteps slowed. Then she resumed her lead like a gladiator going into battle. Whatever she had to face, she wanted it done and over, but she wouldn't avoid the fight.

Another fence made of interlocking chains stood many meters high. Four strings of sharp-edged wire had been added at the top. It glistened in the sunlight, a warning of the harm it could inflict. Beyond the fencing, a clearing circled a large pit. His stomach turned at the realization that the dots of color lining in the pit were people. Children in tattered garments. They were the source of the death and decay overwhelming his nose and filling his lungs with every breath. He'd seen many terrible things in the arena, but he'd never seen so big a massacre. The children's flesh was gray and loose on the thin, bony frames. Some were recently dead. Others had been lying in the pit long enough to decay to rotten meat and bones. At the edges, he could see signs of the bed of ash and charcoal below.

The fence made a circle around the open grave, stopping only where it attached to the back side of one of the factory's buildings. Fee had led him to the other, not so public, side of the complex.

In the distance, a man dressed in black leather, face covered, stood with his hands tightly grasping the wire fence. When he looked up and saw them, the man lifted a hand in the air, like a friendly wave. His body language was anything but friendly. He was still and stiff.

Beside Jupiter, Feeona pulled her hand from his. She jogged to the fence and wrapped her fingers around the links in the chain, mirroring the leather clad man. She stared into the pile of bodies as if the strength of her gaze could bring the dead back to life. What she could hope to find he couldn't fathom. And then her body went still and stony. Jupiter stepped up behind her, pressing his warmth against her back to let her know he was there for her. He wanted to drag her away from the hurt that tightened her hands to a white knuckled grip on the fence.

Her gasp caught him by surprise. She looked to the man who'd waved at them. And lifted a hand just as he'd done. The man nodded then squatted down as if he intended to stay by the fence indefinitely.

She seemed to shrug away her pain. "It's okay." She patted his shoulder as if he'd been the one clinging to the links. "They'll take care of him."

"What?"

"The boy." She pointed into the pit of death and Jupiter followed the line of her arm, searching the frail decaying bodies. A tiny movement caught his attention. He listened, tilting his head to the side. And then he heard it. Beyond the movement of scavengers, he heard whimpering. Someone was alive. A child.

"He'll wait until dark." Fiona spoke like she was talking to herself. Reassuring herself. "At nightfall he'll climb the fence and take the boy to the riders.

"The riders?" Jupiter turned her to face him.

"Yes. They're a group of survivors that live outside the city. They run messages, parcels, anything they can carry on their thrust-bikes, to the nearest town. People here don't have the funds for planetary transports. It's dangerous to cross the chemi-desert, but the riders are fast and they get paid well for their services." She paused then her lips tipped in a half smile. "They're a little wild, a little rough around the edges, but they're good people. They'll take care of him. Nurse him back to life. Then he'll be a rider like them."

At her description of the riders, he wondered how she would describe him and his brothers. Wild? Violent? Pitiful? Jupiter realized he was scowling and tried to calm. "They all came from this pit?"

"I'm not sure. Most, I think. Some might have been runaways.

Maybe drifters from the badlands."

"You admire them?" Jupiter didn't like the jealousy that stirred.

"Yes. Yes, I do." She laughed but the sound was bitter and broken. "I'm grateful for them. For what they do."

Jupiter wrapped his arms around her. He wanted to take away her pain but didn't know how.

"This whole planet is owned by Petro Corporation. They founded the colony back when the Alliance didn't patrol this sector." She shook her head. "Petro shipped people here to carve out the towns and build their factories. When they'd done that, Petro told them they still hadn't finished paying back their passage. Roma aren't the only ones guilty of making slaves of people."

"These children, were slaves?"

"Yeah. I guess you could say that. They call it a tax. It's the price you pay for living on Petro-5. Every family gives their first-born child to the factory."

He hadn't thought his opinion of humans could sink any lower. "The people of this world give their own offspring to this factory?"

She nodded. "That's the way it's always been. No one questions. At least not publicly. It wouldn't be so bad, if the children worked a few years and then went back home. But that's not the way it works. Parents hand over the child then forget about them. They don't care that they work from the time they wake until they can't stand. That they cry for the first few days and then never cry again because crying takes energy they can't afford to waste."

Her voice cracked on the words that came from somewhere deep inside her. Jupiter didn't know how to comfort her. He could only hold her.

"They work until they're not able to work anymore. Then they're brought here, to the pit. Nobody cares if they're dead when they get here or if they die lying on the ashes."

Jupiter turned her in his arms, pressed her face against his chest, and pressed his lips to her forehead. He understood now. He understood what she wasn't saying. "You were the first born. They sent you to the factory."

Her nod brushed against his lips. The moisture of her tears soaked into the thin material of the shirt she'd given him as her hands fisted in the fabric. "But you survived. You're a survivor."

"No, not really. I was saved. Rescued."

Jupiter remembered her love of the man who'd raised her. After she'd escaped this hell, he realized. "Your Roland?"

"Yes."

He lifted her chin, forcing her to meet his gaze. "Why did you want me to see this?"

Tears overflowed her warm brown eyes and clung to her cheeks. "I just…It's part of me. I wanted you to know me."

When she tried to look away, he wrapped his hands around her face and held her there. He wanted her to see his feelings for her in his eyes. "This is a part of you. Your past. But it's not all that you are. I've been coming to know you every day since the moment we met. From the moment you rescued me."

He thought she'd argue. He could see what she wanted to say lodged in her throat and choking her. She swallowed it down and the moment was lost. She gathered her strength around her like a cloak, her shoulders back, her spine straight. Jupiter rubbed away her tears with the edge of his thumb.

She smiled—no hint of her grief left on her face—as she stepped back from him and patted one palm against his chest.

"Keep that in mind the next time you feel like killing me."

She turned and led the way back and Jupiter followed, confused and saddened, not by what she'd said, but by what she hadn't. Despite her claim that she wanted him to know her, she still hid from him.

They found a booth in the Crooked Path and waited for Toolman. Feeona did her best to hide her impatience. She didn't like being in town and out in the open. They had too many people looking for them. And Jupiter's hooded cloak stuck out more sitting inside.

He sat across from her with a local beer sitting in front of him. He hadn't liked the taste. One sip and he'd been done. Her whiskey was half gone, but it hadn't done a thing to slow her heart rate or dull her heartache.

She liked that Jupiter didn't enjoy the taste of beer. It made her smile when she wanted to scream at the universe for making her choose between this man and the kids.

The sound of the door swinging open drew her gaze just as it had every other time it had opened since they'd arrived. Some part of her still hoped Toolman would arrive and that she'd be able to talk him into giving her the kids on credit.

Her stomach twisted. It wasn't Toolman.

There were two of them. She recognized one. He'd been with Morgan the last time she'd seen him. Morgan's men were here early. Damn. Damn. Damn.

Her heart pounded like the wings of a wild bird caught in a trap. She could hear the rapid beating in her ears. Jupiter's ears pricked and his body tensed. She reached across the table and grabbed his wrists.

She pleaded with her eyes. "Don't fight them. Please. Don't fight them and they won't hurt you." It was a stupid thing to say. There was nothing better to be said.

She expected him to fight. Despite her warning, she expected him to fight. Instead, he sat stone still. There was hurt in his eyes. Disbelief.

A shadow fell across the table. "Hello there."

The man whose name she couldn't remember stood with one hand on the weapon he wore on his hip. The other man held a hypo-injector and stood at Jupiter's shoulder. Jupiter's arm twitched, moving the wrist beneath her grip. Beyond that he didn't acknowledge Morgan's goons. His eyes never left her. She wouldn't break down again. She created this drama and she would play her role, even though it would cost her Jupiter.

She wanted to tell him so many things. She was sorry. She hadn't thought it would come to this. None of it mattered. She'd betrayed him. And whatever was between them was over. She couldn't expect anything different. And she couldn't give away her feelings for Jupiter. Morgan's men couldn't believe she was weak. Couldn't know she had skin in the game. Feeona pulled her hands back and turned away from Jupiter. "You're early. My contact isn't here yet."

"Never count on a thief. A lesson someone should have taught this one." Morgan's man indicated Jupiter with a thumb in his direction.

"You're a real charmer, aren't you?"

The man, she remembered now his name was Ibor, shrugged. "I wasn't expecting him to be so cooperative."

Feeona forced her gaze back to Jupiter. Her heart crumbling into smaller pieces with every minute. "You're going to cooperate, right?"

"They're not from Roma?" A muscle ticked along Jupiter's jaw.

She shook her head. "No. They're not."

"If they were, they'd have darted me from the door." A threat rumbled at the edge of his words.

They couldn't take him. Even now, he could best them. She'd known that. She needed him to give himself up. "Understand one thing—it had to be *you*. There wasn't any other choice."

His eyes narrowed and then his chin dipped so subtly she might have missed it, if she hadn't been studying his face like a navigation chart. She wasn't giving them Seneca. That was all that mattered to him.

She looked up to Morgan's man. "He's going to cooperate. And you're going to honor my bargain with Morgan."

"Right. He won't be harmed. Just as Morgan promised." His steady unflinching agreement reassured her less than she would have hoped.

With a thought, she used her implant to send Toolman's account number to Morgan's man. She'd used it plenty of times before and Ibor stood close enough that she had no trouble hacking the com unit he was carrying.

"I just sent you the account number. Go find a booth. Wait until I signal. When my contact's here you'll pay him directly."

"Yes ma'am." He said it, sounding agreeable. But the man behind him stepped forward and slapped Jupiter's shoulder with the hypo-injector. Jupiter never jumped. Never made a sound. He'd been expecting it and he'd let it happen. She hadn't. She'd hoped for a moment more to explain herself. It had been foolish. It didn't matter. When you betrayed someone, it never helped to make excuses. Besides, he wasn't hers. Never had been. So why did it hurt so damned much?

Jupiter slipped into unconsciousness and Ibor slid into the booth beside him, pushing him against the wall. It wouldn't do for the whole restaurant to notice a man falling unconscious onto the bench seat.

"I'll just sit here with you, keep you company until your contact arrives." With a wave of his hand, he dismissed the other thug. "My friend will wait outside."

Feeona pasted a smile on her face. "Sure. Why the hell not?" Her sense of control was slipping away, replaced by self-loathing and a burning rage at the universe.

CHAPTER TWENTY-THREE

Petro-5
Earth Alliance Beta Sector
2210.160

Watching Morgan's men carry Jupiter away was the hardest thing Feeona had ever done. It was no comfort that she had guarantees he'd be safe and well treated. There was an empty ache inside her that wouldn't go away. Retrieving the kids Toolman had smuggled out of the factory had been bittersweet. She was glad to see them, alive and whole. Most were weak and frail, but the life she would deliver them to would help them grow strong. They'd breathe fresh air and have all the farm fresh food they could eat. She hadn't been able to save the girl that had shared her blanket with her during her first winter at the factory. Or the boy that had kept quiet when he saw her stealing a piece of a ration bar from one of the guards. She could never lift the weight of their deaths from her soul, but these kids would not add to that burden. They would not be left to die.

Feeona looked over her shoulder to make sure all of the kids were staying close as she led them through the forest to the clearing where she'd landed the *Hawley*. She'd coached them all using the same rules, almost the same words she'd used every other time.

"Angel." A small voice whispered.

Feeona held up a fist in the sign for stop and all the little feet came to a halt. Feeona squatted down to the wisp of a girl who'd called to her. It was the first time any of them had spoken without being asked a question. "What is it, sweetheart?"

"I need…" The girl pressed her lips together and shifted her eyes away.

"It's okay. You won't get in trouble. You can tell me. You need…" Feeona pushed a sweaty clump of hair from the girl's face.

The brown haired, brown skinned boy beside her stepped closer. "She needs to piss," he whispered. "Wouldn't go when Toolman told us to. She was scared."

There was no malice in his tone. He was matter of fact. Practical. It was a good trait for a factory kid and probably accounted for his relatively good health. He'd probably learned fast to take from the dead—extra layers of clothes or blankets that the dead had no need of. That's what had kept her going. She noticed the girl had put her small hand in the boy's and he'd taken it as if it was a long habit.

"Do you think you can do it in the bushes, honey?"

She nodded.

"Okay. We'll wait here. Be quick and don't go far."

The girl nodded again then ran off into the bushes. Fee squatted down next to the boy. "What's your name?"

"Toby."

She liked that he'd given her a real name and not his factory designation. It was a good sign. Most of the kids lost their identity in that place, but those usually weren't the ones Toolman brought her. It might seem cruel to someone else that they only helped the strongest kids, but she couldn't afford to give a chance to a kid that might never recover from their experiences in the factory.

"Toby, when we get to my ship, I want all of you kids to stay hidden in the underbrush until I have a chance to talk to the man that's waiting there. Can you keep an eye on them for me? Make sure none of them run off?"

"Sure, I can do that." Toby's face scrunched in worry. "Is he a bad man?"

"No. He's a good man, but he's going to be upset. He has good reason. And he doesn't know you all are coming. So, I just need to talk to him before you meet him, understand?"

"Yeah," Toby acknowledged, but he didn't look happy about it.

The girl came back looking more relaxed, but she still slipped her hand into Toby's.

Feeona gave the kids the signal to move forward and follow. She led them to the edge of the clearing where the ship sat and indicated they should huddle down and wait. She winked at Toby then set off across the clearing alone.

The *Hawley's* hatch whooshed open and the ramp came down. Seneca was on the ramp looking worried by the time she reached the ship.

"Where's Jupiter?"

Feeona focused on keeping her breathing steady. "Let's talk inside, okay?" She didn't want the kids to see the full wrath of his reaction. It would make it harder for them to trust him.

"If he's in trouble, we go now." He was firm and more aggressive than she'd ever seen him.

"Jupiter's okay. There's nothing we can do right now. Let's go inside and I'll explain."

Seneca's attack took her totally by surprise. He slammed into her, carrying them both to the ground. Her back smacked hard against the hard packed dirt. Pain exploded along her shoulder blades and at the base of her spine. The air rushed from her lungs and before she could get her breath, his hand wrapped tight around her throat. She couldn't breathe.

"What have you done?" Red rage flushed his cheeks and darkened his eyes.

Her lungs burned. She pounded her fist against his shoulder. Air rushed in as he loosened his grip. She sucked it in greedily.

"Tell me!" He showed his teeth as he waited for her response.

Her heart pounded loud in her ears. She couldn't lie, but she wanted to. In that moment, she wanted to do whatever it took to get his hand off her neck, but if she lied now it would be worse when he learned the truth. For all his lazy smiles, she had no doubt he was capable and willing to kill.

She grasped his sides and met his eyes. "We'll get him back. I swear, we'll get him back."

For a handful of heartbeats, he studied her. Hope and rage at war battling in his features. Rage won. "What. Did. You. Do?"

She wanted to scream that she hadn't had a choice, but that would be a lie. She had chosen. It had been her best option. But how could she make him understand.

He leaned in and growled centimeters from her face. "Your tears won't save you."

Was she crying? "You need me to get him back."

Seneca shook her, tightening his grip on her neck. "Answer. Or I'll crush your windpipe and leave you to suffocate while I track your scent back until I find him or his scent trail."

The edges of Feeona's vision dimmed.

A shrill scream swelled into a shriek. Seneca jerked above her as something hit him from the side. His hold on her throat tightened, but his attention had been temporarily pulled away. It should have been a moment to escape, but shadows crept further into her vision.

"Stop!" The voice seemed small and far away.

Seneca growled.

The boy shrieked again. "He's killing the Angel," Toby shouted. "We gotta stop him!"

A cacophony of inhuman noises swirled in her ears.

Seneca jerked again as something thudded against him. And again.

The children. Their small bodies swarmed Seneca like angry ants. Feeona's heartbeat thundered in her chest. Don't hurt them. Please, don't hurt them. Her vision had faded away and she couldn't move her limbs to fight.

The crushing pressure at her neck lifted. Her lungs filled with robust, planetary air. The shroud of darkness fell aside. Seneca's weight shifted away. She lay still, just breathing for a moment. The sound of snarling and snapping swelled, drowning out the children's screeches.

Rough hands gripped her arms and pulled her to her feet. Seneca shook her once. Her eyes blinked open. His face was close. A red splotch surrounded a small gash on his temple. Were the children okay? She couldn't see anything but his face and she still couldn't lift her arms.

Her voice shuddered and broke as she spoke. "I had to trade him for the credits to save the kids."

The growling Seneca pulled her impossibly closer, his breath hot against her face. "If you chose him to sell to Roma, because you thought you'd be safer with me, you're going to regret it before I let you die."

She shook her head, her strength returning bit by bit. "Roma doesn't have him." She set her jaw. "And WE. WILL. GET. HIM. BACK."

His grip on her arms tightened to pain. "If not Roma, then who?"

She turned her head enough to see Toby crouching a few meters away. He held a rock in his hand. His clothes were dirty and rumpled and his hair stuck up in odd places, but she didn't see any sign of serious injury. The other children were clustered behind him. When he noticed her looking at him he stood up, moving slow but steady. She opened a palm and waved him off with a tiny motion.

Seneca shook her again. "Who?"

"A slaver, but—"

Seneca hissed. "Slaver?" His eyes narrowed. Deep grooves formed in his wrinkled forehead.

"Yes. An independent one. We have a deal." She reached out and dug her hands into Seneca's sides. "He's keeping Jupiter safe until I can buy him back. I promise. We'll get him back. Unharmed." She wanted to wrap her arms around him and feel his arms holding her back. He loved Jupiter as much as she did and that somehow made her feel like he would be the one person to understand both her conviction and her terror. "Morgan wants a connection with me badly enough to stick to my terms... and he knows I'll kill him if he breaks his word."

"Did Jupiter agree to this?" A new pain had entered his voice. That was a worry she could lift from his heart.

"No. He'd never have left you without telling you. He loves you." She stepped closer and wrapped her arms tight around him.

Seneca exploded into motion, shoving her away.

She landed on her ass on the ground at his feet. With Jupiter around, Sen had always been the smaller Dog. From her position on the ground, looking up the full length of him, he was a giant.

His face had gone from fiery rage to icy stone. "If I didn't need you to get him back, you'd be dead."

She nodded, grief and loneliness weighing down her shoulders and hollowing out her insides. Fee shifted her gaze to the ground and focused on the mundane reality of the hard packed dirt beneath her. She sent a silent command to recall Bug from the sky overhead. Brushing the dirt from her palms, she buried her emotions and shifted her attention to the kids. She couldn't give up now, not after she'd sacrificed so much.

CHAPTER TWENTY-FOUR

The Hawley
Earth Alliance Beta Sector
2210.161

Seneca watched Feeona settling the children into beds and on to benches and sleeping mats. She'd gotten them back into space without alerting the authorities and managed to get them re-supplied by doing what she called *off-the-books* trading with other nearby ships. All proof and reminder that she lived her life outside the law. He hadn't minded that before, because the law wasn't on their side. But sharing an enemy didn't necessarily make them allies. She'd seemed good for Jupiter, something else he'd gotten wrong.

With the ship safely back in skipspace, she'd assessed the health of each child, comforting them and getting to know them as she gave them each a nutrition booster and saw to their scrapes and minor injuries. They called her Angel. The part of him that wanted to hate her for her betrayal didn't want to understand why, but it was impossible to ignore her efforts to take care of them. Or the fatigue weighing her down as she leaned over to cover a child with a blanket.

"If you hurt her again, I'll kill you." The boy called Toby

stood a meter away. His threat was calm and convincing, despite his young age.

The other children kept their distance and avoided eye contact, but Toby's gaze rarely left Seneca. The boy had decided it fell to him to be Feeona's protector. The other children looked to the boy as a leader.

"Understood," Seneca acknowledged.

"She said you had a good reason to be mad." The boy's hands fisted at his sides as he spoke.

Seneca nodded, surprised she'd made excuses for him.

"No reason is good enough to kill an angel." Toby puffed up his chest as if he were trying to look intimidating.

Seneca well understood the human mythology of heaven and hell and angels and demons. One of the men who'd kept him like a pet for a time told him stories of ancient, winged beings that had been favored by God or fallen from his teachings. He'd also told Seneca they were both going to Hell for what they did together. The man's self-loathing had only made Seneca want to send the bastard to his God all the more.

Seneca squatted down to the boy's height so they could better look each other in the eye. "You don't believe she's truly an angel."

Toby scowled. "Don't matter. She saved us just like the stories said she would. Flew us right off the world. That's good enough for me."

But where was she taking them? That question had been circling in Seneca's mind. She'd admitted knowing a slaver and had sold Jupiter to the bastard. She could easily be planning to sell the children as well.

Seneca kept those thoughts to himself. "You trust too easily. She could be a demon in disguise."

"Naw." The boy clutched at a leather loop hanging around his throat. "I've seen demons before. She ain't one." The boy hitched a thumb over his shoulder in her direction.

Seneca looked up to see her approaching. Angel or demon?

"Everything okay over here?" The makeup she wore was smudged, leaving hints of her true skin tone showing. Purple bruises he'd put there ringed the soft skin of her neck.

Seneca pushed up to his full height. "Fine. Toby and I have reached an understanding."

Fee's eyebrows shot up. "Is that so?"

"Yup." The boy crossed his arms over his chest. He looked Seneca up and down then gave Fee a friendlier nod. "Night, Angel."

With that he strode off to his assigned spot on one of the benches in the ship's common space.

"Come on." Fee led Seneca toward the ship's pilot station. "I arranged for us to check in on Jupiter."

That surprised him. Not only that she would've made the arrangement, but that it was even possible. "You said before that it was difficult to communicate in skipspace." Had she lied about that, too? Is that why she'd been able to setup her betrayal without their notice?

"Difficult, but not impossible." She sighed as she settled into her seat. "I set us up for a skim, so I can drop us out. It's inefficient resource-wise, but we have plenty of fuel. We might have to wait. We took longer than I expected and they might have gotten tired of waiting." She swiveled one of the seats to face a view screen. "Sit here. I want to keep you out of the vid."

Seneca sat and watched her. She repaired the ornate braid she'd formed her hair into that morning and touched up her makeup to cover her bruises with a small spray bottle. She was full of tricks. "Why bother with that?"

She didn't meet his eyes when she answered. "I need them to believe in me."

"You humans are vain and shallow creatures." He'd seen it in the pleasure houses and in the arena.

"Perception is everything with a con. I need them to think I'm strong, in control, and cold enough to smuggle slaves." She turned back to the control console. "No matter what, stay quiet and out of the vid. So far, Morgan doesn't know there are two of you." She pulled up data on one of the screens. "That won't last forever, but I'd like to keep him in the dark on that as long as possible."

Seneca studied the commands she entered manually into the navigation system. The transition from skipspace was smooth enough that the children probably wouldn't notice the change. Very different from the damaged resistance ship.

"Alfred, adjust the lighting to keep everything but me in shadow, please."

"I'll take care of it, Captain."

Seneca sat, stiffly. He didn't want her to see how starved he was for the sight of Jupiter.

A small tone sounded and the vid display came on.

"Well, if it isn't Feeona Traveler. About damn time." A human male, midlife, muscular and impatient. "We've been waiting out here for hours."

"I had a few things to do." She spoke dismissively, but Seneca could see the stiffness of the muscles of her neck and shoulders.

"We've got effing things to do," said the man. "Hang on and I'll transfer the com to the hold."

The screen flickered. Another man about the same size and age appeared then stepped aside to reveal Jupiter pacing in a cage behind him.

"There's your boy. Unharmed, as promised."

Seneca's chest tightened. He wanted to throw his head back and howl. Rage still burned in his gut, but seeing Jupiter looking whole and healthy turned the heat down to a simmer.

Jupiter stopped his pacing and turned to face the vid camera—his face a blank mask. "You should not have done this."

Feeona looked into her own camera with a face just as expressionless. "Never trust a thief."

"I didn't trust just any thief." Jupiter never flinched. "I trusted *you.*"

Feeona couldn't sleep. She studied the constellations painted on her ceiling. *I trusted you.* Jupiter's words had been stuck in her head like a never-ending loop. After he'd said that, he'd turned his back and sat on the floor of the cage. She remembered their conversation about cages when they'd been locked in the *Salley Ho* brig. Jupiter had been freed after a lifetime in a cage and she'd been the one to lock him up again. No matter what it took, she'd get him free, but then they'd part ways. She wished she could have held on to him a little longer. Despite the ship full of new arrivals, she'd never been more alone.

Seneca had moved into Roland's room and several children had made their way up the stairs to sleep on Feeona's floor. A few had staked a claim on her bed. It was plenty big, and she could never deny the frightened ones the extra measure of security they found in sleeping near the Angel. In their eyes she could do no wrong. What a lie.

Feeona slipped out from under the covers and pulled on

pants and a top in the dark. The kids deserved all the sleep they could get, but she couldn't stand to be in that bed a moment more. She took the cabin level passage over the common area below and climbed down the ladder to the pilot's station.

She pulled Jacky from his storage compartment then hugged him against her middle as she settled into her chair. She stroked her fingers through the soft pink fuzz of the unicorn's mane. "How are we doing, Alfred?"

"Everything is functioning satisfactorily and we are on schedule, Captain. I would have alerted you if there was anything needing your attention." Alfred was the only thing that allowed her to fly the ship without a crew.

"I know." She sighed. "I just need someone to talk to."

"Mr. Seneca is also awake."

Her heart squeezed. She didn't want to think of him tossing and turning with worry for Jupiter. She was doing enough worrying for them both. "I meant you, Alfred."

"I am at your service, Feeona. But I'm surprised you wouldn't rather talk to a person."

Her heart ached. Something it was accustomed to when it came to the kids, but this was different. With Jupiter gone, a piece of her soul was missing and the one person who was probably feeling the same rightly blamed her. She'd lost Jupiter forever, but she would get him back to Seneca and see them both safe.

Feeona huffed out a frustrated breath and pushed Jacky back into his bin. "It wouldn't be polite to approach Seneca when he doesn't want to talk to me."

"Of course." Alfred paused and Feeona was left with her thoughts. "He is already talking to young Toby, so perhaps you are right."

Why was Sen talking to Toby? She was on her feet before the question fully formed in her thoughts. They'd claimed to have come to an understanding, but that hadn't made them friends.

Feeona strode out toward the common area. She heard whispered voices before she made it out of the hall and down the steps, but they were nowhere in sight. She followed the whispers past sleeping kids and found them in the food prep area. They were sharing one of the fruity treat bars she stocked for the kids. A length of leather with an irregular shaped medallion attached lay on the table between them.

"Hi, guys. Everything okay?" She stopped three meters from the table to give Sen plenty of space. She could still feel his hands around her neck. But she knew he wasn't going to hurt Toby. Even when Toby attacked him, Seneca was the one that had come away with an injury. Toby didn't have a scratch.

"Yeah," said Toby. "We're on the same side now."

"Side?"

Toby sat straighter. "Seneca is going to help me protect you."

That surprised the hell out of her. "Is that right?"

Seneca dipped his head in acknowledgement.

Feeona didn't know what to think of that. Maybe it was just something he told Toby to help the kid relax more around him. Seneca turned out to have a knack for relating to the kids and since she started covering her bruises, most of them seemed to have forgotten the big tussle.

"What's this?" She eased closer then lightly touched the metal. It wasn't an alloy she'd seen before.

"It's mine," said Toby. "Only thing I have left from my mom."

He spoke with fondness when he mentioned the woman who'd given birth to him and then turned him over to the factory. Most of the kids didn't speak of their parents at all after the first few months.

"May I hold it?"

Toby shrugged his narrow shoulders. "Yeah."

She lifted the medallion and considered the size, weight, and density. "I'm not familiar with this alloy. Do you know where it came from?"

His brown eyes met hers. "Mom said her Dad gave it to her. I seen more metal like this in the hills near our village. Most don't have symbols like this. Just old scrap."

She hadn't known Toby came from the hills beyond the badlands. His people didn't rely on the factory. He shouldn't have ended up there. Feeona laid the medallion back on the table. "I'm glad you were able to keep it."

Seneca tapped the table near the medallion. "The symbol is familiar to me."

Feeona's gut quaked at the sound of Seneca's velvet voice. So casual, as if he hadn't come close to killing her. She pulled out the chair in front of her, turned it backward, and straddled the seat. The shapes on the medallion didn't even look like a symbol to her, just random decoration.

"It's part of a larger design the Mothers carved into the walls of the nursery." Sen traced the pattern on the table, his gaze locked on Toby. "Along with this one." Slowly, deliberately, he traced another symbol.

Toby grinned. "I remember that one, too. It means strength." He tapped on his medallion. "The one on my cord is for protection."

Seneca traced another symbol on the table.

Toby screwed up his face with effort. "I… I saw it before, but I don't remember it so well. She painted that one on our tent when my dad died." He looked up without focus. As if he were remembering or trying to. The concentration on his face turned to sadness. "Yeah. It was like grief.... Suffering. That's it. Suffering."

Seneca laid a hand on Toby's shoulder. "Thank you. This is something I didn't know. I am grateful to understand the symbols now."

The sadness in Toby's features lightened. "No problem. Your mother never taught you?"

Seneca shook his head and let silence answer.

Toby looked from him to Feeona, as if he could feel the tension between them. He wrapped his small hand around the medallion and got to his feet. "Goodnight. I'm going back to bed."

Bed wasn't exactly right. He'd been one of the kids sleeping on her floor. As he disappeared down the hall, she realized he must have woken and come looking for her.

"Are the Mothers the surrogates Roma used to carry you?" She'd noticed the way Sen had talked about them and his hesitation to answer Toby. From what Jupiter had told her, they didn't actually have biological mothers.

He leaned back in his chair. "Yes, they were a different species. They gave birth to us but didn't treat us as their children. At least, I don't think so. They provided care, only as much as required by our Master. They never spoke a word except to chant."

Feeona reached out on instinct to put her hand over his on the table. He moved his hand before she could make contact. "I know what it's like to be discarded as a child. I'm sorry you started out that way, too."

"Jupiter told you about the Mothers?"

"Only a little." He'd told her about Seneca's life between childhood and the arena. It had been Jupiter's reason for denying what simmered between the two men.

Seneca bowed his head. "Knowing these symbols makes me wonder about the Mothers. Maybe they cared for us more than I thought."

Feeona pulled her hand back and clasped the edge of the chair back. "Might as well believe the best, since they're not around to disappoint you."

They sat in silence for a moment before Seneca spoke. "Toby told me about the factory. How the Angel comes to save those who believe in her."

She shook her head, vehemently. "No!" It made her sick to think they believed she picked and chose who would survive based on belief. "Toolman, my contact at the factory, chooses the children and sneaks them out. I would take them all if I could."

Seneca stretched to clasp her wrist and pulled it onto the table between them. "Because you were one of them?" He rubbed the rough patch where her tattoo had once been. "All the children have a tattoo just here and so did that young male back on Karona Station. He called you Angel, too."

"Yes, I was one of them and I've been helping kids get out for a long time. I had my tattoo removed, but the memories never go away. It's who I am." Shadows from the past raised tiny bumps along her skin and she pulled her wrist free to rub her arms.

"Did this Toolman help you escape?"

She choked on a laugh. "Hardly. He sold me to Roland—a con man who needed a child for one of his cons. He couldn't have known Roland would be good to me. I got lucky."

His ears flicked. "Toby told me he was caught in the woods and turned over to the factory. His mother died fighting off their attackers."

"That explains a lot about how different he is. How strong."

Seneca stared at her as if he'd just seen her for the first time. "You were like the other children. Your parents turned you over to the factory willingly."

"Yes." Feeona sighed. It was a long time ago and it was the least of her aches these days. "I didn't blame them for that. That's just the way it was. I'd never known anything different. I'd always known I was different from my younger brothers and sisters. They all treated me differently. I'd been taught it was my job to keep the factory running so my younger siblings would have a good life."

He grunted an angry sound in the back of his throat. "They betrayed you."

It wasn't an accusation. There was no disbelief. He sounded certain. Feeona hated feeling pitiful.

She stood up and walked over to the counter, leaving her back to Sen. She wasn't a victim anymore. "You're pitying me. Is that why you've suddenly decided to protect me? Or did you lie to Toby about that?" She blurted it out with more fight in her voice than she'd intended.

Seneca stood quickly, making his chair legs scrape against the floor. "I am not the liar here."

Feeona spun around to face him. "No. I've got that covered. And I don't need your pity."

He scoffed. "You think I pity you? I need you alive until I have Jupiter back. For the moment my needs are aligned with the boy. There is nothing more to it than that." He bit off the last word and scowled.

Feeona nodded. "Fair enough."

Seneca studied her, ears alert and tipping his head to the side. Abruptly, he stalked toward her and gripped her arms. She couldn't stop the wince when he squeezed against her bruises.

"What aren't you telling me?" He punctuated his questions with a shake.

Feeona's eyes widened. "That's a broad question. Liar, remember? Want to narrow it down?"

Seneca growled. "Your story doesn't make sense. Why would I pity you for doing your duty or for escaping enslavement?"

Feeona tried to tug her way free, but Sen's grip didn't give. "It's nothing. Nothing you need to worry about."

He growled quietly. "Tell me."

She bit her lip. Damn him. It really was none of his business, but if he didn't settle down, he was going to wake the kids. So much for that agreement with Toby. She blew out a frustrated breath. "After I did the job for Roland, he offered to take me wherever I wanted to go. I asked him to take me back to Petro-5." Her words spilled out in a rush. "I'd seen how my parents were with the other kids. How they loved them and played with them and kept them safe. I snuck back to my parents' home in the middle of the night. I thought they would finally treat me like my siblings. They seemed glad to see me at first, but after they bundled me up on a pallet to sleep, I heard them whispering. I snuck down the hall until I could hear them clearly."

Sen's grip loosened, but he didn't release her.

He might have let her off the hook at that point, but she couldn't stop. "They were going to take me back to the factory the next morning. The factory thought I was dead. They weren't looking for me." She swallowed to clear the lump that formed in her throat every time she thought about it. She'd wanted to make excuses for them—maybe they were scared the factory would find out and punish them. It was Roland who'd eventually taught her that true parents fought for their children like Toby's mom had fought for him. "I crawled out a window and went back to Roland's ship. This ship. He was waiting for me. He'd known what would happen, but he knew I had to learn it for myself."

Seneca's hands fell away, and his big lavender eyes closed and opened in a slow blink before his gaze drifted down to her neck. "Your voice is roughened by the bruising in your throat. Have you done anything to heal yourself?"

"Yes, for that and for the other bruises." He'd shown no signs of remorse, so his questions surprised her.

"Good," he said. "It scares the children."

She tried to take his words in stride. It wasn't as if she'd been expecting any tenderness. She watched him walk away with that sexy grace of his and stood there a moment after he was out of sight. She stood there and listened to the quiet familiarity of the ship and the small movements of children moving, settling, breathing. She stood there in her now crowded ship, utterly alone.

CHAPTER TWENTY-FIVE

The Abundance
Earth Alliance Beta Sector
2210.163

The shackles that weighed down Jupiter's wrists and ankles slowed his steps and tugged at his joints. He'd never worn anything so heavy, but it was the feather-light band circling his throat that worried him. Head held high, he moved steadily toward the slaver, walking along a silver path on the floor. The man sat in an ornate chair on top of a raised stage at the opposite end of the room. Every man present had to look up to meet the slaver's gaze. The women at his feet stared at the floor, heads bowed.

"That's far enough." The guard at the end of the silver path brought Jupiter to a stop with a cudgel poked in his ribs.

The guard beside him struck the backs of his legs. "Down, dog."

Jupiter made no move to obey. Another blow buckled his legs but he remained standing.

The slaver grinned, showing perfectly white, even teeth. "Now, Thompson. I know I told you this one is special. We must treat him gently." There was little censure in his tone.

"It was just a nudge, Morgan. Not a scratch on him." Thompson smirked. "We won't screw up your chances with that hot little snatch."

Jupiter hid the anger Thompson's words churned up in his gut. Instead of lashing out he noted that the slaver's men didn't fear him, if the relaxed way they spoke to the bastard was any measure. His cruelty must be reserved for the poor souls he bought and sold. The masters of the arena would never tolerate being spoken to in such a way.

The guard between Jupiter and Morgan snorted. "Give him a shock and he'll kneel just like any other slave."

Whatever was coming, Jupiter didn't want to be helpless for it—unable to move in his own defense. That would be the result, if the guard activated the slender shock collar at his throat. Jupiter knelt on the cool silver path. The shackles clicked against the surface as they made contact.

Morgan's neatly trimmed eyebrows lifted. He descended the steps from his throne, halting directly in front of Jupiter. "I see Thompson explained the collar."

"Yes," he growled. The guard on the transport ship had demonstrated its power. The jolt it sent through him at the touch of a button had disabled him completely. He'd been shocked many times before, but the shock whips used in the arena didn't compare to the jolt from the band. He hadn't been able to move for nearly a half hour.

"And he told you about the perimeter transmitters?"

Jupiter resisted the urge to growl again. "Yes." Even if he overpowered his guards before they could engage the band, perimeter triggers would disable him the moment he attempted to leave the slaver's ship.

"Good." Morgan circled around Jupiter like an arena

opponent, searching out weaknesses. "I don't want an accident. The collar isn't meant to cause lasting injury, but it has crippled one or two of our stock. Physiology is so variable. You can never be sure."

Jupiter listened to the sound of the man's boots as they hit the floor. The *clank* of heel to metal changed to a more muffled thud when he stepped off the path. *Thud, thud.* Then back when he stepped behind Jupiter. *Clack, clack, thud.*

"I've heard your physiology is quite unique." *Thud, thud, clack.* "How long was he down when you did the test, Thompson?" Morgan stopped directly in front of Jupiter.

"Half the normal," answered the guard.

"Half? That's impressive." Morgan stepped backward and sat on the top step to his stage.

It put them on a more equal level, eye to eye.

Jupiter tried to lift his hands from the metal floor, but the shackles at his wrists had grown impossibly heavier. He pulled until he got them an inch above the floor then dropped them. *Clank.* It had to be magnetized, but did magnets extend beneath the rest of the floor?

"Don't feel bad Jupiter. That's your name, right? Not Seneca." Morgan shook his head. "You see, Owens has told me all about you. Your strength's your weaknesses. He is eager to have both you and Seneca back."

Jupiter kept his expression blank. "What of your promises to the female?"

"Oh, I intend to keep them. She'll have a chance to bid against Owens. But we both know she's low on funds. The rumors say she tried to hock her ship before resorting to selling you to me."

That gave Jupiter a good deal more satisfaction than he wanted. At least betraying him hadn't been her first choice. "Why would she make you promise, if she doesn't plan to pay?"

"That's a very good question." Morgan slapped his thigh and opened his eyes wide as if Jupiter had sad something to surprise him. "Feeona isn't a fool. She has to know Owens can outbid her. No matter how precious the cargo she picked up on that backwater colony. Owens can afford to buy that whole planet." He stretched out his legs, crossing them at the ankles. "Either she's playing some sort of a con, she is Roland's protégé after all, or she's setting up a double-cross. Maybe she plans to use her body to persuade me in her favor." The man threw back his head and laughed.

Red stained Jupiter's vision. He strained to slide his hands and the shackles a few centimeters to the side. He stretched and strained different parts of his body, hoping to disguise the movement as idle resistance to the restraints.

Morgan's laughter fell away, leaving only a trace of excitement lighting his eyes. "I wager it's betrayal. But who does she plan to betray. You? Me? Owens? Or all of us? I just love her unpredictability. She and I will make great partners." He sneered at Jupiter's seemingly idle movements.

A centimeter more.

Morgan sat straighter. "Are you bothered by that thought? Does it make you agitated?" Morgan huffed as he got to his feet and started circling again. "You still care about her." His voice rose and fell with disbelief. "My God. She already sold you to me," he tapped his chest as he paced. "Morgan St. Germaine, the most ruthless, most renowned flesh trader in the sector. How ignorant can you be?"

Sparks of anger flicked along Jupiter's skin. He strained more obviously. Morgan expected his restlessness now. Jupiter knew his efforts would gain him little. He couldn't escape. Not yet. He should play the ignorant slave Morgan expected. Let the man drop his guard, but the shackles chafed at his dominant nature. Such primitive restraints were only used with the monsters of the arena, not the gladiators. He wasn't the monster here.

Morgan took hold of Jupiter's jaw and jerked his face toward him. "Did you think she was some sort of noble rescuer? She tries to play it like she's above live trade. Like hiding in the shadows is more honorable than being known throughout the sector. But she's just like Roland, keeping her more unsavory trade hidden."

Jupiter jerked his jaw free. "Sounds to me like you're the one infatuated with the woman."

"I always suspected there was more to her and now I know." He poked a thumb into his chest. "I did a bit of digging. Do you have any idea what she was doing on Petro-5?"

Jupiter strained. The shackles moved. Only a little farther.

"She was smuggling children out of one of those factories and it's not the first time. She's been slaving on the side all along." Morgan made a humph sound. "Children. Any idea what happens to child slaves?"

Jupiter remembered. He remembered the young Dogs who died in the dirt on the training field. He remembered the pups led away to be whored out in the brothels. Could Feeona truly be selling children? That couldn't be possible. The same children she cried over in that awful pit. Children like she'd once been. Impossible. This man didn't know anything about Feeona. His Feeona.

One last jerk and his hands slipped over the edge of the metal path. The terrible weight fell away leaving only the inconsequential heaviness of the metal at his wrists. Only the metal path was magnetized.

Morgan's eyes slid down to the floor. His eyes widened in recognition. His muscles tensed and his chest filled with the air that would form a shout. Jupiter swung the shackles over his head and twisted his body. The weight increased, but with some distance between the shackles and the path it was manageable. Momentum carried him toward the guard reaching for the remote tucked into his belt. Jupiter punched toward him, landing a blow to his torso.

The remote slipped from Thompson's scrambling hands. Adrenalin kicked in and Jupiter jerked to his feet, twisting back to Morgan. Jupiter lunged for the bastard, taking them both to the ground. They hit the floor together with a dull thud. They were no longer on the path. Jupiter could move freely and he wasted no time wrapping his shackled arms around the man's neck. He pulled back until the links stretched across Morgan's throat. He pulled enough to make sure Morgan felt the threat but killing him would accomplish nothing. Keeping Morgan between him and the guards, Jupiter growled out a single word. "Stop."

The guard who'd been scrambling for the remote froze. The guards who'd been running toward them followed his lead.

"You might kill me," Jupiter spat. "But not before I kill your master."

Morgan stayed silent, hands locked tight around the chain at his neck.

"Kick the remote over," Jupiter demanded.

The guard closest to the device did as he asked.

"Now that I have your attention, I want you to listen carefully." Jupiter stood, dragging Morgan with him, and spoke directly against the man's ear. "I allowed your men to take me without harming them. I made no attempt at escape on your transport. If I wanted you dead, I'd have killed you already." He was safe at least, until that damned auction. "But you will remove these shackles and cease your useless chatter." He lifted the chain from Morgan's throat and lifted his arms free. He shoved Morgan toward the guard and extended his arms, presenting the shackles for removal. "Then you will lead me to my cell and leave me in peace."

The guards all stood motionless, mouths hanging open like buzz-fly traps. Morgan rubbed at his neck as if he could rub away the shame of being bested by a slave.

Jupiter shook the shackles. "Now!"

Morgan scowled, but he seemed to know there was no point in pretending to be able to control him. "Do it, Thompson."

CHAPTER TWENTY-SIX

The Hawley
Earth Alliance Beta Sector
2210.164

Seneca lifted the small boy called Raf from his shoulders and set him down in a circle of kids throwing a soft ball back and forth. Before he could fully straighten there was another child with her arms extended toward him. "Me next, please."

"Sorry little one, no more rides for a bit."

The girl's face fell until Toby walked over and gave his back to the child. "You can ride on my back, Bitty."

Seneca patted Toby's shoulder and headed to the galley. He'd been waiting for Feeona to come out of her room. He wanted to know more about her plan to rescue Jupiter and sharing a meal would give them an opportunity to talk. But she hadn't. Hadn't come down from her room to eat. Hadn't come down to check on the children. Hadn't come down at all. Early the day before she'd decided he was good enough with the kids that she could leave them to his care. He hadn't seen her since.

"Alfred, she's avoiding me, isn't she?"

"She hasn't said so, Mr. Seneca." Alfred answered without hesitation.

"Why am I surprised she's not more involved with the kids?" The same kids she willingly sacrificed Jupiter to save.

"She normally spends more time with them, but she always tries not to get too attached to them either." The questions had been rhetorical. Seneca hadn't expected Alfred to offer real insight. "She does have me monitoring them. I provide her with a report every four hours."

"I suppose with you around, she doesn't really have to leave her room at all."

"I am capable of flying the ship autonomously, but the ship does occasionally require physical maintenance beyond the repair bots' capabilities."

"I thought she'd at least come out for meals." His disappointment with her absence was entirely due to his need to speak with her about Jupiter. Otherwise, he'd be glad she'd stayed away. Wouldn't he?

He wove his way through the children and headed for the stairs. He'd had enough of waiting. He would just have to confront her in her room.

Alfred surprised him again. "I have been rather concerned that she's not eating. She did go to the galley for tea last night, but that is insufficient nutrition and hydration over several days.

Seneca's steps slowed, then quickened. Alfred would have told him if she was in serious trouble—unless she ordered Alfred not to. No, she was perfectly fine. When he reached her door, he struck it a bit louder than he intended.

No answer.

His heartbeat quickened and whooshed loudly in his ears. "Alfred, tell her I'm not going away until she answers."

"The captain is in the pilot's station. Would you like me to ask her to join you in her room?"

"How the Hell did she get there?" Unless she'd gone there in the middle of the sleep cycle.

"She used the captain's cabin level passage."

Seneca spun on his heel, studying each of the closed doors along the corridors. He'd assumed they were storage. Heat crept up the back of his neck, all the way to the tips of his ears. He jerked open the most logical door and found a narrow hall with several more doors. His ears flicked. He could hear her. Her voice drifted up from an open hatch in the floor at the opposite end of the hall.

He stalked toward her voice, ears forward and alert.

"This is just what I needed. Thanks for coming through for me, Gulliver." The cheer in Feeona's voice sounded forced.

"It was the least I could do. Only the second time you've ever asked for anything and the first time I had to turn you down." The male voice rasped with age and vice. "Glad you found another way."

Who was he and what had he done for Feeona?

"I have to go, Gulliver." The level of strain had multiplied.

The man began to speak, but his voice was cut off before he'd formed his next word. Seneca could hear her making manual entries at her controls then footsteps.

The hatch was plenty wide, so he ignored the ladder and dropped down through the opening with a loud thud. Once down, he realized why he hadn't noticed the hatch previously. Its ladder was tucked into a nook in the corner. It wouldn't be visible from anywhere in the room.

"Seneca?" Feeona appeared in front of him, eyes wide. "Everything, okay?"

Frustration, suspicion and worry warred inside of him. It escaped his throat as a growl.

She put her open palm over his heart. "Whatever you're thinking, stop. There is nothing going on here to worry you."

Her placating only added fuel to his volatile emotions and somehow the fatigue-darkened skin beneath her eyes deepened his anger. He had to talk through the rumble in his chest. "Who were you talking to?"

She turned and walked back to her control panel. "An old friend that I trust. Since Roma has people looking for us everywhere, I had to go through him to get a few things we're going to need. Starting with the engineering plan to Morgan's ship. I found out where it was built and tracked down one of the crew chiefs that worked on it, but I needed Gulliver to bargain for the plans."

She tapped a button and diagrams appeared on several screens.

Seneca could identify patterns that might be the outlines of rooms and corridors, but there seemed to be layer upon layer and swarms of symbols he didn't recognize. "This is where they're holding Jupiter?"

"Mmm." Feeona made the small sound as she flicked through different views of the ship's layout. "Here. This is the holding area."

He directed his gaze where she pointed. It was... He had no idea what he was looking at. "Show me."

She zoomed the picture to show just the area she wanted then traced a line around the screen with her finger. "This is the outer bulkhead for this section. It's thick. Too thick to cut through safely." She moved her finger to trace smaller sections within the larger one. "These are cells. It looks like they're configurable. He can change them around to suit his needs. Complex system, but I guess he can afford top of the line." There was no liveliness in her voice now—neither real nor forced. Only grim determination and exhaustion.

"How will we know which of these cells will be used to house Jupiter?" There were so many. So many cells. So many souls sold into slavery.

"We won't." She rubbed at her temple. "When we get on board, Bug could track him down, but that would take time and would mean we'd have to walk in there without the details nailed down. We'll have to free him when he's on display for the auction." She wrapped her arms around her body. "It would be a hell of a lot better if we could get him out before Roma arrives."

"You believe they'll send a large force to transport him back to Roma?" Seneca considered what little he knew of their owner, Grand Owens. "Or do you think he will send hunters to capture me as well?"

She grimaced. "We'd better assume they'll do both."

The bleakness in her voice darkened his vision with anger. Had she ever truly believed they could do this? "We can't fail."

"We won't." She sighed then dropped her arms and straightened. "I know it might not sound like it, but I am good at this. Really good."

"You'd better be." Seneca squeezed his fists against his need to shake her.

She approached him like she expected him to tackle her again. "I don't give up." She fisted her hand in the loose material of his shirt and pulled him down until their faces were close. "I *will* get him back. Understand?"

He had no reason to believe her, but her resolve steeled his own determination. "*We* will get him back."

She nodded her head and released him. "I was going to start

with the specification for the security and control systems." She strode back to the controls. "But now that you're here, let's take a better look at these schematics." He followed, relieved she accepted his participation.

Feeona rolled her shoulders. "Alfred, keep a closer eye on the kids for us, will you? Report on anything you think I should know."

"Yes. Captain. If I may be so bold—"

"Not now, Alfred." She leaned over the controls, bracing one hand on the panel and adjusting the angle of one of the screens with the other. Her arm shook as she adjusted the screen. She leaned heavily on the console. Glancing at him, she pointed to the screen. "I need you to find every route from both the security level and the auction room to every external hatch. Let me show you how to work the monitor?"

Seneca nodded but lifted a finger to signal a pause. He recognized the signs of fatigue and dehydration. She hadn't been avoiding him out of a weakness of character. She'd been working and skipping meals and probably hating herself for what she'd done. A circumstance he'd lived for years. "Alfred, have Toby bring us protein bars and a couple of nutritional shakes."

"Right away, Seneca."

Seneca dropped the finger and returned her steady gaze. "Now, I'm ready."

Later, when they had a plan and there was nothing more to be done, he would weigh everything he'd learned about her and tease apart the confusing tangle of his emotions about this woman that was Jupiter's mate.

CHAPTER TWENTY-SEVEN

New Hope Settlement
Agrove Colony
Earth Alliance Beta Sector
2210.168

Seneca grasped the armrests as the ship shuddered. He lost his ability to focus on Feeona's landing lesson when the planet they'd been circling became a world with an up and a down, land and sky. It was only his third time landing, second on a planet. The deceleration and the knowledge they were on solid ground both relieved and agitated him.

The external view screen provided a clear view of the line of beast-drawn carts waiting for them in the open field. She'd told them all what to expect. Carefully described the animals and assured them these beasts were gentle, tamed. The children had listened intently as she'd described the new life they'd have. He remembered thinking that he wouldn't believe Fee was telling the truth about her plans for the kids until he saw it for himself. The need to doubt her had faded days before they'd made it to the agrarian planet. He should've been suspicious of these humans who offered a place in their homes in exchange for farm work. He had only Fee's promise that the kids wouldn't be worked too hard, that they'd be cared for and given true homes. Some would have farms of their own one day or leave the farming life, if they wished. And he believed her.

He ignored the nausea that the uncomfortable sensation of landing had given him and cleared his throat. "You're sure this place is safe? Roma…"

"Probably doesn't even know this colony exists." Fee looked over her shoulder. "Independent colonies like New Hope aren't owned by corporations like Petro-5. There isn't even a proper port here. They're self-sufficient. The colonists here work hard, but they work for themselves. They're truly free. And I chose Agrove as our one and only stop because I have the strongest ties here."

There was only patient reassurance in her voice, no defensiveness. That was progress between them. He believed in her, but he knew he hadn't yet earned an equal measure of confidence from her.

She swiveled her seat to face him and laid her palm over his hand. "Sen, I wouldn't be doing this if I wasn't sure."

He'd known, but he'd had to ask. She'd explained that she had arrangements with over two dozen communities that took in the kids she rescued. Normally she would make several stops so no one colony would be overwhelmed with new kids.

She leaned back in her chair with a sigh. "If it will make you feel better, I'll send out Bug for a look around from above us."

He nodded. It would at least give them advanced warning if anything went wrong. "Thank you."

The chatter of the children drifted in from the common room. Seneca reached for the clasp on his safety restraints and got to his feet. He forced away the frown he'd developed from over thinking. "I'll go help them get ready to go."

Her worried face softened into a smile. "Thanks. Just a few things to finish up here."

She sat in the pilot's chair, wearing a hand-stitched tunic with her hair pulled loosely back by a single band and not a bit of cream on her face. It was the simplest look he'd seen on her and anticipation shined in her eyes. Beautiful. He wanted to brush his fingers across the soft skin of her cheek. He wanted, and that was a feeling he hadn't had for anyone since Jupiter. His gut still ached with worry for Jup, but he'd seen the same ache eating at her. She was to blame, and she carried that weight as well. Knowing the kids made it impossible not to understand the difficulty of the choice she'd made.

Seneca pushed that thought aside for later and headed toward the kids. Toby was already helping the others. His mood had been even and content until they dropped out of skipspace. Since then, he'd become distracted and distant. The others were talking and laughing with excited nervousness. Toby was all business.

The kids were lined up and waiting when Fee came to the hatch.

She leaned down to straighten a collar for a pale blond boy. "Are we ready?"

A discordant jumble of "ready," filled the space. She turned to him and lifted her eyebrows.

He nodded. "Ready."

"Alfred, open the hatch and extend the ground ramp."

The soft rumble of the mechanism hushed the children. Their faces filled with expectation and for a moment the anxiety that had plagued them all moments earlier vanished. Seneca's heart beat faster as if their worries had landed on his shoulders. He now knew Feeona carried that burden all the time. He shut his eyes and imagined the weight of Jupiter's hand on his shoulder and his pulse settled.

The humid planetary air filled his lungs and forced open his eyes. The scents were unfamiliar. He had no reference for most of them. Fee stepped onto the ramp. Sunlight painted threads of red in her hair and caressed her caramel skin. She disappeared down the ramp and the children filed out behind her. Seneca lingered, making sure all the children descended, then followed.

"Augie, you old fool!" Laughter filled Fee's voice as the brawny colonist swung her in a circle.

It took all of Seneca's control to approach them calmly and hold back the growl rumbling in his chest. She was Jupiter's mate. No male that wasn't pack should be touching her.

Augie set her on her feet and she patted his shoulder, speaking softly. "That's enough of that."

Seneca moved into position at her side, rubbing his arm against hers.

"Who's this?" The male looked him over, open curiosity on his face.

Augie stood nearly as tall as Jupiter. A dozen shades of brown streaked his short hair. Sun darkened skin covered a fit but modest musculature. He couldn't guess the man's age or his intentions.

"This is Seneca." Fee shifted her shoulder against his arm. "A friend."

"Well met, friend," said Augie. "Let's get these kids back to the farm. The rest of the families are already there with the feast we have waiting."

Feeona and Sen stood in Augie's back yard watching the kids chase after one another in a game of tag they'd quickly learned from an older child. If there had been rules at the start, they'd quickly been forgotten. She'd never want to make a life on the farm, but she loved visiting. "The first time I came here, I was so sick Alfred's emergency protocols kicked in and landed us right behind Augie's house." She leaned a centimeter closer to Sen until they touched. "I spent the first week in bed, completely out of it. Sometimes I still can't believe I let strangers take care of me."

Sen chuckled softly in a way that soothed her aching heart. He'd become increasingly more comfortable around the colonists when he'd seen they were exactly as advertised. Good hardworking farming families.

"By the time I was coherent enough to attempt to leave, it was too late to freak out about it. I stayed another week recuperating and one after that working on the farm to repay the time and expense of looking after me."

While she let her gaze linger on Sen, his eyes followed the children in fascination. "It was good fortune finding this place."

"Yes. Good fortune and Alfred's excellent programming."

"Yes," Sen agreed. "How long will we stay?"

He'd done a good job of hiding his impatience until that moment. "I've already explained to Augie and the other families that we'll be going after the evening meal. The kids are adjusting well, so we don't even have to wait for that, if you don't want to." She lowered her voice. "I worry about him too."

Sen took her hand in his and squeezed. "I know you do."

The small acknowledgment made her heart thump harder, sending a wave of extra warmth through her. They'd been working together more easily, but that didn't mean Seneca had forgiven her for her betrayal.

"I wanna go with you." Determination colored young Toby's

voice.

Feeona's muscles clenched at the sound, but Sen was relaxed. He'd known the boy was approaching.

Fee turned and squatted down to the boy's level. "I like you kid. But this is your home now. Best you just forget about us and look after Sweet Pea." It was the moniker Augie had landed on the young girl Toby seemed always to be looking after.

Toby crossed his arms over his chest the way Seneca sometimes did when he was trying to be stern with the kids. "She's safe here. None of the men look at her in a bad way. I been watching them all day."

"But she'd miss you." She ruffled the boy's thick brown hair.

"She's young. She'll get over it." His voice was flat. His expression deadpan.

Feeona had to resist the urge to laugh. He was only a few years older than the girl.

"This place is nice, but it ain't for me." He jutted his chin out, unwavering.

"I'm sorry, Toby. But if you really don't like it, Farmer Augie will help you find another place. The whole planet isn't a farm, I promise." She accompanied her words with a smile, trying to lighten the mood.

Toby's scowl said he didn't buy it. "I want to go with you."

Her smile slid away. "Maybe you'll find you like it, if you give it a chance."

Seneca squeezed her shoulder. "Feeona... the boy is old enough to know his own mind."

She shot to her feet. "You know we can't take him with us. Where we're going is no place for a kid."

He was solid stone with no intention of being detoured, but he was also calm. "Let me speak with him."

Fee took a page from the kid's playbook and jutted her own chin in Sen's direction. "Toby, give us a minute."

Seneca remained relaxed and unriled. "No, stay Toby."

She bit the inside of her cheek. If he made her say things in front of Toby that would hurt the kid, she'd make him pay. "Can't you just trust that I know a little more about this than you?" Her vision was on the edge of turning red.

Before Sen could answer, Toby pushed between them and turned his determined gaze on her. "It don't matter what you say. I belong with you." He paused a moment. "With Seneca."

Fee's spine softened. She hadn't anticipated that. It wasn't uncommon for some of the kids to want to stay with her. She was their savior. The mythical Angel come to life. They felt safe with her. But of course, it wasn't safety Toby would want. He wanted the loving father he'd lost. He'd made a connection with Seneca on the journey.

Sen watched her as if he could read her racing thoughts on her face. "Please Fee, let me deal with this."

She met his gaze and wished she could read him better. "You can't make promises we won't keep."

Sen dipped his chin in agreement.

Fee bent and kissed Toby's cheek. The little guy was wound tight. "I wish you all the best of life."

Seneca watched Fee walk away, surprised she'd given in so easily.

"You're not gonna take me with you." Toby sounded resigned and disappointed.

Seneca lifted the boy and sat him on the top slat of a nearby fence. "Not now, my friend."

Toby's gaze slipped to the ground. "Because you think I can't take care of myself."

"No." Sen waited for the boy to look up. "Because I need time alone with her. We have things to work out before we take on what comes next."

"The slaver." Toby's face twisted in a grimace.

"You shouldn't be listening to other's conversations."

"I know," Toby agreed. "It's not good manners. That's what Alfred said."

"Did he?"

Toby nodded once. "Yep."

Seneca refocused the conversation. "Not because of the slaver. You could well be a help there."

Toby straightened up with pride. "Then what?"

"The man we're going to take back from the slaver."

Toby nodded again.

"When we get him back, things are going to be… complicated."

Toby's eyes rolled. "Oh geez. It's like that, is it?"

Seneca ignored that. "If things work out that we can, we'll come back to make sure you can decide your life for yourself. It may take us a while to get back, but when we do, if you choose to stay with us, I'll convince them."

Toby's young brow wrinkled with concentration. "Swear?"

"Swear," repeated Seneca.

One corner of Toby's mouth lifted. "All right then." Toby jumped down from the fence and turned as if to go, then stopped and turned back. He took hold of the leather loop that carried his mother's talisman. He lifted it over his head and held it out in his hand.

Seneca leaned forward and let the boy slip it over his head.

"This will keep you safe." Toby explained. "It's up to you to keep *her* safe. Okay?"

Seneca straightened. "She cares for you. You know that?"

The boy grinned as if all the weight of their conversation had been lifted. "I know. She just don't like to show it. Father would say, you got your hands full with that one." He hitched a thumb over his shoulder towards Feeona where she stood saying her farewells to Augie and his family.

Seneca returned the boy's smile then looked to Fee, now heading to her ship. Alone. The afternoon sun sparkled on her hair and made her caramel skin turn golden. "Some things are worth the struggle."

Feeona waited for Seneca in the common room, propped against the back of one of the sofas and Bug safely tucked away until she needed it again. She didn't have long to wait. He got back to the ship, just minutes behind her, giving her an opportunity to look her fill as he approached. The fluid way he moved made the long, loose trousers and tunic he wore look less plain. Even without his white hair and lavender eyes, he could never look ordinary.

"Alfred, start the engines and get us ready for launch."

"Yes, Captain."

She narrowed her eyes and pinned Seneca with a glare. "Tell me you didn't make him any promises."

"I didn't make him any promises." No inflection colored his voice to give him away, but she knew.

"You did, damn you." She shot up and fisted her hands on her hips. "It isn't fair to lead a kid on."

He lifted a single eyebrow. "I made sure he understood it

might not be possible to return."

Feeona shook her head. He didn't understand. "Possible? These kids need certainty. They need to believe they're safe and wanted and settled. They need to see a god damn realistic future. Now, he'll resist settling in."

Seneca still stood, relaxed in front of her. Calm, cool, infuriating. "Toby is old enough to understand I don't have control of the universe. If we're not able to return, he'll understand.

Her body vibrated with a fury all out of proportion. She knew it. She didn't understand it. She wanted to swing out and punch the wall—to relieve some of the senseless fury. "You have him waiting for something that is never going to happen."

"Never?" His query whispered into her ear as if he thought the lack of volume could disguise the anger vibrating through the word.

"Never." Because once they'd freed Jupiter, the Dogs would be joining the resistance and she'd be left trying to hold things together. She plucked a soft pillow from the bench and squeezed it tight in her hands. She hated her increasing inability to control her emotions. To hide her panic. How was she going to continue her work—to free the next batch of factory kids—with a price on her head? And if she couldn't do that, how would she survive losing Jupiter and Seneca?

Seneca's eyes narrowed as if he was trying to read her thoughts in her eyes. When he spoke, it was through a clenched jaw. "If we CAN return for the boy, we WILL."

The flame of her temper jumped and flared. "We?" He had no right to talk about the future as if they had one shared between them. As if he would even want that. "Since when did you and I become a we?"

He was in her face in a flash of movement. He gripped her arms and jerked her so close she could see the sparks in his lavender eyes, feel his breath on her face. "The moment *my* mate.... chose *you*... as his mate."

CHAPTER TWENTY-EIGHT

New Hope
Agrove Colony
Earth Alliance Beta Sector
2210.168

Fee's stomach twisted in her gut and the pillow in her hands fell to the floor as Seneca gripped her arms. He thought she'd taken Jupiter from him. He'd choked on the words as he barked them at her—ache in every syllable. "Sen, I…"

"You what?" He shook her hard then lifted her up until only her toes touched the floor. "You didn't know he was my mate? Didn't know he chose you?" His words softened and came slower, but his chest still heaved with strained breaths. "Don't even try to pretend you didn't know exactly what you were doing every step of the way."

She hung in the tight grip of his hands, their faces close. The heat of him like a flame. Despite the accusation, she knew his words were more pain than anger. She recognized it because she felt it too. They both feared losing the man they loved. The man they both loved. The only difference was that she'd already lost him, with only herself to blame. "Oh, Sen." She reached for him, but his grip didn't budge. She could only just touch his waist. She squeezed against the muscle. "I didn't know at first that your love for each other was more than friendship. I didn't figure things out until we were on that burned out resistance ship. Even when I'd figured out you were a pair, I didn't understand exactly how. Even before I ran out of options that wouldn't push you both away, I knew you both deserved better than a woman with a calling that would always come first."

Seneca set her on her feet and loosened his grip. Eyes dark and cold.

Feeona slipped her hands up to frame his face. With her eyes she pled for him to see the naked honesty she bared. It was like ripping off her own skin, but it was better than seeing him suffering. "Don't you see? I never wanted to take him away from you." Her eyes filled with tears and her throat tightened. A ball of grief lodged in her chest, weighing her down. The weight of a loss that swelled larger every day. She'd already lost Jupiter. Seneca had never been hers, but she was coming to respect him, to count on him, to care for him in a way that added to her grief for what they could never have. "When we get Jupiter back, you'll be free of me. He'll need you more than ever, and I'll be out of the way. He already loves you. He just needs to figure out what it can mean. I thought I could help bring you together. I thought—"

"You thought fucking a woman together would make him see me?" He scoffed. "You aren't that naive."

She fought not to look away from his eyes. She couldn't let him believe she stood between him and Jupiter. "Maybe I am naive, but I thought if I encouraged you to touch him, he'd see you wanted him, and you'd see he isn't blind to you. Not at all. I don't think he even allows himself to think of you that way. He's afraid of reminding you of the past when you had no choice.

Afraid of hurting you, maybe even losing you."

Seneca's eyes melted back to a deep lavender as he rubbed at the place where he'd been gripping her arms, as if he could rub away the hurt. "He told you this?"

She slipped her hands down to his chest and let her palm rest over his pounding heart. "He didn't have to tell me. I heard it in his voice when he told me about your past. I saw the heat in his eyes when you touched him when we were in bed." She let the memories lift the corners of her lips. "He loves it when you touch him, and not in a brotherly way."

Seneca ended up being the first to look away, but not before she saw a flicker of hope lighten those tortured eyes.

"We should get going," he said.

She patted his chest, then wiped away her tears. "Yeah, we should."

His hands still held her arms loosely. "I've probably bruised you again."

She cupped his cheek and managed a friendlier smile for him. "There's a salve for that. Remember?"

He nodded then bent to pick up the pillow she'd dropped. "Mmm hmm. I'll help you with that later."

She thought she should protest—she didn't need his help—but all she offered was a concession. "Later."

Feeona watched the data flicker over the screen as the skipdrive leveled off and their flight became stable. "What do you see?"

"Everything seems to be within the normal range." Seneca tilted his head as if he could read the data better at an angle. Not long after they'd made peace, he'd demanded she teach him about piloting the ship. She'd argued that with Alfred online there wasn't any need. Sen had insisted. His ears flicked. "Did I miss something?"

"No." Feeona reached over and patted his hand. "You got it right. Everything is good."

He nodded, looking satisfied. His silver hair picked up the lights from the control panel, crowning him in shades of ruby and emerald.

She pulled free of her safety restraints and stretched. "Alfred, load the file on the *Abundance*'s security system to this terminal, I want to work on it for a while."

"Yes, Captain. Where would you like the data you requested for Mr. Seneca?"

Seneca raised an eyebrow.

Feeona shrugged. "I had him grab as much data off the long-range feeds as he could while we were transitioning from orbit to skipspace. I figured you'd want to scan for news on your pack brothers."

His eyes widened for a fraction of a second. "Thank you, Fee. Alfred, can you do a preliminary scan of the data?"

"Yes. It would be my pleasure. I have all of the relevant parameters on file."

"Then do it and have it ready for me when we wake. Feeona and I are going to get some rest now. It's been a long day."

"New Hope does have a twenty-eight hour day," Alfred added.

Feeona chuckled. "I think it's sweet how well you and Alfred get along."

His eyes narrowed. "Alfred is a computer."

"I am an artificial intelligence, base program echo-eight—"

"He didn't mean it, Alfred." Feeona interrupted before Alfred could list all of his specs.

Seneca pulled out of his safety harness and offered her a hand as he stood.

She shook her head. "I'll stay here awhile."

He took her hand and tugged. "Later. I doubt you've slept a full night in days."

Reluctantly, she got to her feet. He clasped both her hands, freezing her in place. "You have my apologies for upsetting you about Toby." Seneca pulled her closer. "Perhaps you're right about what he needs. But I could only give him my truth."

She nodded. "There's nothing to be done about it now."

He squeezed her fingers then tugged her toward the ladder that led to the upstairs passage. "You need rest."

"I suppose we're both tired." She wrapped her hand around a rung, with every intention of sneaking back after they parted ways. "What makes you think I'll sleep better tonight?"

He guided her second hand to the rung and urged her to climb. "We'll share your bed and both sleep better for it."

"I don't know whether to be angry at your assumption or laugh at your arrogance." She was leaning toward the laugh, and she feared it was because the idea of having him back in her room made her heart expand with want. Not a sexual want. Just the need to feel close to him.

He put a hand on her butt, still urging her upward. "Why don't you just accept it as truth? We both need the sleep and that is all I am asking for tonight."

Feeona put her foot on the first rung of the ladder and started climbing. "Asking?" She scoffed and muttered to herself. "I never heard a question." But the word that lingered in her mind was *tonight*.

🐾 🐾 🐾

Seneca woke feeling better than he had since they left Petro-5. Feeona's warmth pressed against his chest and wrapped around his right leg. Her breath brushed across his chest and teased his nipple. When he'd fallen asleep, she'd still had her back to him. He liked that she'd turned to him in the night. He looked down at her naked face, relaxed in sleep. There were still dark circles under her eyes where her lashes rested against the tender skin, but they were lighter than before.

She'd worn a sleeveless tunic and lightweight, ill-fitting shorts to bed. He could see the shadow of her nipple through the fabric and the plump curve of her breast pressed against his chest. The nipple was large and soft—evidence that she was still deeply asleep. His dick was awake, but not yet demanding attention. The thought that he should fuck her was a lazy tease that spread more warmth through him. She was Jupiter's mate. Oddly, he was even more certain of that now than before she'd betrayed them. As Jupiter's pack brother, it was his duty to use sex to seal a pack bond between them. Now that his anger had faded, the pull to have her was nearly irresistible, but doing it for that reason didn't sit right. She loved Jupiter. He was certain of that now. How she felt about him was less clear.

It would feel damn good to fuck her, and that might have been enough for him if his own feelings for her weren't such a jumble. She was hurting as much as him. And like him, she was no stranger to hurting. As he watched her chest rise and fall with her breath, it wasn't the thought of the slide and tug sensation on his dick that came to mind and stirred him. It was a need for the skin to skin heat of her body against his, their scents mixing and filling the air, the feel of her arms around him. He shifted a leg to make his now pulsing dick more comfortable.

Feeona's breathing changed and a moment later she stretched as much as she could without moving away from him. Her eyes were still closed, and that brought a smile to his face.

He pressed a kiss to her temple. "Sorry, if I woke you."

"Mmm. You were thinking too loud." Her words came out whiney in the way some of her kids had complained when they'd resisted getting up for breakfast.

Seneca kept his chuckle silent, but his chest shook beneath her cheek.

"Are you laughing at me?" The whiney drag of her syllables was still there, so he knew she wasn't truly upset.

"There's no rush to get up. You only slept about five hours."

After a deep breath and a long exhale, her eyes opened, and she started to pull away from him. "I'm awake now. I might as well get back to work."

He closed his arms around her, keeping her close. "No. Don't go yet."

She studied his face as if she could see something written there. "Okay."

Together they sat up, knees bumping into each other until he scooped her up and positioned her butt in the gap between his legs then pulled her slender legs up over his thigh.

Seneca reached for the salve they'd left on the bedside table and began applying a second treatment to the already fading bruises on her arms. "There are a few things we need to talk about."

"I'm listening."

He could see that, but he could also see her nipples hardening at his touch. "First, you need to understand that I plan to sleep here with you from now on."

She licked her lips, leaving them glistening. "I never told you to stop."

He nodded. "I know. I shouldn't have left. I know it made things harder for you."

She grimaced. "You had every reason to hate me. Still do."

"No. I let anger and fear get the best of me. As our mate, you deserve better from me."

She paled. "What?"

"You are Jupiter's mate and in our way, you and I are also bonded. That is the second thing I wanted to talk to you about. Last night you said that when we get him back, I'll be free of you. That you would be out of the way. I don't know what you're thinking but get it out of your head. Jupiter won't let you go, and neither will I."

She shook her head and tears welled in her eyes. "Jupiter was never mine for keeps. I knew I'd lose him the moment I contacted Morgan."

He brushed tears from her cheeks. "You think he won't forgive your betrayal. Didn't he explain? Arena Dogs mate for life. You're stuck with us."

"I could never ask—"

"You don't have to ask." Jupiter would probably blame himself for not gaining her trust so that she wouldn't *have* to betray them.

Vulnerability made her wide-eyed and raw. Bastard that he was, seeing her this way, without the protection of her sarcasm and her snark, spiked his arousal. He closed the millimeters of distance between them and pressed his lips against hers. She offered no resistance but gave him nothing back.

"Come on, Feeona." He buried his hand in her hair to keep her close. "Kiss me back. We're friends, at least. You can give me that much." He leaned down to her and bit her bottom lip, then licked away the small hurt. "Kiss me."

She conceded, pressing her lips lightly against his. She kissed him gently and he nibbled at her like a thoughtful lover, but it wasn't what either of them needed. She opened when his tongue pressed for entrance to deepen the kiss. She put a hand on his shoulder and her fingers flexed against his muscle as if she needed something to hold on to. He lifted her and brought her down in a kneeling position over his lap. It left her knees at his hips. She wrapped her arms around his shoulders and let him pull her close until they pressed together from groin to chest. He moaned at the heat of her so close but not yet skin to skin. His claim of friendship had come without thought, but it fit. They could be friends, but more than friendship would always tie them together. They were both in love with Jupiter and they each recognized the brokenness inside the other. They could come to need each other the way mates needed each other. Once the thought entered his head, he knew he wanted that. Wanted her.

He kissed her hard and this time she responded.

"Yes," he praised between deep, hungry kisses. "We both need this."

He left her lips to nose along her neck as he slid a hand up her thigh and beyond the wide legs of her shorts.

He palmed one cheek of her firm ass and squeezed.

She groaned.

Seneca let the tips of his fingers follow the valley between her cheeks down to the hidden oasis between her legs. She was warm and starting to become slick. Her scent became thick in the air. "So good," he whispered in her ear.

"Seneca?" She pushed against his shoulders.

He lifted his head. And rubbed his nose against hers. Her scent had become paired with Jupiter's in his mind and it made him long for her. "Tell me what you want, Fee. Anything. I can make you feel so good."

"This isn't what you want," she said. "I'm not who you want."

He chuckled as he nudged his dick against her. "The evidence suggests you're wrong about that."

He slipped his fingers between her wet-slick folds. Avoiding her clit, he stroked along the delicate skin with gentle finesse. The fist in her hair became a cradling hand as he turned her head and started kissing her again.

Again, she pulled away. "Sen, please. You don't want to betray Jupiter this way."

He scowled and shook his head. "Is that what you think?" Seneca frowned then pressed his forehead to hers. "This isn't betrayal. Arena Dogs share mates... Jupiter would want me to reinforce our bond. Don't you see? He's your mate. He chose you. That makes you my link to him."

It was the wrong thing to say. Feeona pushed him away with more force, leaning back to put all the distance between them that she could manage. Seneca growled from deep in his gut.

"Seneca, stop. Please. I can't be your link to him. You two belong together. You don't need me. You're the one his heart wants."

"You're wrong." He fought to keep his words from turning into barks. The words she meant to comfort, poked at his guts like a *guisarme*—a barbed spear that could gut an enemy without getting too close to flying claws. "When an Arena Dog finds his mate his body chemistry changes and becomes attuned to the mate. He can no longer enjoy the touch of another. If Jupiter felt for me as you claim, he'd never have been able to touch you."

She shook her head. "No. That can't be right."

"As much as it pains me, Feeona, I speak the truth." A truth he'd been keeping far in the back of his mind. A truth too devastating to dwell on.

She punched him in the shoulder. "You idiot."

He threw back his head and howled. She was killing him.

She sat up on her knees and cupped his face with her hands. "If that was true and I was his mate, like you say, he wouldn't have been able to stand your touch anymore." Her voice rose as she spoke. "I promise you that was the furthest thing from truth. And since he's your true mate, you shouldn't be able to be with me."

As her meaning pierced his addled brain, time stopped and stretched. His heart didn't beat. Silence surrounded him. And then it all came crashing back into his reality. "That can't be right."

Warm golden flecks sparkled in Feeona's brown eyes. "Seneca, maybe you're just different. You don't look like the other Arena Dogs that came up when I did a data search. Most of them look more like Jupiter. Dark hair, dark eyes, golden or copper skin." She released him and settled back on her heels. "From what Jupiter told me, they didn't make you all the same. Even the guys that look similar have different DNA, right?"

Seneca nodded his confirmation. He couldn't seem to form words. Even his growl had quieted.

"So whatever biology makes this mates thing happen, maybe it is different for you. Maybe even for Jupiter."

His heart swelled. Could it be true? He wanted to love her just for suggesting it. He nuzzled against her, pressing kisses to her jaw.

Fee's breath came faster.

"God, Fee. I need you. I've already spilled all over you… I want inside you, Fee… It's going to be so good."

"Sen, this won't fix anything." Even as she said it, she clung to him.

"Sex never does." He agreed, but that didn't stop him from squeezing her ass again or sliding his fingers through the wet of her.

She gasped as his fingertips slipped deeper, stroking her smooth, slick skin.

She wrapped her arms tight around him and pressed her face into his neck. "Sen, this will only make it harder to say goodbye."

She still thought she was going to let them go. His Dog brain needed to fuck that idea out of her head. The whore in him knew that wasn't the way to strengthen their bond. That might work for Jupiter, but not for him. It wasn't the Dog in him that called to her.

Seneca finally pulled back in frustration. As their eyes met, tension crackled between them. "I don't give a damn about hard or easy. So, unless you really have a problem with having sex with me—"

"I knew you and Jupiter came as a pair, Sen. Having sex with you has never been a problem. But we both know that the sex was never about us."

Her fear, her sadness, her doubt—only made him more determined. "This time, it will be."

Feeona's senses were on the verge of being overwhelmed and he hadn't even fucked her yet. Seneca had kissed and stroked her for so long and so well, she'd lost track of time and the world beyond her room. He'd discovered and excited erogenous zones she didn't know she had. Generous with his body, he let her stroke and tease him back. He sped them up and slowed them down in turns, until her body was taut as a bow string. The man knew what he was doing. Sex with Jupiter had been aggressive and pounding and wholly satisfying. Seneca was showing her a different way. Letting her know this was different. It was about them—not pushing Jupiter out—just adding a new thread to the cord that bound them all together.

She gasped again as Sen stroked his tongue flat against her clit. His silky hair tickled against her inner thighs and her back bowed. She was so close. "Please don't stop this time," she begged.

She wanted to scream when her words stopped him. Damn it. She should have kept her mouth shut.

He moved up her body, tonguing her skin and nipping gently as he went. "Sweet, Fee. Are you telling me you need me?"

"Yes! You know I do." He'd made her more than need him. She would snap if she didn't orgasm soon.

He buried his nose behind her ear then inhaled with a groan. "You smell so good."

She tossed her head, trying to get him to look her in the eye. If he did, he would surely see how desperate she'd become. "Please, Sen. I need you."

"Where do you need me, Fee. Tell me. I want to hear you say it." He ran his teeth along her jaw as he rolled her nipple between his finger and thumb.

"Inside. I need you inside me, Sen." It didn't matter that he'd stopped tonguing her clit. She still felt the throbbing demand between her legs. She spread them wider to encourage him.

"Music," he said. "Beautiful music. Now, give me more, Fee."

"Please." Every twist of her nipple magnified the throbbing between her legs. His cock slipped between her folds and bumped against her clit. She let out a guttural growl. "I need you inside me, now!" It was a demand. No longer a request. She wrapped her legs around his hips and ground against him.

"That's it," he praised.

His words faded away as his cock slipped inside her. She began to spasm and clinch before he was all the way in. Once he made it there, he froze. Buried deep inside her, pinning her to the bed, he kept his body still as she lit up around him. He stroked her skin and urged her on with whispered encouragements.

When she came down from her release, she could still feel him inside, a big stone intruder. He pulled back and slipped free with a crude, wet sound. He nudged her hip. "Turn over." Her legs were noodles, but she managed to roll over onto her front and get to her hands and knees.

"Steady?" He stroked her hips and over her ass as he asked.

"Mmm, hmm." Bliss was spreading through her urging her to collapse on the bed, but the knowledge that he hadn't cum kept her from giving in. She wanted him to move inside her and she wanted to hear him, feel him, when he found his own release.

She was so wet, he slipped inside her easily. "Damn, you feel good. Hot and wet and squeezing my dick just right." He hummed his delight.

She jumped when the flat of his hand came down on her ass with a loud smack. She must have clenched, too.

He moaned and rubbed the spot with the palm of his hand. "So pretty and pink. So tight."

He smacked her ass again and she moaned arching her back and lifting her butt even higher. It hurt but it also felt good—a sting that warmed into ecstasy beneath his palm. He grabbed her hips and began long deep strokes in and out of her. His thumb stroked between her ass cheeks and found the tightly closed entrance to her ass. He dipped his thumb down, drawing up some of the moisture from her pussy. He stroked gently around the entrance and then pressed solidly against the opening. Her tension flared back to life and grew stronger with each stroke. She was going to come again. It happened fast, before she even considered fighting it and it left her boneless and exhausted. She collapsed onto the sheets, Seneca following her. His hips thrust as his release coated her lower back.

He pulled her into his arms and pressed his lips against her temple. "You are Jupiter's mate, but you are also mine."

The words stuck another painful pin in her heart.

CHAPTER TWENTY-NINE

The Hawley
Earth Alliance Beta Sector
2210.190

They'd come out of skipspace at the prearranged coordinates and found Morgan's enormous ship already surrounded by smaller vessels. It worked to their advantage that Morgan hadn't kept the auction just between Feeona and Owens. Security would have its hands full and there would be too many witnesses and collateral damage for Owens to risk killing them outright. The slaver was heartless, not stupid.

Feeona sat cross-legged at the edge of the bed. Seneca stood in front of her as she used her body sprayer to paint a wolf that stretched from his hip bone and to his opposite shoulder. "Be still."

His abdomen rippled. "I'm trying. It tickles."

She smirked. "Where's that amazing control of yours?" Something she'd benefited from for the last week.

"You already told me I'm not getting sex after this. I only put forth that much effort when there's something in it for me."

She lifted her finger off the sprayer's trigger and swatted his thigh. "I'm past the worst part. Turn and put your hand on my shoulder."

He obeyed and she went back to work. His thumb stroked across her collar bone. "Do I get to do you next?" His rich baritone raised bumps all along her arms.

With effort she kept her focus on the wolf. "No body-art for me, but you can do the metallic sheen I'm going to use across my shoulders."

He turned a step further. "Shouldn't it go on your cleavage? Trust me, in that dress, that is the only place Morgan's going to be looking."

"The gold spray is only for the entrance. I need to look rich as Midas."

"Who?"

"Not important." Her mind jumped from Midas to Jupiter. Jupiter hadn't known about his name. "Do you know who you were named for?"

Seneca shook his head. "Master Owens named me. It's just a name."

She kept her eyes on her task as she talked. "Seneca was an ancient Earth philosopher and poet. I remember liking some of his work, but I don't have anything memorized. We can read more about him, later. Alfred has a great library of Old Earth classics, history and literature." With Alfred's help they'd gone from nursery rhymes to fairytales—the original versions. Neither of them had been in the mood for anything too perfect.

"Later," he agreed. "I like the sound of that." His voice was soft and husky.

Feeona sighed. He wanted her to accept that he and Jupiter would be sticking with her. She shouldn't mislead him. She didn't want him to feel like she expected that. She didn't. And she wanted him to leave her without bad feelings between them. If she had her way, Jupiter would finally be the mate to Sen that he always should have been.

"It'll take a few days for me to get you some place safer, after we take Jupiter from Morgan. We'll have time then."

Sen squeezed her shoulder. "Will you check for news of Mercury and our other brothers before we go onto Morgan's ship?"

As of the last time they'd checked, they still hadn't found any news of them. "If we have time. There won't be anything we can do about it until after, anyway."

She turned off the sprayer, then removed the paint canister. After putting it back into its slot, she started cleaning the nozzle. "You can put your arm down now. It dries pretty quickly but try not to rub up against anything for a few minutes."

He lifted his hand and wove his fingers into her hair. The defined muscles of his bare arm and shoulder flexed. He bent and pressed a kiss to her forehead. "Everything will work out, you'll see."

At least he no longer doubted her ability to get Jupiter back from Morgan. *She* wasn't even convinced the A plan would work. Sen walked over to the clothes rack and grabbed the barely-there costume they'd chosen for him.

He didn't know her fall back plan. She hated that she was still keeping secrets. Sen was practical. Could she tell him? "Hey, Sen."

He looked up from fastening the modified briefs carefully around his hips. "Yeah?"

She plucked the next paint from the case, then shifted it out of the way. She patted the spot on the bed. "I need you sitting for the next part."

"Right." The wolf moved with his muscles as he walked. Sexy

as hell.

He sat down and pushed her hair behind her ear. "What worries you, love?"

Love. Such a beautiful word. It didn't matter that he didn't mean it the way her heart heard it. He did care for her. Maybe he even loved her a little. Their attraction and affection for one another had turned into a bone deep bond that went beyond friendship.

She gave him a smile. "After I put the rest of this paint on, you might just be lethal."

He didn't give her an answering smile. "You can tell me, Fee."

She sighed. "After the paint."

"That bad?"

She nodded. She adjusted the sprayer settings and put a finger under his chin. "Close your eyes and keep them closed until I tell you to open them."

He lowered his long pale lashes and relaxed his face. She moved the sprayer carefully across his eyes. A lighter setting across his cheekbones.

She put down the sprayer and dipped a finger into a pot of lip color. "Keep them closed. I'm going to touch your lips," she warned.

He didn't move.

She stroked the vivid color over the sensual curves. It hadn't been easy to find a color that looked good with his skin and eyes, but she'd gotten it right. She could tell now. Jupiter was going to see Seneca in a whole new light.

The color across his eyelids and lashes would be dry, but it was easier to say it without him looking at her. "If something goes wrong—"

"We'll adapt," he interrupted. "We'll make it work."

She huffed out a breath. God, she adored him. "I have the coordinates for the Resistance's secret base."

His eyes popped open. His gaze traced her features and his head tilted. "How?"

She licked her dry lips. "I hacked the resistance ship. I stored the information in my neural unit."

His eyes closed. "You've had it all this time." He wasn't asking, but he hadn't tackled her to the floor either.

"Yes."

He opened his eyes and shook his head. "Thank you for telling me." He reached for her hand and wove their fingers together. "But you're not giving it to Owens."

"If there's no other way, I will. I'm not letting anything happen to Jupiter or to you."

"Jupiter wouldn't want you to save him that way."

She acknowledged that truth with a nod. "Last resort."

She picked up the collar they'd designed for him and fastened it around his neck.

Sen tugged in a futile attempt to adjust it. It was never going to be comfortable. "You should just...erase the data now."

"Is that what you want me to do?" She bit one lip between her teeth as she waited for his answer.

He was silent a moment and she knew she had him.

"No." He squeezed her hand.

"Good," she let her lips curve the barest fraction. "Because I'm keeping the coordinates and I'll use them if I have to."

"It won't come to that."

"We'll make sure it doesn't," she agreed. "But if it does..."

Sen met her gaze with hard resolve bright in his lavender eyes. "We save Jupiter."

CHAPTER THIRTY

The Abundance
Earth Alliance Beta Sector
2210.190

Jupiter stood in a gilded cage, wearing little more than a cloth draped around his hips. The only consolation was that Creek was dressed the same. All the better for the bidders to look them over. Creek had been a surprise. The Arena Dog had already been in Morgan St. Germaine's slave hold when he'd arrived. It had taken days just to get the Dog to speak to him. Creek still hadn't explained how he'd gotten off Roma except to say, "same as you, I expect." He hadn't identified his House. Wouldn't speak of it at all. There were several Owners of Roma, each with his or her own training house and each with different specialties. Today, all his questions were set aside. Today, they shared the same circumstance and on the subject of St. Germaine's guests, they agreed. The humans there were disgusting. So far, they'd done a good job of scaring most of them away.

His first sight of Feeona sucked the air from his lungs and drove all the blood in his body to his loins. Then it all came crashing back to his heart, pounding with fear. He'd half hoped she wouldn't come for him. He didn't want her anywhere near the slaver. His senses reassured him that Seneca was with her even though he couldn't see his pack brother.

"I take it that change in your scent means the female came as you said she would." The normally stoic Creek stepped up to stand at his shoulder. He barked a low, brief sound of interest. "*That* is your human?"

Jupiter couldn't stop the growl that vibrated up from his chest. Instinct screamed that he didn't want Creek looking at Fee. Especially not as she looked now. The velvet black dress she wore clung to her curves and showed off her gold-dusted, caramel skin. The dress clung to her breasts as if by magic. Two slender strips of cloth twisted down from the top to connect to a skirt that hung from her hips and barely covered the curve of her ass. A gem sparkled in her navel. It matched the gem studded pins in her hair. She'd tamed the mahogany mass into an intricate design atop her head. A sparkly strip of smoky amber spread across her eyes, but that and the gold across her shoulders was the only makeup she'd worn. Without the chemical she'd used to cover her skin when they met, he could smell her natural scent across the room.

Mate. Mine.

The mate bond he'd barely accepted before she'd betrayed him, flared through his senses like a jolt from a shock stick. Her scent together with Seneca's twisted him up inside.

Creek shifted on his feet. "You didn't tell me your pack brother is a pleasure slave. How is that even possible?"

Jupiter shook his head to clear it and then searched for Seneca. He stood just beyond her shoulder. Jupiter barely recognized him. It wasn't just the animal that leapt across his muscled torso, covering his body above tight black shorts. It wasn't the silver circlet that ringed his throat, connecting to a chain that led to Fee's hand. Or the heavy color lining his lavender eyes, making them look large and exotic. The way he moved, oozing sensuality, the way he averted his eyes in submission, the way he stood a step behind. Jupiter wrapped his hands around the bars of his cage and squeezed. This was a Seneca he'd known about, but never seen.

As the other bidders greeted his Feeona they ogled Seneca and he seemed to bask in their attention. If Jupiter believed Feeona had truly taken Sen back to that abused creature he'd once been, he would have been enraged. He didn't believe it. Their scents told him what he needed to know. They were equals, working together to free him. He should have been outraged that they would put themselves in danger, and he was. He should have been outraged even more that they would use their bodies to distract and draw the attention of the slaver. Even now the man was smiling delighted at the sight of them across the room. But all Jupiter could think was that he wanted to take them back to Feeona's ship and have them play out their roles for him. He would fuck them until they couldn't move.

His pounding heart skipped a beat. The moisture in his mouth dried up like fallen leaves under a brilliant sun. He didn't just want to fuck Feeona. He wanted to fuck them both. They were his. Both of them. He had not one, but two deceptive, secretive, dangerously sexy mates. He threw back his head and howled. He was aware of the crowded room going silent around him. He let the power of the howl hollow him out and fill him up again. He rolled through it and started again. Seneca's howl joined his. And then Creek followed. The Dog that claimed no pack howled with them—the sound pulled from him as if he couldn't resist the call.

Jupiter let the howl fall away, then looked for his mates. Creek stayed blessedly silent. Fee and Sen were making their way through the guests and toward Morgan's stage. The large room looked very different from the day he'd arrived on the slaver's ship. Eight male aliens up for auction were shackled and held in place along the silver path. The large green men were barrel-chested with muscular limbs. They had flexible snouts and four eye stalks that moved independently.

In addition to the guests, servants wrapped in white togas offered food and drinks. In the long expanse between the cage and Morgan's stage, waist high pillars dotted the floor, serving as tables.

"That was impressive." The voice resonated with power and health despite the man's age. The old man stood in front of Jupiter's cage, smoky haired with cynical eyes. Too close.

Jupiter had been too distracted. He bared his teeth and growled to back the man off.

The man showed no fear. "I've seen you fight in the arena." His tone turned sad. "With my Seneca."

His Seneca? Muscles tight, his fists clenched, Jupiter growled again.

The man shook his head. "Speak like a man."

Jupiter didn't understand the tone. There was plenty of arrogance, and the voice was instructive, but nothing at all like the whip-masters who'd trained him. "Who. Are. You." It was hard to form the question through clenched teeth and over the growl that still vibrated in his throat. He was afraid he knew exactly who the man was and the thought enraged him.

"Andre Cervenka. Perhaps Seneca has mentioned me?" His features softened when he spoke of Sen.

Disgust made Jupiter's stomach twist. "He never mentioned the names of any of the humans who abused him."

Cervenka's tidy eyebrows lowered. "Abused him?" He shook

his head, then smiled. "I loved him. Still do. And he loved me."

Feeona and Seneca's scents pulled at Jupiter. The knowledge that they approached kept him from reaching through the bars and ripping the man's throat out.

Feeona stepped up alongside the man. "Children do learn to love their abusers."

Jupiter admired her ability to confront the man in a way he could not. He relied on his might to communicate his feelings. He didn't have the words for insults.

Cervenka's face tightened. "You don't know what you're talking about." He turned his gaze on Seneca, at Fee's side. "Ask Seneca. He'll tell you."

Seneca stood like a statue with his head bowed in submission, but Jupiter scented his fear and his fury.

St. Germaine stood with them, looking amused.

Fee stepped into Cervenka's space. "If you don't get out of my sight, you'll be missing the very body part you like to use against the children you rent and abuse."

Sincerity colored Feeona's voice, but the idiot seemed unaffected. Jupiter was affected. He loved her tough attitude and the softer side hidden beneath. Memories from when they'd first met rushed back and reminded him why he'd been unable to resist her.

"It looks like you may have fierce competition for the bidding after all, Feeona." Morgan's chuckle broke into Jupiter's thoughts. "Unless Cervenka, you're more interested in Creek. Another fine specimen."

Feeona made a show of looking Creek up and down. "They're both too old for this bottom feeder."

Jupiter bit his tongue to keep from barking.

Cervenka ignored them all and instead spoke to Seneca. "You

weren't supposed to be here."

Sen raised his head. The lavender of his eyes had darkened to near black. Cold rage poured out of the inky depths and sarcasm dripped from every word he spoke. "Forgive me for living after I grew too old to interest you." Jupiter could see the role Sen played weighing him down when he'd rather have dug his fingers into the man's eyes.

"Well..." After a moment, Cervenka turned away. "I can be gentleman enough to give you some space—for now."

Morgan rubbed the back of his hand down Fee's bare arm. "I can see why you haven't been more successful in your business. You need me, Feeona." He sighed dramatically. "But I need to go calm my buyer. The man has a large fortune to spend." St. Germaine turned on his heel to follow Andre Cervenka through the crowd.

The moment the men were out of earshot, pain bled through from the back of Feeona's eyes. The smoky color striped across her face made them appear large and bright, exotic and mysterious. She stood straight and tall. The black boots she wore had thick heels and clung to her legs, stopping just above her knees. They drew his attention to her bare thighs.

"Costumes and disguises are part of my lifestyle." Her voice was low and husky. "But I'm still me, Jup."

That final syllable jerked his gaze back to her face. "You've never called me that before."

"Seneca calls you that all the time." She wove her hand in Sen's and he squeezed it in return. His mates were united.

The movement in Fee's hair caught Jupiter's attention. Bug launched into the air and flew toward him, landing on his shoulder. It crawled closer to his throat and latched on to the shock collar he wore.

"I've studied the design," said Fee. "But it will take me some time to hack both your collars." She tipped her head to indicate Creek. "Where did he come from?"

Creek remained silent, apparently willing to let Jupiter speak for him. "He was here when I arrived."

"And we can trust him?"

Jupiter raised an eyebrow at her question. "He has shown no love for St. Germaine."

Feeona gave up a manufactured smile. "I can't imagine he would."

Too aware that the slaver could return at any moment, Jupiter rushed out a warning. "Morgan expects you to try to steal me. He'll be ready. He doesn't believe you have any credits."

The news didn't seem to affect her at all. "What about Owens? I thought he'd be here, waiting for us. Have you seen him?"

"No. Not yet."

"Huh." She looked over her shoulder as if she thought he might appear at that very moment.

"Problem?" Jupiter shifted his weight, restless to be on the other side of the bars of his cage.

Fee shrugged her gold-dusted shoulders. "No. Even if it was, I always have a back-up plan."

"Yes." The word vibrated in his throat. He could no longer hold back his anger. "But you also like to keep your problems and your plans hidden."

Her mask wavered. "You have to know, if there were any other way—"

"If you had talked to me, we would have MADE another way." For a moment she looked so vulnerable and full of ache. It fed his anger. He should have known there was a problem. He should have earned her trust.

She grabbed hold of the bars of his cage and leaned in. "I couldn't risk it."

It was all he could do not to reach through and wrap his arms around her. He longed to comfort her, but he wasn't ready to forgive her yet. "Afraid you'd miss out on your opportunity to pick up your cargo?"

Her knuckles whitened where she clutched the bars. "Kids. They were kids."

He shouldn't be so damned jealous of those children. Even though he understood, his heart whispered that if he'd been a fit mate, she would have shared her burden with him. He ignored his heart and forced his voice to the firmness his pride demanded. "Morgan told me. And did you make enough profit from selling them to satisfy your greed?"

She paled, but it was Sen who flinched, as if the blow had bounced off her and struck him. "I don't sell them, Jupiter. I free them. You can't believe—"

He didn't, but his anger had been bottled up too long. Indulging it seemed better than admitting his own failures. "You sold me to Morgan."

Tears rolled down the smoke grey of her cheeks. She couldn't have been more stricken if he'd hit her. Then she would have been fighting back. Despite his anger, he hated that he'd hurt her.

Her fists flexed and tightened on the bars. "I deserve your anger. I know that. But you saw the pit. I try to save the ones I can before they end up there. I'd already made arrangement with the man who gets them out of the factory for me. If I hadn't taken delivery, my contact *would* have sold them to a *real* slaver. Or worse." Her eyes were wide and pled for understanding. "I love you Jupiter, but I couldn't abandon them the way my parents abandoned me. I..." Her mouth snapped shut. Her lips pressed together as if she could stop the words she'd already said.

There was a story there. One he needed to hear when they were all safe. She'd confessed that she loved him and that helped to cool his temper. How could he lash out his anger when he knew the failure was his own, and she'd obviously been punishing herself. He reached toward her and wrapped one of his hands around her much smaller one. "That is a story for another day." He spoke softly, but his voice was rough with emotion.

She nodded, turned on her heel, and was three strides away with Sen in tow when he stopped her.

He barked softly. "Feeona."

She looked back over her shoulder.

"Thank you." The words were easier to say than he'd have expected. "For not giving them Sen."

Seneca tensed, but she just dipped her chin, lips pressed tight. She hesitated, then sighed. "You know he's strong enough to handle anything?"

He studied Sen's stiff back for a brief moment. "Yes." And he did know that. It surprised him more that she knew. And if she did, that meant the reason she'd turned him over instead of Seneca was that she knew he would want it that way. Feeona and Seneca walked away, and Jupiter indulged himself in watching the way they moved together. Fee had betrayed him, but in some twisted way she'd done it for him.

"A strong female." Creek patted his shoulder. It was the first time the man had ever touched him.

"Yes," he agreed. But not always as strong as she appeared.

🐾 🐾 🐾

Feeona and Seneca worked their way back to Morgan's stage. The number of admirers hovering near him only made it more frustrating. She strode through the crowd and climbed the steps as if she belonged at Morgan's side. Seneca kneeled at her feet, eyes on the floor, playing his role perfectly.

"So well behaved," said Morgan. "I'm impressed. The others are a bit too cocky for my taste."

Fee curved her lips in a hint of a smile. "You just have to know how to handle them."

"I suppose you're going to tell us that your fighter Dog would behave as well for you as this one," Morgan waved a hand toward Seneca. "If we let him out of the cage."

Fee watched her breathing and forced herself not to answer too quickly, too eagerly. "Of course." Luckily, Morgan wasn't watching her. He was busy playing to his audience, feeding off their attention. "He's been following my instructions well so far."

"Your instructions?" This time Morgan threw a chuckle in after his question and the others laughed along.

Feeona refused to let them get to her. "Yes. The ones I gave him before I sold him to you." She took a dramatic pause and stroked the top of Seneca's head, reminding them all that they had an uncaged Dog in their midst. "You've had Jupiter for some time now and he hasn't eaten any of your guards, has he?"

The laughter that followed her challenge quivered with universal discomfort from the crowd. Morgan wasn't taking the bait. He wasn't letting Jupiter out of the cage. She hadn't expected him to, but she'd had to seize the opportunity to try. She knew better than to push him.

Feeona widened her smile and touched Morgan's cheek.

"Have I told you how much I admire a man that can take a bit of ribbing? Roland always said you were a good sport."

Sen leaned into her, pressing his shoulder to her thigh. His inaudible growl vibrated against her. Oblivious to the power of the man at his feet, Morgan took her hand and pressed a kiss to her knuckles before launching into a story about one of the adventures he and Roland had shared. The story was for his audience more than her, and she gladly faded out of the spotlight.

Morgan's story gave Fee time to study the crowd as they hung on his words. Using her neural link, she identified each of them. A few had been to the Roma Rex resort, but only Cervenka had a direct connection to any of the owners of Roma. Her quick search revealed that Cervenka lived on Roma in a villa owned by Owens. It was enough to make her think she needed to be careful not to underestimate him.

When everyone was laughing at the end of Morgan's story, Fee drew his attention back to her. "My friend, when is my competition arriving?"

Morgan looked her way, but his gaze stayed well below her shoulders. "There is no one to compare to you, Feeona. But if you're asking about Owens, he's sent his regrets." He lowered his voice. "Rumors are that there was a huge fiasco in the arena. Second one this quarter. This time, some of his property escaped. He's trying to hush things up, but you can't keep something like that out of the data stream." He chuckled as if he thought he was clever to point out the obvious. "A lucky thing for you, though." He indicated Fee with a wave of his hand. "With more recent public escapes, Owens seems less interested in your Arena Dog. You might have a chance of making the winning bid."

Morgan started as if he'd move closer to her side, but found

Sen in the way. Cervenka shifted behind the other guests as if preparing to leave the crowd. She liked him better where she could keep an eye on him.

Feeona lifted her voice to be heard. "What do you think, Cervenka? Do I have a chance of winning the bid?"

The crowd between them parted. "Why ask me?" His expression said he knew exactly why she was asking him.

She lowered her sparkling eyelashes and gave him her best flattery-will-get-me-everything look. "You look like a man in the know."

He lifted his eyebrows and dipped his chin in Seneca's direction. "I'd say you know a great deal about the worth and sweet temptation of Arena Dogs."

With the way Sen was dressed and kneeling at her feet, Cervenka had to think she'd been abusing him. And despite what Sen meant to her, she supposed she *had* been abusing him from the moment they met. She'd set out to help Jupiter and Seneca, and so far, she'd failed spectacularly.

She was too good an actor to let the sudden rush of regret and grief show, but it sat heavily in her belly. Regret for what she'd had to do was bad enough, but the grief devastated her. She'd been fooling herself these last weeks with Sen. Giving in to that sweet temptation. Fee had let herself have him and now she'd be losing both the men she loved.

She had a duty to the children of her world. That would always be in the way. Jupiter and Seneca deserved better than she could give them. They deserved to have each other the way they were meant to be. If she could give them nothing else, she'd give them that.

"I've come to see the value of having an Arena Dog at my side." She tugged on the silver chain still clutched in her hand.

Seneca rose to his feet like a canine uncurling from a nap. She turned to meet his gaze and pulled him close against her side as she spoke. "Seneca already feels like a piece of me."

Sen buried his nose in her neck, giving her leave to turn her attention back to the others. Morgan stared at them with fascination. The rest of the crowd were either entertained or aroused. Of all of them, Sen's admirer was impossible to read.

Morgan adjusted the ruffled cuffs of his sleeves, then clapped his hands to summon a servant. "Drinks for my guests."

The servant walked up with a tray of something golden and bubbly.

Morgan waved the tray to Cervenka, who'd made his way forward through the crowd. "Feeona is here to bid for Jupiter just as you are."

Andre accepted the glass but didn't drink. "You're mistaken. The Arena Dogs you have available hold no interest for me."

Seneca shivered against Fee's skin. Something about the man's words had hurt him.

Morgan frowned. "Perhaps the Dreat then? They excel at physical labor."

"Mmm." Cervenka didn't answer. Instead, he took a sip from his drink.

Something wasn't right. Feeona wished she knew what. She needed to get the plan moving along. "Morgan, this is a fabulous ship. I saw some of your impressive armaments as we arrived."

"I have all the security a ship could need—outside and inside." He nodded and lifted a hand. Armed men seeped in from every entry to stand along the walls. Guests clustered into groups and shuffled away from Morgan's private guards. "You can feel completely safe here."

"I've never felt safer." The size of the lie almost made it stick in Feeona's throat. "I'd love a tour. After the auction, maybe?"

Morgan took the bait. "Why wait? We have plenty of time." He put out an arm, like an Old Earth gentleman offering aid to a helpless lady.

"Wonderful." And if things went to plan, she'd teach him a thing or two about helplessness.

CHAPTER THIRTY-ONE

The Abundance
Earth Alliance Beta Sector
2210.190

The tour of the ship led to Morgan's private office more quickly than Feeona had expected. It had probably been too much to hope he'd show her the security station first. What she hadn't been prepared for was the speed with which his arm had changed from a gentle assist to an immovable chain around her waist. Sen's jaw was locked so tight she worried he might break it. The moment Morgan's office door closed behind them his hand had gone straight to her ass.

"Hey, no need to be so grabby." She tried to fend off his hand in an effort to calm Seneca down. Watching Morgan's passes had him beyond agitated. He'd been too good to show it, but her skin prickled in warning.

Morgan's slim face scrunched in frustration. "No more playing hard to get." He grabbed her upper arms and yanked her to him. He thrust against her, pressing his arousal against her belly. "You've made me wait years already."

She didn't fight him, but she let Sen's silver chain slip from her hands. He was already starting to growl.

Morgan rocked his hips against her again. "Sounds like we should have put your pet in a cage like the others."

"Sen." She spoke calmly and clearly, afraid he might be too far gone to listen. "Anyone outside the door?"

"No." There were a lot of teeth in that one word. He'd shed the submissive posture and once again stood proud and defiant.

Feeona savored the moment Morgan realized his mistake in seeing Seneca as no threat. Sen was behind him in a blink, ripping Morgan away from her.

Sen threw him against the wall, then stood over him where he sprawled on the floor. "You will *never* touch her again."

The idiot climbed to his feet. He tugged his shirt into place and brushed at his trousers. Blood marred his lip. "You're not getting off this ship alive."

The door to the room slid open behind them.

Before either of them could reply to Morgan's melodrama, a plasma blast obliterated his face. Fee spun around to see Andre Cervenka slipping a blaster inside his coat. The man who'd once paid to abuse Seneca, looked casual and relaxed despite the body he'd just put on the floor… and the wall.

Seneca stayed silent. If Feeona had the capacity to growl like the Arena Dogs, she would have.

"Cervenka." Feeona called his name to get the man to stop staring at Sen, but it didn't work.

"Seneca." Cervenka's voice was wistful and lover-like. "I've missed you."

Sen stayed silent and somehow managed not to leap across the room and rip out the man's throat.

"Well, damn." Feeona wanted to slug the older man in the nose. Of course, it wasn't the first time she'd had that impulse. "Why in hell did you do that?"

"He was going to die anyway. Don't be ungrateful, Miss…?"

"We had things under control." She strode to Morgan's com station and sat in his chair. "He's no help to us dead."

"I seriously doubt you need him. But you do need to know an unauthorized ship just appeared in the landing bay. Whatever you're planning to do, you should make it quick."

Seneca stood next to her. He vibrated with aggression, but he didn't make a move toward Cervenka. "Can you hack in from here without Morgan's codes?"

She looked at Sen over her shoulder. Despite everything else that was going down, she was way more worried about Sen. "Maybe. But I might have to go to the central security station. But Sen—"

He squeezed her shoulder softly. "I'm okay, Fee. Now isn't the time."

He was right. They had a rescue to pull off. "Okay. Good to know. But we need to find the code-key for the cage." She shot Cervenka a look. "And I am not searching that mess of a body."

Sen bent over the body to search for the small crystal-like object that was key to getting Jupiter safely out of the cage. They'd done their research well and knew Morgan carried it with him during auctions.

Feeona pushed away from the terminal and stood. "Cervenka is right about the ship. I'm getting chatter on the com about an invasion force in the bay." She stepped into the old man's space. "Are you going to be more of a problem?"

Andre sighed in a way that rolled through his whole body. "I'm afraid our intentions are at cross purposes."

Fury flashed through her. She poked her finger into his chest. "You're never getting your hands on Seneca again."

He smiled sadly. "He's safe from me." He placed a hand over

his heart as he shifted his focus to Seneca who now stood with the code-key in hand. "I'll always love you my boy, but I am content with my memories." His gaze slid back to her. "As you surmised, at a certain age my young loves no longer satisfy my physical needs. Even so, Seneca was hard to let go."

She wanted to cut his balls off. She counted to ten before she could speak normally.

"Besides being a pervert, what are you doing here?" Her attitude probably wasn't helpful, but the man didn't react to her provocation. "My old friend Grande Owens sent me here to clean up his mess." His eyes shifted back to Seneca momentarily. "I told you I was a fixer. It's just not broken things I fix, only broken situations. I never lied to you, my boy."

"He's a man now," Feeona snapped. "How exactly are you supposed to fix things?"

He frowned. "I have a team planting explosives at crucial points in the ship. Grande wants no survivors to go telling tales. He wants to kill the rumors of escaped Arena Dogs."

Seneca finally allowed disgust to slip over his face. "He'd kill everyone on this ship to do it?"

Andre shrugged. "Mmm. Barbaric isn't it."

"Evil," said Seneca. "This isn't your sort of sin, Andre. You can't seriously mean to kill all these people."

"Sadly, I do." Cervenka shifted his focus back to Feeona, suddenly serious. "But I refuse to kill Seneca. I don't care about the other Arena Dogs or you. Don't give a damn if the rest of you manage to escape the explosion. I don't imagine you're planning to be very visible after this. So, you get Seneca off this ship and we'll agree to stay out of each other's way in the meantime."

"Staying out of your way leaves too much up in the air."

Feeona eyed the built-in terminal on Morgan's desk. "So, bring me up to speed."

She pulled up a map of the ship on the screen. Cervenka stood beside her and pointed to several areas. "These are the locations for each member of the team. They're targeting strategic bulkheads, the main power relay stations. The team leader is quite expert at this sort of thing."

Feeona had studied the ship's systems enough to agree. "Call them off, Andre."

He shook his head. "I can't do that. Why do you care about any of these people? They're all in the slave trade. Criminals. You have plenty of time to get off the ship."

She would never work for a slaver, but her hands weren't clean enough to condemn every crew member onboard. Some of which had nothing to do with Morgan's business and might be there as a last resort. And then there were the slaves. "How long, Andre? How long before these explosions go off?"

He checked his very snazzy palm display. "Fifty minutes."

"I can work with that."

"So pleased to hear it." Andre's words dripped with boredom.

Seneca growled. "Don't be. That means she doesn't need you anymore."

Cervenka's face twisted in confusion. "Seneca—"

"I can't let you hurt another boy." Sen was on him in a flash. There was a sickening snap and the older man's body slid to the floor.

Seneca took a deep breath then locked his gaze on hers. If he was looking for condemnation, he wasn't getting it from her. He moved cautiously forward and took her hand. "I did love him, or thought I did at the time. I hated him for that most of all."

"He manipulated you and you were young. Men like him are

experts at ensnaring the vulnerable."

Sen nodded then seemed to shake off thoughts of Andre. "We can do this. Together. We're a good team."

"Yes." She wove her fingers with his. The instant rush of their connection steadied her. Muted the anxiety of everything that could go wrong. She could only hope it was the same for him. She smiled through the hurt in her heart. They made a good team, but their time together was almost done. Letting go of the two men she loved was going to break her. "Let's go. We need to check out the so-called invasion force."

"You don't think they're real?"

Feeona shook her head. "There is someone there, but the ship they came in on is too small for an army."

"Let's find out." Sen led her through the winding corridors and back to the auction room. They didn't need to go any further than that. The invasion force had started a war with Morgan's security team.

🐾 🐾 🐾

Seneca scented them before they walked through the entryway. Blood rushed through his heart in an adrenaline fueled rhythm. His body buzzed, ready for battle. Fee froze the moment they crossed into the room. He tightened his hand on hers. "It's okay. It's our pack."

She didn't answer. Her eyes were blank.

A plasma blast hit a wall near them. He grabbed her and carried her to the floor in a nook behind Morgan's stage. "Fee?"

"Jupiter." Her eyes remained blank, but her voice was strong.

Seneca's gaze shot to the gilded cage where his other mate crouched. A lean human male with spiky white hair and dressed in gray trousers, a matching pullover and heavy worker boots stood by the cage door trying to hack the lock. Or rather he would have been, if he wasn't dodging Bug. Fee was keeping him away from the lock that would explode if opened without the code-key tucked into Sen's waistband. The man clearly wasn't a guard or a guest, but he was about to kill himself and take Jupiter and Creek with him.

Seneca tucked into a crouch and launched himself over the stage. Where he landed, guests huddled together on the floor in front of him. He chose a target, a sturdy looking man next to one of the short pillars. One step. Two. Then he bounded off the man's back onto the top of the table and flew. His muscles stretched and his body twisted. His shoulder hit the corner of the roof of the cage. He rolled across and dropped to the floor between the human and the door. He landed in a crouch and barred his teeth in a warning growl.

The man put his hands up, palms out. "Whoa. Whoa. Friendly, here."

Seneca quickly took in the rest of the room. Security guards arced around a central cluster. A guard flew from the center, crashing into the guests. The sound of screams and bones snapping reverberated beneath the shouts of the guards. Security officers were also taking cover in various areas across the room with their blasters. One was currently climbing a service ladder built into a wall to get a shot at the Arena Dogs below.

"I was just trying to help your friends get out of the cage." Pleading strained the man's voice. "We could use them out here."

"Sen." Jupiter's voice was calm and close. "What's wrong?"

"The cage lock is rigged to explode." Seneca spotted a guard aiming at them. He barked an alert to Jupiter and Creek and dove toward the hacker, taking him to the floor. A blast struck the floor where they'd been standing.

The man tangled up with him stared at the ceiling. "The things I do for a stubborn, half-pint—"

Seneca shook the man until he shut up. He pulled the code-key from his waistband and shoved it into the man's hand. "Use this."

The man nodded furiously. "Yes, yes. Use this."

Seneca pushed him aside and ran for the guard on the ladder. Instead of climbing, he ran up the wall, flipped, and kicked the weapon from the man's hand. Mid-air, he twisted and reached out for a rung. He ignored the jerk that stressed his shoulder joint and his collision with the wall as he locked his grip on the guard's leg. He yanked hard and threw the man to the ground. The human survived the fall but didn't get up fast enough to escape when Sen dropped down into a crouch beside him. One punch ended his foe's ability to breathe.

He shot a look to where he'd left Fee. She'd pulled herself into a ball on her side and so far, she'd escaped notice. He looked for Bug, but the small flying machine had disappeared. She must be using it to try a remote hack into the security system.

A scream brought his attention back to the center of the auction room and the large green aliens. They were free and using the strength of their bulky bodies to shove the guests into the now empty cage. Jupiter and Creek had run up behind the cluster of guards that surrounded what sounded like two of his pack brothers, Mercury and Carnage. Looking strong and powerful despite his time being held prisoner, Jup easily pulled a guard out of the fight and ended him. Creek did the same. One by one they were improving the odds for Mercury and Carn.

Sen heard Diablo, his third pack brother, bark then he appeared from the far side of the cluster. He leapt into the air and, looking weightless, bounded across the heads and shoulders of the crowd of guards. Jupiter was ready when Lo landed in the platform he'd made of his hands. Jup, biceps bulging, threw him up into the air and Lo landed atop the cage. He stood tall and fearless and healthy.

Seneca didn't know how his pack was here, but their presence filled a hole in his heart. Lo's gaze met his and he saw relief and joy flash into those red-black eyes. He hadn't seen anything close to joy from Lo for more than a year. With a few quick barks they'd sorted out their targets among the scattered guards Seneca had spotted earlier. Lo leapt from the roof, then ended the nearest one with a slash of claws across the guard's neck. Blood spurted onto the floor.

Seneca ran for his next targets. His muscles sang and the primitive part of his brain roared with the pleasure of doing what he'd trained for, what he'd done along with his pack brothers over and over. Ever-victorious in the arena until that last fight when they'd been forced to battle each other. The more civilized parts of his brain worried for his brothers and his mates. He flipped through the air to avoid the guard's blaster pulses. When he'd eliminated that threat, he scanned the area and spotted his next target, a guard working with a remote. Sen followed the man's line of vision and saw several of the green aliens fall to the floor. He went for the guard, with one eye on Fee. She hadn't moved in a long time. The sounds of battle and death were thinning. When he'd taken down the next guard, he barked an alert to tell his brothers he was out of the conflict and headed for Feeona. He crouched over her, listening to her breathing—shallow and fast. "Fee?"

"Busy." Her voice was barely audible and the word came through a locked jaw.

He put a hand on her back to offer his support.

A bark alerted him to Diablo's approach. He looked up to see his brother striding in their direction. Splashes of blood dotted his arms and chest. Behind him Sen could see Mercury, Carn, and Creek aiding the green aliens to their feet. Jupiter was jogging across the room toward them. The battle was over for the moment.

Lo tilted his head and held his ears alert as he watched Fee. "Is the human broken?"

Sen shook his head, but his eyes were on Jupiter. He yipped reassurance to let Jup know their mate was safe.

Jupiter fell to his knees beside her. He brushed her forehead with the back of his hand. His fingers smeared blood across her caramel skin. "Talk to me, Fee."

She turned her head into the caress, but her eyes stayed shut tight. Her jaw flexed, then she spoke through gritted teeth. "Using the security system to lock down the crew and keep out reinforcements."

Mercury and the others came to stand with them. Merc's gravelly voice rumbled in his throat. "Let them come."

Her eyes snapped open and she took in the group. "Oh, my." Her eyes shut tight again. She stretched out a hand and Sen took it. "Explain it to them."

Jupiter worried over the strain in Feeona's face. He'd seen how using Bug and her neural implant could fatigue her before, but there was something else. She was stretching beyond her usual abilities and she'd lost weight since Petro-5. Earlier he'd been too distracted by the glory of seeing her and Sen again to notice her condition.

Seneca wove his fingers with Fee's momentarily and they both seemed to draw strength from it. As he released her and stood, there was no sign of the submissive role Sen had played before as he addressed their Alpha. "I assume you eliminated the security team in the landing bay, but there are at least another dozen guards that were assigned to other areas of the ship. The ship also has a crew of fifty. And we don't know how many of them will defend the ship. This ship carries plenty of arms and any person can pick one up and do damage."

Lo yipped. Mercury nodded and Lo took off toward the landing bay. "My mate and Hera are still in the shuttle with the pilots. Lo will make sure they are safe."

Mercury had a mate and Hera was with them. Jupiter soaked in the wonder of it. Their pack was together and free. They would not be defeated this day.

"Fee will make sure Lo can get back to them," Sen assured them without consulting her. Making it clear they had planned and prepared for their rescue mission together. Their bond had grown strong.

"What *is* she doing?" Carn rumbled the question.

Jupiter answered from where he still knelt at Fee's side. "She has a neural implant that allows her to interface with computers. She's using it to control the ship's security systems."

"Icy!" It was the human hacker that spoke. "So, she was the one controlling that drone earlier. Wha—"

Mercury silenced the man with a look. "Even if the humans fight, a dozen trained men and fifty untrained humans are no match for six Arena Dogs."

There was a swell of noise from the green aliens. Creek waved a hand at them to quiet them down. "And eight Dreats."

Mercury looked at him with raised eyebrows.

"Just telling you what they said. They want to help."

Sen barked respectfully to regain their attention. "There's also a small team of mercenaries, sent by Roma, planting enough explosives around the ship to destroy it. We must have less than thirty minutes now."

Mercury growled in disgust and concern. "Then we warn the ship's occupants and leave now."

The Dreat grunted and muttered. Creek spoke over them. "There are more Dreat in the slave hold." He rolled his shoulders. "And some humans." He shifted his weight looking eager to move. "I can take the Dreat and we can retrieve the slaves."

Mercury frowned. "Is there time?"

"Yes," said Seneca.

Mercury nodded toward Fee. "The female can give them a clear passage to this slave hold?"

Sen answered with another, "yes."

"Good," said Mercury. He hesitated a moment with a look they'd all seen before. Strategy was whirring in his head. "Can we stop the explosions?"

Seneca nodded. "Yes. With Fee's help."

Mercury chuffed a pleased noise in the back of his throat. "The ship will be a good asset in the fight to free our people."

Jupiter's heart skipped. That meant it would also be a good asset for Fee to save her children. He and Seneca helped Fee to a sitting position as she peeled her eyes open. "I need to get to the security station. I can control things much better from there."

"I can help," the hacker chipped in.

Feeona blinked her eyes several times. "Great. With two of us we should be able to use the ship's sensors and intercoms to help our strikers as we go." She managed a smile with those words. Jupiter swelled with pride at his mate's spirit. "Sen," she said. "You'll have to go after Andre's men and the explosives. You know where—"

"Mercury is faster."

Mercury nodded. "I'll go. What else must be done?" He showed no hesitation in relying on Seneca and a human. He led from a place of caring for his pack not from a need to control or reign supreme over them.

"I'm interfering with the bridge crew's actions," said Fee. "As well as I can, but we need someone up there to stop the pilots from engaging the skipdrive."

Sen met Mercury's gaze. "I'm familiar with piloting controls."

"Excellent," said Mercury. "You and Carn go to the pilot station then."

Jupiter could see that Mercury was about to assign him a task. "I'll stay with my mate and the human to make sure they are safe while they work. You can see this work leaves her vulnerable."

Mercury nodded and turned his attention to Creek. "Freeing the slaves is no longer a priority. We can do so after the ship is secure."

The Dreat chattered wildly.

Creek calmly met Mercury's waiting eyes. "The slaves could still be a help in securing the ship."

Their pack leader addressed the aliens. "You seem to understand us well enough."

They chattered with nodding heads.

"Good. And Creek seems to understand you," said Mercury. "Free the slaves and restrain the crew. We don't want them dead unless they resist. Some may be useful in running the ship after we take it. Can you handle that?"

Again, the aliens nodded in unison.

"Understood," said Creek.

Jupiter scooped Feeona up in his arms.

Mercury clamped a hand on Seneca's shoulder. "Can you lead the way to the security station?"

"Yes," Sen answered.

Creek yipped and the Dreat focused all their eye stalks in his direction. "Slave hold is in the opposite direction."

"Wait here then until she clears a path for you. Make sure someone stays here to keep an eye on our new prisoners and the fallen guards. Not all are dead."

"Got it," said Creek.

"Okay," said Mercury. "Let's move."

Feeona snuggled her face into Jupiter's neck as he began to walk. "Feels like old times." Her words whispered against his skin. She felt right in his arms.

"Humph." Jupiter's chest shook softly with a suppressed chuckle. "It is a good thing I never got around to killing you."

CHAPTER THIRTY-TWO

The Abundance
Earth Alliance Beta Sector
2210.190

Jupiter's words were a small thing, but they melted Feeona's heart. Maybe when they went their own ways, he would remember her with affection. She would remember him with a love so deep it would never let her go. His watchful presence was a comfort as she worked with his pack to secure the ship. Even if she suspected he wasn't just there to keep her safe but to make sure she didn't try to steal the ship out from under them. She couldn't blame him. If she thought she could control the enormous ship singlehandedly, she would have considered it.

"Seneca was right. Mercury is fast." She'd been using Bug to work with him to locate the mercenaries and disarm the explosives. Unfortunately, Bug's energy-pack was draining fast with such intense use.

Jupiter grunted in response.

The hacker, whose name was Knock, made a distracted sound of agreement. He wore a headset that covered one ear and positioned a microphone to the side of his mouth. Primitive, but functional. He'd been working with Creek and the freed prisoners to lock down the ship's crew.

She'd been keeping an eye on Seneca, but he and the mountain sized Carn had the bridge under control.

Jupiter moved closer. "Is everything okay?"

He'd picked up her concern over the last bomb and the low power warning flickering in the corner of her vision. "As fast as Mercury is, we won't be able to disable that last bomb if Bug can't make the distance. I don't think I can talk him through a manual disarm."

"Can the ship survive if it explodes?"

"Shit," said Knock. "Did you say bomb and explode?"

Jupiter growled. "Concentrate on your own tasks."

Knock waved his hands in the air. "Yeah, yeah. Okay. Just give me a heads up if we're all going to die."

"The ship can survive, but it would be a rough ride. We might have damage in the landing bay."

Jupiter made a concerned noise. "Mercury and Carn's mates are still in the landing bay."

"And the shuttle pilots." Knock had clearly not stopped listening. "You need a hand?"

"Mercury." Feeona spoke to him through the ship's intercom to conserve Bug's power. "I'm going to land Bug on your shoulder. We're losing power too fast."

She waited for him to nod. There was never a break in his stride.

"If Bug goes dark before you get there, you need to run directly back toward the bridge to get clear of the blast."

Somehow, he managed to pick-up his pace.

It wasn't going to be enough.

The flashing low power warning stopped.

She grabbed Jupiter's arm. "I need to go there."

Without question, he scooped her up and swung her onto his back.

"Knock, warn Mercury." She tossed it over her shoulder as Jupiter launched into motion.

She directed him through the endless taupe corridors from memory, unable to keep her connection with the ship's systems. His feet pounded the floor and his chest rose and fell in a steady rhythm. He was there and he was real... and he'd trusted her again. She wasn't worthy of his trust. She wanted to press her face to his back and soak in his warmth while she still had him in reach.

Instead, she kept her eyes open, concentrated on the reality of the moment, and gave him directions. "Next right."

His ear twitched as her breath brushed it.

They had to make it in time. The goon with the explosives hadn't planted them yet. Maybe the explosives weren't armed. Her breathing accelerated, even as Jupiter's held steady. How long would it take her to disable the bomb without Bug? "I'll find a way," she muttered.

Jupiter made a grunt of agreement. "You always do, my mate."

His mate. The words started an ache in the pit of her belly. She wasn't meant to be his mate. She could never put him first as he deserved. Seneca was the one to do that. But what if Sen had been right about mates being forever? If she'd condemned him to needing her when his heart should belong to Seneca, she wouldn't be able to live with herself.

The long hallways started to blend together. God, she was tired. "Next left. He should be right around the corner."

"I smell him. And Mercury." As he approached the corner, she could hear Mercury and the mercenary fighting. There were no words. Only the heavy thud of blows.

Jupiter swung her off his back and plopped her on the floor. "Stay here until it's clear."

Then he disappeared around the corner as a blaster pulse zipped past. She edged toward the corner, twisted, and peeked around.

Damn. The man had just thrown a second armed drone into the air. Her first instinct was to hack it, but without Bug she'd have to get closer.

If his explosives were armed, time was ticking.

She saw Mercury, his body a blur of motion, dodge another blast.

Jupiter ran toward the fight, kicked off a wall and flipped into the air. He swung out and swatted down one of the drones. Cervenka's man reached out and grabbed Jupiter's leg. They ended up grappling on the floor together and a black bag came off the mercenary's back and slid down the corridor. It was the only storage the man had been carrying.

And the explosives had to be in there.

Feeona belly-crawled along the floor. The sound of the blast pulses was getting closer.

She snatched the bag and scooted back around the corner. She could feel Jupiter's eyes on her, but he didn't or couldn't come to defend her. She was glad of that.

She pulled open the bag and her heart sank. The bomb was armed and had more explosive power than any of the others. Damn. She lifted it carefully out of the bag and examined the mechanism. Damn. Damn. Damn. *That* was different, too. She closed her eyes and, using just her neural implant, tried a near-field hack.

Oh, God. She couldn't even connect.

She looked up and down the hall for something, anything she could use to keep the thing from killing them. A bomb-proof lock box would be handy.

She struggled to her feet. "Knock." She knew he'd be monitoring. "Patch me through to Sen."

A brief pause, then Sen's voice. "Fee, what's wrong?"

"I can't disarm the bomb. The only thing I can think to do is to get it as far away from Jupiter and Mercury as I can." She didn't know what else to say. She'd just wanted… So many times they'd complained that she hid her plans from them.

She took one last look toward Jupiter. The last remaining drone had Jupiter and Mercury penned down. It had to be running on AI without a kill switch command, because the mercenary was very dead. They were using his body as a shield. They were going to be okay. She had to believe that they would be fine, if she could just get them clear of the explosion.

She got to her feet and ran.

"Fee!" It was Seneca. "There's an emergency airlock, not far. Will that work?"

"Yes!" She'd even headed the right direction on instinct or luck. Hope renewed her strength and added speed to her pace. Her lungs burned.

The hatch came into view and she pushed harder, faster. She slammed into the wall next to it, panting for air. She grabbed the manual emergency access ring, turned, and pushed.

Nothing happened. A wave of nausea hit her. That shouldn't be possible. It was an emergency airlock. They were never shut down.

Eyes fixed on the red glowing light over the sealed interior doors, she initiated a hack. The interior hatch opened, giving her access to the airlock itself.

She could see the blackness of space through the small porthole in the exterior door. Sliding the bomb carefully into the lock, she looked for a way to reclose the door just short of a seal. She wanted enough air to be able to escape to push the bomb far out into the black.

The mental equivalent of tripping over a wire shook her. A rush of panic squeezed her heart. "Knock! Something just happened. I'm locked out of the airlock controls." How could she not have seen something like that in any of her data on the security systems? "Knock!"

"Looking!"

He had to find it and shut it down. "It has to be some kind of master override implemented recently."

"Shit." Knock's voice wavered. "I haven't even dug into the part of the system that deals with airlocks."

Over the rush of her pulse pounding in her ears, she heard Jupiter calling her. They'd dealt with the drone. That was good.

No! Not good. "Knock, keep Jupiter and Mercury away from here."

"I can't do two things at once."

"Do it." She shouted it to make it absolutely clear. A gut-wrenching snap and another then cursing signaled the Arena Dogs slamming into a security field.

"Fee." Seneca was still looped in and he sounded blessedly calm. "You have to let Jupiter help you."

Nothing could happen to Jupiter. She couldn't live with that. "Knock?"

"Nothing yet." Panic filled his voice.

How much time had there been left on the bomb? "Knock, lock off this corridor with the safety system."

"But, I—"

"This! Do this." If the bomb exploded it would minimize damage to the ship.

"Feeona!" Jupiter sounded furious.

"Fee!" Seneca's voice boomed through the intercom. "Don't you die on me. I'm coming to you, now."

Jupiter and Seneca shouted again but this time they were threatening Knock if he didn't let them through. No! Her mind screamed it. But she had to set it aside and trust Knock to keep them safe.

Fee stepped into the airlock, dropped to her knees, and pulled off an access panel to the plasti-sealant conduits. The essential material was right there, running through transparent tubing, in easy reaching distance. Poor design.

Pulling one of the alloy styling pins from her hair, she grabbed the nearest safety handle with her other hand. She worked her arm under and wrapped it around the bar.

"Knock," she had to concentrate to keep her voice steady. "If Jupiter and Mercury aren't behind a sealed door, tell them to hang on to something."

They were strong. They would be okay.

She crouched down, took a deep breath, and smashed the pin through the conduit.

Jupiter slid into her, slamming her body against the bulkhead. "Fee?"

"No time. Hold on."

The whoosh of air registered first. Then pain. It was so big it filled her mind. It took her a second to remember why she was clinging to the side of an emergency hatch. After the powerful jerk on her body, she was definitely feeling the emergency. She felt it in her shoulder and where Jupiter's arm wrapped around her waist like an alloy safety band. He shouldn't be there. I didn't want you to die, big guy. She wanted to tell him, but she had no air to speak. The sound of it venting into the vacuum of space screamed in her ears. It felt as if an enormous hand had reached in and was trying to rip her out of the ship.

Light began to bleed out of the corners of her vision. She let her chin fall to her chest and watched her feet swing above space. Her boots were gone—what an odd thing.

There was no way to close those external doors.

Jupiter's heat was a beacon, the only warmth in the cold, cold airlock. He should let her go. With his strength he might be able to climb free.

Vibrations rippled through the ship. The bomb.

Jupiter pulled at her body, pressed her back against the bulkhead and covered her mouth with his. He breathed into her mouth and she sucked the small traces of oxygen into her lungs. She lost track of time. She had a sense of movement, of things happening around her, and then she slipped away.

Jupiter paced in the *Abundance's* med-bay. It was a large room with beds for several patients at once. He thought he'd lost her— Fee. She lay in an aftercare bed, curled on her side, blue cushions under her head, supporting her back, and keeping her arm and shoulder comfortably aligned. The bed was wider than a typical med-bed and he wanted to crawl into it with her. He would have if Mercury's small, lively mate wasn't sitting on the side of the bed. Her name was Samantha, and she'd been brought there to supervise Morgan's medics, whose allegiance was uncertain. When they'd found no damage except Fee's dislocated shoulder and bruises, he'd taken over the task of moving her bones back into place. It seemed right. After all, she'd taken care of his injuries back on the *Salley Ho*.

Six weeks. It had been six weeks since he'd woken up on the resistance ship. Six weeks since he'd first seen her. When she'd slipped into unconsciousness in that airlock, he'd feared she was gone. As his brothers worked to drag them past the interior hatch so Knock could shut it, he'd shared the oxygen his lungs were so efficient at using and conserving. Then he'd had to stop and help get them clear.

Seneca appeared in front of him. He'd been leaning against the wall, watching him pace. A gentle anger had dominated his expression since they'd gotten Fee to the med-bay. "We are fortunate she is so strong."

"Yes, but I would rather she did not risk her life so readily."

A muscle in Sen's jaw twitched. "If we're to keep our mate safe, you'll have to accept that she will always risk herself." There was censure in his tone.

This was a side of him Jupiter had rarely seen. It confused him coming from the sensual, painted Sen. "Were you nude when she painted that dog on your chest?"

Sen didn't blink. "Yes."

Jupiter humphed for lack of a better response. He flicked his ears forward, studying Sen closely. "You said *our* mate."

"I did." Sen pressed his lips together in an unyielding line.

"Good." His instincts and his body liked the certainty in his mate's voice.

Sen's eyes widened. "Samantha, can you watch over Feeona while she sleeps? Jupiter and I need to talk."

The female brushed a lock of hair from Fee's shoulder. "Of course. She'll be safe with me."

And Lo would be watching over Samantha. He currently

stood watch in the hallway. He seemed glued to the woman's side.

The moment Sen had his answer, he strode to the door. He looked over his shoulder, spearing Jupiter with his exotic eyes. "Follow me."

CHAPTER THIRTY-THREE

The Abundance
Earth Alliance Beta Sector
2210.190

The room Seneca led Jupiter to was just down the hall and barely the size of the cell he'd shared with Feeona on the *Salley Ho*. Its dominant features were pale blue walls and a bed similar to the aftercare bed in the med-bay.

"Feeona." Worry pulled her name from his lips.

Seneca grabbed his arm and pulled him around so they were chest to chest. "Feeona is alive and safe and getting the rest she needs. Right now, you need to deal with me."

Jupiter wanted nothing more than to *deal* with him. Waiting for a lecture or some as yet unexplained source of Sen's anger, his eyes devoured his sensual mate. Seneca and Feeona. Funny how needing one did nothing to lessen his need for the other. He must have stood staring too long at Sen's sleek muscles and the damn dog leaping across his chest. Seneca shoved two hands against his own unpainted chest hard enough to send him flying. He landed hard on his back. Good thing the bed occupied most of the floor space. He was sprawled across it with Seneca crawling up his body.

Jupiter's cock hardened in an instant.

"I'm tired of waiting." Sen spoke through a low growl that stroked along his skin. Seneca slid a hand down Jupiter's torso, ending cupped around the part of him he wanted to shove inside Sen. But the need to go carefully won out. The only thing that had kept them apart all these years was his soul deep need not to hurt Sen. Something he wasn't going to be able to avoid, unless he got Sen's hand off his cock. Now.

He grabbed Sen and rolled, putting the smaller Dog beneath him. He pushed up to get some space between them. Sen struggled. Jupiter caught his wrists and pinned them over Sen's head. The memory of the day they'd struggled in Feeona's gym almost stopped him. Sen had been desperate to get away from him that day.

Jupiter looked down at the Dog he was ready to claim as mate. Sen still struggled, twisting and trying to tug his hands free. This time there was no fear in his face. His movements seemed designed to brush against Jupiter as much as to break free. Sen's struggles stroked Jupiter's need to dominate, to claim. He threw back his head and howled. Sen's howl answered, ripping Jupiter's attention back to Sen's lavender eyes and soft lips. He didn't see fear, only frustration.

Jupiter leaned down to press his forehead against Sen's and he chuffed softly in the back of his throat. "Tell me what you want, my mate."

Sen's body stilled. His panting breath brushed against Jupiter's ear. "Touch me." He hissed through clenched teeth. "Oh, God. Please touch me, Jup." Sen's back arched as if to prove his need to be closer to his body. Sen angled his head and nipped at his lips. "I've waited so long."

Jupiter could no longer resist. He thrust his tongue into Sen's mouth and stroked. Sen did not lay passive. He dueled with Jupiter, their tongues battled and tasted and made love. Sen tasted spicy-sweet. Jupiter wanted to know if Seneca's skin would taste the same.

I've waited so long. That's what Sen had said. The memory of Sen's rough tongue against his skin when the younger Dog had lain weak and dehydrated flashed through Jupiter. It magnified all his senses and rewired his brain, turning every casual touch they'd ever shared into something full of promise.

He dipped down to lick along the cords of Sen's neck, following them to his chest.

"Yes." Sen moaned softly as he turned his head, baring his throat to give Jup more access. What was a gesture of submission among Dogs became a sensual promise of trust. Sen was his. Jupiter's heart pounded. He was Sen's, too. They were mates.

Jupiter lowered his body onto Sen. All their bare skin, sharp edges, and hard muscles pressed together in a sensation that was pure sex. Sen wrapped his legs around Jupiter's thighs and adjusted his hips. The movement settled their cocks together in a pressure that was so good it was almost pain. Sen thrust his hips up and Jupiter's eyes rolled back in their sockets. The sensation, the pleasure, the need it created—they drove him mad. On instinct he scraped his teeth against Sen's shoulder. His mate whimpered sexily, but his thrusts didn't stop.

Jupiter released Sen's wrists and the smaller Dog immediately shoved him, rolling them across the bunk until their positions were reversed. Sen positioned their hips perfectly to keep that delicious pressure where they both wanted it. Sen's tongue and hands stroked over Jupiter's body. Tracing his scars and squeezing his muscles.

Sen's hips kept up a continuous motion and Jupiter joined in, finding a rhythm that distracted Sen's wandering tongue and held them both slave to sensation. "Jupiter," he moaned against his neck. "Love you. Love you, so much."

"Yes." Jupiter had loved Sen forever. He'd known Sen loved him, but not like this. Hearing it from Sen in that sexual, needy moan sent shivers along his spine and made his heart expand in his chest.

He stroked his hands down Sen's ribs and reached around to slide his fingers under the fabric of his costume. He squeezed Sen's ass and reveled in his answering groan.

He had just discovered he could urge Sen and guide his movements in a pace that dragged their cocks together in just the right way when Sen pulled back and rolled away.

Leaning up on his elbows, Jupiter watched Sen rip his costume off until he was bare. He was back over Jupiter in a flash of motion and he pulled and pushed at Jupiter's costume until his cock sprang free and into Sen's hands.

The sensation was exciting but brief. Sen quickly released him. Jupiter pulled his eyes away from the sight of their cocks jutting so close together to raise his eyebrows at Sen. "What?"

"Can I... touch you?"

Jupiter grinned and threw himself back, arms wide. "I am yours, Sen. Do what you will."

The feel of not only Seneca's hands but also his cock pressed up against his own startled him, tensing his muscles. Seneca had his hand wrapped around both their straining organs and he stroked them both up and down. It went on and on until he thought he might die of the pleasure. Sen's moans and whimpers played a chorus in his ears. When he couldn't take it anymore, he wrapped his hand around Sen's and urged a faster pace.

His heart raced. His throat dried from panting. His spine

tingled and his balls drew tight. "My mate," he muttered. "Cum with me."

Sen was panting when he tried to speak, but the words seemed to break in his mouth and then they both came. And came. Hot, wet, cum coated their bellies, the sticky sensation unreasonably erotic as their hands slipped away leaving nothing between them.

He wrapped his arms around his mate. "I'm sorry it took me so long to see, Sen."

The curve of Sen's lips brushed against his shoulder. "I love you, Jup."

"I love you," he answered back, lethargy seeping into his muscles.

Sen pressed a kiss to his throat. "That's all that ever mattered."

They laid silent so long, Jupiter thought Sen had fallen asleep. He knew that wasn't the case when Sen gripped him tighter. "She'll leave unless you stop her."

Jupiter sighed. "She'll try to steal the ship or something else of value first."

He expected a chuckle from Sen, but there was no humor in Sen's tense body. He leaned back so he could see Sen's face. There was real worry there.

"Our mate has needs," said Sen. "She NEEDS to aid the children of her world. That's why she betrayed us. Her past drives her beyond the needs of her heart."

Jupiter stroked a hand along Sen's cheek. Truth be told, Sen had spent more time with their mate than he had. He would know better what drove her. "I saw the factory on her world. I saw the dead children dumped in a pit there. I will not soon forget the moment she chose to trade me away rather than trust me."

"She—"

Jupiter silenced him with a finger to his lips. "I understand why she did it." He took a deep breath and let his gaze drift to the ceiling. "We will figure something out… with *our* mate. She let us in, with the bomb. We will teach her that we can be unbeatable as a pack so she will never make another decision without us."

"She called for me. It was progress for her." Sen rested a hand over Jupiter's heart. "If she chooses to leave, I'll go with her."

Sen's words surprised him, but he felt no anger over them.

Jupiter chuffed softly. "As will I."

Whatever good or bad Feeona had done, she'd shown his Sen another side of his strength. Strength of the heart. For that, and for so much else, Jupiter would always love her.

CHAPTER THIRTY-FOUR

The Abundance
Earth Alliance Beta Sector
2210.191

Feeona woke in an unfamiliar bed. Unfamiliar but comfortable. A beautiful pixie with brown-gold hair and a friendly smile stood over her.

"How are you feeling?"

Fee started to sit up, but cushions had been wedged around her arm to immobilize it.

"Oh, let me help you with that." The woman gently moved the cushions away. "There is a sling for you. You should wear it for a day or two."

As Fee managed to sit straight and swing her legs over the edge of the bed, she realized she really didn't feel too bad. "Thanks. I think I'm going to live." She still wore the velvet outfit that really didn't look sexy anymore. "I could use a change of clothes."

The woman turned and lifted a set of Fee's clothes from a table and laid them on the bed next to her. "Seneca picked them out." She indicated the floor. "He brought shoes, too. And this." The woman pushed Jacky the Unicorn into her arms.

Feeona smiled through the rush of happy tears. "I didn't think he knew about Jacky."

The woman shrugged, but she seemed happy with the effect Seneca's thoughtfulness had on her. "I'm Samantha."

"Mercury's mate," she guessed, squeezing Jacky tight.

"That's right." She smiled and the skin across her collar bones flushed golden.

"Pleased to meet you. I'm Feeona."

"Yes, I know. And I hate to rush you, but the rest of the pack is waiting for us. Would you like me to step out while you change?"

Feeona slipped off the edge of the bed. Her legs seemed to hold under her. The floor was cold beneath her bare feet. "Suit yourself. I'm not shy." And she didn't want to put Samantha in an awkward position if they'd told her not to leave her alone.

"I used to be," mumbled Samantha mysteriously.

Five minutes later they were striding into what she hoped wouldn't be a firing squad. Lo followed them. He'd been waiting in the hall outside the med-bay. Strangely, she knew who all of the Dogs were—had even worked with them in a life or death situation—but she didn't really know anything about them at all.

The room turned out to be a large mess hall. Dozens of circular tables were scattered around with some pretty comfortable looking chairs. The walls and ceilings were decorated with tasteful art. At least Morgan had used some of his success to take care of his crew. The smell of recently cooked steaks made her mouth water and her stomach rumble.

The Dogs were clustered around the nearest table, but on their feet, not sitting.

Seneca broke away and came to meet her. He stopped so close in front of her they were breathing the same air. His lavender eyes were enormous. Then he reached for her, pulling her into his arms. Lips against her ear, he whispered. "It's going to be okay."

He released her and escorted her to the rest of his pack. She only had eyes for Jupiter. His big body blocked everything, everyone from her sight. She resisted the urge to fold her arms around her like armor, as if she could protect herself from the pain his words could inflict. She'd worn the damn sling, but her shoulder was already starting to ache from the tension in her muscles.

Jupiter stepped closer and she had to look up to meet his gaze.

"So." The worry inside her stretched so tight she thought she would break. "If you wanted to kill me, that whole emergency hatch, bomb thing would have been a good time." She managed to lift one side of her mouth in a semblance of a grin.

His expression never wavered as he shook his head and held her gaze. "I can't kill you now. That would be like slicing off a chunk of my soul."

Feeona's heart stopped… then beat like the wings of a hoverbird.

His arms opened and she leaned into him. As he folded her into him, she pressed her ear against his chest and listened to the solid thud of his big heart.

"When I saw you running with that bomb, I feared I'd lost you." Jupiter's chest rumbled as he spoke in that deep bass of his. His hand brushed gently up and down her back.

She clutched him tighter. "I'm sorry. For everything. For Petro-5. I should have found a better way."

He loosened his hold on her and tugged on her hair until she looked up at him. "We're mates. You're not alone anymore. We figure out what to do together from now on."

Seneca stepped up beside her and she was surrounded by them. "We're mates," he repeated.

The joy and the sorrow almost knocked her to her knees. To have everything she wanted offered and to be unable to accept. Her pulse raced. Her muscles tensed. She needed to get out of there. She needed to run. "I can't. I... You deserve more than I can give."

"We won't let you go, Fee." Seneca's rich baritone stroked her insides. "We would never expect you to abandon the children of your world."

"But... Your people—"

Jupiter put his fingers under her chin and his claws pricked gently against her skin. "We will work it out."

"Your pack—"

"Would never stand in the way of mates." The source of that voice stood nearby. Mercury, their leader had tucked an arm around Samantha. Lo stood on the other side of her. Midnight black hair in a silken curtain brushed their shoulders. Alert ears flicked as she took them in. Lo was all dark brooding good looks with reddish black eyes. Mercury was almost as big as Jupiter, but not as beautiful as Seneca. He released Samantha and stepped forward with a smile. "We haven't been properly introduced. I am Mercury. Welcome to our pack."

"Thanks, but—"

Mercury laughed, a sexy rumble that rolled through the room. "Stubborn." He lifted his gaze to Jupiter. "You are blessed my brothers. A stubborn mate can bring great joy to your life."

"We are well aware," agreed Jupiter.

Mercury nodded then returned his attention to Feeona. "Jupiter and Seneca have told me about your world. Cruelty, it seems, is not limited to Roma."

She'd seen far too much cruelty in every corner of the sector. "No. It isn't, but there is also kindness everywhere."

Over her shoulder, Jupiter muttered. "Optimist."

"Thank you for that reminder, my sister." Mercury leaned back and rubbed at his neck. "Nevertheless, it seems we have much work ahead of us. Both our people need us."

"No matter what I do," she said. "It never feels like enough."

"I understand the weight of your burden. This I know," Mercury met her gaze directly. "Together we are stronger. Together we will do more than we could do apart. Together we will find a way to free them all."

They each understood the burden and they each needed to do more. It was a solid foundation for an alliance.

They all closed in around her. That's when she realized Creek and Knock were missing, but she supposed someone had to be minding the ship.

Mercury barked loud and strong. "Together we will free your people and mine. We will do what it takes or die. As Arena Dogs."

CHAPTER THIRTY-FIVE

The Hawley
Earth Alliance Beta Sector
2210.193

They'd all been working non-stop for several days. Feeona liked them all. It felt good to be part of a team and she hadn't seen any sign of mistrust from any of them. It surprised her and made her want to be worthy of that trust.

They'd put her in charge of handling the auction guests they'd captured on that first day on the *Abundance*. The fact that they'd all been there to buy slaves won them no friends among the Dogs. She'd released them all… after extorting as much treasure as she could from each of them. If they were going to war on two fronts, they would need all the funds they could get. The Dogs saw the logic of that.

Samantha, with the help of the human pilots that had been traveling with her, had taken charge of the *Abundance* and its crew. In addition to being a pilot herself, Samantha seemed to understand how a big ship ran. Which staff was essential and which were not. The Dogs had helped her screen the crew and decide who could be trusted. The rest were being put off at the closest port they could reach.

Tonight, though, she and Seneca and Jupiter were back on the Hawley. Home. And heading back to the Agrove Colony. They were visiting or picking up Toby—his choice—before they rendezvoused with the others at the resistance base. They were safely in skipspace and would be for another thirty-six hours.

Feeona wrapped her arms around Jupiter's neck as he carried her up the stairs to her room... their room. She liked the sound of that. Unlike weeks ago when they first met, this time Seneca led the way. He had the door open and a shower already running when Jupiter set her on her feet. She reached out and pressed her hand over his heart. His heartbeat was strong and steady. Hers was weak with want. She wanted them both every moment. "Can you have truly forgiven me?"

"There was nothing to forgive." He lifted her tunic and pulled it up over her head and off.

"Fucking would be a good way to move past it," Seneca volunteered with a snicker.

She mock-scowled at him over her shoulder. "You just want sex."

His slender white eyebrows lifted. "Doesn't everyone?" He chuckled and they all joined in.

But she couldn't let it go. When their laughter quieted and the steam from the shower warmed the room, leaving a fine layer of moisture on her skin, she framed Jupiter's face with her hands. "You can't mean that. It can't be that easy to forget what I did."

Jupiter wrapped his big palms around her ribs, just below her breasts. "I respect your need to keep your obligations to the children. And through it all, you did the best you could to keep us safe."

Seneca came up behind her and slipped his arms around her. His hands moved to the fastening of her pants. "But you're our mate now." He nipped her ear before pulling her pants and briefs down her legs. His hands caressed her thighs as he straightened and pressed his naked skin against hers. "From now on, no secrets. We work as a team."

Jupiter, whose hot gaze had been following Seneca's movements as he undressed her, moved his hands up to cup her breasts. His thumbs flicked against her nipples. They hardened and Sen's cock hardened against her hip.

Sen's lips pressed close to her ear. "You want to let him undress while we get started showering or do you want to watch me undress him?"

An uncontrollable smile spread across her face. Her cheeks were impossibly tight with happiness.

Sen's chest vibrated with mirth against her back. "I think she is speechless with anticipation."

"Of course, I am," she answered.

Jupiter smirked. "Enough talk, time to clean up." With that, he made the decision for them, stripping himself with efficient motions.

Seneca drew her under the water. The warm spray soaked them and she had to rub the water out of her eyes to see them.

Jupiter. Despite his growly attitude when they'd met, he'd effortlessly slipped past her defenses and into her heart. His hard, sculpted body had surprisingly little to do with it. It was just a bonus. One hell of a bonus. As Seneca fingered shampoo into her hair, she watched Jupiter move toward her. Wide shoulders tapered to defined abdominals. Deep grooves ran from his hip bones down to frame the perfect representation of his masculinity.

She reached for him and he filled her grip. The distance between the base and tip of his cock was a long, slow stroke. She brushed the veins along his length with her fingertips and palmed the head of him. His moan of appreciation drew her gaze up to his. She wanted to press kisses to his cheekbones and tongue that little indention at the base of his throat. That would have to wait for later when he was lying down and she could actually reach him.

He brushed a thumb over her cheek. "What are you thinking, Fee?"

"I'm not sure you can call it thinking." Both males chuckled. She ignored that and let her fingers tease the slit at the top of Jupiter's cock. He stopped laughing and his breathing quickened. She loved seeing him this way, warm and open and aroused. "My head is playing out all the ways I want to make love to you," she told him.

Behind her, Seneca stroked cleansing gel along her spine and down her ass. "There is all the time in the world, now that we're together."

"Yeah." She sighed dreamily. "Time for everything."

Seneca um-hmmed approvingly as he wrapped his hand over hers on Jup's cock.

Jupiter choked. "Wash her faster." He captured her mouth nibbling at her lips until she stepped against him, pressing her nipples against the hard wall of his chest. Seneca went back to soaping her, his motions brisk until he'd washed all the ordinary parts of her. When there was nothing else left and Jupiter had switched to offering Feeona deep, tongue-thrusting kisses, Sen stroked cleansing gel between her legs. His fingers stroked her feminine folds and teased her clit. She moaned into Jupiter's mouth. The big Dog lifted her and pulled her legs around his hips. The position opened her more to Sen's exploring fingers and he pressed the advantage. He pushed his fingers deep inside the place that had been so empty without them.

Struggling to pull enough air into her lungs to keep up with her racing heart, she pulled away from Jupiter's kiss. He looked set to complain, then she felt the withdrawal and brush of Seneca's hand between her legs. Jupiter grunted and shifted his stance to give Sen room to fondle his balls. It had to be that, Feeona realized with a surge of arousal, because there was no space between Jupiter's cock and her belly. She luxuriated in being with them again. Together, but differently than before.

Seneca stepped back. "Let me rinse her." He pulled her out of Jupiter's arms and set her squarely under the spray. She sputtered and punched his shoulder. "Ass."

His grin met her curse. "Is that an invitation or a request?"

When Seneca had thoroughly washed away the soap from Feeona's flesh, Jupiter took control once again, guiding her from beneath the water and beyond its reach, where he wrapped one of the big, soft towels around her. When he seemed satisfied that she was adequately dry, he ducked back beneath the spray with Sen. They washed quickly—such a missed opportunity that Feeona frowned as she watched them. Her gaze on them only seemed to quicken their quest to finish their shower.

Still, she enjoyed the brief peep show. She enjoyed seeing them so comfortable with each other. They might not be touching purposefully, but they weren't avoiding it either. And they looked... lighter. They moved as if no weight held them down or tired them. Their eyes sparkled and they smiled easily.

She pressed her fingers to her cheek. The wide grin she wore seemed there to stay. She didn't deserve them, but she was going to keep them. She was theirs and they were hers.

When they shut off the spray, she handed them towels. Sen practically bounced over to her shelves and started digging through her things.

"Thank God." He waved a tube of lubricant in the air.

Her mouth dropped open. She hadn't realized he knew she had it. Jupiter was arching an eyebrow at her. She ignored him and frowned at Sen.

He laughed and tossed the tube to Jupiter, then bounced back over to Feeona, took her hand and tugged her toward the bed. "I love this bed. So roomy."

Jupiter followed to lift her damp hair off her shoulders and towel away some of the water clinging to the heavy curls. "It's like you were destined to have two mates."

"Ha!" She laughed. "Roland just believed in comfort. That's all."

"Maybe. His bed is equal in size." Sen hopped onto the mattress and urged her on as well. "Or maybe he also enjoyed more than one lover at a time."

Feeona covered her ears. "I'm not listening to that. That isn't a picture I need in my head right now."

Sen took advantage of her hands being busy to guide her down to the mattress where he wanted her. He positioned himself above her head on the bed and she tipped her head back to frown her confusion.

"Jupiter's first."

Jupiter caught her hands in his and pressed them to his ribs. "I want your touch, Fee."

When she stroked her palms over his skin, he slowly lowered himself down to her and she opened her legs for him. The weight and heat of him comforted her even as all the nerve endings in her body sparked back to life. He stroked a hand down to her belly then took hold of himself, as if ready to guide himself into her.

"Foreplay, Jup," Sen scolded from the top of the bed. "For fuck's sake, you can't just—"

And then Jupiter did. He filled her smoothly, stroking every pleasure point. He pressed kisses to her face as he held himself motionless inside her. "She is always ready for me. Isn't that right, Fee?"

She gave him a halfhearted scowl, but when he moved his hips, sliding his cock slowly out then in again, she broke. She had to admit it. "Yes," she panted. "That's right."

Jupiter palmed her breast, squeezed it gently before lightly pinching her nipple. She couldn't stop the moan rising in her throat as she arched her back in a plea for more.

She reached a hand back, blindly searching for Sen. "You don't...have...to..." Jupiter was dragging in and out of her with that same slow roll of his hips. She found it difficult to keep a thought in her head.

Sen squeezed her hand. "Don't worry, Fee. I'll get my turn."

"Sounds..." Her voice trembled. "Like you h-have a plan."

"Enough talk." Jupiter pressed down harder against her and changed the position of his hip so that his cock pulled across her clit with each stroke. He kissed her over and over until she thought she'd go mad. Then he lifted his mouth from hers just barely, his quickened breaths rushing with hers. "Now, you may say things like *more, Jupiter* and *harder, Jupiter.*"

"Arrogant," she whispered. No way would he put words in her mouth.

He wrapped his arms around her, snugged their bodies tight together, and thrust harder. Her breath escaped in a huff. The next time she was prepared and she met him with equal passion, wrapping her legs around him and digging her feet into his calves, leaving herself completely opened to him.

Her heart raced, her body became a raw nerve and she craved everything he could give her. "Harder," she begged. "Deeper."

"I've missed you, Fee." His lips were close to hers and he was panting, too.

He thrust even harder. She screamed as pleasure exploded inside her. Trembling, Jupiter went still and held himself deep within her. His piercing gaze sought and held hers. "You feel so good squeezing my cock. I love you, my mate."

Her eyelids were so heavy, her pleasure-drunk mind tripping on the edge of consciousness, she couldn't form a response. But his easy, soulful words nestled inside her, putting her world to rights.

Still painfully hard, Jupiter pulled out of Feeona and moved to lie beside her. She managed a groan of complaint at his departure, but then Sen was between her legs, pressing kisses to her thighs. Jupiter's heart raced as he lifted himself onto an elbow to watch Sen gently open her folds and blow across her sensitized flesh. Somehow it made him shiver.

"So pretty and pink," Sen praised.

Jupiter could only watch. His throat went dry, his breath quickening with anticipation as Sen flicked his tongue lightly along Fee's swollen flesh then moved to press kisses on the ticklish skin below her belly button. Her stomach jumped. Her muscles twitched. This was the foreplay Sen claimed was so important. Jupiter could see the benefit.

He stroked Fee's arm and urged her hand closer to his complaining cock. She happily obliged, circling him with lazy strokes. He rewarded her efforts with his own gentle caresses across her collarbone, her breasts, the pulse point on her neck.

He wanted to touch every centimeter of her.

Seneca's graceful body bowed as he slid lower, pressing his belly and hips to the mattress as he returned to her folds, pressing kisses there. Polite, closed lip kisses at first. Then nibbling, licking, sucking kisses that made her arch and squirm. Watching Sen using his lips on her female flesh was almost more erotic than Jupiter could bear. He couldn't resist the urge to wrap his hand around his cock and stroke as she writhed under Seneca's attentions. A few mindless strokes and he was on the edge of coming when Sen pressed his tongue against Feeona's clit. She clutched at his hair with her free hand. "Sen, you're killing me."

"Cum for me, Fee." Sen gave her a boyish grin. "Cum for me, then I get mine."

Despite the humor, his tone was demanding. Something Jupiter had only recently heard from the younger Dog.

Sen's tongue stroked directly over her clit and circled as he slipped two fingers inside her. The moment he touched her exactly where and how she needed it, she flew apart all over again. This time they gave her no time to recover. Sen was up and over her in a heartbeat, his cock pushing inside her. He held himself still and kissed her as if he would never get enough of her tongue and her taste and her love. It was the same for him, Jupiter thought. He would never have enough of either of his mates.

The moment he rose on his knees behind Sen, the other Dog stopped kissing Fee and glanced over his shoulder to catch Jupiter's gaze. His breath was coming so fast, for a moment it almost seemed like fear. But when Jupiter gently set a hand on Sen's hip, seeking permission, Sen's eyes darkened to a deep purple. There was tension in Sen's tightly muscled ass and legs, but that, he knew, was arousal. Jupiter's heart soared as Sen shifted and let his head drop to Fee's, leaving Jupiter to seek his pleasure.

Jupiter found the lube and coated his fingers, then shifted closer to stroke the pink skin around Sen's opening. The younger Dog was breathing harder, his chest expanding with each labored breath. Fee's arms went around Sen, drawing him down to cradle his head against her breasts. Her eyes were open as she stroked his silken white hair and met Jupiter's gaze. Trust and pleasure and love drifted together in her mysterious brown eyes.

She smiled and mouthed the word "foreplay."

Jupiter's heart skipped with love for her. For her and for the magnificent Dog between them. Sen had told Jupiter about the importance of readying him. Jupiter had even let Sen dull some of his claws with a file for this. Focus and control would be important here. He slipped a single finger inside the tight heat of Sen's body. There was a clench of protest, then Sen's muscles eased and his back arched, tilting his ass higher for Jupiter. After a few strokes, carefully, he added a second finger. He worked his fingers gently, beckoning pleasure, until Sen began to squirm.

Feeona moaned as Sen moved inside her.

Sen pressed back on Jupiter's probing caress. "Please," he begged. His voice sounded quavering and needy and maybe a little afraid.

Jupiter wrapped his hand around his cock and nudged the entrance to Sen's body.

Sen hissed and Jupiter pulled back.

He settled a hand on his mate's back. "Are you okay?"

"Yes." Sen muttered the word against Fee's skin.

Jupiter applied more lube to his fingers and pressed against his opening again, but it was closed tighter than before. Sen moaned and drove his hips forward, pushing deeper into Feeona.

She gasped, but her face told Jupiter it wasn't a bad thing. She was probably still over-stimulated from their earlier love play. Sen's cock had to feel good inside her.

Jupiter clasped Sen's hip tight. Love and lust and too much thinking warred in his head. He released his grasp only to stroke Sen's spine. With care, he soothed his mate with touches and chuffing noises until his body eased and he squirmed against Fee.

It was the first time Sen hadn't seemed confident about sex since they'd started. "Talk to me, Sen. You know all you have to do is say the word, and everything stops."

Sen groaned again, but a different sound. Frustration. "No. Don't stop. I want this. I want you. I'm not thinking about the past. I'm not afraid you'll hurt me. I know you won't hurt me."

But Jupiter could hurt him, he knew. Sen had told him much about this type of loving. He leaned over and pressed his lips against Sen's back. "If you want more, tell me. If you don't, you can tell me that, too."

Sen pushed up on his forearms, but his eyes were on Fee. He cupped her cheek. "Sorry, love. This isn't the way I envisioned things going."

She laced her fingers with his. "It's perfect, because it's us."

Jupiter wrapped his arms around Sen. Fuck, he loved his mates.

Sen leaned back into the embrace, wrapping his arms over Jupiter's. "You know you don't have to do this, right, Jup?" He sounded so solemn. "I don't need this. I don't need anything more than you have to give."

The words shocked Jupiter. Did Sen think *he* didn't want the physical side of their love? He tightened his arms around the Dog that was so much a part of him. "Think, Sen. You know I'm not doing anything here that I don't want. I love you. And I want you. I've always wanted you."

Sen's answer was slow in coming. "But if you don't, it's okay. I just need you to know that."

Jupiter gave in to a chuckle. "Says the Dog who's been whispering in my ear about how good this is going to be."

Sen looked over his shoulder, meeting Jupiter eyes. "Good for me." He grinned shakily.

Feeona was still holding his hand. Her eyes were on Sen, watching, making sure he really was okay. Together. They would get through this together. Jupiter guided Sen back down to Fee. She wrapped her arms around him, still cradling him inside her.

This time when Jupiter lubed his fingers and stroked Sen's ass, everything was different. He teased Seneca playfully and met far less resistance. He moaned, but it was a good sound and he flexed and moved against Jupiter's touch. Below them, Feeona moaned with him.

"Enough. I'm ready, Jup." Seneca sounded more confident, more eager.

Jupiter pressed his lubed cock at Sen's entrance. "I think this is the time for that deep breath you talked about."

Sen dragged in a lungful of air and Jupiter pressed forward. Sen's ass resisted for a moment, but he drove steadily on.

Sen shook beneath him. "Fuck. Fuck. Fuck. Don't stop. It just stings like a…"

And then Jupiter was through the tight ring and swearing a few of his own choice words. Despite all the effort he'd put into relaxing and loosening Sen, the other male was tight beyond imagining.

Emotion and sensation screamed through Jupiter. The tight stroke along his cock, the endorphins of muscular exertion as his body moved against Sen, the scent of his mates surrounding him.

"So, good, Sen," he growled. "You feel so fucking good."

He fucked harder, faster, and Sen rewarded him with moans and whispered pleas to never stop, his hips moving in counterpoint to Jupiter's. Beneath him, Fee's eyes were fluttering with pleasure, her chin up, the tendons in her neck tight. She was more than with them for the ride. She was a part of it, a part of them.

Jupiter loved everything about fucking Sen. He loved everything about having both his mates beneath him. He wanted more. He wanted to take them in every way possible. He wanted to surrender himself to them in just as many. There would be time. They would have time for everything.

His balls slapped against Sen's ass until they tightened too much to move. A tingle formed at the base of his spine and he thrust harder, deeper.

Sen cried out. "Yes, yes. God, Jup. You feel so big inside me. Make me yours."

"You're already mine," Jupiter murmured in Sen's ear.

Fee was his, too. Theirs. And she was panting beneath them, but she wasn't as close to coming as they were.

"Fee," Jupiter rumbled. "Touch her clit. Make her come with us, Sen."

Sen rushed to do as instructed, and Feeona screamed her pleasure. A bright white light exploded behind Jupiter's eyelids.

Sen howled. His ass clenched, draining Jupiter.

Jupiter threw back his head and howled. For a thin second, the world was bright and shiny and perfect. Every moment of their love wouldn't be so perfect, but they would always be perfect for each other.

Slowly, they eased apart and collapsed onto the bed together, limbs tangled. Glorious exhaustion weighed Jupiter down. Sen somehow managed to slip out of the bed and came back with cleaning cloths. He cleaned them up and pressed fresh cool cloths against their necks.

"Alfred, lower lights to dim." Feeona sounded like she was already half asleep. Jupiter pulled her into his embrace and when Sen returned from getting rid of the cloths, he pulled him in as well. He had both his mates in his arms and they were all well and truly sated for the moment.

Each of his mates was special to him. Each held a piece of his heart. And they gave their hearts to him and to each other. It flew in the face of all they knew about the mate bond. It didn't matter. They loved each other and that was everything. It shouldn't be possible. Jupiter certainly hadn't done anything to deserve them, but it was true. Incredibly, wonderfully true. "I love you," he whispered.

They echoed the sentiment back to him.

Sen reached across him to touch Fee. "Love you, Fee."

She wove her fingers with his. "Love you, Sen."

Today Jupiter had his mates and the rest of his pack were safe.

One day all of Fee's kids and all the Dogs would be free. Together they were unstoppable.

Each day until then and each day after, Jupiter would count himself lucky for the mates that slept in his arms.

A NOTE FROM THE AUTHOR

Ready for more Arena Dogs? Check out Book 3: Healing Creek, to find out where the pack is going next.

If you enjoyed reading Tempting Jupiter, I'd love for you to help others enjoy it, too. You can help other readers find this book by recommending it to friends and readers' groups or by reviewing it online.

To be eligible for exclusive giveaways and get new release announcements, sign up on my website: www.charleeallden.com.

Thank you for giving my books a try!

Charlee

ACKNOWLEDGMENTS

This book has been made better through the encouragement and generosity of author friends, wonderful readers and my loving family.

To readers Lori S, Jannie S, Christine S, Monica R, Angela, and Brandy B; your kindness and encouragement have been a warm beacon to light my way. Thank you!

To authors Abigail Sharpe, Lis'Anne Harris, Priscilla Oliveras, Shelby Reed, Leah M, and Savannah; your generosity and companionship mean the world to me.

To every reader who's taken the time to get in touch, review a book, or hang out with me online and for every author friend who has offered encouragement, I thank you all whole-heartedly.

Any deficiencies in this book are entirely my own.

Charlee

ABOUT THE AUTHOR

Charlee Allden is a longtime fan of love, adventure, and happily-ever-after. She is the award-winning author of sexy, intense, out-of-this-world romance, including the popular Arena Dogs science fiction romance series. She loves to hear from readers at charleeallden@gmail.com. You can also connect with her online at: www.charleeallden.com or find her on Facebook, Pinterest, or Instagram.

www.facebook.com/CharleeAlldenAuthor
www.pinterest.com/charleeallden/
www.instagram.com/charleeallden/